OUTSTANDING PRAISE FOR MARY BURTON AND HER NOVELS!

MERCILESS

"Burton just keeps getting better!"
Romantic Times

"Terrifying . . . this chilling thriller is an engrossing story."
Library Journal

SENSELESS

"This is a page-turner of a story,
one that will keep you up all night,
with every twist in the plot and with
all of the doors locked."
The Parkersburg News & Sentinel

"With hard-edged, imperfect but memorable
characters, a complex plot and no-nonsense dialog,
this excellent novel will appeal to fans of
Lisa Gardner and Lisa Jackson."
Library Journal

"Absolutely chilling!
Don't miss this well-crafted spine-tingling read."
Brenda Novak, *New York Times* bestselling author

Please turn the page for more RAVE reviews!

Before
She
Dies

Books by Mary Burton

I'M WATCHING YOU

DEAD RINGER

DYING SCREAM

SENSELESS

MERCILESS

BEFORE SHE DIES

Published by Kensington Publishing Corporation

Before
She
Dies

MARY
BURTON

ZEBRA BOOKS
KENSINGTON PUBLISHING CORP.
http://www.kensingtonbooks.com

ZEBRA BOOKS are published by

Kensington Publishing Corp.
119 West 40th Street
New York, NY 10018

All Kensington titles, imprints, and distributed lines are available at special quantity discounts for bulk purchases for sales promotion, premiums, fund-raising, educational, or institutional use.

Special book excerpts or customized printings can also be created to fit specific needs. For details, write or phone the office of the Kensington Special Sales Manager: Attn. Special Sales Department. Kensington Publishing Corp., 119 West 40th Street, New York, NY 10018. Phone: 1-800-221-2647.

Zebra and the Z logo Reg. U.S. Pat. & TM Off.

ISBN-13: 978-1-4201-1021-0
ISBN-10: 1-4201-1021-7

First Printing: February 2012

10 9 8 7 6 5 4 3 2 1

Printed in the United States of America

Prologue

Eighteen Years Ago

He could pinpoint the day, the hour, even the second when he'd chosen his first kill. In that sacred moment, fear, rules, and consequences ceased to matter and long nurtured fantasies elbowed aside judgment. The switch had been flipped. And a line would be crossed.

He raised his gaze to the blindfolded young girl tethered to the wooden chair. She was slumped forward, unconscious from the drugs he'd administered. A curtain of lush dark hair covered her pale oval face, cascaded over tight full breasts, and grazed a full waist and gently rounded hips. Not more than seventeen or eighteen, the girl worked at the carnival. She was the psychic. The seer. The seducer. For the average person she was a delightful diversion or a harmless amusement. But he was a rare breed, empowered with gifts that allowed him to see beyond her youth and beauty to the timeless evil.

The decision to kill her had come seven days ago

when he'd visited her carnival tent. On that night, he'd patiently waited in the line that trailed outside her tent. He'd been nervous, edgy, and still clueless that his life was about to change.

When he'd finally entered her domain, candles flickered in shadowed corners, soft music drained from unseen speakers, and the heavy scent of incense clung to the air. She'd been sitting behind a gilded desk and had worn a bright red flowing gypsy costume. A dark wig framed a lovely face half hidden by a black domino mask. He'd felt the rush of excitement as he'd stared at her and sat across the table from her.

"Madame Divine," he'd said.

Nodding, she turned his hand over and exposed his palm. "Yes."

"You look so young."

"Do not be fooled by my youth." Confidence dripped from each word as she traced his jagged lifeline.

He wasn't deceived. "I saw the line. You are quite popular."

Green eyes bore into him. "What is your question?"

Her abruptness stoked his anger but he was careful to keep it checked. "Did she love me?"

Nodding, Madame Divine traced another line on his palm. "I can answer that question for twenty dollars."

His skin tingled as he pulled his hand free, dug a rumpled twenty-dollar bill from his jeans pocket, and laid it on the velvet-draped table. She set the timer at her side before she again cradled his hand. Her skin was soft and warm. Sweet, subtle perfume drifted around her and mingled with the heavy stench of scented candles. She closed her eyes and asked the spirits for guidance.

As he stared at the delicate frown that creased her

forehead, he imagined what it would be like to strip the clothes from her body and beat her until she wept. How would her voice sound when she begged? He imagined she'd beg, cry, and plead. And when he wrapped his fingers around her neck, how long would it take for the life and warmth to drain from her body? He wondered all these things as she traced the lifeline on his palm and spoke of prosperity and good fortune.

And then suddenly she straightened as if she'd been kicked by the Devil. Tension rippled through her fingers and her breathing grew shallow. She released his hand as if it had burned her flesh. She stared at him, fear glimmering in the green depths.

In this panicked moment, he *knew* that she saw his true intent.

The realization rattled him. No one had ever seen beyond his veneer. She was a true seer. A witch.

She was The One that God wanted him to kill.

"Are you okay?" he said.

"Yes. Yes. I'm fine." She moistened her lips. "Tell me about this woman you love."

He smiled, knowing he could be charming when it suited him. "We met at the university. We're in the same class."

"What's her name?"

"Carrie. I loved her very much. Why didn't she love me back?"

The predictable question coaxed some of the tension from her shoulders, and she eased forward a fraction. She smiled but he knew her fear, as visible as the sweat on her brow, lingered. "Carrie loves you, but she is afraid of . . . her emotions."

Despite his resolve to be strong, her soft voice speaking

Carrie's name drew him in closer. He wanted to believe Carrie had loved him. "She said she hated me."

"She doesn't hate you. She loves you. You must go to her and tell her that you care."

She spouted more nonsense about good fortunes and happiness, but when the timer buzzed, she immediately released his hand.

His open palm lingered. He yearned for her touch. Emotions demanded he take her now. *Kill. Kill. Kill.* But logic kept him on a tight leash. *Wait. Prepare.*

And so he quietly left the tent and used the next week to prepare his room for her. She was his first kill and he wanted the details to be perfect.

On the seventh night after his reading, he'd waited in the shadows. When she returned from her whoring in town and ventured to the carnival bathroom by the wood's edge, he grabbed her and covered her mouth with his gloved hand. An injection in her arm had immediately rendered her silent and compliant. He easily dumped her in the trunk of his car and brought her to this hunter's cabin, nestled in the hollow of the Virginia woods.

Now moonlight streamed through the small windows and mingled with the glow of three lanterns. The only concession to luxury in the rough cabin was a water pump, which fed into a deep basin. Furnishings were limited to a long wooden table and a few straightback chairs by an old soot-stained hearth. Those who inhabited this place were prepared for a monk's life, an idea that appealed to him.

Eagerness churned inside him. Too many years of fantasizing and dreaming were about to become reality, and it was hard to maintain control. His skin tingled. His stomach clenched. If he didn't soon unleash the raw energy brimming inside him, he'd go insane.

Unable to wait for her to awaken, he grabbed a bucket of cold water and poured it on her face. She awoke cussing, screaming, and sputtering. The hint of panic behind her screams enhanced his excitement. He stared at her silk blouse, now wet and plastered to full, full breasts.

Breathless, his own muscles aching with want, he retreated to the cabin's corner and sat down. He'd not expected so much desire. He'd always considered himself a chaste and prudent man, but she made him crave dark, evil passions.

Anticipation burned through his body, and he knew if he didn't rein in his desires, he'd break his covenant with God.

She must confess and be purified first.

As she coughed, he muttered a prayer for patience. Retrieving the small Bible from his pocket, he gently kissed the gold cross embossed into the well-worn black leather. The Bible had been a gift from his mother on his tenth birthday. Though not fancy or substantial in size, the book provided him with answers, insights, and in times of stress, it was a guiding force.

With trembling fingers, he flipped through the pages, scanning and rereading passages. As he focused on the words, he suddenly felt her gaze through the blindfold. Her head was tipped back and cocked in his direction. Water dripped from her hair and face over a gold chain and down between the cleavage of her breasts.

Tied up, cold and wet, she should have been contrite and scared, but instead she possessed a dark, brooding bearing that unsettled him. He didn't like her absence of fear.

"Don't stare at me," he said.

She shook her head. "I'm blindfolded. I can't see anything."

"You are looking at me."

"So what if I am?" Her voice was rusty, seductive.

"You are Satan's child."

She actually smiled. "So I've been told."

Fury scraped at his nerves. He crossed the room and grabbed a fistful of her hair. He pulled a knife from his back pocket and pressed it to her neck so she could feel the sharp tip. Her jugular pulsed under the blade.

He was a half-second from slicing her throat when reason shoved its way to the front of his mind. "I need you to confess your sins to God so you can be released from this earth clean and pure."

A defiant set to her jaw said as much as her words. "The clean and pure days are long gone for me." The girl's tone resonated a lifetime of experience.

"I need your confession. I need to send you to God pure."

"Then I guess it's your bad day." She cocked her head.

This close, he could smell the hint of a spicy, no longer sweet, perfume mingling with the stale scent of the threadbare gypsy costume. He turned her face roughly to the side so the lantern light caught the high slash of cheekbones. She was pretty, but she possessed a callous aura that would grow more insensitive with time. By thirty, she'd be washed up and spent.

Why had she seemed so different a week ago?

"It's just you and me, baby," she whispered. "Why

don't we play instead of fight? Some boys like to play rough but I promise gentle is better."

The grip in her hair tightened. "Don't call me baby."

She reminded him of a cat toying with a mouse. "Why not? I'm good and you'll like what I can do for you."

Tempted by her honeyed words, he dropped his gaze to her breasts, so round and full. He ached to touch and suckle them. The balance of power was shifting. "Shut up."

"Be my baby, and then I promise you'll forget all about the whip and this cabin."

He pulled her hair until she cried out. "Whore. Harlot."

Tears of pain, not fear, ran down under the blindfold's creases over her cheeks. "Baby, just take me. You know I'll be good. I'm always good." She had enough range of motion in her bound hand to brush his jean-clad thigh with her fingertips.

The faint touch sent an explosion of sensation through him and immediately he grew hard. Honeyed words, as sweet as a siren's call, tested his resolve and summoned him to temptation's edge. Though he was the one with power over life and death, she'd somehow mesmerized him with her soul-stealing eyes and a simple touch.

"You don't have to hurt me, baby," she said. "We can be good together. Untie me and you'll see."

"Do you think I'm stupid?"

"No." Her supple lips belied the word. "But we better get busy before someone catches us."

It was his turn to smile. "No one is going to bust in on us. Only a handful know about this cabin, and those

that do wouldn't bother with a visit until deer season."
He stroked her hair. "And that is still weeks away."

She moistened cracked, dried lips and this time a
faint tremor rippled under her words. "Kiss me. I know
you want to kiss me."

And God help him but he did. He'd dreamed about
taking her since he'd first seen her seven nights ago.
It had taken repeated razor cuts to his thighs and belly
to keep himself chaste and controlled until the right
moment.

He leaned forward and tasted her rosy lips. They
were soft, salty, and before he thought, he greedily
cupped her full breast in his smooth palm. He squeezed
her nipple until she wimpered. He grew harder and
fantasized about releasing her bindings and taking her.
Perhaps he could keep her a few weeks in the special
box under the floorboards where he hid his toys. There
she'd be safe, secured, and always at the ready to play.
Maybe given more time, this Delilah could be cleansed
and sent to God pure and clean.

And then in the distance he heard the Voice, sum-
moning him back to his path.

*"She is a witch. She will steal your soul if you give yourself
to the temptations of the flesh."*

He jerked back and stepped away from her. He
swiped his mouth with the back of his hand.

She must have sensed his panic because her smile
radiated arrogance. "It's okay, baby. You can love me.
Let me free, and I'll show you what real fun can be."

He'd dreamed and fantasized about killing. He'd
chosen his victim. He'd planned. And now, when he
should follow through, he was faltering. What was
wrong with him? He backed away from her, snatched
up his Bible, muttered random prayers, and reminded

himself that he was a soldier of God. "I am not weak. I am stronger than your temptations."

She moistened cracked dried lips. "Let me love you, baby. Let me love you. You don't even have to take the blindfold off."

He set down the Bible. "'Thou shalt not suffer a witch to live.'"

Scorn pulsed from her. "I love you, baby. I just need you to unchain me so I can show you."

"You are a sinner. You need to confess." His voice, roughened by desire, was unrecognizable.

"I have nothing to confess."

"We are all sinners, baby."

She moistened her lips and shifted her body so her breasts gently bounced.

His erection throbbed.

He pressed his hands to the fresh cuts he'd made to his chest that morning. Pain seared his senses, and for a moment he struggled with his breath as the desire leaked from his body. "'Thou shalt not suffer a witch to live. Thou shalt not suffer a witch to live.'"

The words from Exodus rolled off his tongue, again and again, half statement and half prayer. He'd been born to destroy the wicked, not be drawn in by their earthly temptations.

His own blood dampened the front of his white shirt and his hands now. In the moonlight, the blood had darkened from red to black. He smeared it on the woman's forehead, mingling his blood with her own. The scent and smell of their blood was sweet, indeed.

He turned and moved to the pump and bucket in the corner. He cranked the pump's lever until the water spat and then flowed free.

She turned her head toward the water. "What are you doing, baby?"

He filled the bucket and transported it to a long metal tub near the woman. He repeated this process until the tub was full and brimming with water.

With fumbling fingers, he untied her wrists. "It's time to play."

"Good," she said. "You'll be glad. We'll be good together."

Hefting her slight form, he carried her toward the tub and forced her to her knees. He grabbed a shock of her hair and dangled her face above the water's rippling surface.

"What are you doing?" Bravado could no longer hide her terror.

"Confess and be free of your sins."

"Confess what?"

He shoved her face into the cold water, savoring the way her body flailed and squirmed. Only when he saw bubbles rise to the surface did he draw her head back. She coughed and sputtered and gripped the edge of the tub with trembling fingers.

"Are you ready to confess?"

Wet strands of black hair draped her face and hid her expression as she coughed, sputtered, and tried to pull free.

She screamed.

The sound ricocheted off the log walls and swirled in the air above his head. "No one can hear."

Her cries slowed and stopped. "Why are you doing this? I've done nothing wrong."

He shoved her face so close to the water's edge the tip of her nose touched it. "You know why, *Witch*."

She yanked at her bindings and shook her head. "Why do you keep calling me a witch? I'm not a witch!"

He shoved her face in the water, counted to thirty, and then lifted it. She coughed and gagged. "I saw you coming out of the sorceress's tent tonight at the carnival. You held my hand a week ago and spouted your evil."

She jerked her head and tried to break his hold. "We're just stupid carnies. The fortune telling is just for fun."

"You read palms. You do the devil's work."

Her black, thick hair clung to her face like a spider's web. "You know it's all bullshit. None of that stuff is real. It's all a show. An act."

He loomed over her. "You were right about too many things."

"I'm good at the game. One of the best. But there's no magic." She shook her head. "People pay us a few bucks and we tell you a little about yourself. No magic. It's bullshit."

This time he held her face under water for the count of forty-five. "Liar. Heretic."

She gagged and rolled her head to the side, frantically coughing and expelling the water from her mouth and lungs. "You want me," she said. "I feel it. Let me make you feel better."

"I don't want you anymore."

"You do!" Bitterness tangled around the words.

Defiance still lingered in her rusty voice as her face loomed over the water's edge. It made sense that she would be strong. She'd been raised among the carnival people, traveling demons that moved from town to town.

This time when he shoved her head under the

water, he held it there until her body stopped flaying and went limp. When all the fight had leeched from her body, he jerked her free and turned her on her side to allow the water to drain free. He checked her pulse, and when he felt that it had stopped, he panicked. "She needs to confess."

He tipped her head back and started mouth to mouth. After several chest compressions, she inhaled sharply and her eyes opened wide. She vomited water from her lungs.

He ripped off her blindfold. He wanted to see her eyes. He wanted her to see his face.

When she looked at him, recognition and shock glistened. "Christ, man, why are you doing this to me? I thought you liked me."

Contrition. It was the first step toward salvation.

"Why are you doing this to me? Please." Her voice sounded hoarse and raw.

He leaned forward and brushed the wet hair off her face. Her skin felt cold, clammy. "What are you sorry for?"

Vibrant blue eyes bore into him. "Whatever I did. I'm sorry. Just don't punish me anymore."

Again, her gaze caught him off guard. It lured him in as it had before and made him want to forget about crusades and righteousness. He simply wanted to sink inside her warmth. As he'd dreamed of so many times, he kissed her gently on the lips and smoothed hair from her eyes. "If you don't know what you did, then how can you be sorry?"

Renewed panic replaced the silent pleas. "You called me a witch."

He'd never deny that she was a smart, clever girl. "I did."

She licked her lips. "You're not the first. Other men have said I bewitched them."

He traced his hand over her flat belly. The idea of other men staring and leering at her troubled him. She was his and his alone. "So you admit you are a witch, a sorceress, a stealer of souls? I wouldn't be driven to this if it weren't for your magic."

Her gaze remained locked on his as she laid her hand on his. "Yes. I'm a witch and whatever else you said."

He tightened his fingers on her breast and squeezed. She winced but continued to smile. This one understood the powers of her body and how best to wield them. "And you repent? You swear that you are evil?"

"Yes."

For a moment he laid his head between her breasts and listened to the rapid thump, thump of her heart. "Praise be."

"Let me go," she said. "I won't tell. I won't. And I can still make you feel real good. I swear."

He closed his eyes. "After what I just did to you, you still want me?"

"Yes. I want you. Just us, baby, no one else."

He still longed to suckle her breasts and shove inside her softness. As he lifted his eyes and prayed for strength, his gaze settled on the cracked mortar sandwiched between the logs of the cabin's wall. He likened the cracks to his own soul. Flawed and damaged, they were still strong enough to carry the burden. With trembling fingers, he combed her hair back. She stared up at him, vulnerable, scared, and ready.

Before he could surrender to temptation, he shoved her head under the water. She fought him, straining and twisting her body as her fists flailed. She tried to kick him with her feet, but he used his weight to render her immobile. Slowly, he counted away the seconds until her struggles lessened and she stopped fighting. Bubbles gurgled to the surface and still he held her face firmly under the water until the three-minute mark.

This time when he released her, her body slumped to the dirty floor, pale, cold, and dead. "Go with God, Grace."

"Mariah!"

Grace Wells screamed her sister's name even before she was fully awake. She sat up in her twin daybed searching the dark as she grabbed her throat. She struggled to breathe and to catch her breath. Slowly, she hauled in enough deep breaths to calm herself.

She searched the dark room of her trailer for signs of her sister's return. Light seeped into the small window and illuminated the flowered coverlet, stuffed animals, and a poster of Brad Pitt in a scene from *A River Runs Through It.*

She pulled at the frayed edges of her pink nightgown and struggled to calm herself. She'd endured endless nightmares since her mother had died three years ago, and for the most part she'd gotten used to waking up alone and terrified. But this night terror was different. She saw no faces and heard no sounds except for Mariah's cries for help.

Grace pressed trembling fingers to her temples and stared out the window. The grassy fairgrounds were located on the outskirts of town. The ground had been soft when they'd arrived and the carnival's trucks had left deep ruts in the ground and torn away large patches of grass. This field looked much like so many other fairgrounds in cities she'd long forgotten.

The carnival's Ferris wheel and flying scooter sat still and .dark. The flaps to the rifle shot, ringtoss, and basket jump shot games were closed, and the ticket booth's window was shuttered and locked.

All normal.

She crossed the room she shared with Mariah to the small crib and peeked in on the baby. The girl, Sooner, was just five days old, and already looked so much like Mariah.

The baby's deep even breathing did little to ease Grace's fears. Grace should have been working tonight, but she'd not felt well so Mariah had agreed to take the shift. Because the carnival would be closing in four days, they'd all anticipated big crowds.

You owe me, kid.

I know. Thanks.

Don't wait up for me. I've got a date.

Mariah had met another boy. A prince, this time, who was most valiant and who just might be The One. But the boys that lingered around the carnival weren't looking for lasting love.

Theirs was a gypsy's life with no regular address, schools, or roots of any kind. Not for the first time this season, she longed to move on to the next stop, thinking that maybe it would be better.

The room chilled with loss and grief. She hugged her arms around her chest. "Oh, God, Mariah, what have you gotten yourself into this time?"

Chapter 1

She had a power over him.

In this room, alone with her, words failed him. Here he followed her lead, moving with an economy of motion, undressing quickly and falling into bed before reason spoke. Their sex was always urgent. Hot. And it left his heart punching against his ribs.

This time, like every time before, she rose out of bed, his scent clinging to her, and dressed in silence. He knew what would follow. She'd manage a quick fix of her tousled auburn hair, they'd share obligatory, if not embarrassed, pleasantries, and she would leave, never suggesting that there should be a next time.

However, this time when she rose, Daniel wasn't content to just let her leave. He rolled on his side and watched her trembling fingers smooth the bunched cream silk slip down over her naked hips. She moved to the mirror and inspected once well-applied makeup now sinfully smudged and pale skin, crimson with sex's afterglow.

He wanted her back in bed, curled at his side, but he hesitated to ask. She'd been clear from the beginning that she'd only signed up for good, hot sex. She didn't want a lover or a boyfriend or anything that involved commitment.

That first time he'd agreed to her terms, counting his lucky stars and fully expecting little more than satisfaction and a pleasant memory. But from that initial release until now, he couldn't get enough of her. The more she gave, the more he wanted.

And the line she'd drawn between professional and personal had entirely faded—for him.

Manicured fingers slid over the slip as she glanced at the clock on the nightstand, sighed, and collected her scattered clothes from the floor.

He made no effort to hide his fascination with her. They'd shared this motel room five other times now, but he'd yet to see her fully naked. She had a long sleek form, creamy skin, a narrow tapered waist, and a nicely rounded bottom. He wasn't sure what she hid from him, but found the mystery more consuming each time they had sex.

Last time he'd seen the scar marring her side and thought he'd discovered her secret. When he'd asked her about it, she'd shrugged and said, "I was shot."

Curious, he'd pulled the police file and read the details of the shooting. It had occurred three years ago. She'd been working late. A client's hit man had entered her office and shot her because she'd been considered a loose end. Bleeding and alone, she'd escaped to a bathroom and locked the door. The shooter, unable to reach her, had barricaded her inside and left her for dead. It would be another eight hours before she would escape and call 911. The crime scene photos had stirred primal anger in him. Even now he could vividly recall photo images of her blood staining the bathroom's carpeted floor; the door hinges she wedged free with the tip of her high heels; and her bloodied silk blouse left behind by EMTs.

"Do you think about the shooting?" he'd said as he'd kissed the scar.

She threaded her fingers through his hair. "No."

"It's got to bother you."

Her fingers stilled. "I never dwell on the past."

If she weren't hiding the bullet hole scar, then why not take off the slip? Last night when he'd tried to tug it off her, she'd resisted. What else was there to hide?

She slipped on her blouse and efficiently buttoned it. Sliding on a pencil-thin black skirt, she tucked in her shirttail and with the flick of the zipper was again all elegance and class. Maybe some old lesson from charm school kept her from stripping totally.

Thinking about that slip and what it hid gave him another hard-on. "Why don't you stay?"

She found her panties and, facing him, tucked them in her purse. "We both have early calls."

"You gave your final summation yesterday. The pressure is off until the jury comes back. Go in to the office late today. You've earned it."

She arched a neat eyebrow. "I've never been late before."

He propped his head on his hand. "Be late."

"Why?"

"Once is not enough when it comes to you."

She readjusted her pearl necklace so the diamond clasp was again in the back. A smile played with the corners of her lips. "I wish I could stay for an encore. Really. But I've got appointments."

"All work and no play makes Charlotte a dull girl, counselor."

"All work keeps Charlotte liquid and her bills paid, detective."

Naked, he rose off the bed and moved toward her until he was inches away. Towering, he fingered the pearls around her neck. She smelled of Chanel and him. "We should have dinner sometime."

She grinned. "We just had dessert."

"I'm talking about real food. Tables, chairs, forks, knives, and spoons."

She didn't pull away. "I don't think so."

"You've got to eat sometime."

"We drew a line. It has to remain fixed and secure."

He curled the pearls around his index finger. "The defense attorney doesn't want to be seen with a cop?"

"Maybe the cop shouldn't be seen with the older defense attorney."

"Three years doesn't count as older. And I don't care who sees me with you."

She untangled his finger from her pearls. "We are judged by the company we keep."

The wistful, if not sad, edge surprised him. She wasn't talking about him. But who? Another mystery. Another reason to want her.

As she picked up her purse, he pressed his erection against her backside. "Stay just a few more minutes."

She tipped her head against his chest. Tonight there'd been more urgency in her lovemaking, which he'd attributed to the murder trial's conclusion. "I can't."

"That sounds halfhearted." Sensing a shift, he pushed

her hair aside and kissed her neck. Her sharp intake of breath pleased him.

"I have to go." The trademark steel in her voice had vanished.

He turned her around and unfastened the buttons of her blouse until he could see the ivory lace of her slip. He kissed her shoulder, her chin, and the top of her breast.

"We have rules about avoiding tangles."

"Fuck the rules. And the tangles."

She wrapped her arms around his neck and kissed him. When she broke the connection, she was breathless. "I really have to leave in twenty minutes or I will be late." The whispered words gave no hints of the woman he'd seen on the courthouse steps late yesterday. Swamped by reporters, that woman had been cool, direct, and flawless ice.

The contrasts added to the mystery. "Have dinner with me."

Her fingers wrapped around his erection. "No time for talking, detective."

He swallowed, struggling to hold on to clear thought. "You are avoiding the question."

Her hands moved in smooth, even strokes. "Nineteen and a half minutes."

Until now she'd called the shots. But that would change. Soon.

Dinner and power plays relegated to another day's battle, he kissed her as he scooped her up and laid her in the center of the bed. Straddling her, he reached for the package of condoms on the nightstand. Urgency blazed through him. He tore open the pack with an impatient jerk and slid on the rubber.

As she wriggled under him, tugging up her skirt, he

thought he'd explode. There was nothing else in the world that mattered more now.

When he nestled between her legs, his beeper vibrated on the nightstand. Fuck.

She glanced at him expectantly. "Do you need to get that?"

"They can wait," he growled.

She gripped his shoulders as he pressed into her. "You sure?"

"Very."

They both forgot about deadlines, clients, and responsibilities.

Chapter 2

Tuesday, October 19, 6:45 a.m.

Detective Daniel Rokov pulled up at the crime scene and shut the car engine off. He got out of the car and retrieved his suit jacket from the hanger in the back-seat. Sliding it on, he took a moment to adjust the jacket collar, and then do a quick check of his gun, phone, and badge, which hung on his belt. He shook off his lingering drowsiness and closed the squad door.

The scene was at The Wharf, an abandoned restaurant sandwiched between Union Street in Old Town Alexandria and the Potomac. The faded white building was square and set eight feet off the ground on stilts. The exterior had been neglected since the place had closed over a decade ago, and the wooden deck-ing and stairs looked as if they'd tumble in the next real windstorm. The place had been a popular restaurant back in the day, and the roof top dining had offered some of the best views of the Potomac River in the area. He'd heard that the city had purchased the building and planned renovations, but given a tanking economy and a dwindling tax base, that wasn't likely.

The trees along the river had turned from a deep green to a mixture of oranges, browns, and yellows. The air was a cool sixty degrees, which compared to the summer's triple-digit numbers, felt phenomenal.

The paved parking lot, fenced off from Union Street by a ten-foot chain-link fence, was filled with a half-dozen white Alexandria Police marked cars. The city's forensics van was parked on the side of the building, and the vehicle's back-bay doors were open. He surveyed the area and searched for any orange cones used to indicate stray shell casings, tire marks, or anything else that might be considered evidence. He didn't see any.

A handful of tourists had gathered. This was the height of the tourist season in Old Town. Ghost and historic tours ran nightly, and it was common to see large groups of people shuffling past as a guide pointed out the buildings where troubled spirits lingered past their exit dates. He'd taken a date on a city tour about six months ago. Monica. She'd been with the tourism bureau and had suggested the excursion. He'd been out of his divorce less than a year, but backbreaking hours had left him little time to date so he'd still been rusty. The tour had been more interesting, but Monica had been more concerned about incoming text messages than him. By the end of the date she'd called him rigid. *Rigid.* Because he'd expected common courtesy. Shit.

"Danny-boy, is that the suit you wore yesterday?"

The rusty voice belonged to his partner, Detective Jennifer Sinclair, a tall brunette who tended to wear jeans with a black turtleneck and a worn leather jacket. Today, as most days, she'd swept her thick hair into a bun at the base of her neck. Only on the rare occasions when she wore her hair down did its lush ends brush the middle of her back. She liked to work out at the gym, had an athlete's physique, but swore she didn't enjoy sports. Raised by a single cop father, she moved among the detectives and uniforms easily, never falling prey to jabs and jokes and always able to toss back what she received.

Rokov rested his hands on his hips. "I can't wear a suit two days in a row?"

"You only wear your best suits to court. Court was yesterday. Not today."

Early this morning, he'd walked Charlotte Wellington to her car parked outside their motel room, left her with a very public kiss, and then snagged his Dopp kit from the trunk of his car. He kept the kit stocked with an electric razor and other essentials. He'd been presentable in ten minutes, but there'd been no time to drive to his apartment and collect a change of clothes. "You're a regular calendar. You gonna hit me with a weather prediction next?"

Rokov and Sinclair were two detectives in a four-person homicide department. They had been in court yesterday along with the other two members, Deacon Garrison and Malcolm Kier, to hear the summations in the Samantha White murder trial. White, a thirty-year-old housewife, was accused of murdering her husband. Most would have bet the young woman, who'd confessed to crushing her husband's head with a golf club, would easily be convicted of first-degree murder. None of the public defenders had wanted the case. And then Charlotte Wellington had stepped into the picture, and all bets were off. Wellington had insisted her client had acted in self-defense, and the slam-dunk conviction had dissolved into uncertainty by trial's end.

"So you gonna ask her out?" Sinclair said.

"Who?"

"Charlotte Wellington. I saw the way you were staring at her in court yesterday. Very intense."

The jab would have gotten another male cop a threatening glare, but Jennifer reminded him so much of his kid sister all he could manage was a shrug. "Maybe I was paying attention to her summation. Try it sometime."

Jennifer grinned, unfazed. "So you are gonna ask her out?"

His gaze roamed the lot around the building. "Why would I ask her out?"

"'Cause you got a thing for her."

A brackish breeze billowed the folds of his jacket. Hands on hips, he asked, "And what birdie told you that?"

"Don't need a birdie, man. I can read you like a book."

He smiled, more relieved than amused. She was fishing blind. "Sinclair, as much as I love girl talk, we got a victim who might like some of our attention."

A half smile raised full lips covered with no lipstick. "Whatever you say, Danny-boy."

They ducked under the yellow crime scene tape and passed a collection of cops and cars with flashing lights. Rokov found the uniform that had been the first responder and secured the crime scene. The guy was mid-forties, short, stocky, and sported a dark crew cut and a thick mustache.

Rokov extended his hand and introduced himself. "You're Jack Barrow, right?"

"That's right." Hearing the sound of his own name relaxed the guy a fraction. "Heard you had a talent for remembering details."

"Naw, not really. I just remembered you got that service award last spring for working with the kids in the Seminary District."

"Right again." Barrow hooked thick thumbs into his waistband.

Sinclair shook hands with Barrow. "Your wife birth that baby?"

"Not yet," he sighed.

"Damn, boy," Sinclair said. "What does this make, number four?"

"Five." He glanced at Rokov. "This gal's old man trained me when I was a rookie. I think she was in elementary school then."

Sinclair shook her head. "Please, no visiting the dark ages."

Barrow tossed her a friendly wink. "She tossed a mean softball."

"We're not here to talk about me or your old self," Sinclair said. "Give us the rundown."

Barrow's gaze turned toward the building, and his expression grew somber. Few outsiders could understand how cops could joke in times like this. Cops, however, understood it was the jokes that got them through times like this.

"This one is a real freak show. Sure to give cops nightmares and land on the ghost tour when the details leak out." Barrow glanced at Sinclair, all traces of humor gone. "I'm sorry you're gonna have to see it."

Sinclair cocked her head. "I can handle it."

"Break your old man's heart to know you do this kind of work."

For the first time, Sinclair had no quip.

"What drew you to the building?" Rokov said to Barrow.

"Saw a light in the second-story window. Like a candle flickering. The place is locked up tighter than a drum because it's unsafe. City bought the building. Supposed to be torn down. Anyway, thought we might have vagrants or druggies so I called for backup and we went to check it out." He rubbed the back of his neck with his hands. "We didn't find anyone there except the victim."

"Male or female?" Rokov said. He pulled a notebook from the breast pocket of his jacket and a pen.

"Female."

"You see how she died?"

Morning light cast shadows on Barrow's face and deepened the creases. "No. The scene makes me think of, well . . . better you just go up there and see for yourself."

"Sure," Rokov said.

"Watch the stairs. They're old. Not too stable."

"Thanks."

He moved past Sinclair and took to the stairs first, knowing if they gave way, he might have time to warn Sinclair off. Plus he couldn't shake the thought of Sinclair's old man cringing when his baby girl entered the scene.

"I could have gone first," she said.

His partner didn't appreciate chivalry, so he did his best to downplay it. "Then move faster next time."

The stairs creaked and groaned and shifted slightly as they climbed past the first floor to the second. Sunlight streamed into the first floor, but instead of cheer, it added an eerie quality that deepened and extended the shadows.

There was only one other cop on the floor and the forensics tech. No doubt, there'd been some concern about structure as well as foot traffic in the dusty room. Plus, the fewer people up here, the better.

Both detectives put on paper booties and snapped on rubber gloves.

They moved toward the tech, Paulie Somers, a crusty guy in his late forties who didn't tolerate interruptions well. Paulie wore a jump suit, booties, and gloves. Snapping pictures, he didn't bother with greetings.

Paulie could be difficult to work with but he was meticulous and a master at finding evidence a less experienced tech could miss. He would spend a good deal of time snapping pictures and documenting every inch of the crime scene before collecting data.

When Paulie stepped to the left, it gave Rokov his first real full-on view of the victim, who lay on her back, her hands outstretched, her palms up. Her hands and feet had been nailed to the ground with wooden stakes. A neat white powdery substance neatly encircled the victim's body.

He'd learned to put aside emotion when he viewed a crime scene. His job was to accumulate facts, details, and anything he could use to catch a killer. And so he focused on the details.

The victim was young, twenties maybe, and she had a thick shock of black hair that swooped over the right side of her face. Her skin was as pale as caulk. Below the roughly hewn stakes, her fingers were curled upward as if she'd been trying to claw free. She wore a black dress and a red leather jacket.

He glanced around the body and the walls for signs

of blood: a spray, droplets, pools, something to tell him more about the death. But there was nothing.

"There's no blood," Sinclair said.

"No."

"She wasn't killed here."

"That's my guess," Rokov said.

"Which means she was dead when she was staked to the ground."

"Yes." Gratitude could blossom at the direst times, Rokov thought as he stared at the body.

"Rigor mortis is well established," Paulie said. Rigor mortis began three hours after death, but the slow stiffing of the muscles didn't peak until the twelve-hour mark, when the process then began to dissipate.

"Eight to twelve hours since she died?" Rokov said.

"Give or take. And have a look at her legs." Paulie lifted her skirt to reveal her ankles now stained a bluish purple by blood that had settled under the skin. "Note the lividity. She was upright when she died. Sitting maybe. Sat there for at least an hour before she was moved." When the heart stopped beating, blood traveled to the lowest point in the body, darkening the skin. "I haven't been able to get a good look at the underside of her arms, but there appears to be lividity under her forearms as well."

Rokov studied the victim's neck for signs of trauma. There was some bruising. "Was she strangled?"

"I don't know. That's for the medical examiner to figure out."

"Knife wounds. Bullet holes."

"First glance, nothing. But until I remove the stakes, I can't process and examine like I should."

"What's the circle made of?" Rokov said.

Paulie squinted as he glanced through the view-finder of his digital camera. "I think it's salt."

"Salt?"

"Everyday regular iodized table salt."

Rokov squatted and studied the circle. He could sense Sinclair's gaze. "Any thoughts, partner?"

"Assuming the substance is salt?" Her voice sounded rough with emotion.

"Sure."

"Salt has lots of uses. Keeps bugs away. Maybe the killer didn't want the ants on her."

Rokov rose. "It's also used in magic spells."

She arched a brow. "That's kinda far-fetched."

"This whole scene is far-fetched. In fact, when we get the go ahead to walk around, check the corners of the room, and see if there are any bits of salt there."

"You're joking, right?"

"No, I'm not."

The deep tenor of Rokov's voice erased whatever amusement she'd allowed. "Witches. Really? I thought the Samanthas and Endoras of the world were just fiction."

"I'm not saying this woman was a witch. But that doesn't mean the killer didn't believe she was a witch. He could have put salt in the corner to seal the room."

"How would you know something like that?"

"I've heard tales from my grandmother."

"She grew up in Russia."

"Where superstition reigns."

She opened her mouth to argue but then stopped. They'd seen a lot of crazy shit over the last eighteen months as partners.

Rokov turned to Paulie. "Any other observations?"

Paulie snapped three more pictures before he

straightened. "There are ligature marks on her neck, and the underside of her hair and her collar are damp with what appears to be water."

"Cause of death?"

"Ask the medical examiner."

The tech was always careful not to weigh in with an opinion. His job, he'd often said when prompted for a comment, was to collect data. He left the fancy figuring up to the detectives.

"Identification?" Sinclair knelt by the body and stared into the woman's face half cloaked by her hair.

"No ID. No jewelry. And there are red marks on the side of her neck. Looks like he got her with a stun gun several times." Paulie knelt down and examined the hair draping her forehead. He snapped more pictures and then gently moved the hair back. "Have a look at this."

Sinclair squatted and glanced down. "She's been tattooed with the word *Witch*." The bold letters covered most of the delicate forehead skin, still puckered red and raw from the tattoo needle. "Shit."

Rokov's half-baked theory had been correct, but it gave him no pleasure. "She have any other tats or markings?"

"Not on the exposed areas. But there could be other body art under the clothes."

"I can't imagine anyone willingly doing this to themselves," Sinclair said. "But we've seen all kinds of oddities."

Rokov glanced around the room. The flowered wallpaper was peeling off in frayed strips, and the ceiling was soiled with a dozen watermarks. All the furniture had been stripped out, and a shadow imprint on the back wall suggested there'd been a bar at one point. A thick coating of dust covered the room. "Footprints?"

"Two distinct sets," Paulie said. "The first I identified as Barrows. He was kind enough not to trample all over the floor, which left me with clear impressions of the second set." Paulie pointed to the window. "The best impression is over by the window, and I've marked it with a cone. I've got an electrostatic dust print collector. It will pull an impression."

Rokov moved toward the footprints carefully to mirror Barrow's path. "It looks like a size eleven or twelve." He studied the grooved pattern. "Sneakers?"

"That's my guess, but it will take time to narrow the brand."

"The impressions are clear and defined. He walked carefully and with precision."

Paulie shrugged. "You know I don't make impulsive calls."

"I'm not holding you to it," Rokov said.

"That's what they all say. I'll have a report by to-morrow."

Rokov studied the impression. "Inside back right heel looks worn. He's favoring the foot."

Paulie snapped more pictures. "Could be an injury or he could have had a wart at one time, and it changed the way he walks. Doesn't mean he noticeably favors the foot now."

"So he moved her here," Rokov says. "Positions her, stakes her, and then moves to the window to stare at what?"

"The river. The full moon. It was a clear night last night. He stops to enjoy the full moon. Maybe he heard a sound."

"If he's got a thing about witches, the moon makes

sense," Rokov said. "The full moon has a lot of power in some circles. Stands to reason he'd be drawn to the moon."

Sinclair rose. "We need to figure out who she is. I'll head downstairs and put a call into Missing Persons and see what they have."

"Good." Rokov turned to Paulie. "Does she have defensive wounds? Did she fight for her life?"

"I'm going to bag her hands. Hopefully, the medical examiner will find something under her nails."

Rokov knelt by the victim's right hand and studied the crude stake that had pierced the flesh of her palm. It would have taken tremendous force to drive the wood through flesh. He wondered if she'd known her attacker. Most murdered women knew their killers. Lovers. Husbands. Boyfriends. Love could turn vicious instantly.

"I wanted you to see her before I pulled the stakes. If I can pull them out now, I can roll her over."

"Need a hand?" Rokov said.

"I got it." Paulie slid on workman's gloves over his surgical gloves and grabbed a hold of the stake. "The floor boards are rotted." He pulled hard, and the stake wriggled free of the floor and the victim's palm. Carefully, he moved to the other side and repeated. Then it was on to the feet. The last stake proved stubborn and it took assistance from Rokov to free it.

Paulie laid the stakes out and photographed them. Then very carefully, he turned the body on its side. The victim's jacket was embossed with the word *Magic*. He checked the jacket's label. "Tanner's."

Rokov recognized the retailer. "Tanner's is a shop in Old Town. It has a solid reputation of making custom leather jackets."

Rokov pulled a notebook from his pocket and wrote down the detail along with the dozens of others he'd noted since he entered the room.

"Okay. You keep doing your thing here," Rokov said. "Sinclair and I will beat the streets. Maybe somebody saw something."

Outside, Rokov found Sinclair by the car on her radio. She looked pale but determined. "Thanks. If you get a match, give me a call."

"No matches."

"Not yet. But she might not have been missing twenty-four hours yet."

"Her jacket is unique. The seller is located in Old Town. I'll double check, but I think he opens at ten."

"Good." Sinclair rubbed the back of her neck. "Last night was a Monday night in late October. The streets would have been packed with tourists taking ghost tours and hitting the bars."

"The retail shops would have been closed by ten, but the bars would have been open until twelve, one, or two."

"Give or take a few hours, she died last night about one."

"Yeah. There's O'Malley's on the corner. It's as good a place as any to start. Maybe someone saw someone here."

Rokov waved to Barrows, Sinclair nodded, and the detectives made their way across the parking lot. Quick strides got them across the street to O'Malley's.

The pub was on the corner of Union and Prince in a three-level town house that had been built a hundred-plus years ago. Built of old brick, the building had a large glass window with gold lettering and green café curtains. The historic look appealed to tourists.

"This is ground zero for the city's tourist industry," Sinclair said. "The press is going to eat this up."

Rokov glanced back at the murder scene. "They'll be here within the hour, and the story will be on the news by lunch." He worked hard to push aside circumstances that he could not control. But when it came to the press, his success rate was mixed. "The only way to diffuse the story is to solve the case as quickly as possible."

"A closed case would be a great way to start the week."

Rokov glanced inside O'Malley's, and when he saw the flicker of movement in the back, he pounded on the front door with his fist. For a moment, the bar's interior went silent, and then footsteps sounded inside.

A tall, lean man, sporting a black five o'clock shadow, stopped about twenty feet short of the door. He wore a white apron over T-shirt and jeans. A bar towel hung carelessly over his right shoulder.

"We're closed until three," he shouted.

The man was already turning toward the kitchen when Rokov tapped on the glass and held up his badge. The barman turned, his face dark with frustration.

"We have a few questions," Rokov said.

The man hesitated and shook his head, as if the cops were the last complication he'd expected or needed. Finally, he moved toward the door and unlatched the deadbolt. Bells jingled above as the door opened, and the smell of stale beer and cigarette smoke rushed out to greet them. "Someone filing a complaint?"

"Should they?" Sinclair said.

The barman shifted his gaze to her and let it roam slowly and freely up her frame. He didn't smile, or

leer, just absorbed every detail of her. Sinclair arched
a brow but didn't flinch.

"You got a name?" Rokov said.

"Richardson," he said, pulling his gaze from Sinclair.
"Duke Richardson. I own O'Malley's."

"So is there a reason someone would file a complaint?" Sinclair repeated.

"And you are?" Richardson said.

Sinclair pulled out her badge. "Detective Sinclair.
This is my partner, Detective Rokov."

"Big guns," Richardson said. "I'm guessing you're
not here for me, then."

"Why's that?" Ten years on the force had taught
Rokov never to trust anything at face value. He'd
solved more than a couple of crimes by pure chance.
Once as a traffic cop he'd pulled an SUV because of
a broken taillight. The driver, a thin man with a plaid
shirt, had been nervous and unable to stop fidgeting.
Rokov had called the plates into dispatch, learned
there'd been no priors, but the guy had just been too
damn squirrelly. He'd asked the guy to get out of his
car. The man had opened the door abruptly, trying to
drive it into Rokov and knock him into traffic. Rokov
had dodged the assault, stumbled, and righted himself
just as the guy pulled a gun. Rokov fired and killed the
man with the first shot. Turns out, the assailant had
murdered his wife and was fleeing the state.

Rokov still had moments when those tense seconds
came back to him in a flash. He could recall each
detail as if the film had been put in slow motion. The
way the guy's eyes had shifted to the left. The way his
own hands had trembled very slightly as he'd gripped
the handle of his gun tighter. The way the assailant
had reached under a newspaper on the front seat and

pulled out a Berretta. Rokov could remember the sound of a horn blaring as a car passed behind him, the rust-colored stain on the man's jeans and the sweat beading on his upper lip. It had felt like a lifetime but in reality was mere seconds.

Without realizing it, he had already eased his hand to his belt and draped his fingers over his gun handle.

Duke glanced at Rokov's hand and then held up his own. "Hey, I don't want trouble."

Rokov's own heart raced and for a moment he said nothing. He'd not been shot but he still had lingering moments of stress related to the incident. Charlotte had been shot, and yet she insisted she was just fine. No fucking way she'd walked away unscathed.

Rokov cleared his throat and lowered his hand. "We have a few questions. There was a problem across the street last night."

Duke folded his arms over his chest. "I was open until midnight. Slammed until a half hour after that. I never got more than a few feet from the bar. What happened?"

Rokov let the question pass. "See any customers that might have aroused your suspicions?"

"Yeah, a lot of them."

"Particulars?" Sinclair said.

Duke shrugged. "A couple. One dude had to be cut off, and I called a cab for him. He didn't appreciate either gesture and told me so in so many four-letter words. And a gal, tall, dark. She sat at the corner of the bar and drank until about midnight. She didn't say much, but just sat and stared."

"Either of them use a credit card?" Rokov said.

Duke shrugged. "The chick paid cash. Twenties. But the dude used plastic. Name was Matt Lowery."

"You remember the name?"

"Sure. I took his keys. I tried to take his license, but he screamed identity theft. So I wrote down his address and gave the license back to him. Planned to mail the keys back to him this morning with a note telling him to stay clear of O'Malley's."

"You take keys often?"

"When I have to be sure. I don't mind anyone coming here and enjoying a few drinks, but no one is going out of here hammered with car keys. I don't need that kind of trouble."

"You said you got an address for Mr. Lowery?" Sinclair said.

"Sure." He turned and moved toward the bar and retrieved a padded envelope. "You can deliver his keys. Chances are he's still sleeping it off."

Whoever had positioned the victim had not been drunk, but that didn't mean he'd seen the killer. A long shot, but a shot. "Just give me his address."

The bartender scribbled down the address on an order pad and handed it to Rokov.

"He give you any other reason to remember him?" Sinclair said.

"Talked to himself. Was a real pain in the ass. But he didn't break any laws."

Rokov took the slip of paper. "Queen Street. Just a few blocks from here. What time did he leave?"

"He arrived an hour before closing and the cab picked him up about twelve thirty."

"Where's his car?"

"Parked on the street, I guess. Judging by the keys it's a Toyota."

Rokov made a note. If they found the car, they

couldn't search it without a warrant, but they certainly could have a look inside from the sidewalk. "See anything across the street in the old restaurant?"

"The Wharf? That's been closed for a decade. The city owns it now. No one goes there."

"Someone did last night," Rokov said.

Duke shrugged. "Sometimes I see homeless people hanging around. The city keeps the place locked up pretty tight, but sometimes someone gets inside. Someone overdose?"

"No overdose, but we had trouble in the building."

Duke stared at Rokov expectantly, waiting for more of an explanation, but when none came, he said, "Like I said, I didn't see anything. Way too slammed. But this Lowery guy might have a word or two for you. I put him outside around midnight to cool off and sober up while he waited for the cab. There was a mix-up on my end and my waitress didn't call the cab, so Mr. Lowery sat outside for almost an hour. He might have seen something if he didn't pass out."

"How drunk was he?" Rokov said.

"Stinking drunk. Too drunk to stand. Even if he had his keys, he wouldn't have been able to get back to his car. I doubt he'll be much of a witness."

Eyewitness testimony was sketchy even under the best of circumstances. "What about waitresses or waiters?"

"Can't help you with that. If anyone saw anything, they didn't tell me. Come back this evening and ask them if you like. We'll have the same crew on for tonight."

"Right," Rokov said. "What other stores would have been open last night after midnight?"

Duke's gaze narrowed. "What happened across the street?"

Rokov pushed out a breath. It would be all over the news soon enough. "A woman's body was found in the building."

"I'm judging by your expression that it wasn't drugs."

"It was not."

Duke pushed long fingers through dark shoulder-length hair. "Damn. You got an ID on the woman?"

"No. Not yet. She was wearing a red jacket with the word *Magic* on the back. See anything like that?"

Duke shook his head. "No. Can't say. But who the hell knows? Like I said, last night I was slammed." He rested his hands on his hips. "Check with Just Java across the street. They're open to midnight. Stella runs that place at night and she keeps an eye on all."

Rokov glanced through the front window to the little coffee shop in the town house building painted a bright yellow. "Thanks." He pulled out a card and handed it to Duke. "Call me if you think of anything."

"Yeah, sure. Will do."

They moved toward the door and Rokov opened it for Sinclair.

"Do you think it'll take long to solve this one?" Duke asked.

"We'll try," Rokov said.

"News is going to be all over it," Duke said.

"That they will."

Duke shook his head. "Shit, first it's the economy and now a body. Karma does not like this place."

Rokov let the door close behind him. The sun had risen high in the sky, prompting him to pull Ray-Ban sunglasses from his breast pocket. "Let's check out coffee lady. See what she knows."

"I hate the door-to-door knocking, the endless questions and the endless vague answers. It's amazing how much crap we have to wade through to get a few nuggets of gold."

He shook his head. "Beats sitting in court and having an attorney railing on my ass."

"Ah, let's face it, Rokov, you want Ms. Wellington to rail on you."

They paused as a minicooper buzzed past and then crossed to the coffee shop. "You're like a dog with a bone, Sinclair. What set you off today?"

"The new suit for court. Super fancy, even for you."

"Dad made the suit for me for my birthday."

"Your birthday was in February."

"So, maybe it was just time to dust it off."

"Right."

"Get it through your head, Sinclair. The suit ain't about Charlotte Wellington."

As Rokov opened the coffee shop door, the rich scents of coffee and pastries greeted them. Three customers waited at the register as a kid working behind the counter looking frazzled hustled to fill drink orders. They held back.

"And just for the record," Sinclair said, "if Samantha White's husband really beat her as the witnesses during the trial testified, I can't say I'm against her. Wellington wins points in my book for taking the case on pro bono."

He pulled off his sunglasses. "I'm sure the good attorney will be relieved to know you approve."

She chuckled. "She doesn't give a crap about what anyone thinks about her. She is pure ice."

Charlotte had been cool and reserved when they'd first met at a cancer fund-raiser a month ago. Her law associate, Angie Carlson, who was married to homicide detective Malcolm Kier, had hosted the event. Rokov had gone as a show of support to a fellow cop's wife and the cause. Charlotte Wellington was there to support Angie as well. They'd been fish out of water at the festive event and had struck up a casual conversation. At the event she'd been reserved and cool. He'd suggested coffee and somewhere along the way they'd ended up naked in a motel room.

"So you gonna see her again?" Sinclair said.

"There can't be an again if there wasn't a first."

Sinclair nudged him with her elbow. "Come clean."

"Buzz off."

The morning crowd at Just Java had cleared, and Rokov reached in his pocket for his badge. He flashed it as the kid looked up at them. "Five-O. What's the deal?"

"Stella here?"

"Yeah, just a second." The kid vanished in the back and seconds later returned with an older woman in tow.

She tucked stray strands of gray curly hair behind her ear. "Figured when I saw the cops down the road earlier there was trouble. Kids using drugs this time or vandals? We've had trouble with both since that building was abandoned."

"A woman was found murdered," Sinclair said. "Her body was left in the building."

"And you are?" Rokov said.

"Stella Morris. I own the place."

"Were you here last night?"

"Normally I have Monday nights off but I got a call from the kid who was working the last shift. He was sick and had to go home, so I came in to work the last couple of hours and close up."

"You see anything? Odd customers? Trouble. A car that didn't belong?"

Stella rested her hands on her hips. "A few buzzed guys from O'Malley's wandered in before midnight. And there was a homeless guy who stops by when he can scrap together enough coins." She raised a finger. "I was closing up around twelve thirty, and I did hear someone shouting."

"Shouting what?"

"Couldn't make out the words, but it kinda sounded like howling. Like a wild animal. I figured it was a drunk."

"What direction was the sound coming from?" Sinclair said.

"By The Wharf. That's why I thought to mention it."

"And that was about twelve thirty?" Rokov said.

"Twelve thirty-six as a matter of fact. The sound kind of spooked me. Sent chills up and down my spine and I glanced at my watch because I wanted to remember the time."

"See anything?"

"Nope. Saw nothing."

Rokov pulled out his card and handed it to her. "Ever seen a woman around here with a red leather jacket that says *Magic*?"

"That sounds like Diane."

"Diane?"

"I don't know her last name. She used to come in here a lot but I haven't seen much of her the last six months. She does something with computers."

"She ever use a credit card?"

"Sure, I guess, but it's been a while since she's been here. I'm gonna have to dig."

"Would you do that?" Rokov said.

"Yeah, sure. Why not." She flicked the edge of the card. "I'll call you."

They thanked the woman and moved back down the street toward the car. "Let's stroll down the street and see if we can find Lowery's car."

"The Toyota?"

"Sure." Sinclair took the north side of the street and Rokov the south side. They walked a block and a half when Rokov spotted the silver Camry. Sinclair crossed the street. "This the car?"

"Could be." On the front seat was a briefcase. The cup holders between the seats held two empty cups. "He's lucky no one smashed the window to get the briefcase."

"Maybe he was in a hurry to get to the bar."

"Let's pay him a quick visit."

"Will do."

The detectives walked back to their car and for an instant Rokov nearly cut to Sinclair's door.

"If you go for my door, Danny-boy, I'm breaking your fingers," Sinclair said.

Rokov held up his hands. "I learned my lesson." When the two had first started working together, Rokov had opened Sinclair's car door. She'd demanded to know which medieval century he'd just returned from. He'd laughed, blaming the door-opening habit on his parents' old country manners. They'd settled on a compromise. He'd not open the car doors, but she'd allow the occasional shop door.

Sinclair slid into the passenger side seat and Rokov behind the driver's wheel. As he fired up the engine, the first television news van pulled up outside the crime scene. "The media is going to love this one."

"I'm afraid you're right."

The drive to Lowery's took minutes and soon the two were standing on the doorstep of his town house. Painted white with black shutters, the town house was modern but fashioned to look colonial. A planter on the front porch sported drooping marigolds and several cigarette butts.

Rokov rang the bell once. After a pause he hit it again, and when that didn't produce results, he banged with his fist. Finally, they heard shouts and the stumble of footsteps. The door snapped open.

A man wincing against the sunlight greeted them with an angry glare. Dressed in suit pants and V-neck T-shirt, he had greasy dark hair that stuck up in the back and a dark beard shadowing his lantern jaw. A thick cross hung from a thick gold chain around his neck. "What the hell do you want?"

Rokov held up his badge. "You Matt Lowery?"

"Yeah."

"You at O'Malley's last night?"

"Sure. And if you're here to ask, I didn't drive home drunk. I took a cab."

"So we hear," said Sinclair. She glanced beyond him to a foyer warmed with Oriental rugs and a landscape on the wall.

"The bartender tells us he parked you outside on a bench last night."

He rubbed a bloodshot eye with his knuckle. "Damn near froze my nuts off while I was waiting."

"You see anything?" Rokov said.

"I was pretty hammered."

"Unusual people? Odd sounds," Sinclair prompted.

Lowery shoved out a sigh as if pushing through the fog of his hangover. "I thought I saw someone at the old restaurant across the street."

Rokov tensed. "What did you see?"

"Shit, I don't know. It was late and dark, and like I said, I was hammered. I just figured it was a couple getting busy."

"A couple."

"Saw a man with a woman at his side on the top floor. They went in and a light came on."

"You see the guy or the woman?"

"No. Just their outlines. He was holding her close and kissing her like he couldn't wait to get her alone." He sniffed. "So what's their deal?"

"She's dead. And we think he killed her."

Chapter 3

Tuesday, October 19, 9 a.m.

Charlotte Wellington's heels clicked against the sidewalk as she turned on her BlackBerry and checked her messages. Two clients. Her realtor. Clerk of the court. The apartment manager of the Seminary Towers. And a number she did not recognize.

As she walked the block toward her office, she called the clerk first. His message had been in response to a call from her. No verdict in the Samantha White case yet.

"Good," she muttered. "They have questions and are thinking."

She dialed her realtor and two rings later heard a perky, "Hello, Charlotte! How are you?"

"Great, Robert, as long as you have not had other problems with my condo sale."

"It's nothing huge this time. The man buying your condo called to say the home inspector has two issues. He says there is a leaky faucet in the second bathroom and the lock on the exterior storage closet rattles. He wants you to fix them both. He also wants to move the closing date up to the thirtieth."

"Robert, I've made enough price concessions to this guy. I agreed to be out the middle of next month and now he wants two weeks and two minor issues fixed? He is officially a pain in the ass. The place is stunning, one of a kind. He should be grateful the place came on the market."

"Five years ago, I'd have agreed. These days, just be grateful you got asking price. Besides, Charlotte, these are minor changes. You could hire a handyman to take care of both issues in an hour. And the new move-out day is only fifteen days earlier."

"Fifteen days is a lifetime for me this year." Given a different set of financial circumstances, this last request would have been the final straw. She'd have pulled the condo from the market and told the buyer to buzz off.

But she needed the money from the condo sale more than extra time to arrange the move. The law practice had hit a dry spell that she fully expected to ride out in the long run. But short term, cash flow was strangling her. "I don't have the time to track down a handyman. And I haven't even called a mover."

"I'll call the handyman and a mover that I trust. My guy can have the minor repairs made today, and my other guy can have you safely moved out in fifteen days."

She tightened her grip on her briefcase handle. "I don't like being pushed like this."

"This is a huge sale, Charlotte. It would be a shame for you to lose out. And I know you really want this."

People chose Robert because he was aggressive and

had a reputation for quick, high-dollar sales. His customers either needed cash or a quick move. Seeing as she wasn't leaving Alexandria, it didn't take a huge leap for him to figure that money drove this sale.

Life had backed her into a corner before, and she'd learned that survival depended on adaptability. "Fine. Get your man in to fix the problems and find me a mover. One way or the other, I'll be ready to move out by the new date."

"Great. Great. This will be worth the effort."

"It needs to be." She said her good-byes and hung up. As she walked, she called one client and left a voice mail. She was dialing the second when her phone rang. Her realtor. "Robert."

"You're good to go. I've taken care of everything."

"Great."

"Plan to close in fifteen days."

"Okay."

"It's going to be fine." The soft edge in his voice suggested unwelcome pity.

"It's going to be better than fine, Robert." She hung up, moving down the tree-lined brick sidewalk past the historic town houses.

When Charlotte arrived at the office, she unlocked the front door, which always remained secured. She'd never fretted over security and enjoyed an open-door policy until a man had waltzed into her law offices three years ago and shot her.

She'd returned to her office one week after the surgery to inspect the installation of her office's new security system. She'd insisted that she was recovering nicely and had no lingering issues after the shooting, but the truth was worry stalked her constantly. Her world became smaller and smaller, and she'd begun to feel quite alone in it.

Perhaps it was that self-imposed isolation that had driven her to Rokov and why being with him was exhilarating and addictive. If she still saw her analyst, he'd have had quite a field day with her choice to finally break a four-year dry spell with a cop—a protector.

She found her receptionist grinning like a little girl. Iris was a fifty-plus, silver-haired woman who dressed in pinks and madras. Generally stoic, she was efficient and had the office organized down to the last paper clip.

"Hey, boss." Iris was grinning when she offered Charlotte her standard morning greeting.

Charlotte paused, taken back by the unexpected grin. "Whose birthday did I forget?" She didn't celebrate holidays and often forgot her own birthday. Consequently, she wasn't good about remembering most milestone events that were so important to others.

Iris grinned. "No birthday."

"There is something. What did I miss?"

"You didn't miss anything. Angie decided to surprise us." Iris handed her a half-dozen pink message slips.

She wasn't fond of surprises. "Why?"

"Relax, surprises can be good, Charlotte."

She flipped through the messages. "So you keep telling me. So what is the good surprise?"

"Angie has brought in a cake and we're having a minicelebration."

"The celebration is for?"

"Her fund-raiser for the American Cancer Society. She just received several pledges late yesterday that are going to put her near the million-dollar mark."

Angie, a cancer survivor, had suggested a fall Hal-

loween fund-raiser for the children's cancer ward at
Alexandria Hospital. To make the event happen, she'd
twisted arms, including Charlotte's, and called in
favors. She'd transformed a once sleepy event into a
big costumed Halloween party that was going to be
not only a moneymaker but The Event of the year.

"So we eat cake."

"We do. Now put down your bag and get into the
conference room. And don't tell me you have work.
You always have work."

Charlotte rarely took time to celebrate milestones
like this. So consumed with success that the instant she
reached one hurdle, she set her sights on the next.
Angie was teaching her to slow down if only a little,
every so often.

She slipped into her office, set down her briefcase,
and touched up her lipstick. She found her staff in the
conference room. Angie Carlson Kier stood at the
head of the table wielding a knife over a large pumpkin-
shaped cake. Beside her was Zoe Morgan, their new
paralegal. Tall, lean, with black hair that grazed her
shoulders, she had been a dancer in her teens but had
suffered an injury that had ended her career. She'd
worked for several nonprofits but had accepted a job
here five months ago. So far, she was turning into a
real asset.

Charlotte smiled and tried not to calculate the billable hours idling in this room.

Angie's smooth blond hair hovered around her jaw
line. She wore a simple cream-colored suit and a white
blouse. Since Angie had adopted her son, David, she'd
cut back her hours to forty a week, part-time for a
lawyer. Angie had declined partnership on the heels of
Charlotte losing her original partner, Sienna James, to

a lover in Texas. Sienna's buyout, Angie's inability to buy into the firm, and the lost billable hours to the White case had created the crippling cash flow crunch.

"I can hear the wheels turning in your brain, Charlotte," Angie said. "We will take just a few moments to have this minicelebration and then it's back to work."

Charlotte relaxed her shoulders and eased the tension from her face. "No rush."

Everyone laughed.

"I don't see the humor," Charlotte said.

Angie grinned. "You not rushing is funny. And by the way, you did a stunning job with summations yesterday. You've the makings of a great criminal attorney."

She'd been pleased with her closing comments yesterday. And judging by the jury's body language, she'd planted real seeds of doubt. "So I hear you've reached a new high in fund-raising?"

"We've passed the million-dollar mark with our fund-raiser. We've shattered all expectations, and we've not even held the party and auction."

Charlotte clapped, her smile genuine now. "You've a lot to be proud of, Angie."

"Thanks."

Pragmatic, even calculating to a fault, Charlotte recognized that this event benefited not only the community but also Wellington and James. She'd learned at an early age that those who weren't always scraping for the next morsel went hungry.

Angie cut the cake and doled out pieces to everyone. Charlotte bit into the chocolate cake and savored the hidden flavors of espresso. Angie had been raised in an affluent home and knew all the best caterers and bakers in town. She also knew the best schools, the best dance studios, and the most prestigious social events. Not that Angie focused on such things. She didn't. But it struck Charlotte that what came so naturally to Angie had required painstaking research for her. She built her list of The Best one name at a time. It was very important to her to cultivate the impression that she, too, had grown up in a world similar to Angie's.

"So, how is the baby?" Zoe asked.

"David is great," Angie said. "He's walking and tearing up everything in his path. Malcolm has the day off so the two went to the park. Malcolm said it's a male bonding kind of thing."

"What does that mean?" Iris said.

"Who knows? Likely they take off their shirts, paint their faces, and run through the woods at the park hunting squirrels."

Zoe's eyes widened. "You're kidding."

Angie laughed. "Yes, I'm kidding. Most likely it's an ice cream at the carnival and a few games of chance there. Then the afternoon in front of the television watching the Dallas game that I taped for him while he was working."

Zoe shook her head. "I'd read that the carnival opened last Friday, but I hadn't thought to go."

"For David and Malcolm, it will be great fun. For me, not so much. I was never a fan of carnivals. Too dirty."

Charlotte glanced at her cake and poked it with her fork. *Too dirty.*

The front door buzzer sounded and Iris moved to answer it.

Charlotte raised her hand. "Sit. I'll get it." She set down her cake, almost untouched, and moved down the hallway. As much as she enjoyed her staff, she understood that there would always be distance between them because she was the boss.

She checked the security camera behind Iris's desk and spotted a man, his face turned partway from the camera. The ends of his flannel shirt hung over the painfully narrow waist of faded jeans. He had gray hair and what looked like a scruffy beard. He finished the dregs of a cigarette and then crushed it out in a stone planter filled with white mums.

"Nice," Charlotte muttered. She considered calling the cops just as the man turned and faced the camera. He grinned as if he sensed she was staring at him.

She jerked back and for a moment could barely breathe. Time had weathered the face and grayed the hair, but there was no mistaking the sharp gray eyes that had been a fixture in a childhood she'd worked hard to erase from her memory. She stepped back from the screen, her heart knocking against her chest.

"What the hell are you doing here, Grady Tate?" The carnival was in town, but she'd stayed away because she did not want to see him. He must have seen the news coverage of the trial yesterday.

As if she'd spoken directly to him, Grady rang the bell again and then again. His arrival was clearly no accident, and he was not going anywhere.

Iris appeared at reception. "Who is ringing the bell?"

Pure, sharp panic cut into Charlotte's belly. "I'll take care of it."

Iris glanced at the monitor. "He looks like something the cat dragged in."

"He has that effect on people."

"Who is he?"

Charlotte smoothed hands over her black pencil skirt. "Nobody."

Iris folded her arms. "Really? Well, *Nobody* has rattled your cage."

"He has not."

"Your lips are blue."

She moistened her lips and offered a smile too brittle to be amiable. "Just go back to the party and enjoy your cake."

Iris tapped a manicured finger on her forearm. "I think I'll stay right here and make sure *Nobody* isn't a problem."

Charlotte did not want Iris to meet Grady. Past colliding with present promised disaster. But making an issue could require more explaining down the road. "Eat your cake, Iris. I'll shout if I need you."

Plucked brows knotted. "I don't like it."

"I know. Thanks. But go. Please."

"Fine."

Swallowing the tension in her throat, Charlotte crossed and opened the front door. Grady's fist was poised in the air ready to knock again. For a moment, he stared at her, stunned into silence. She'd changed—a lot—since the long-ago night he'd put her on the Metro bus to Alexandria. His gaze moved over her, assessing and calculating, before a slow, dangerous smile curved thin lips. "Hello, Grace."

Blood rushed to Charlotte's head, making her temples pound. She'd not heard that name in eighteen years. "My name is Charlotte Wellington."

"Yeah, I saw you on the television last night. Sounds like you tore it up at that trial yesterday. Got to say

I was surprised to see you. I always figured you'd have left the area after all these years."

Tension seared her nerves. "What do you want, Grady?"

If he noticed her unease, he didn't seem to care as he glanced beyond her into the reception area. "Aren't you going to invite me in? Looks mighty fancy inside."

She shifted and blocked his view. "What do you want, Grady?"

His gaze thinned, the pretense of civility melting like ice on a scorching day. What emerged was the hard cold man who had been her stepfather. "You always could piss me off in no seconds flat."

"Get to the point or leave."

"I raised you to respect your elders better than that, didn't I, Grace?"

"You tracked me down after all this time to issue a lesson in good manners? I find that a hard one to swallow."

He slid gnarled hands in the pockets of his jeans and leaned forward. "Invite me in and make nice, or I swear everyone in this town will know you are not some fancy attorney but a lowlife carnie who did what she had to do to put pennies in her pocket."

The scents of the carnival—tobacco, cotton candy, popcorn, and grease—wafted off him, and instantly she was transported back to a time when she'd lived her days in fear and want. Despite half a lifetime of creating Charlotte Wellington, Grady could smash her image with a few words.

"Come inside. But do not call me Grace."

His smile flashed again, quick and razor-sharp. "Now that is more like it . . . Ms. Wellington."

Charlotte stood back and waited for him to enter her reception area. Past and present had merged, and eighteen years' worth of fear, regrets, and dread came to fruition. "What do you want, Grady?"

He took his time surveying the room, taking in the oil landscape paintings, the Oriental rugs, the sleek mahogany receptionist desk and the gold-embossed sign that read *Wellington and James.*

"Mighty fancy, baby girl." He sniffed and shook his head. "Mighty fancy."

"Don't call me baby girl."

"You liked it when I called you that back in the day."

She folded her arms over her chest. "I never liked it, and if you haven't noticed, back in the day is long gone."

He shook his head and winked at her. "You can rewrite your past for all your fancy friends, but you and I both know the real story."

Tension coiled in her belly. "What do you want, Grady?"

"Can't I just come and see you, baby girl?"

Grady had entered her life when she was eight and her sister Mariah ten. Her mother, reeling from her latest breakup, had met Grady when the carnival had come to Knoxville, Tennessee. Before it broke camp three weeks later, her mother had moved them into his RV. By the age of eight, Charlotte had been in five different schools and lived in nine different motels in nine different towns. This move in her young mind was as temporary as the others. But for reasons she'd never understood, Charlotte's mother and Grady had forged some kind of bond, and before Christmas of that same year, they married. Her mother, Doris, had started working in the carnival's Madame Divine tent as the resident psychic, while Grace and Mariah did odd jobs around the carnival.

It had gone fairly well for a time. Her mother was happy. Mariah had begun sleeping again. And she'd been able to finally keep the books she'd accumulated at yard sales. But within seven or eight months, Grady rediscovered the bottle and proved to be a nasty drunk. Her mother and Grady shared five years of explosive bliss, and when Doris died, her daughters remained with Grady. The time would have been miserable if not for Mariah.

Laughter from Charlotte's coworkers drifted from the back conference room, prompting her to lower her voice a notch. "You never do anything without a reason. What do you want? Money?"

He glanced toward the laughter and then grinned, still taking pleasure in her unease. "I don't need your money. Though it sure does look like you're doing real fine for yourself."

Nothing she could say would drive him faster to the point he'd come to make. Grady would take his sweet time.

"You were always a prickly one. The worrier of my two girls."

"You were good at giving me enough to worry about." Bitterness dripped from the words.

"Maybe. Maybe." He walked to the receptionist desk and picked up a crystal paperweight. For several seconds he studied it. "I've been sober for eighteen years."

"Good for you."

He tossed the paperweight like a worn baseball. "I need your legal help."

The paperweight had been a gift to Iris last year. It

had been hand made by a glassmaker at Alexandria's Torpedo Factory, an artist enclave on Union Street. It had cost six hundred dollars.

She took the paperweight from him. "I saw the article in the paper and know the carnival is in town. Did one of your boys get arrested?"

He curled his empty fingers and lowered them to his side. "I could see where you'd think that. The boys do tend to mix it up from time to time."

"Drunk in public. Theft. Fighting. Your employees have a talent for getting into trouble. And I have no intention of helping any one of them."

He arched a brow. "You got some attitude in you, girl."

"And your point is?"

"Maybe I could bring you down a peg, and let the folks in the back know that you didn't come from such refined stock. Maybe I should tell them you was born a low-life carnie just like me."

Threats were par for the course for a defense attorney. Most either rolled off her back or amused her. This one struck at the core.

But she also knew Grady well enough. If she showed weakness or caved in to his demands, he'd own her. She'd buy his silence for a time, but there would be more and more favors. He'd worm into her life like a cancer, and in the end still tell everyone about the past she wanted to forget.

"Go ahead. Tell them. And when you're finished, get the hell out of my life."

Gray eyes narrowed and glared as if he were dealing with a disobedient child.

When she'd been a kid, that look had scared her—

it still did a little—but she'd gotten much better at bluffing. "Now or never."

He hesitated. Waited.

She waited, barely blinking.

Finally, he nodded, grinned, and bowed his head slightly. "Now, baby girl, I did not mean for this to turn into a pissing match. I've come with hat in hand to see if you can help me. For old times' sake."

This victory of wills was small, but a first. Grady never did anything hat in hand. "I won't help you or any of your carnies get out of jail. I'm done with that life, Grady. There is no going back for me." Her normally controlled voice had slipped back into an accent she'd worked so hard to destroy.

"I wouldn't be asking for me or any of those slobs that pretend to work for me."

She shrugged. "Then why are we having this conversation?"

"I came about Sooner."

Hearing the name smacked her gut like a one-two punch. She could feel the color drain from her face as she scrambled to remain stoic. The last time Charlotte had seen Sooner, the girl had been eight days old.

Regret and sadness scorched her, and for an instant she couldn't draw in a breath. She'd thought about that baby often and of the night she'd left her behind. "You didn't give me a choice, as I remember."

"It wasn't hard to get you to leave. You'd been dreaming about leaving for years."

"Mariah had died. I couldn't handle staying."

"You didn't have the grit to stay."

"I was sixteen, Grady. Not more than a child myself."

"Tell that to the baby girl who looks so much like Mariah that it'll take your breath away."

Tears welled in her eyes, and for several seconds she could not speak for fear her voice would crack. "You told me you were going to put Sooner up for adoption. You said she'd have a real home."

He rubbed his clean-shaven chin. "I decided it was best she stay with me."

"What?" Her head spun. Of all the scenarios she'd imagined over the years, this was not one of them. "You swore on Mariah's grave you'd give her a real home."

"I gave her a real home." He straightened his shoulders. "I did right by the girl."

"If you kept her, you didn't do right by her."

"She turned out all right. She's smart and quick."

Bitterness soured her stomach as she imagined that innocent baby growing up in the grit and dirt of the carnival. "Where is she now, Grady?"

"Got herself arrested for shoplifting from a store owner."

"What kind of store?" Dark, heartbreaking scenarios swirled through her mind.

"Crystals, cards, bracelets. Knickknack shit. She's always liked that kind of stuff. Makes sense I suppose since she is the new Madame Divine."

Anger choked her throat. "You put her to work in the tent?"

"She wanted to work."

"Why isn't she in school?"

"She got herself a good education. Homeschooled but it's worked out fine. She's smart as a whip."

All the hopes and dreams she'd had for Sooner

dried up and blew away like dust. "Not so smart. She's been arrested."

"She didn't do it. She said the shopkeeper made a pass at her, and when she told him to fuck off, he got mad. He called the cops, whining about stolen crystals. He held her until the cops showed."

To cope with emotions too extreme to name, she focused on the facts. Her mind clicked through the consequences of shoplifting. "What was the item?"

"Some fancy crystal. Expensive from what I hear."

"Does she have an arrest record?"

Gray eyes thinned. "No. She's a good kid."

"Where is she now?"

"In court. Arraigned today. Maybe right now."

Charlotte stared at him a long moment. Nothing could have dragged her back into Grady's world. Nothing. Except Sooner.

And he knew that.

"I'll get my briefcase."

"I'll go with you."

"No, don't. In fact, I don't even want to see you near the courthouse. You don't mix well with cops, and I don't need to deal with your temper on top of everything else."

"I won't lose my temper."

That made her smile. "Of course you will. You always do."

Grady slid his hands into the back pockets of his jeans. "You'll take care of it then?"

"I will." She checked her watch. "What's her full name?"

"Sooner Mariah Tate."

"Tate."

"Sure. It's a good name."

Facts. Think about the facts. Morning court will be in session for at least another hour. "If I hurry, I might catch her case."

"Thank you."

"Don't thank me, Grady. Just stay away from me."

Chapter 4

Charlotte reached the courthouse fifteen minutes later. She hustled up the front steps in her heels and dashed up to the line for the metal detectors. Normally, the wait irritated her. Today it made her want to scream. A man in front of her kept setting off the scanner, which required him to return and empty more from his pockets.

When it was Charlotte's turn to pass, she made it through without a glitch and then quickly grabbed her personal items and briefcase as they passed through the scanner. She dashed up the stairs to the second floor courtroom and quietly slipped inside general court. Taking a seat in the back, she scanned the room. There were at least six girls being arraigned. Three were dressed like hookers, one wore ragged jeans with slumped shoulders, one looked drunk, and the last sat alone and quiet facing the judge. The last girl had long dark hair that brushed the middle of her back. Instantly, Charlotte's gaze went to the last girl. The hair, the narrow breadth of her shoulders, and the way she tilted her head to the right instantly reminded her of Mariah.

The courtroom melted away for a second and she was transported back to an afternoon when two teenaged sisters sat in the trailer.

"God, Grace, do you have to brush my hair so hard," Mariah wailed.

"Stop being a baby. You said you wanted tight braids to go with your Indian costume, and that's what I'm giving you."

"Not that tight."

"Stop. I'd kill for your hair."

"You would not."

"I would." The thick mane was so black, blue highlights shimmered in the strands when the light hit just right.

Once they'd dressed, the sisters were going to a Halloween party at the local high school. Mariah was the Indian and Grace was the cowboy. Neither attended regular school, and though it never bothered Mariah, it did bother Grace. Whenever they were in a town, Grace would check to see what functions were being held at the area schools. They gravitated toward the big fall and spring events: football games, plays, homecoming, and prom, knowing blending would be easier. They'd dress, hitch a ride to the school, and for a few hours they'd mingle and pretend that they were regular kids.

"The next case is the Commonwealth versus Sooner Mariah Tate. She's been charged with credit card theft, petty larceny, and resisting arrest."

Charlotte glanced at the bailiff and then to the judge. What was the judge's name? Rosen. Judge Silvia Rosen. The graying pale woman didn't raise her gaze from the papers on the bench. "Will the defendant rise?"

The girl with the long dark hair rose and for a moment turned her head in profile. Charlotte's breath caught. The girl was the image of Mariah, and for a few seconds it felt as if Mariah had returned from the dead. Tears choked Charlotte's throat.

Charlotte swallowed, shifted her gaze to the judge, rose, and moved with purpose and direction down the center courtroom aisle. Clearing her throat, she moved beside the girl, who now stood in front of the judge.

"Judge Rosen," Charlotte said. "Charlotte Wellington. I am counsel for the defense." She didn't offer a glance in Sooner's direction but sensed the girl's confusion and relief.

The judge lifted a somewhat surprised gaze to Charlotte. "Ms. Wellington, this isn't your normal beat."

"No, it is not, Your Honor. But I've been retained to represent Ms. Tate."

"Very well, Ms. Wellington. How does your client plead?"

"Not guilty. And I move that the charges be dropped."

Silver bracelets jangled from Sooner's wrist as she dug long fingers through her hair. She shifted her stance as if she wanted to speak.

The judge made a note. "Why is that?"

"This is my client's first offense. She just turned eighteen a week ago."

"And the creep tried to assault me," Sooner said. Her voice had the same rusty quality as Mariah's. "He planted those crystals in my purse. I didn't even know they were there. He's just mad because I wouldn't sleep with him and I called him fat."

A rumble of chuckles passed through the court-room, prompting the judge to raise her gaze and silence everyone with a look. "The police report mentions your complaint that he attempted sexual assault, but there is no evidence to support the claim."

"It's the truth," Sooner said.

Charlotte held up a manicured hand, silencing the girl. "I know the court's dockets are full and there are more important cases to consider."

The judge stared at the attorney with a cynical eye. They both knew that this case, a first offense, did not warrant a great deal of her time. "All right, counselor, I'll bite. What do you suggest?"

"Charges be dismissed."

The suggestion seemed to amuse the judge. "Just like that?"

"She has no priors. And she is young. But if the court wishes, I can prepare an extensive case on her behalf."

The judge studied Charlotte. "Why her? Why now?"

Because I never should have left her with Grady. "My practice is dedicating more time to pro bono work."

"Yes, I heard your summation was something to see yesterday. However, this case won't get you much publicity."

"Nevertheless, I am fully committed to the defense."

The judge drummed her fingers on the bench. "All right, I'll concede. But your reputation is bailing this kid out, counselor." The judge didn't hesitate and rapped her gavel. "Charges are dismissed, but if Ms. Sooner Tate gets into trouble again, it's your hide, counselor."

"Agreed."

The judge hit her gavel on the bench. "Case dismissed."

Sooner looked at Charlotte, her dark eyes searching and angry. "Did I just admit that I did it?"

As the bailiff read the next set of charges, Charlotte took the girl tightly by the arm and led her out of the courtroom.

Outside in the busy hallway, Sooner pulled free and glared at Charlotte. "I didn't do it."

"The charges were dismissed."

This close, standing face to face, Charlotte got her first real look at the girl. She had long dark hair and olive skin like Mariah's, but her eyes were as green as Charlotte's. She was slender, as tall as Charlotte, and held herself with surprising poise. Her billowy loose dress was sleeveless, revealing not only a slender figure underneath but also a tiger tattoo on the inside of her right forearm.

"Yeah, but it sounds like I'm on some kind of watch list for the next year."

"We both are." Charlotte had a thousand questions for the girl about her life. "If you keep your nose clean, then we won't have a problem."

"Hey, I was just shopping." Sooner's raised voice caught the attention of several passersby. "The creep expected more because I work at the carnival."

"Lower your voice."

Sooner folded her arms over her chest and looked almost as if she were pouting like a kid. "He was gross."

"Maybe it's time to find yourself another job."

"Working the Madame Divine tent is a good gig. And it sure beats slinging fast food or straightening the bottles at the baseball toss."

Anger, grief, and sadness swirled around her and

she raced to keep ahead of them. "I don't know what to tell you, Sooner. The tent is not the best place for a kid. Neither is the carnival."

Sooner shrugged. "Beats the streets."

"That sounds like something Grady would say." Bitterness added bite to the words.

Her eyes narrowed. "Grady said I had an aunt who was a fancy attorney but I didn't believe him."

"He said that?"

"Yeah. But if you know Grady, he says a lot of stuff. So why would a fancy attorney/aunt like you do something Grady asked?"

"I did it for you."

She'd often wondered what she'd say to Sooner if she ever saw her again. She'd assumed she'd feel love or tenderness, not irritation. "How about you just thank me for keeping you out of jail?"

"They wouldn't have sent me to jail."

"You don't think so?"

"Grady said not to worry when he came to visit me in jail."

Charlotte snorted. "And we both know Grady never lies."

"He has to have something. Aunt or no, a fancy woman like you doesn't mix with people like me."

I was a girl like you. "Just do us both a favor and keep your nose clean."

"You look upset."

"I'm not." Heat rose in her body and tears burned the back of her throat. It was too much seeing Sooner . . . seeing Mariah. There was so much to say and no adequate words.

Overwhelmed, she hurried down the stairs, telling herself that it was okay to run. She'd done her good deed for the day. She and Sooner might have connected a very long time ago, but clearly Sooner was all grown up, no doubt wise beyond her years. She didn't need Charlotte.

And still when she reached the front door of the courthouse, she glanced back. Sooner's head was turned and she was talking to a man. He was grinning and clearly his interests in her were not very pure. Sooner's stance suggested that she understood exactly what kind of effect she had on him.

Mariah had been like that. Even at sixteen Mariah could make any man, no matter how straightlaced, old or young, want her.

Charlotte turned from Sooner, and for a moment wondered how different their lives would have been if she'd stayed with the carnival or taken the child with her.

"Focus on what you can fix," Charlotte muttered as she pushed through the front door of the courthouse and headed down the steps.

As she glanced down the steps toward the street, she spotted a very familiar set of broad shoulders. Detective Daniel Rokov. His tall build set him head and shoulders above most in a crowd, as did the finely tailored suit that tapered so perfectly from his broad shoulders to his lean waist. He'd worn that suit yesterday. He'd answered that page and realized he'd not have time to go home and change.

Early this morning just as she'd reached for her purse at the motel room, he'd grabbed her by the hand, tugged her toward him, and kissed her. She'd leaned into his warmth as if she'd never been touched. Encouraged, he'd cupped her face and kissed her a second time. She'd wanted him so much.

"Have dinner with me," he whispered by her ear. "And no dodging the question this time."

Her perfume still clung to his skin. "You didn't seem to mind my artful dodging."

"I want to know more about you."

"Getting to know each other isn't part of the deal."

"What is the deal?"

I don't know anymore. "Sex."

He traced her jaw with his thumb. "Maybe it's time to start thinking outside the box."

The easy freedom they'd promised in the beginning had vanished. And that was not good. Sleeping with a cop was one thing but dating one—especially one like Rokov—was another. He wouldn't be content with pieces of her. He'd want everything: present, future, and past.

"We shouldn't see each other anymore."

His pager went off again, and when he'd glanced at the number, his face had darkened. "This isn't over, counselor."

He was the last person she needed to see right now. Her nerves were raw, her defenses down, and Rokov would detect the weakness and use it.

Charlotte pulled her dark sunglasses from her purse and put them on as she moved toward him. Of course, there'd be no avoiding him. But then why should they dance around each other? They were adults. His partner, Jennifer Sinclair, said something, and it prompted a smile that softened the warrior's visage.

However, when he glanced up and shifted his gaze to her, the smile faded. Dark sunglasses covered his eyes and tossed back her reflection. A slight ripple of tension moved through his body as he took a step toward her.

She hesitated, managed a professional smile, and quickly riffled through the endless small talk topics at her disposal. Weather was safe. Cases were not, even if she was tempted to ask what had summoned him away this morning.

Sooner Tate stepped into Charlotte's line of sight, cutting off her view of Rokov. "Hey, thanks for what you did in there. I know I was a bit of a bitch and I'm sorry."

She glanced beyond the girl to Rokov. He tossed a questioning look her way and then turned his gaze back to his partner.

Charlotte focused on the girl and was grateful he hadn't approached. "It's okay."

An awkward silence settled as they stared at each other. Sooner rubbed long fingers, sporting rings and black nail polish, over worn jeans. "I need a little help."

"Are you in more trouble?" It was like Grady not to tell the whole story.

Annoyance flashed in Sooner's green eyes. "Why do you say that?"

"Look where we are, Sooner. I just got you off a theft charge."

Sooner's jaw tightened. "I don't need your elitist bullshit."

Charlotte didn't rise to the bait. In fact, she found the girl's flare of temper amusing. "Sounds like you do need my elitist bullshit."

"I don't need you or anyone else. I can do what I need to alone." Her tone had risen and a few folks around them glanced in their direction.

"Sooner," Charlotte said in a softer tone. "What do you need?"

Sooner flexed her fingers and then with a conscious effort released the tension from her body. "I want to open a shop. A place where I can put down roots. Read fortunes. Crystals. I'm tried of traveling with the carnival."

The ambition didn't really surprise Charlotte. In fact, she was proud of it. "Does Grady know about this?"

"No, and I'd like to keep it that way. He can be controlling."

Charlotte couldn't disagree. "He doesn't want you to leave."

"No."

"According to the papers, this is the last season for the carnival," she said.

"Don't believe it. Grady uses the last season angle to get us more press. He's been playing that card for a couple of seasons."

So like Grady. Always playing an angle. "And when he hits the road again next year?"

"He'll come up with something. He always does." She rubbed the back of her neck with her hand. "The thing is, I'm tired of the road. I want a real life."

She'd felt the same way at that age. "And a shop is the answer."

"I've got money saved. And I'm good with the cards. I get a lot of repeat customers."

"That doesn't mean you can make a living."

"I'm the biggest draw at the carnival." Sooner spoke directly with no bravado. "I can turn this into a business."

She admired the girl's ambition. She might be naïve, but she wanted to go places. She was Charlotte eighteen years ago. "So what do you need from me?"

"I don't know much about leases. And I don't

want to put my name on a contract without someone reading it."

"You want me to read the lease agreement."

"Yes. And I'd like you to see the space."

"Why me, Sooner?"

"You're all I got, Auntie Charlotte." No missing the edge. "Nobody at the carnival could help me, and if they did, they'd tell Grady. And he'd do something to screw it up."

"Nobody gets out unmarked." Mariah had voiced those same words often.

"You know Grady well."

She swallowed. "I know his type."

"If you're my mother's sister, he's what, your step-father?"

"Not anymore." Her grip on her briefcase handle tightened. "I'll help you with the lease. When do you want to meet at the site?"

Sooner's eyes narrowed. Clearly her curiosity of Charlotte and Grady warred with her desire for help. Desire and ambition won. "Anytime Thursday would work. I just have to tell the guy a time."

Charlotte fished her BlackBerry out of her briefcase and checked her calendar. "How does one work?"

"I don't have to be at work until five."

"One it is. Do you have the address?"

"It's 101 Washington Street."

"Nice area." And right smack dab in the middle of her world. The past had arrived in Alexandria and had set up shop.

"It's a small space in a bookstore, but it's in a high tourist area. And traffic is king."

"You've learned a few lessons from Grady." She'd learned her own share of lessons from Grady. Most weren't good lessons but a few were. Like it or not, the guy knew how to work the crowds, and he knew how to spin a profit out of nothing.

However, the comparison didn't sit well with Sooner. "I'd like to think I figured out a lot for myself."

"Don't be offended. It's a compliment. See you Thursday."

"Sure. Thanks, Aunt Charlotte."

"Please, just call me Charlotte."

A small grin lifted full lips. "Charlotte it is. And Charlotte, I won't horn in on what you've got going here. I can see that I make you uncomfortable. It's a big enough city, so we won't ever have to see each other."

"I don't have a problem with you being in town." The first hit of shock had eased, and her mind was already crammed with more questions for Sooner.

"Sure you do. It's written all over you. But it's okay. It'll be like we never met after Thursday."

She watched the girl walk away, already knowing she'd go to the mat for the kid.

"So who was the girl?" Rokov's deep baritone voice hovered above her.

Charlotte remembered why she and Rokov would never make it. One day she'd have to lie to him. And that day was today. "She's a kid I represented in court. Pro bono work."

"You're doing a lot of that lately." He smelled of motel soap and his own aftershave.

"Seems so." Did she imagine that he'd sensed the lie?

"What was her offense?"

"Shoplifting." Sooner vanished around the corner.

"She guilty?"

She arched a brow. "None of my clients are guilty, Detective Rokov. You know that."

"That's right. I forgot."

"So what brings you to the courthouse?"

"There's a shop down the street that might be able to help me with a case. I'd just parked and was passing by when I saw you."

"And so you stopped." Her BlackBerry buzzed, snagging her attention down at the screen. *Unknown Caller.* "Hey, I need to get back. I'm burning the candle at both ends today."

He frowned. "Sure. See you soon, Charlotte."

"Sure thing, Detective Rokov."

"Detective Rokov?"

"It's your name."

"Kinda formal."

"It's the agreement."

He leaned forward a fraction. "Time to renegotiate, counselor."

Her phone buzzed again in her hand. "I really do have to go."

"Run along."

She walked away slowly and carefully as if she didn't have one regret or worry. She glanced at her text. *Appreciate the help. G.T.*

G.T. Grady Tate. "Son of a bitch."

What were the chances she'd seen the last of Grady Tate? Slim to none.

Rokov and Sinclair entered Tanner's on King Street just as the owner flipped the *Closed* sign to *Open*. The owner was in his mid-sixties and had been in the custom leather business for decades. Rokov's father had once said the man was an artist, and judging by the collection of leather jackets hanging from the wall, he didn't doubt it.

"Mr. Tanner," Rokov said, pulling his badge from his pocket. "Mind if I ask you a couple of questions?"

The old man lifted his gaze from a gray leather jacket sporting a jagged rip and peered over half glasses. Gray wisps of hair framed his thin face. "Daniel Rokov?"

"Yes, sir. I didn't think you'd remember me."

"Of course I remember you. You worked for me for two summers."

"That was a long time ago. I must have been a freshman or sophomore in high school."

The old man smiled. "You've filled out, but you are much the same." He glanced at Sinclair. "He was quite the conscientious young man. Never late. Never complained."

Sinclair grinned. "I've always said he was a Boy Scout."

Mr. Tanner nodded. "How is your father, Daniel?"

"He's well, sir." Mr. Tanner and his father had been friends for thirty years. His father had gotten Rokov that long-ago summer job.

"I've not seen him in a while. This economy keeps menders like your father and I busy. Good for business but not so good for friendships."

"Better to fix the old than buy new." How many times had he heard his father utter those words?

"A notion that is again popular." He set down the jacket and rose, shifting his stance from side to side as if working out kinks. "What can I do for you?"

Rokov unclipped his cell phone from his belt. "I'd like you to look at a picture of a jacket."

"Sure."

Rokov pulled up the picture. He'd been careful to snap just the jacket and not any part of the victim. "You know I'm with the Alexandria Police."

"I do indeed."

He held out the phone to Mr. Tanner. "It's got your name on the label."

He adjusted his glasses and leaned closer. "It was a custom piece. One of a kind. I worked on it for a month."

"Who was it for?"

"A young woman with dark hair." He held up his finger. "But I will have to look up the name. Just a moment. You will wait."

"Of course." He replaced the phone back in its holster.

The old man disappeared through a curtained doorway.

Sinclair glanced around the shop and moved to a black leather jacket. "So you worked here?"

"That's right. I delivered pieces to clients, picked up supplies, ran whatever errand Mr. Tanner needed."

"I thought you worked for your father."

"I did that as well."

She touched a brown jacket's soft leather sleeve. "If I worked here, I'd be broke because I'd be buying all the stock. Gorgeous work."

"Mr. Tanner's work is top of the line. A piece from him will last forever."

She flipped over the price tag. "I don't think I can afford forever. The best I can do is the immediate future."

"So it is with most."

Mr. Tanner reappeared holding a white index card. "Her name is Diane Young. And she lives on Beauregard." He rattled off the address. "So what has happened to Ms. Young?"

"It's not good."

Mr. Tanner frowned. "I am sorry. I remember her now. She was a nice lady. She told me she read fortunes. She said I would live to be very old. I laughed and said I was very old."

Rokov wrote it down. "Thanks, Mr. Tanner."

"Of course, Daniel. Tell your father I said hello."

"I will."

They moved back outside into the sunlight and each put on their sunglasses. "Do you think identifying the victim will be that easy?"

"Let's hope."

He sat in his office watching the video on his computer, earplugs tucked in his ears. The monitor was faced away from the closed door and he could easily minimize the image if someone entered unexpectedly.

The picture was crystal clear, and when he watched the scene on his computer, he felt almost an intimate connection. The world around him faded away, and he imagined he could crawl inside the computer and relive the event.

His hands around the witch's throat, he stared into her eyes. They'd been playing their games for several days, and with each passing day her fear grew, heightening a thrilling sense of power.

But this last time he was not playing any longer. This time, he was here to end their journey together and absorb the power of her magic.

He pushed her head under the water and held tight as she kicked and grabbed at his wrists. A muscle twitched in his jaw as he held her down. Her pulse throbbed faster and faster under his palms. Soon the energy would leave her body and enter his own.

He held so tight to her neck, the small bones of her throat snapped in his hands. Her feet kicked once. Twice. And then her heart stopped.

He closed his eyes, moaning as in a great rush the power hit him like a rough wave. He leaned forward, pressing his forehead to the fresh tattoo on her forehead, savoring the surge that rippled his body with tension.

He held tight to her limp body. His own arms and legs trembled as the flow of magic shot into him again and again until he could no longer endure it.

Finally, he released her, relieved as if he'd just made love. He cupped the witch's lifeless face and then leaned forward and kissed her cold lips. "Go in peace."

He reached for a straight-edge razor on a table by the basin and held it up for inspection. The overhead light caught the edge of the blade, making it wink. He raised his T-shirt and then made a slow slice across his belly.

The need to kill again was already strong. In years past, he could go months or even years between kills, but this time the urges had returned almost immediately. Why was his appetite so voracious? What in the universe so tempted him?

He touched the still tender wound on his belly, pressing until the welcomed pain distracted him from the Need. His heart raced and a bead of sweat appeared on his forehead. The pain would keep him focused. Keep him from killing too soon.

He'd discovered this blade therapy by accident when he was young. He'd been battling the urge to kill in those days, still fearful of crossing the line from light to dark. He'd been watching a woman through her bedroom window, studying her, and fighting the urge to kill. Someone—a neighbor, he supposed—had spotted him and shouted. His heart racing, he'd run through the backyards toward the woods. He'd been disoriented and so frightened. In his haste to get to his car, he fell on his palms and landed against the sharp edge of a rock. When he raised his hands, he saw the blood made black by the moonlight.

In the dark, as he'd stared at the blood, he'd felt sudden relief from the Need. The pain rolled through his hands up his arms. It wrapped him in a tender embrace that blocked out all worries and fears. As long as the pain of the wound had lasted, he'd been able to resist the kill.

He dug his thumb deeper into the wound. Pain pulsed from the long thin gash. He managed a smile and a deep cleansing breath.

The cell phone in his pocket vibrated and pulled him back to the world of the living and the real. He fished out the phone and checked the message. He texted back a response.

He rose, wincing joyfully as the wounded skin pinched and stretched. He grabbed his jacket and slid it on. Most did not understand the importance of his trade. Most did not know there were men like him who kept the world safe. But working anonymously was the secret to his success. As long as the world looked past him, he could continue to hunt.

Chapter 5

Commonwealth Attorney Levi Kane was a well-dressed man. His suits were hand tailored, as were his shirts. His gold cuff links were Dior, and his shoes had a fine polish that always caught the light. He had never had the look of an overworked civil servant but a man who saw the job as a stepping-stone to the next level. He was out to make a name for himself.

So when Charlotte's phone buzzed and Iris announced that Kane stood in the lobby, she wasn't totally surprised. She'd basically kicked his ass during the summations yesterday.

"Give me a minute and then escort him back." She raised her gaze from the doodles. She'd written *Mariah* and *Sooner* on her legal pad and circled both dozens of times. She tore the top sheet, crumpled it into a tight ball, and tossed it in her trashcan. Rising, she pulled her jacket from the back of her door, checked her hair in the bathroom mirror, and touched up her lipstick.

Calm. Cool. Reserved. Nothing can touch you.

When Levi entered her office, she was smiling and waiting, hand extended. "Mr. Kane. To what do I owe the honor of this visit?"

His grip was firm. "I think you know why I'm here, Charlotte."

"Why don't you have a seat?" She moved behind her desk as if to suggest the question wasn't really a question at all but a command.

He checked his watch. "Sure."

She leaned back in her chair. "So how are your wife and children? Last you spoke about them, your wife was in nursing school and the girls were in elementary school."

He set his briefcase beside his chair and smoothed his hand over his red tie. "I'm always amazed how you keep tabs on everyone."

It paid to know the competition. "I like you, Levi. It's natural for me to ask."

"Thanks. And all three are good. My wife will graduate from school in December and the girls love school. Mattie plays soccer and Josie wants to be a ballerina." He pulled a photo from his wallet and showed it to her. "My three angels."

The three had very bright, eager smiles. The littlest one had dark hair like her father and a gleam in her gaze much like Sooner. Sooner likely hadn't played soccer or taken dance lessons.

Charlotte hesitated and then handed the photo back to Levi. "Lovely."

Carefully he tucked the picture back in his wallet. "Now that we've played nice, let's cut to the chase. You know why I'm here. The Samantha White trial."

She folded her hands on her desk and willed all the

distractions from her mind. "What would you like to discuss?"

"Your client is going to be convicted."

It always amused her when someone told her what the future held. "Really?"

"The jury is going to come back with a murder one conviction."

"I don't think so." Feigned smugness aside, she didn't know any more about the trial's outcome than Levi. Juries could be fickle.

He crossed his leg over his knee and adjusted his cuff. "I want to talk again about a plea deal."

She'd hoped her summation yesterday might have prompted a deal. "Let's hear it."

"Samantha killed her husband."

"No one is contesting that. The issue at hand is if the killing was cold-blooded murder or self-defense."

"I've read the files, and I know the woman suffered at her husband's hand. I'm not an unfeeling bastard when it comes to these things. Between you and me, I think his brutality drove her to desperation. But the fact is no one can take the law into their own hands."

"What are you saying?"

"I want to be generous. Second-degree murder. She does fifteen years with credit for time served."

Charlotte's laughter sounded genuine and might have been if she weren't fighting for a woman's life. She wiped away a pretend tear. "You know, Levi, I've already had a trying day, and I was just thinking how nice it would be to have a good laugh. And bless your heart, you have done just that."

He arched a brow. "It wasn't meant to be funny."

"Of course it was," she said, letting the humor drain from her gaze. "In fact, I need to believe it was a joke, otherwise I might take it as an insult. Because no one in this town is naïve enough to believe that I am going to let my twenty-nine-year-old client, the mother of an eight- and ten-year-old, spend the next fifteen years of her life in jail and miss every important moment of her children's lives."

"I'm sorry for those children. I really am. But she killed her husband."

"In self-defense. Stan White was a brutal man who systematically abused his wife the entire ten years they were married. When he tried to murder her in cold blood, she defended herself and he died as a result. She does not deserve to serve one more day behind bars. She deserves to be with her children. And judging by the jury's faces yesterday, she won't go to jail. She will be acquitted."

He sat back in his chair, his expression curious and probing. "Why are you doing this?"

"Doing what?"

"Defending a nobody. I've seen some of the clients you've handled. Big bucks. Big money. Why did you ride in on your white horse to defend this woman? You are pissing away your valuable time on Samantha White."

A nobody. The words rattled in her head. "I appreciate your concern, Levi. But my time is my own to manage as I see fit."

He leaned forward, a conspirator's smile on his lips. "I'd hate to think of all the billable hours that went down the toilet on this case. I mean, an office this fancy has got to cost a fortune, and with less income coming in, well, I'm wondering how long you can hold on."

As long as it takes. "Again your concern touches me so deeply but I can promise you the firm is quite solid and prepared to back Ms. White even through an appeal."

"An appeal? You've got to be kidding. Samantha White is going to do jail time."

"No, she is not."

Annoyance flashed in his eyes. "I always figured you for a smart woman."

"Good for you. Underestimating me is always a mistake."

He tugged at his shirt cuffs. "Are you going to take the plea deal or not?"

The scrapper in her wanted to reach over the desk and smack him hard. But she'd learned that acting out led to unfortunate consequences. She smiled brightly and rose. "Not."

For a moment he did not rise but studied her with narrowed eyes. "So you're going to ride this out to a very bitter and disappointing end?"

"I suppose you will be disappointed when you lose, won't you?" She moved toward the door. "Now if you will excuse me, Levi, I've got work to do."

He stood, his posture stiff with annoyance. "You're making a mistake."

"Have a nice day, Levi."

"Voluntary manslaughter. Eight years with the possibility of parole in five years."

She hesitated. He'd sweetened the pot, another indication he was worried. Next year was an election year, and he wanted the conviction on his record.

"You owe it to your client to tell her about this deal. Five years is a hell of a better deal than life."

Five years would be painful but it wasn't a lifetime. And she owed it to Samantha to tell her about the deal. "I'll pass it on."

"Deal is on the table for twenty-four hours." He moved past her in quick strides.

When she heard the front reception door close, she gripped the edge of her office door so tightly her knuckles ached. She wanted to slam the door over and over again until the wood splintered. Anger had been a constant in her life, and she'd long ago learned to control it. So, she released her grip, carefully removed her jacket, and hung it on the back of her door.

Angie appeared in her doorway. "So what do you think that house call was all about?"

"He's scared."

"He didn't sound scared."

"He was. I could smell it on him. He's offered a plea. Manslaughter. Eight years with the possibility of parole in five years."

"Damn. That's a long way from life for murder one. You want to tell Samantha or do you want me to?"

"I'll do it." She shook her head. "He's not usually the kind to cave."

"If you plea, he has a conviction, and his record remains pristine. He's got ambitions. And that makes him predictable."

"Maybe. He said he felt sorry for Samantha."

"Do you really believe that?"

"No."

Rokov and Sinclair had gone to Diane Young's apartment but it was locked tight. There were no signs of forced entry or break-in and neighbors had reported nothing out of the ordinary. She ran a business from her house, one neighbor had said, and it wasn't unusual for her to go days at a time without being seen. Without a search warrant they'd have to wait to enter the apartment.

None of the neighbors had pictures of Diane, so he'd contacted the Department of Motor Vehicles and requested a picture of her driver's license. The contact at DMV had complained the computers were again down but promised an image by end of business.

Now as the day wound to a close for the nine-to-fivers, Rokov cut down a side street toward the medical examiner's office. Jennifer Sinclair reached for a power bar in her purse and ripped open the wrapper.

"How can you eat that?" Rokov said.

She glanced at the bar as if searching for a problem. "What? I'm hungry."

He shook his head. "Do you ever sit and eat a meal?"

"I'm sitting now."

"At a table."

"Hey, I've conquered half the battle." She bit into the bar.

"I'm talking about eating at a table with chairs and a hot meal."

"Please. I'm single. I eat in front of the computer, on the fly, or if I'm lucky, with the television."

"You never sat down with your family to share a meal?"

"Good Lord, no. Dad and I always ate in front of the television. TV was our version of family interaction."

"What about discussions on politics or family matters?"

Her eyes sparkled with amusement. "I know you got the Old Country thing going with your family. But that's not the way of with Clan Sinclair. Dad and I were the masters of avoiding any deep conversation. I'd venture to say if not for the television, World War

Three might have erupted in our home between me and my dad."

"Shameful."

"Did you and your ex sit at the table?"

He frowned. "Sometimes. But she was on the go with her job, so we rarely were in the same city together."

She peeled away more of the bar's wrapper. "Was it her job that broke you two up?"

He shot her a glance. "Kinda personal, don't you think, Sinclair?"

She shrugged. "Hey, we've been partners over a year, and you've never mentioned her."

He tapped his left hand on the steering wheel. The tan lines of his wedding band had finally faded. It had taken longer because he'd refused to remove the ring until the divorce was final. "She wanted to live in California. She loved her work. And she did not want children. We both realized we wanted very different things out of life."

"No room for compromise?"

He shrugged, wondering how they'd ended up on this line of conversation. Partners shared more with each other than their own families, but he had never discussed his divorce with anyone. "Not for her."

"Do you miss her?"

The question caught him short, and for a moment he thought carefully about the question. "No."

She nodded her approval. "So now that you're officially single, have you been out there tripping the light fantastic?"

"Not much time," he said.

"You still living with your grandmother?" The teasing edge added bite to the words.

He felt no need to apologize. "I have my own place.

I've been with my grandmother the last couple of weeks because my sister, Anna, is out of town. Anna has lived with Grandmother since her fall."

She shifted in the seat toward him. "It's touching. the way you all look out for her. But isn't it weird living with your grandmother?"

"I usually stay with her one night, Sinclair, so Anna can get a break. But for the record, if my grandmother needed me more, I'd be there. She took care of me when I was little and my parents worked eighteen-hour days. Now it's my turn."

"You're a good guy, Danny-boy. Some chick, maybe someone like Charlotte Wellington, is gonna snap you up." She frowned and pretended to think. "Of course, Ms. Wellington has got high maintenance written all over her."

Charlotte wasn't like his ex. On the surface there were similarities. But under the glitz there was more to Charlotte. "Sinclair, you care way too much for my private life."

"I'm living vicariously through you, Danny-boy. My love life is a wasteland. Plus, I like to watch you get revved up when I mention her name. Charlotte. Charlotte. Charlotte."

"Amusing." He drove down the parkway and soon pulled up in front of the regional medical examiner's office. "Do you remember that woman who was talking to Charlotte Wellington?"

"Tall, olive skin, dark hair."

"Yeah. It strike you as odd that Wellington would be representing her?"

"She's doing the pro bono thing more, I hear."

"No, her partner is. She's only committed to the Samantha White case."

"So she's doing another case. What's the dif?"

"Wellington tensed up when the girl started talking to her. She looked almost . . . sad."

"Maybe she feels sorry for the girl."

"It's more than that."

"How so?"

"Don't know yet." He parked the car and turned off the ignition. "I called in to the clerk of the court and got the girl's name. Sooner Tate. Eighteen. Arrest report said she works for the carnival."

"Really?"

"Got charged with shoplifting."

"So how did she hook up with Wellington?"

"That's the mystery. The clerk said Charlotte just appeared and told the judge she was counsel for the defense."

"And why do you care?"

He shook his head. "Good question."

"You just got out of a marriage with Ms. Career. Now you're sniffing around another."

"Doing no such thing." Annoyance snapping, Rokov grabbed his notebook and got out. His partner had a knack for finding the right nerve and twisting.

"Good because the image of you two cuddling over wine . . ." She pretended to shudder. "Twilight Zone."

"We haven't been on a date." Technically true.

"Good because, dude, good working men and princesses don't last."

"You're getting to be a pain, Sinclair."

She grinned. "I do try."

He opened the front door of the medical examiner's office for her and she walked past. "Diane Young bills herself as a fortune teller. You believe in fortune tellers?"

She barked a laugh. "No and hell no. Tell me you don't."

"My grandmother is considered a Seer. Many in the Russian community come to see her for advice."

"Ever occur to you that she's just an experienced older woman with good common sense?"

"She told my cousin last year she'd have two boys before the year ended. We all laughed because Sue said she never wanted kids. She gave birth to twin boys last week." They walked up to the front desk, showed their badges, and signed the visitor's log. Rokov led the way to the elevators and punched the down button.

"I've met Sue. She talks tough but is a marshmallow when it comes to babies."

"Grandmother said my brother would injure his leg when he went to college. He broke it in three places."

"He was a soccer player. A forward center, if I remember. Not a stretch."

"She said you will be married by this time next year."

"Oh, she did?" Sinclair planted her hands on her hips. "So she tell you anything else about my Prince Charming?"

"No."

"Too bad." Sinclair folded her arms over her chest. "She's got good instincts. Not special powers."

"We'll see." The doors opened. "Time to go to work, Sinclair."

They moved down the tiled hallway toward the double set of metal doors. The air had grown thicker with the scent of bleach and cleaners as they'd traveled deeper down the hallway. Above, a fluorescent light buzzed.

"Dr. Henson said she'd start the autopsy by five," Rokov said.

Sinclair checked her watch. "Which is right about now."

Rokov pushed through the door, and they found Dr. Henson standing beside the stainless steel gurney, which held the sheet-draped body of their victim. Henson's red hair was tucked up in a surgical cap as green as the gown, which covered scrubs, and she wore gloves and booties over her feet. On the other side of the gurney was her similarly garbed, though short and heavier, assistant.

The gurney was situated over a drain and pushed close to a sink. The tiled back wall sported a stainless work counter outfitted with a gruesome collection of saws and other instruments.

Henson pulled back the sheet covering the victim. "Just in time, detectives. Suit up, and we can have a look at your victim."

The detectives donned gowns and gloves and moved toward the table. Both stiffened just a little as Henson dragged the sheet from the victim's naked body.

Suspended from the ceiling was a microphone, which Dr. Henson could control with a pedal under the examine table. The doctor pressed the button with her foot and said in a clear voice, "It's October nineteenth, five p.m. and I have in attendance, Detectives Jennifer Sinclair and Daniel Rokov with the Alexandria Police Department and my assistant, Nancy Farmer. I have rolled the victim's prints and submitted them to forensics, and we are waiting for an identification."

"We might have a possible on her identity," Rokov said. "I'm waiting on a picture from DMV."

Dr. Henson reviewed the victim's stats for the tape recorder as she moved up to the head of the table.

"There is trauma to her hands and feet, all caused by wooden stakes being driven through her extremities. Judging by the wounds, I'd say those assaults were done post mortem."

"What about the tattoo on her head?" Rokov said.

"It's fresh. There's slight bruising around the letters, which tells me she was alive when this was done. The letters are in a crude block style." She pulled a ruler from the exam tray. "And measure one-and-a-half inches in height. The letters stretch the full length of her forehead."

Rokov drew in a breath at he stared at the dead woman's pale, sunken face. The skin on the face was particularly thin so receiving a tattoo would have been painful. Judging by the thickness of the letters and the careful lines, he guessed the act took several hours. "What about cause of death?"

Dr. Henson shook her head. "No gun or knife wounds. Bruising around the throat but her windpipe is not crushed. There is water in her lungs. I'll know better when I open her up and run blood tests."

And so they stood watching the doctor complete a thorough external examination. She noted scars, bruises, other tattoos, moles, and any bit of information that could catch a killer. No telling what piece of evidence would be the one that would eventually catch the killer, so it all had to be collected and noted.

Henson studied the victim's hand and then, using a clipper, snapped off bits of nails painted hot pink. She studied the nails under a microscope. "We might have a little DNA, folks. Looks like she might have scratched him."

Rokov watched as she bagged the clippings. "Great. You think you can rush through the results?"

"Backlog is high now, but I'm sure I can make a compelling argument. Still, it will be at least a week."

"As soon as you have DNA, I'll run it through CODIS." CODIS was a national database containing DNA profiles from unsolved crimes, missing persons, and the convicted. "The killer is so careful and practiced, I'll bet money this is not his first time."

Once the evidence had been tagged, the doctor continued with her external exam. Only when she'd inspected the body fully did she reach for her scalpel and make the Y-incision on the victim's chest.

Though stoic, Rokov reminded himself that the body on the table no longer carried the soul or life of the woman. She felt nothing. She was beyond this world. And her body was no more than evidence that would help him catch her killer. And yet as the sharp tip of the blade breached the skin, he could not quite quell the anger and sense of violation. The killer had violated and terrorized her, and now it felt like they were doing the same.

Dr. Henson reported that the victim's heart, lungs, liver, and other vital organs all were a healthy weight. When she opened the lungs, she said, "It looks like she drowned."

"Drowned?"

"There is water here. But blood tests will give me a better idea."

"Drowning has got to be one of the worst ways to die," Sinclair whispered. "I nearly drowned as a kid, and I'll never forget the sensation."

Rokov glanced at his partner, and for the first time, she looked upset. However, a tender word would be met with scorn, so he ignored the comment. "She was drowned in one location, brought to the abandoned restaurant, and staked to the ground." Rokov made notes in his book.

Dr. Henson continued her autopsy with a vaginal examination. For this Rokov did drop his gaze and waited to hear the doctor confirm what he already suspected.

"She was sexually assaulted," Dr. Henson said.

Sinclair muttered an oath. "Any semen?"

"No. He was careful to use a condom. I would suggest that, based on the damage, he raped her several times."

A heavy silence filled the room as she finished taking swabs and then covered up the lower half of the body. When Henson pronounced the autopsy complete, the detectives moved toward the door. They pulled off their scrubs, dumped them in a laundry bin, and moved into the hallway.

Sinclair pressed fingers to her temples. "He's going to do it again."

"What makes you say that?"

"He went after her like he was on some damn holy mission. And fanatics on a mission don't stop at one."

Rokov often played devil's advocate. "A bad breakup or divorce. Emotions run hot."

"Hot? Shit. This goes beyond regular anger and frustration. This is crazy-guy behavior."

"No argument." Rokov's cell buzzed. He removed it from the holster, and checked the caller's identity. "It's Kier."

Detective Malcolm Kier was partnered with the senior member in the unit, Deacon Garrison. Kier hailed from the southern part of the state and last year had married Angie Carlson, Wellington's associate.

Rokov opened his phone. "Rokov."

"I got your DMV picture. Where are you?"

"Medical examiner's office."

"I'll send it to your phone."

"Thanks."

"The magistrate says if the photo matches this victim, you'll have your search warrant right away."

"Good." His phone beeped. The image of Diane Young's driver's license photo appeared on the screen.

He held the DMV photo next to the victim on Dr. Henson's table. Dark eyebrows, round face, full lips. It was a match.

Rokov raised the phone to his ear. "Tell the magistrate the photo is a perfect match."

"I'll get the warrant," Kier said.

He checked his watch. "It's past seven so the traffic should be gone. I want to search her place tonight. The sooner we catch this nut, the better."

Chapter 6

Tuesday, October 19, 7:30 p.m.

The detectives arrived at Diane Young's house just after ten p.m. Forensic technicians were backlogged at another crime scene but had said they'd follow within the next half hour.

Diane Young lived on the top floor of a three-story brick apartment complex in New Market Apartments off Beauregard Street. The three-hundred-plus-unit complex was constructed mostly of brick and had plenty of grass and well-established trees for shade. Located on the border of the city of Alexandria and Arlington County, it had been built in the late seventies and was considered nice and affordable.

A single light illuminated the top level and the metal doors that led to the four different units. Each of the doors had either a wreath or a welcome sign, including Diane Young's, which sported a piece of stained glass artwork fashioned into a half-moon.

Rokov pulled on his rubber gloves, and then using the master key from the complex manager, he opened the front door. He flipped on the light just inside the front door. He glanced inside the apartment, taking note of parquet floors that led to a galley kitchen, and then to a dining room.

An eleven-by-fourteen painting featuring the sun and the moon hung on the wall just inside the small foyer, and below it a small table sported a basket and a cell phone charger. No doubt, like him, Diane put her keys in the basket and her phone on the charger in the same place every time when she returned home.

"She's got a thing for the sun and moon," Sinclair said.

Rokov nodded. "Records show that she owned a business called Beyond. Apparently she reads horoscopes and tarot cards for Internet customers."

Sinclair flipped on the lights in the kitchen. A pot rack filled with copper pans dangled from the ceiling, and a rich maple dinette set filled the corner nook. "Looks like business might have been good."

"According to the city business license department, she made six figures last year. And the business owns three top-of-the-line computers, a scanner, and printer."

Moving through the kitchen into the dining room, they noted the furniture was made of a rich fine-grained wood. A china cabinet was stocked with fine crystal and china. More paintings on the walls featured the sun and moon theme. They rounded a small corner and into the living room filled with a brown leather sofa, two club chairs, a coffee table, and a wide-screen television. An oval Oriental rug pulled the space together.

The magazines on the coffee table were neatly

stacked. Rokov picked up a copy of a fashion magazine. Diane had dog-eared the pages of the articles she wanted to read. Not surprisingly, she'd made notes in the margins on the horoscope page. "*JV! Wrong! Too general.* Looks like she didn't have much use for the monthly horoscope column."

Sinclair picked up another magazine. "She's done the same here. I guess she was always tracking the competition."

Other than Diane's notes in the magazines, the place was eerily put together. Not a pillow was out of place or a picture askew. "She liked things neat."

Sinclair picked up a picture of Diane and another woman who shared her blue eyes and black hair. "Think this is her sister?"

Rokov glanced at the photo. "Good bet. I've got an officer trying to track down next of kin."

Walking through a victim's home always left Rokov feeling like the interloper. A week ago, Diane had been alive and well and sitting on this couch, watching TV, eating a snack, and marking up her magazines. Now she lay in the morgue, a Y-incision on her chest, waiting for next of kin to claim her. "Let's have a look at the back two rooms."

The first room, listed as the unit's den, was set up as a bedroom. A twin bed, covered in a silk comforter, hugged one wall. Beside the bed stood a nightstand with a pair of glasses, a half glass of water, and a bottle of sedatives. Pink slippers peeked out from under the bed. The room's small closet was crammed full of her clothes and shoes.

Rokov picked up the pill bottle made out to Diane Young, prescribed by a Dr. Wexler seven days ago. He opened the bottle. Only three pills remained. "She's taken more than her share in the last week."

"What or who could have stressed her?"

"That might be the million-dollar question."

The next room, considered the master bedroom, had been set up as an office. The walls were covered with astrological charts, stars, moons, and inspirational quotes. In the center of it all was a circular desk equipped with three top-of-the-line laptops. In the corner was a high-capacity printer and fax machine and next to it a shredder. A lush purple carpet warmed the floor, and a pale plum coated the walls.

"So she's all about tradition in the other rooms, but here it looks a little like a mystic's shop."

"That's what she was for lack of a better description." He sat down in Diane's chair and glanced at the blotter covered with jotted notes. Most of the notes were restaurant names and numbers. "Most of these places offer takeout. I bet she almost never cooked."

"Welcome to my world."

Rokov shook his head as he clicked on the computer. The screen popped up and immediately requested a password. "Looks like we'll have to wait for the computer guys to do their thing."

Rokov heard the squeak of the front door and immediately he and Sinclair drew their weapons and moved toward the hallway. Adrenaline popped and snapped through his body. Forensics was expected but he never assumed a visitor was a friend until confirmed. It wouldn't be the first time a murderer had returned to collect damning evidence.

"Hello! Diane. Are you here?"

The woman's tentative voice gave him pause as it

bounced off the walls and down the hallway. The voice was tinged with fear and worry.

Rokov rounded the corner, his gun in hand. "Alexandria Police. Identify yourself."

The woman screamed and jumped back. Her gaze darted between Rokov and Sinclair. "Who are you?"

Immediately, he recognized the woman from the framed photo on Diane's end table. He lowered the tip of his gun but maintained a firm grip. "Alexandria Police. I'm Detective Rokov and this is my partner, Detective Sinclair. Please identify yourself."

Dark hair swept over narrow shoulders and accentuated pale, pale skin. Frown lines etched her forehead, and her lips were drawn and thin. "I'm Suzanne Young. I'm Diane's sister. What are you doing here?"

Rokov let out a breath and lowered his gun. He pulled out his badge and showed it to her. "Ma'am, may I see some identification?"

He tucked his badge back in his pocket as she fumbled in a sac purse and dug out a black wallet. With trembling fingers, she pulled out her driver's license and handed it to him. Her name was listed as Suzanne Elizabeth Young, aged twenty-six of Arlington, Virginia. He handed the license back to her and holstered his weapon. Sinclair did the same.

Suzanne gripped the wallet in her fist as she stared at them. "What are you doing in my sister's apartment?"

"Why don't you come into the living room and have a seat?" Sinclair said. The detective could hold her own with the department's toughest cop or face down any assailant and still possessed a surprising knack for dealing with victims and their families.

"Lady, I do not want to sit down," Suzanne said. Tears welled in her eyes. "What are you doing here?"

Death notices were never easy, and Rokov had learned years ago from a veteran detective to make them as quick as possible. "Ms. Young, your sister's body was found early this morning in an abandoned building. She'd been murdered." The gruesome details would eventually be revealed to Suzanne, but for now he'd spare her.

Tears spilled down her cheeks. "What do you mean, she's dead? You've got it wrong. Diane cannot be dead."

"We're very certain, ma'am," Rokov said.

"How can you be certain?"

Sinclair stepped toward her. "She was wearing a very distinctive red jacket. We located the seller, and he gave us your sister's name. The woman we have in the morgue matches your sister's DMV photo."

"You could have made a mistake."

"It's no mistake. We've taken prints and plan to match them to ones found in this apartment."

Suzanne dragged trembling hands through dark hair that looked so much like her sister's. "There has got to be a mistake."

"No mistake," Rokov said.

She looked to the picture taken of the two sisters. Her eyes brightened as if clinging to a happier memory. "We had that picture taken this past summer. Diane almost never got out of her apartment and I was able to coax her out. We went into Washington, had lunch, and saw a show."

"You said she didn't go out much?" Rokov said.

"Her work kept her busy."

Sinclair closed the gap between her and Suzanne and cupped her elbow with her hand. "Come and sit down. Let me get you a glass of water."

Suzanne allowed the detective to lead her onto the living room sofa. Rokov went into the kitchen and pulled a glass from the cabinet and filled it with water. He moved into the living room and handed it to Suzanne, who accepted it with trembling hands. She made no move to drink the water but held the glass tight. *Pale and fragile* would have described her best right now.

"Can you tell us a little bit more about what your sister did?" Rokov took a seat in one of the club chairs. Knowing his height could be intimidating, he leaned forward and dropped his gaze a fraction.

"She ran a website."

"*Beyond*," Sinclair said.

"That's right. She read cards and did charts. She'd become widely popular in the last year. Hits on her site were over a half a million last month."

Rokov had never heard of *Beyond*, but knew that rate of visitation would have put her on a lot of people's radar. "Is that why she didn't go out much?"

Her gaze shifted slightly as she stared at the water glass. "She said it was the work that kept her here in the apartment. She said she always had more and more requests to fill. She said it was all she could do to keep up."

"But work wasn't the only reason she stayed in the apartment."

When Suzanne raised her gaze, he knew he'd hit a nerve. "It started a couple of years ago."

"What started?" he coaxed.

"She got more and more nervous about driving on the Beltway. She said the traffic was driving her nuts. That's when she founded *Beyond*. She'd work on the site on weekends and evenings. It seemed to really calm her nerves so I thought it was great. And then the site took off and she was able to quit her job as a secretary and devote all her time to it. She was so happy that I didn't really put two and two together. Then one day I asked her if she wanted to get lunch in two weeks, and she said she'd likely have far too much work to make it. That's when I realized she had a problem."

"There were sedatives on her nightstand."

"She needed those to sleep and to just walk to the mailbox."

"The bottle was almost empty."

"She'd said on the phone last week that she'd been considering meeting one of her clients for a date. He e-mailed her a lot, and she was kinda falling for him."

"You know who this guy was?" Rokov said.

"No. She just mentioned him in passing. He said he wanted to take her to the carnival that had just arrived in town. He was really into astrology and energy healing. It never occurred to me that she'd really go on a date." Suzanne shook her head. "I should have pushed this homebound thing more with Diane. I talked to several doctors about her and even a lawyer. They all said she was over twenty-one, was working steadily, and didn't appear to be a danger to herself. They said there wasn't anything I could really do unless she tried to hurt herself."

"She ever try to hurt herself?" Rokov said.

"No. Never. Diane really did enjoy this world she'd created. Here, she said, she was the queen."

Someone or something had coaxed her outside. "Did she have any tattoos?"

"Yeah. A few. She had a snake on her arm and two

bands around her ankle. There is also a long string of stars tattoo at the base of her spine."

All matched the autopsy findings. "Any words?"

"Like what?"

"Any kind."

"No."

"When we found your sister, she had the word *Witch* tattooed on her forehead."

Suzanne frowned. "Diane did not have the word *Witch* on her forehead. Are you really sure you have the right person?"

"Yes, ma'am. Very sure." Had Diane summoned the courage to get out of her apartment in the last week and get the tattoo or had the killer done it?

"She had a thing about the skin on her face. It was part of her getting out of the house problem. She didn't want the sun to ruin her skin. She took pride in how smooth and pale it was." Her eyes watered up again. "Do you think whoever killed her did that to her?"

"That's what we're trying to figure out."

"How did she die?"

"She was drowned."

"What? She doesn't even swim. She hated the water and never goes near it."

"That's what the autopsy revealed."

She closed her eyes and shook her head. "This doesn't make sense. Why would anyone want to hurt Diane? She had her quirks, but she was kind."

"Do you happen to know the password for her computer?" Rokov said.

"It's 1985diane. The year she was born plus her name."

"I'd like to have a look at her computer and see if

I can open her e-mails." The question was a courtesy. With or without her permission, he was going to look.

"Sure. Go ahead."

As he rose, Suzanne moved to stand as well. "Why don't you stay here with Officer Sinclair?"

Sadness and sincerity rolled off her. "I might be able to help."

"I appreciate that. Really. But until I know what I have, it's better that I have a look first." He felt for Suzanne Young, but at this point he didn't know much about her or her relationship with her sister. And until he understood the players, he'd maintain strict control.

As he moved down the hallway, Suzanne's soft weeping followed him. He sat at Diane's desk and typed in the password. It worked and in seconds the main desktop screen appeared.

The desktop had twenty folders. Tarot. Horoscope. Clients. The Star. Moon. It would take hours if not days to dig through all that she'd created.

He opted to open the e-mail and see who'd been talking directly to her. He hit *Get Mail* and waited for the latest messages to load. If Diane had been dead twenty-four to thirty-six hours, it had been at least that long since she'd checked her messages. It took nearly a minute for all the messages to load, and by the time the ticker had stopped counting, he had over one thousand two hundred unread messages. He sat back in his chair. The last time she'd checked messages had been Friday, October 15. She'd died on Monday night. Had the killer held her for three days?

He arranged the messages in alphabetical order and scanned to see who had sent her the most messages. This wasn't necessarily going to give him the killer's contact information, but it was a place to start. The top three contenders for the most e-mail were *CelticLove2*, *SmithAB*, and *Wolf-Woman Six*. He opened the last message from *CelticLove2*.

> Beyond,
>   Where r you? I need advice! Should I marry
> him or not?

All of *CelticLove2*'s other messages were much the same. She wanted love advice.

SmithAB was next in line, so he opened the last message sent. He seemed to be searching for financial advice. He needed stock tips and advice about dealing with his mother. And *Wolf-Woman Six* was trying to decide if she could take a new job. All everyday questions that required thought and common sense, not a card reader.

His grandmother had once said many young girls would come to her with silly questions about love and marriage, and his grandmother always advised them to look at the facts. Make a list of pros and cons, so to speak. The most frequent e-mailers could have benefited from this advice.

None of the most frequent e-mailers' messages sounded threatening or dangerous. And none mentioned the carnival. The computer expert would have to dig through his haystack of leads and hope there was a needle of evidence.

Mariah and Grace huddled in the bed together, staring out the trailer window at the crystal blue sky.

"I've never seen a stomach so big." Mariah smoothed her hand over the taut belly.

Grace smiled, her gaze a mixture of sadness and fear. "Kinda gross if you think about it. Like Invasion of the Body Snatchers."

A kick fluttered under Mariah's hand. "It moves a lot."

"Yeah."

Mariah kept her gaze on the stars. She'd never been good at speaking her mind and didn't know how to voice all her thoughts and fears now. "I'm scared."

"Me, too."

Charlotte startled awake and for an instant didn't recognize her surroundings. She blinked and searched for familiarity. Slowly, the elements in the room made sense: robe over the edge of her blue comforter, wide oval mirror over a dresser filled with cosmetics, and teacup on a glass table by the chaise. This was her bedroom and she was lying on her chaise by the window. Around her were rows of boxes, some fully packed and others still empty and waiting for her attention.

Files strewn on her lap, she rubbed her eyes and glanced at the clock beside her bed. One forty-one. The last thing she remembered was that it was midnight and she'd been proofing briefs. She must have drifted asleep.

She'd not dreamed of Mariah for years and in the last week she'd dreamed of her twice. The first time she'd been screaming for help. And this second time they'd been talking about the baby. Carnival. Grady. Sooner. All had invaded her life and she supposed dreams of Mariah would be natural.

Charlotte swung her bare feet off the chaise and pushed her papers off her lap. Standing, she glanced out the picture window that looked out over the river. She would dearly miss this view, which offered her a sense of peace on the endless nights when sleep avoided her. This sweeping vista of the Potomac had been the reason she'd bought the condo.

And next week, she would lose it forever.

She'd gotten another voice mail from Robert today, and he'd told her he'd lined up a carpenter to fix the few minor annoyances the buyer wanted repaired. She wasn't keen on having a stranger in her apartment, but Robert had assured her that the man was very reputable.

Charlotte glanced up at the sky and let her gaze settle on the North Star. She'd wished on that star as a kid. Then her wishes had more to do with her mother's outbursts. But no matter how much Grace had wished, begged, or pleaded with the heavens, her mother had never improved. In fact, she'd gotten worse.

By the time Grace left the carnival for good, she'd learned that wishes were for fools. And if she wanted something to happen, she had to get out in the world and hustle for it.

Seeing Sooner today had been jarring. Over the years she'd thought about the girl and wondered what she looked like, how she wore her hair, and how her voice sounded. But staring at her today had been a shock to her senses. It had been like staring at a ghost.

It shamed Charlotte that she'd not told Sooner the entire truth. The girl had a right to know. They were blood. And Charlotte had denied her.

* * *

"Tell me again what we are doing here?" Sinclair rubbed gloved hands together as she glanced around the dark, deserted parking lot.

Rokov opened the trunk of his car and glanced at the heavy cloth bag filled with sand. "When we saw the crime scene this morning, it was in daylight."

She burrowed her chin deeper into the black scarf wound around her neck. "What's wrong with daylight?"

"The killer would have seen this place at night." Rokov set the one-hundred-and-twenty-pound bag by the car. "We walked up those stairs. But he lugged up one hundred and twenty pounds of dead weight plus some kind of bag to hold all his goodies." He retrieved a backpack.

She glanced at his running shoes. Paulie, based on the shoe impression he collected, guessed that the killer had worn a narrow running or cross training shoe. "You're going to walk in the killer's shoes."

"That's right." He slammed the trunk closed.

"Do you really think you'll learn something?"

"Won't know until I try." He slung the backpack up on his back and hefted the bag of sand. "You talked to the property manager of this place?"

"I did. And I asked him about the lock on the top floor. He said it was dead bolted when he checked it four days ago."

"So the killer picked the lock last night or sometime in the last four days."

"Exactly." He glanced at the stairs.

"You want me to follow?"

"No. Use that camcorder and tape me. Who knows what we'll see."

She nodded, scanning the lot. "We know that the first-floor door was secured so the only way to the second floor was by the exterior staircase. And the upper door was bolted shut."

With the weight on his shoulder, Rokov moved toward the stairs. Sinclair hit record. He tested the weight on the old stairs and took his first step. The stairs moaned painfully under the added weight of the "body," and his own body shifted. He grabbed for the railing to steady himself before continuing to climb.

In the dark, maneuvering the shaky steps wasn't as easy, and his pace was much slower than it had been that morning. The slower pace coupled with the weight left him winded whereas the morning's climb had been effortless. The old staircase kept moaning and groaning, and several more times he had to readjust the "body" to maintain his balance. Halfway up he paused on the first landing to catch a breath or two. He considered himself fit, but the added dead weight was taxing. From here, he had a clear view of the river and the moon, which dripped light on the calm waters. Had the killer been winded? Had he stopped?

He continued the climb to the top floor and paused at the door. The door had been dead bolted and so to open it now would require setting the body down and then working on the lock. But a search around the small landing made that theory improbable. There was little room to move around let alone stash a body and then pick the lock. The killer must have been here before. He'd come within the four-day window and broken into the building.

Rokov opened the door and moved inside the main room. The moon was nearly full tonight as it had been last night. Weather conditions were similar so he could trust that the light he saw now was similar to what the killer saw. Moonlight streamed into the room, illuminating the spot where they'd found the body, now marked by the red crime scene tape.

Rokov moved to the spot and laid his weight down. His shoulders were stiff and his back ached. This kind of work was not an old man's game. If the killer weren't young, he'd have to be incredibly fit to maneuver the shifting stairs with such a weighty burden.

From his backpack he pulled out a candle, and he lit it as he imagined the killer did. He placed it at the body's head just as they'd found the original. Then he dug out a flashlight and photos of the body. The killer had taken great time with the body, so he'd not felt rushed, as if he knew exactly what he was doing. Lay the body down. Fix her hair. Straighten her skirt. Stretch her hands and feet out. Stake them to the ground. Sprinkle the ring of salt.

Paulie had found footprints by the window. Rokov moved to the window. It was a nice view. The water. The lights on the Maryland side of the Potomac. The boats in the water. Had he first spotted his location from the water? Maybe the shoes weren't cross-trainers but boating shoes.

Strong. A locksmith. A boater.

He checked his watch. It had taken him fifteen minutes to scale the side, enter the room, and lay his body down. He returned to the body and imagined the killer pulling stakes and salt from the backpack. The bar owner had seen the candle flickering about twelve thirty.

The killer would easily have been here an hour.

"You weren't in a rush at all, were you?" He rose from the salt circle. "This is all a part of the ritual of death, isn't it?"

He squatted and studied the scene. It would talk to him eventually. When it was ready, it would tell him what happened. His cell phone rang. "Rokov."

"What gives?" Sinclair said. "You see anything?"

"What am I missing?" He glanced around the scene, absorbing what the killer saw. *Talk to me.* But the room remained stubbornly silent.

"I don't know. Yet."

Chapter 7

Grady let the cigarette smoke trickle from his mouth and nose as he leaned back against the seat of his pickup truck. He stared across the street at the offices of Wellington and James, feeling a surge of resentment. His girl Grace had done right well for herself and made good on all the teenage proclamations he'd discounted. He'd always figured she'd grow tired of fighting, trade on her looks, and sell herself to a rich husband.

But she'd not sold herself to the highest bidder. No, his smart-mouthed girl had gotten herself a fancy education and built herself a fine business. "You got more grit than I imagined."

When she and her sister had been little, he'd kept a close eye on them, knowing the young bucks in the carnival would have used them up good. He'd kept them away from those hounds because he'd considered them special. Turns out he'd failed both his girls.

Despite his failures, he'd kept tabs on Charlotte all

these years. He might have let her leave, but he'd made it a point to know where she lived, whom she dated, and where she worked. He'd always figured she'd leave this area as soon as she could, but she never had. He reckoned that had more to do with Mariah and Sooner. Alexandria was the last place she'd seen both, and maybe deep in her gut, she figured if she stayed, she'd see them both again.

Grace always had been his sentimental one.

It didn't take a genius to see the way her lips curled with disgust yesterday when she'd first laid eyes on him.

Well, she might have thought that she'd left the carnival behind, but she'd not. She was as much a part of the Family today as she was as a kid. No breaking that link.

He took another drag on the cigarette and savored the way the smoke burned his lungs and nose. This time when he exhaled, it triggered a coughing fit that overtook him for nearly a minute. When he finally got a hold of himself, he stared at the glowing tip, annoyed.

She might not want anything to do with him but that was just too damn bad.

Grady cupped the filtered tip between his lips and let the smoke rise around him. This time he avoided inhaling deeply as he checked his watch. "Come on, girl, I ain't got all day."

The carnival sales numbers had been brisk last night, and he'd been pleased to see they'd break even. Folks were anxious to see the carnival, knowing it would be its last season.

His lips curled. Last season. The ploy had boosted ticket sales in city after city and proved that there was one born every minute. And announcing to the press that Sooner could solve murders had been a stroke of genius. No matter what town they had visited, he'd found an unsolved crime and claimed Sooner could close the case. The local cops hadn't appreciated it, but it had pulled in the customers.

Grady spotted the stock of auburn hair and immediately sat up a little straighter. He jammed the butt in the ashtray and got out of his car. He waited until the door to the law offices opened before he called out her name, "Grace."

Her shoulders stiffened and tensed. It pleased him to know he could still rattle her cage. It was important that she remember her roots and who had been there for her when she was young.

Slowly, she turned. She wore all black and a string of pearls around her neck. In the last seventeen years she'd slimmed down, and he realized the words *fancy* or *uptown* did not do her justice.

"You remind me of your mama when I first met her. Full of fire and spunk, she never shied from a fight. Course, the years robbed her of that spunk."

If he'd hit his mark, she showed no sign of it. "What do you want, Grady?"

"I came to talk to you."

"We talked yesterday. Aunt Charlotte helped Sooner, and she won't be going to jail. We have nothing more to discuss so get the hell off my property."

God, but she could still piss him off faster than anyone. "We got a lot to talk about."

She jammed her key in the lock and opened her front door. "Leave."

"Or what, baby girl? You gonna call the police on your uncle Grady? Be a shame to do that, wouldn't it?

Then I'd have to tell them about all the money you stole from the till."

Her lips flattened and she stilled.

He'd gotten her with that tidbit. "You think I'd forget how you stole that money from me before you ran away? When I saw that empty till, I was fit to be tied. I nearly chased you down."

"Why didn't you?"

"'Cause I had a carnival to run and Baby Sooner to raise."

Her face paled with fury. "I left the carnival because Mariah was dead and you swore Sooner would have a real family."

"I gave you a choice. Go without her. Stay with her. Nobody gets their cake and eats it, too."

That barb triggered the wince he'd wanted. She stepped over her threshold and held the door open for him. "Come inside."

He was about to make another crack when another woman walked into the reception area from the back. She was blond, tall, and well dressed. He wouldn't call her stunning, but she was a fine-looking woman that he'd never have refused.

"Charlotte?" the woman said.

Grace straightened her shoulders. "Angie, this is Grady Tate. He had a few questions for me." She kept her gaze away from him as she said, "Grady this is my associate, Angie Carlson."

Grace's words were refined and polite enough, but her rigid stance all but shouted, *Fuck Off*. And it also wasn't lost on him that she'd not told Angie about their relationship. Uppity girl was ashamed of him.

"How you do, Ms. Angie." He wiped his right hand on his jeans and then extended it to her.

To Angie's credit, she accepted his hand, but the gesture did not lesson the wariness in her gaze. "And who are you, Mr. Tate?"

"Back in the day, I was married to her mama before she passed. God rest her soul." He grinned. "Charlotte's not one for remembering her roots, so I reckon she's not mentioned me."

Angie glanced to Grace, but said nothing. Grace made no move to deny or add to his comment, but he supposed if she'd had a gun right now, he'd have a bullet between his eyes. "No, she has not mentioned you."

"Grady," Grace said. "We don't need to hold Angie up. Come back to my office, so we can talk in private."

"Sure, baby girl. Sure." He followed her down a hallway of plush carpet and fancy paintings. The deeper he went into her world, the more he felt out of his element. She was doing a fine job of making him feel second-rate. "So you've never told anyone about your past?"

"No." She set her briefcase on her desk. "And I want to keep it that way."

"You're ashamed of your past."

Her lips lowered into a thin smile. "Let's just say, it wasn't the best of beginnings."

"It wasn't all that bad. You never went hungry. I did well by you."

"I guess in your mind you did."

"You're pissed because my place wasn't fancy."

"That's not why I hated living with you and you know it. Now tell me what you want, or you can tell it to the police. I'm tired and irritated and quite happy to share a few dirty secrets with the cops."

Grady grinned, holding up his hands in surrender.

"No need to get nasty, baby girl. I just came by to thank you for helping Sooner."

"You did that by text yesterday."

"That kind of favor deserves a personal thank-you."

Her eyes narrowed. "Due diligence done. Now go."

"Aren't you curious at all about the girl? Seems to me after a night to rest on it, you'd have lots. You was always one for questions."

She hesitated. "If I have questions, I'll ask Sooner."

"She looks like Mariah but she's wired like you."

"Why are you telling me this?"

"Just thought you'd like to know."

"Really? Or maybe you see a chance to hurt me. As I remember, you liked hurting people when life wasn't going your way." Acid dripped from the words.

"You should be nice to me, baby girl."

"Or what, Grady? You'll go to the police about the money I stole. Try making that charge stick, old man."

"I came with hat in hand, hoping things could be different between us."

"Oh, it's different all right. If it's possible, I hate you more."

His gaze narrowed. "You're gonna be sorry you treated me so poorly today."

"I'll take my chances. Now get the hell out of my life."

A bitter smile twisted his lips as he moved to the door. "Ain't no getting rid of me, baby girl, until I say so."

Samantha White sat in the visitor's waiting area of the regional jail waiting for Charlotte Wellington. Like her, the other prisoners sat on benches mounted to three-by-five tables constructed of a thick worn plastic that was as gray and lifeless as the walls and tiled ceiling. The furnishings, like the women, looked haggard and worn down and the entire place had a sick-sweet smell that she would never forget.

At the table to her right sat a tall buxom woman with thinning black hair and rotting teeth. A meth addict accused of robbery, she leaned forward whispering to a guy who was just as thin as weary as she. At another table a heavyset black woman with corn rows and full cheeks spoke to a woman who wore her graying hair in a neat bun and lace around her collar. The older woman held a Bible in her hand as she listened to the inmate, shook her head, and whispered, "Help her, Jesus." And at still another table sat a mother smiling anxiously at her teen children. The oldest of the children, a girl, kept her body stiff and rigid whereas her little brother's body danced with excitement.

Samantha's handcuffs clinked as she knitted her fingers together and dropped her gaze to the table. When she'd first been arrested, her mother had offered to bring the children to visit, but Samantha had refused. She didn't want her children seeing her locked up.

"It wouldn't be forever," she'd told her mother. "And I don't want the memory of their mother in handcuffs burned in their brain."

"They miss you," her mother had said.

"I miss them."

"They miss their father."

Samantha had dropped her head, pain and bitterness eating at her stomach. "It's not their fault."

"I should tell them what he did."
"No. Not now."

Samantha had not seen her children in thirteen months. She conjured the photo image of the girls she kept in her cell. How much had they changed? What moments had she missed that would be lost to her forever? Did they even think about her anymore?

A sadness rose up inside her as it had so many times since the night her husband died. Despite it all, she missed not only the girls but Stan as well. They'd had a good life, and she still couldn't quite accept that he'd wanted to kill her and the girls. That last desperate moment they shared felt like a nightmare and not reality.

She raised her gaze toward the clock. Ms. Wellington was five minutes late. Worry burrowed deeper into her brain. Ms. Wellington had called the prison for an appointment yesterday, but had not been given a visitation time until today. Had the jury come back?

Since the trial had begun, she'd questioned every glance, every word that was spoken and unspoken. Did the jury believe her story? Did the judge appear angry with her? Did the guards know if the jury had returned with the verdict? The guessing was driving her insane.

A shift in the guard's attention had her sitting straighter, and she watched as the matron beckoned someone forward. Samantha moistened her lips and tucked a stray wisp of hair behind her ear.

To her relief, Charlotte Wellington appeared, and when the guards buzzed her in, she walked into the room with such bearing everyone noticed. Ms. Wellington scanned the room only once before spotting Samantha.

She offered a smile that she hoped conveyed gratitude without hinting of arrogance. Stan had hated that kind of look. "Ms. Wellington."

Ms. Wellington smiled. "How are you doing, Samantha?"

She wanted to rise, but the rules didn't allow it. She nodded. "I'm doing well, Ms. Wellington."

The attorney wore a dark tailored suit that hugged a slim figure and accentuated long legs. A bright blue silk top added a pop of color to skin that might have looked washed out if she'd chosen a less bold color. Auburn hair was swept up into a neat bun that showed off her high slash of cheekbones.

There'd been a time when Samantha had dressed well. Days spent shopping casually and recklessly were now a distant memory in a life that had died with her husband.

"You're holding up well?" Ms. Wellington pulled files and a yellow legal notepad from her sleek black briefcase.

"I'm fine. I haven't heard from my mother in a few days. I'm worried about the children."

"I spoke to your mother this morning when she called the office to see if the jury has returned. She's taking the kids out of town. They're spending the next few days at the beach. They'll be back by the weekend."

"Is everything all right?"

"Yes. Why wouldn't it be?"

She glanced from side to side before saying, "I've been receiving letters. Some are quite hateful."

Ms. Wellington sighed. "Your case got a lot of media attention, which can pull out the crazies."

"Mom hasn't mentioned any trouble?"

"None. She just thought the beach would be a nice change for the kids."

"You'd let me know if there was a problem?"

Ms. Wellington arched a brow. "If you haven't noticed, I am brutally honest."

Samantha rubbed the strained muscles in her forehead. "I know, I know. I'm just worried. My kids feel like they are slipping away."

Her expression softened. "They haven't forgotten you. They love you."

"How do you know that? Have you seen them?"

"It's been a month."

She closed her eyes. "I've forgotten what it feels like to hold them. I can't remember how good they smelled after a bath. I'm losing them."

Uncharacteristic emotion softened her attorney's gaze. "You're not losing them."

Ms. Wellington's hourly billable rates rivaled the best in the city. When Samantha had written to Angie Carlson asking for help, it had never occurred to her that Carlson's high-powered associate would take the case.

"Why did you take my case?" Samantha said.

The question shifted Ms. Wellington's attention temporarily away from whatever thoughts she'd been ruminating on. "My partner showed me your letter. She knew with her new baby she couldn't give you the defense you deserved, so she asked me."

"But why take me on? You could have said no."

"The case appealed to me."

"Why?"

Green eyes narrowed. "It doesn't matter." Ms.

Wellington unscrewed the top of her gold pen. "The prosecutor offered you another deal yesterday. Manslaughter two. Eight years."

"Eight years is a lifetime. The last year has put so much distance between my children and me. In eight years, they will have forgotten me."

"If the jury comes back with a guilty verdict, then it could mean life behind bars."

"I'd also be admitting that I planned to kill my husband." She shook her head. "I was defending my kids. Myself."

Ms. Wellington sat back, staring at her with eyes so keen she nearly squirmed. "So you are rejecting the offer?"

"I don't want any deals."

"It's a good deal, Mrs. White. Mr. Kane won't make a better offer."

Samantha shook her head. "I saw the way the jury was looking at you on Tuesday. You had their full attention. They were mesmerized."

"I'm good at what I do but I've lost cases before. If I lose this one, then you go to jail for twenty-plus years."

She risked never seeing her kids again, versus them hating her. "Do you think we'll lose?"

"I don't know."

She leaned forward. "If you had to guess. What do you think they'll say?"

"I felt good about my summation on Tuesday. We have jury members who must be on our side. And we don't have to convince them all. Just a few. But that doesn't mean their minds can't be swayed by the others."

"There's been no noise from the jury?"

"None."

"That's a good thing, right?"

"It means they've got some reasonable doubt."

"Which works in my favor?"

"Yes."

Samantha dropped her gaze to her handcuffs and nervously picked at the lock. "I'm going to take my chances."

"You are sure?"

She met Ms. Wellington's questioning gaze. "Yes."

Ms. Wellington put away her notebook and closed up her portfolio case. "Okay. I'll relay that to the prosecutor."

Chapter 8

Thursday, October 21, 5 a.m.

Rokov had worked until past 2 a.m., sifting through witness statements and tracking down the waitresses from O'Malley's. The waitresses had been too busy to notice much more than their overcrowded sections.

Rokov normally would have showered at the station and kept pushing, but it was his night to check on his grandmother. Alexa, his sister, would be in Texas another few days. He'd called his grandmother several times earlier in the evening, she'd assured him she was just fine, but he needed to get by the house and touch base with her.

So instead of going to his own apartment, he drove to his grandmother's house. She'd left the back porch light on for him as well as the light above the kitchen sink. A plate of sugar cookies sat on the counter by the stove. Snagging a couple of cookies, he ate them as he moved toward the spare room. He tugged off his shirt and collapsed back against the pillows.

He awoke at seven to the sound of his cell phone

alarm. Pushing up on his elbow, he dug fingers through his short dark hair.

He showered, changed into khakis and a fresh shirt, and wandered into the kitchen. He was surveying the contents of the refrigerator when his grandmother appeared.

Irina Rokov had a petite slightly bowed frame, thick graying hair, and a wrinkled face. She had been born in Tver, a city a few hours north of Moscow. She'd lost family members in Stalin's labor camps and seen all her brothers die on the eastern front during World War II. She'd been pregnant with her only son when her husband had gotten drunk and fallen in front of a train. She'd birthed her son days later and soon after took up needle and thread to earn a living for both. When her son had grown and married, he'd taken his mother and his very pregnant wife to the United States. Unlike many of her generation who'd emigrated, Irina had learned English and also how to drive a car.

"You came in very late last night," she said.

"I'm on a case."

Instead of telling him he worked too hard, she nodded. "You must eat."

"I'll grab a sandwich."

"Sit at the table. I will make you a decent meal."

His head throbbed from lack of sleep so he grabbed a cold soda from the refrigerator, popped the top, and sat down. He took a long liberal pull, closing his eyes as he drank. He finished off the can, and before he could rise to get another, his grandmother set a new one in front of him.

"This case is bad," she said.

"Yes."

"I saw the news. A woman murdered."

"Yes." She'd not ask for details of the case and he'd not give her any. But just knowing she paid attention to his work lifted his spirits.

She took a thick dark loaf of rye and cut off two even slices with a long serrated knife. With bent fingers that had clutched a needle and thread too many times, she smoothed thick mustard on the bread and then covered it with slices of roast beef she'd no doubt made for a dinner he'd missed. She cut the sandwich into neat even pieces and then set it in front of him.

He bit into the sandwich and smiled at her. She nodded back.

As he ate, she made a second sandwich and wrapped it in waxed paper. Next, she set her kettle on the stove and filled a tea ball with loose black tea. When the water boiled, she poured it into a pot and let the tea brew.

"The woman that died," he said. "Had a business. She used a computer to read horoscopes and tarot cards."

His grandmother sat at the table and looked at him. "If she needed a computer, then she was not for real. A seer needs no computer or cards for that matter. They just see."

As many whispers as he'd heard about his grandmother's insights, he'd never really asked her about them. As a kid, he'd loved her but her sternness had kept him and his brothers and sisters at arm's length. Now that he was older and had seen horrors on the job, he understood that her losses had taught her to guard her heart, even from her son and grandchildren.

Now as a grown man and a cop, he recognized that

he was much like her. Closed. Guarded. He did not invite people into his circle easily, and when they betrayed his trust, he was slow to believe again.

"Is that the way it works with you?" he said. "Do you just see things that will be?"

She shrugged a stooped shoulder. "I just see."

"And what have you seen lately?"

"Not too much. But I am old and my energy is not what it used to be. When I was young, I saw too much."

He wasn't sure if she referred to her psychic talents or life in Russia.

"So did you see that woman?" she said.

"What woman?"

"The redhead. The one you watched on television the other night."

"How did you know?"

She looked almost bored. "You wore your good suit to court."

Damn, what was it about the suit? "I like to look professional in court."

"You do not always wear the best suit for court. You wore the best Monday."

He chuckled. "You don't miss much."

"She likes you."

His smile eased. "How can you be so sure?"

"She would be a fool not to."

"You are thinking like a grandmother."

"Maybe. I think that she enjoys being with you. And I think she is not the type to say when she likes a man."

"How do you know that?"

Her eyes danced with the unexpected light of amusement. "Don't wear that shirt today. I like the blue shirt better. It sets off your eyes."

"It's in the laundry."

"It is clean. You left it here last week." She pushed off from the table and rose. "Now your tea is ready, and I must get back to bed. Take that sandwich with you. You will be hungry."

"Thanks."

She raised a finger. "And don't forget we have a family dinner next Thursday."

"I won't forget."

"Bring your partner. I have something to tell her."

"Sinclair? What do you have to say to her?"

"It's for me to say to her." And his grandmother walked down the hallway, her thick blue housecoat billowing around her thin legs.

Rokov rose and poured himself a cup of tea. The brew carried a much-needed kick of caffeine, guaranteed to get him through the rest of the morning. He and Sinclair would be going nonstop until they had a break in this case.

He sighed and pinched the bridge of his nose, then slowly rose. He found his pressed blue shirt, changed into it, and then hooked his cell, badge, and gun to his belt. By seven thirty he was refreshed enough so that he could think clearly. He checked his watch. Time to find out what the computer forensics team had discovered for him.

"It didn't take a great deal of digging," Audrey Sanders said as she glanced up from Diane Young's laptop. Audrey had short black hair cut in an odd asymmetrical way, wore dark rimmed glasses, and a pink turtleneck over worn jeans. She was in her late twenties and had a hummingbird tattoo on her ankle, which showed in warmer weather when she traded jeans and high tops for sandals and capris.

Rokov and Sinclair moved into her office. Every bit of flat surface in her area of the forensics department was covered with some kind of CPU, laptop, keyboard, or jumble of wires.

Sinclair, freshly showered, had changed into a chocolate brown turtleneck, slacks, and flats and had tied back her hair. Her face had a rosy glow, no doubt a by-product of a sleepless night and too much coffee.

Cops were accustomed to going nonstop when they had an active murder investigation.

"So what did you find?" Rokov said.

"Clearly security was not a priority for her. Her pass code was the only security measure she employed. Using her name and birth year was not smart or original. Even if I didn't have the codes, I could have cracked it in a half hour. Anyway, client files, with names and addresses, were clearly marked, as were her income spread sheets." She shook her head. "The lack of security is so naive."

"She had several locks on her apartment door," Sinclair said.

Audrey glared at Sinclair. "She made her living on the Net, which has doors just like apartments. For all intents and purposes, she might as well have propped open the screen door on her computer. The Net is the fucking Wild West and no one seems to care." She raised her hand. "Sorry, pet peeve."

Rokov grinned. "Duly noted."

"Here is a printout of her clients. I've prioritized them in two ways. First alphabetically and then by frequency of use."

Rokov scanned the list. There had to be over two

hundred names on there. "What else can you tell me about her?"

"She had about twelve blogs she followed. All did the woo-woo psychic stuff like her. She had a thing for erotic book downloads. And she did most of her shopping, including her grocery shopping, online. She must have had a steady stream of delivery people coming to her door. And she was a bit of a gamer. Even entered a few tournaments."

"You ever cross swords with her?" Rokov teased.

"If I did, she didn't last long. I remain undefeated."

Rokov understood that Audrey was a big deal in video realms, but that world was totally foreign to him. "Diane Young make any enemies that you could see via the games or e-mails?"

"None."

"Well, she caught someone's eye," he said.

"And he lured her out of the apartment," Sinclair said.

"We'll start first with the clients and see if any had issues with her."

Just after 3 p.m., the homicide team assembled in the windowless conference room on the third floor of police headquarters. The room was decorated in pale beiges that looked closer to brown than white and furniture that was at least a decade old. A large white board hung behind the head of the table, and on the credenza under it, a coffeemaker spat out its third pot for the afternoon.

Rokov had been on the homicide team two years now and he had worked his share of murders not only with Sinclair but with each of the three other detectives.

"So what do we have?" Garrison said, settling. He shrugged broad shoulders as if working out the stiffness.

"Sinclair and I have spent the better part of the night trying to piece together Diane Young's last days. Audrey dug through her computer. No suspicious e-mails or calls so far, but she gave us *Beyond*'s client list, and we are going to dig through that."

Malcolm Kier pulled a pen from his breast pocket and laid it beside his notebook on the table. "How many on the client list?"

"One hundred and six. We have identified the top ten users of *Beyond*. These folks have the highest billing rates of last month. And six of those made the top ten for the last three months. One woman paid out four thousand dollars to *Beyond* in September."

Kier shook his head. "You telling me there was a woman who paid four grand to have her stars and cards read?"

Rokov nodded. "Her name is Sandy Tennyson, age fifty-seven. We spoke to her first thing late this morning." He flipped through the pages of his notebook. "She has bone cancer, and according to her, the doctors had not given her more than six months. She did a random purchase with *Beyond* four months ago. Diane said that all her troubles would be vanquished by the end of this year."

"Did Young know Tennyson had cancer?" Kier said.

"Tennyson swears no," Sinclair interjected. "But to hear her speak, it wouldn't take a psychic to figure out she is sick."

Garrison tapped his thumb on his yellow notepad.

"Is that what Young did? Did she string this woman along and make her believe there was hope?"

Rokov shook his head. "I don't know. Only Young could answer that. But she collected a lot of money from Tennyson."

"Would piss me off if someone gave me hope and then snatched it away," Kier said.

"Even if Tennyson figured out this was a scam, she doesn't have the strength to drown a woman, even one as small as Young, and then drag her up to that abandoned warehouse," Rokov said.

"And she does have an alibi," Sinclair interjected. "As do her two sons, both in their early twenties. She and her husband are divorced, and there seems to be no other relatives." Rokov scanned his notes. "The other top five clients have similar stories. Illness, job loss, one even has a missing child."

Garrison's expression turned grim. "Who has the missing child?"

"Her name is Abby Powers. She was the other client we saw today. Her daughter Bia went missing in the early eighties. The kid vanished from their apartment in the middle of the night."

"I remember that case," Garrison said. "My dad worked it." Garrison's father had been a thirty-year veteran of the department and still remained a resource on old or cold cases. "Tell me she did not give this woman hope."

"According to Ms. Powers, Diane believed Bia was alive. Ms. Powers agrees with Young and was working with Young to find out who took the child."

"Any leads?" Kier said.

"Ms. Powers said that Ms. Young never was able to give her anything, but that didn't stop her from asking."

"Or stop Young from billing her." Kier's words dripped with disgust.

Rokov nodded. "Young made a good living mostly on the worries and fears of others."

"Makes for a lot of enemies," Kier said.

"Powers has no relatives. She lives a hermit's life in Arlington. We are still checking alibis from the other top clients. It's going to take a while." He checked his notes. "There is another guy in Leesburg. Paul Stanford. He plays the horses and consulted Diane for guidance. He's next on our to-be-visited list."

"What did Audrey tell us about Young's last few days?" Garrison said.

Rokov rose and went to the white board. "We know that the last day she logged on to her computer was Friday, October fifteenth, at six in the morning, and she remained on her computer until four in the afternoon. We have records of the e-mails she sent to clients as well as the website copy she was writing for her November forecasts, which she planned to post in a couple of weeks. She appears to have shut down her computer for good that same afternoon."

"Her body was found on Tuesday. When does the medical examiner estimate the time of death?" Garrison said.

"Liver temperature suggests that she died on Monday just after midnight," Sinclair added.

"So what happened to her between Friday afternoon and Monday?" Kier said.

"Surveillance cameras at her apartment building show her leaving the building just after six on Friday evening. She gets in her car and credit card receipts show that she gassed up fifteen minutes later on Route 7."

"We have footage of her filling up her car and then safely driving off. She was headed west toward Bailey's Crossroads."

"And?" Deacon said.

"And then she stopped by her branch bank and withdrew five hundred dollars from her bank account, which she seems to do regularly each month." Rokov moved to the television and turned on the DVD disk. "The bank's ATM camera does show a man walking up to her." They all watched as a man wearing a hoodie approached her. The man's face and race were obscured, but it was clear he had a medium build and was about six feet. Diane grinned up at him when he knocked on her window. She unlocked her door and he climbed into the front seat of her car. Then they drove off. "And that is the last she's seen," Rokov said.

"Until she shows up dead in the abandoned building," Kier said.

"Exactly."

"We showed the tape to her sister, Suzanne Young. She does not recognize the man, but did mention that her sister had been in great spirits lately."

"Any mention of a man?" Kier said.

"Sister thought Diane might have a guy but they'd had no real discussion," Rokov said.

"Are there any other cameras that pick this guy up near the bank?"

"There is a pizza place next door, and we see him arrive on foot. He crosses the lot directly in front of the camera, but again he's careful to hide his face. It was as if he had planned this moment down to the last detail."

Garrison rubbed the back of his neck with his hand. "What else did the medical examiner say?"

Rokov opened his file and read Dr. Henson's clinical words that detailed the trauma. "The victim was sexually assaulted several times, both vaginally and anally. She has ligature marks on her wrists and ankles and there is bruising on her arms. The real kicker is the water in her lungs."

"He drowned her?" Kier said.

"Her ribs were cracked and her heart was damaged as if it had stopped and been restarted several times. We think he drowned her and then revived her."

The words washed over everyone and settled a heavy weight on their shoulders.

Rokov posted pictures taken at the crime scene of the salt circle as well as the pentagram. "Read your witch trial history, and you'll find that it wasn't uncommon to elicit confessions by trying to drown the victims."

Kier leaned forward. "You mean to tell me that the killer is some kind of witch hunter?"

"Right now, all I know is that there are signs of the occult at the murder scene, my victim told fortunes, and my victim was drowned repeatedly."

Garrison hooked his thumbs in his belt. "How much does the media have?"

"Only that police are investigating the murder of a young woman. We were going to release her picture today and identify her. My hope is that someone might have seen her and her killer in that bank parking lot."

Garrison nodded. "Do you realize this kind of story is going to pull the crazies out of the woodwork? I don't even want to consider the tips that will come in on the tip line."

"October and witches," Kier said. "Doesn't get any more entertaining than that for the press."

Garrison rubbed his neck. "Identify her and let the

media know what she did for a living. But let's still hold off any crime scene details."

"Will do," Rokov said. "Sinclair and I could use you both. The sooner we track down clients and neighbors, the better."

"Whatever you need, Rokov," Garrison said.

Charlotte pulled up in front of the New Age shop located on Washington Street in Old Town. The brick town house wasn't old like the buildings near the river, but had been designed to mimic the old world colonial style. This was a busy street, and the shop looked like it would see a good bit of traffic. Points to Sooner for choosing the spot.

She set the parking break on her BMW as her mind drifted back to the call she'd just ended. Levi had not been thrilled about Samantha turning down his plea bargain.

"If she thinks I'll make a better deal, she can forget it." *Levi's voice had been ripe with tension.*

"She doesn't want a better deal."

"She's a fool. The jury is going to come back with a guilty verdict."

"I don't agree."

"When she is taken away from her kids for the next twenty years, this will be on you, Charlotte."

Charlotte carefully slid on her sunglasses and scanned the busy street for Sooner's tall frame and dark hair in the sea of passersby. Seconds and then minutes passed, and there was no sign of Sooner. Charlotte checked her watch. The girl was twenty minutes late.

Tamping down irritation, she considered bagging this entire venture and leaving. Time was money, literally for Charlotte, and she could not waste either now.

Who are you kidding? You'll wait as long as it takes.

Her BlackBerry buzzed, and she checked the number. Angie. Charlotte hit send. "Angie. What can I do for you?"

"I wanted to remind you that I have a fund-raising meeting this afternoon. We've got about a week to go before the big event, and there are too many details to wrap up."

More lost time and revenue. "Angie, remind me why I let you give away so many billable hours?"

Angie chuckled. "Because you like me and because your heart is not as black as the world might think."

A hint of a smile tipped the edge of her lips. "Don't bet on it. I'm evil to the bone."

"You've a core of marshmallow. But don't worry, I won't tell."

"You're fired if you do."

"Hey, have you gotten your costume yet?"

Horns blared as a car screeched to a halt at the intersection down the block. The driver yelled obscenities and Charlotte's gaze tracked the direction of the driver's raging fist. Sooner hurried across the street, her short red skirt, black sweater, leggings, and long dark boots hugging every inch of her frame. Dark hair flowed behind her as she glanced toward the driver and gave him the finger.

The driver studied Sooner a long moment then shook his head.

Charlotte cringed. "My what?"

"Costume. You need to wear a costume to this event."

Sooner reached the corner and shouldered her way through a group of tourists. "You never told me I had to wear a costume."

"I did. Twice. But I suspect, like now, you were half listening. Where are you anyway?"

Charlotte turned from Sooner and refocused her attention on Angie. "It's a long story. I'll fill you in later."

"I meant to ask you about Grady Tate. He was the one profiled in the paper on Sunday. He runs that carnival."

Tension slithered up her back and coiled around her throat. "He is the one."

"Think he'd help us out with the Halloween event? Maybe send us a couple of clowns or something?"

"Angie, don't ask Grady for any favors. When he gives a little, he takes a lot."

"I'm a big girl. I think I could handle him."

Sooner spotted Charlotte and raised her hand in greeting. She moved with a confidence few girls her age possessed. Charlotte certainly hadn't had that kind of panache at eighteen. She'd woven the threads of her confidence together by studying other women she admired. "Believe me, you can't. You play by the rules. Grady does not. Do us both a favor and stay away from him."

"One day you're going to tell me why."

"Not likely." They said their good-byes and Charlotte hung up just as Sooner reached her. "You're late."

"Ten minutes. I know. We had a last-minute meeting at the carnival. Grady was giving a big speech about putting on great shows this week."

"He still does that?"

"He's obsessed with creating a magical illusion at the carnival." She brushed a strand of hair from her face, giving Charlotte a glimpse of a star tattoo on the underside of her wrist.

"It's why he's been in business so long."

Sooner rested a fist on her narrow hip. "Sounds like you're defending the guy."

"Not in the least. But I learned a lot from him. When it came to running a business, he is smart and he knows how to work a crowd."

"He's a pain in the ass. He is driving me crazy." Sooner huffed as if that was something done by a grown-up, exasperated woman. However, the sound reminded Charlotte more of a girl pretending to be a woman.

A question that had been festering since yesterday begged to be asked. "Was Grady good to you growing up?"

"He was okay, I guess."

"What does that mean?"

"He didn't beat me or anything. But he was a hard ass about dating and me having any kind of freedom."

"He said you were homeschooled."

"If you can call it that. I knew more than the teachers."

Two men approached Sooner from behind and cast appreciative glances at her backside. Charlotte's gaze narrowed as she glared at them. They spotted Charlotte and both had the good sense to look away.

Sooner chuckled. "Were you just doing the maiden aunt thing for me?"

Charlotte frowned. "Not at all."

Her denial amused Sooner. "Oh, but you so were. You scared those dudes shitless."

"I did not." She had and took a perverse pleasure from it. "Ready to have a look at your new space?"

"Yes. I really want to show it to someone who can tell me if I'm full of shit or not."

"You don't need to curse."

Sooner laughed. "Why? They're just words."

"They leave a lasting impression. Ask yourself if you want statements taken seriously or dismissed."

Sooner laughed. "So who died and left you in charge of me?"

"Nobody. Just friendly advice." She could have critiqued the girl's outfit as well. *Tone it down. You don't need to grab attention all the time.* But she'd said enough. Sooner was right, no one had died and left her in charge of anyone. "Let's see the space?"

"Yes." Sooner crossed the sidewalk to the front door of Ageless. The sound of New Age music mingling with the scents of incense greeted them. With even greater confidence, Sooner called out, "Mark!"

Charlotte glanced around the shop and with a critical eye assessed walls covered with shelves stocked with crystals, books, incense, and any other talisman or superstitious gizmo anyone would want to own. Charlotte lifted a "magical" crystal on the checkout counter and inspected it. Lovely the way it caught the light, but the stone was about as magical as a strip of asphalt or a brick.

"Mark!" Sooner glanced at her. "He must be in the back. I'll find him."

Charlotte set the crystal down and picked up an angel pendant much like the one Mariah wore. She held the angel up to the light and watched as the afternoon sun made the fake gold sparkle.

Her mind tripped back to when Mariah and she were in their mid-teens. Sooner was just weeks away from birth.

"So who gave you that?" Grace stood at the stove and opened a can of tomato soup, which she poured into a stainless steel pot.

Mariah fingered the angel necklace. "It's just a present."

"I can see that. But from who?"

"You are so nosy."

Grace set the stove on warm and, grabbing a wooden spoon, slowly stirred the soup. "Maybe I have to be to learn anything from you. Lately, you've got too many secrets."

That coaxed a smile. "Mama always said a woman needed secrets if she was gonna keep her man interested."

"You think that's working so well for you?"

Mariah stuck up her nose. "It ain't like you're a virgin."

"It was just the one time."

Mariah laughed. "You'll get wrinkles and look old before your time if you keep frowning." She pushed up out of the chair and stretched. "I can't wait to have this kid out so we can get on with our lives."

"You don't mean that, do you?" She wasn't anxious for the child's birth.

"I sure do. I want us to run around like we used to."

Grace dropped her gaze to the soup, which had started to simmer. They'd been a team since day one. But not so much anymore. "I don't think we'll ever get back to where we were."

"The baby won't change things."

"The baby changes it all."

"Charlotte," Sooner called out. "I'd like you to meet Mark Rogers. He owns Ageless."

Charlotte set down the angel and looked toward the sound of Sooner's voice. She found the young woman standing next to a reed-thin guy who was a few inches taller than Sooner. He wore a black T-shirt, faded jeans, white high-top tennis shoes, and long hair tied at the nape of his neck. An endless menagerie of tattoos formed sleeves up and down each arm, and on the side of his neck was the image of devil's horns. His left earlobe sported ten stud earrings.

Charming.

Sooner grinned proudly and she coaxed Mark forward. "We met at the carnival. He came into my tent and asked me to read his fortune. He said I did a great job and asked if I wanted a more permanent gig."

"Is that so?"

Davis glanced at Charlotte's icy stare, and then let it drop to the rings on his fingers. "She can really pull in the crowds."

"I've no doubt," Charlotte said. "So are you renting space to Sooner or hiring her?"

"He wanted to hire me," Sooner said. "But I've had enough of working for people. I want my own business."

"Working for him would certainly simplify things for you, Sooner. No social security taxes or business taxes."

"That stuff can't be that hard," Sooner said. "I mean, don't you go down to the courthouse and just file papers or something? I sure tagged along with Grady enough times when he had to file papers for the carnival."

"It's a little more than that. Can I see the space?"

Sooner's eyes danced with excitement, and for the first time the girl's youth really shone through. "It's upstairs. Mark, you want to lead the way?"

"Sure."

Charlotte could see that Sooner had cast some kind of spell over the guy. And that spell didn't have anything to do with magic. It was about his hormones clashing with the sight of young full breasts, a sleek figure, and a lovely face.

Following Sooner and Mark, she climbed the narrow staircase to the second level. The space was not subdivided but open. There was one closet and two windows that overlooked a back alley that connected to another set of retail shops. The walls were a pale white and the floors hardwood. It looked more like a storage room than retail space.

"I know it needs work," Sooner said. "But I think if I paint the walls a pale purple and put down rugs, find the right table and chairs, then I will be in business. Mark said he'd have a sign made for me and put it out front."

Charlotte had to admire the girl's ambition, which mirrored her own at that age. "It could be lovely."

"And I'm thinking once the business takes off and starts to turn a profit, I can start selling a little merchandise. I've already talked to Mark, and he said I could if we shared the profits."

"How generous." Charlotte walked to the window and stared at the abandoned alley below and the green Dumpster. "So how much is the rent?"

"Fifteen hundred a month."

"Is there a bathroom up here?"

"Down on the first floor," Mark said.

"Running water?"

"First floor."

"And the rent is fifteen hundred a month." She didn't hide her disdain. "That's a lot of debt for you to take on right now, Sooner."

"It's what a lot of the other shops in the area are asking," Mark said.

"He's right. I've checked around, and I know I

might be eating peanut butter and jelly sandwiches for a while, but it will be worth it if I can get some steady clients."

Sooner stared at Charlotte, her eyes wide with excitement while Mark stared only at Sooner. Not surprising. "Mark, do you mind if I speak to Sooner alone?"

He frowned. "What do you want to talk to her about?"

Charlotte's smile was cool. "I'm her attorney and it's my job to give her advice about this contract."

"It's all legal."

"I didn't say that it wasn't. I just want to talk to Sooner about it in private." Charlotte had devolved an icy stare over the years that left little room for discussion.

Mark, as she expected, dropped his gaze and took a step back. "I'll be downstairs if you need me."

"Thanks."

Sooner grinned at Mark. "You're the best, baby."

He cast her a glance reminiscent of a naughty boy and disappeared down the stairs. Charlotte waited until she heard the steady thud of his high-top shoes move to the front of the door.

"So do you love this place or not?" Sooner said.

"Not."

Sooner cocked her head. "You don't like it?"

"It's expensive. It doesn't come with a bathroom or running water, and I'll bet Mark wants you to pay for painting."

Sooner pouted. "A gallon of paint is not that much money."

Charlotte shook her head as she scanned the space a second time. "You can do better."

"Don't count on it. I don't have any kind of credit history and I'm just eighteen. No one in this area is willing to take a chance on me. No one. But Mark. He says I'm worth the risk."

"He wants to get in your pants, Sooner."

"You think I don't know that? I do." She dropped her voice a notch. "And he can do all the wanting he wants, but he ain't getting nothing."

"You're going to be spending a lot of time in this shop alone with him. You don't know him."

"I can take care of myself. If Grady taught me anything, it was how to deal with a customer who gets a little out of hand. And believe me, I've handled my share at the carnival."

Charlotte had handled her share as a teenager. Boys, and men for that matter, from town trolling for whatever woman they could find. She'd watched her mother flirt and fence with many and then it had been her and Mariah's turn. Her mother had managed. She'd managed. Mariah had trouble saying no.

"I want to talk you out of this," Charlotte said.

"You won't. I'm leaving the carnival, which means I have to find work."

"I can help you find a job."

"I don't want an office gig with nine-to-five hours. Schedules kill me. I need to do my own thing, and I am signing that lease one way or another. What I need from you is to make sure old Mark isn't screwing me in some way."

"So we're agreed he's got a bad vibe."

She dropped her voice to a whisper. "Oh, totally. I can't stand him. But he will do for now."

"How long will you be here?"

"A year. I know I can build a good book of business in that time and find my own place."

"And then you open your version of Ageless."

"Something better and classier. But yeah. And then from there I'll just have to see."

She stared at the firm set of the girl's jaw and understood that there'd be no changing the girl's mind today. The best she could do was look out for the kid. And who was she to say what Sooner could or couldn't do?

"Do you have the contract?"

Sooner pulled a rumpled piece of paper from her fringed purse. "It's all yours."

Charlotte folded the contract, sharply creasing the edge with her fingertips. "I'll read it tonight and call you in the morning."

Silver bracelets jangled as Sooner pushed her fingers through her hair. "I was hoping because it was so short you could read it here and I could sign it."

"I can't read it now. I'm late for another appointment. But I'll call you in the morning. Do you have a cell number?" She opened her phone to contacts.

"Mark said he couldn't wait on this long." Sooner rattled off the number.

Charlotte typed and saved the number. "I'd bet my last dollar that Mark will wait quite a while for you."

She grinned. "He does have a thing for me, doesn't he?"

"He does. And you need to be careful."

"He's a scrawny guy."

"Don't underestimate him."

Chapter 9

Thursday, October 21, 6 p.m.

He glanced out the coffee shop window to the abandoned Wharf, still blocked off with yellow crime scene tape. He had to concede that life had a strange synchronicity to it. One kill had been left here and another soon would be taken from here.

Vanquishing the witches shouldn't have been such a thrill for him. But if he were to confess his sins to God, he would admit that the Hunt gave more satisfaction than the final confession.

He spent endless hours watching the witches, learning their patterns, friends and family. He studied the best places to take them. He knew traffic patterns, cameras, and choke points. In the end, he knew all there was to know about his witch and the best way to capture her.

And so it was with this next witch. He sat in the corner of the coffee shop watching her sit at a table with several of her girlfriends, laughing as they all sipped coffee and shared a large slice of chocolate cake.

She was a pretty one. Her dark hair draped over her shoulders and down her back. He knew from his research that she was in her mid-forties. She'd divorced her husband two years ago and moved out of their Arlington home to live in an Alexandria apartment. She taught women's studies at the local university, drove a green Volvo, liked to buy organic food at the farmer's market, and visited the library every Friday. He'd read the books he'd seen her reading and watched the movies she watched.

He'd written his final dossier on her last night and felt certain he knew her better than her friends and family.

Planning was his best defense if he never wanted the cops to discover his true work. This kind of meticulous planning had been what he'd done with the last witch and the one before and all the others before her. With each kill he'd honed his skills to razor sharpness.

Excitement bubbled and the energy that always hummed before a kill grew. He laid his fingers over his forearm and squeezed the spot where he'd made a clean cut this morning. Pain shot through him and doused the energy.

He sipped his coffee and dropped his gaze to the paper he'd picked up at the newsstand. He'd not read a word, but for a man alone to come into a coffee shop and to be seen staring at women, well, that was the kind of behavior someone noticed.

In his peripheral vision, he saw the waitress approach. This would be the second time she'd offered to warm up his coffee, and it was his cue to leave.

The waitress, a college kid with blond hair and a pink T-shirt that read *Just Java?*, smiled down at him. "Ready for more?"

He leaned back in his chair and patted his stomach, which he'd padded to look fuller. He'd also added gray highlights to his hair and chosen an old tweed jacket more suited for an older man. People rarely, he'd discovered, looked beyond the surface. "No thanks. I'm about done here. Thanks."

He rose, pulled out a tip that was exactly fifteen percent. To leave more or less would stick in the waitress's memory, and he didn't want to stick in anyone's mind.

As he sauntered out, he glanced back one last time at the witch. She tossed back her head and laughed as did her friends. Let her enjoy her coven a little longer. The inquisition would begin soon enough.

He noticed the hint of blood on the cuff of his shirt and frowned. He'd squeezed too hard and opened the wound. Quickly he cupped his hand over the blood-stain and hurried to his car.

He reached inside his glove box and retrieved gauze, which he always kept on hand. Carefully, he wound it around the wound. He thought back to the table in the café. Could he have left droplets of blood behind?

He couldn't be sure.

And he had to be sure.

"Damn."

He glanced at the café, weighing the risk of return-ing versus hoping that he'd not left traces of blood behind. People remembered blood.

He finished bandaging the wound and pulled the long cuff of his jacket over the bloody sleeve. He got out of the car and resisted jogging back. Instead, he moved slowly, like an older man should.

As he opened the door, the witch and her coven were walking outside. He stepped aside, nodded his head, and waited for them to pass. As they did, he got a whiff of perfume that was so sweet and pure that it caught him off guard. A witch should have a spicy scent. She shouldn't smell like roses and flowers.

When they passed, he hurried inside to his chair. The waitress had cleared away his table and wiped it clean. He glanced toward the floor and spotted the single drop of blood. Damn. Pulling a handkerchief from his pocket, he knelt down and wiped it up.

"Can I help you?" The waitress had spotted him and returned.

This time he found her cheerful smile and face annoying. "I dropped my handkerchief," he said as he rose and tucked it in his pocket. "It's a favorite, and I didn't want to lose it." He glanced at her name tag. "Thanks for asking, Katrina."

She studied him closely for the first time. "Sure. No problem. And thanks for the tip."

As she turned and walked away, he watched her and wondered if he'd just made a critical error. His return had made an impression. And impressions were a bad thing.

Back in his car, he did not turn on the dome light to supplement the fading afternoon light as he pulled out his notebook and turned the pages until he found a blank one. He wrote down the date, time, and the name *Just Java*? Under that he scribbled the waitress's name: Katrina. He circled the name three times.

"I might just have to keep an eye on you, Katrina."

After Charlotte left Ageless, the day moved along in a frenetic blur of meetings, calls, and briefs. It was well after eleven that evening when she finally rose from her desk, set the alarm on her building, and crossed the street to her car.

The drive home along the parkway, which snaked along the Potomac River, was particularly beautiful this evening. The sky was full of stars and the moon cast a soft, simmering glow on the water. The lights on the north bank winked like diamonds.

She was going to miss this drive. But nothing— a home, a lover, or a friendship—lasted forever. This ingrained lesson learned from her nomadic child-hood was simple: attachments led only to heartache. And so she'd been careful never to fully invest in people or places. Though she couldn't mark the day or time when she'd begun to anticipate this drive home, she realized she now did. She wasn't going to miss the condo as much as the views of the river's me-andering waters, which had a way of washing away the day's stresses.

She also wasn't sure when she'd grown to anticipate Daniel Rokov's touch. The first time she'd suggested the motel room, it had been Mariah's thirty-sixth birthday. She'd thought a tryst was about basic sex and a need to banish Mariah from her thoughts.

Basic sex. A smile tipped the edge of her lips. Sex with Rokov hadn't been basic at all. It had been so ex-traordinary that the memories had lingered through a succession of fifteen-hour days. Finally unable to resist, she'd called him and suggested another round. He'd quickly said yes.

Have dinner with me?

"So tempting. Just not so wise, detective."

She pulled through the gated entrance of the Cen-tury high-rise complex and parked in the under-ground garage. She waved to the guard stationed in the lot and then moved through glass doors to the elevator. Seconds passed, and it seemed her briefcase grew heavier with each moment. Her heels dug into her feet, and her back ached. The doors dinged open, and she gladly stepped into the car, which she rode to the top floor.

She unlocked her front door, dropped her briefcase and keys by the entrance as the door clicked closed behind her. A note on a sticky dangled from a large mirror by the entryway. Robert's card sat on the table, as did the card of a local mover. There was a note taped to the entryway mirror. *Ms. W. Finished repairs on back window and molding in back bedroom. Mr. Delango.* He'd also attached his business card.

Frowning, she studied the bold handwriting. Robert had vouched for him, but still she didn't like the idea that he'd been in her space.

Shoving aside unease, she kicked off her shoes and padded into the kitchen and switched on the lights. Granite. Stainless. Italian marble floors. Custom-painted walls. She'd believed a well-designed kitchen was a matter of status. The few times she'd entertained clients here, the caterer had marveled at the equipment. Any real cook would weep if they knew she kept only frozen meals in the freezer and used the eight-burner professional stove only to heat tea.

She'd bought and decorated this place when she'd landed a few high-rolling clients. At the time, it seemed the money would be coming in forever. She should have known better. If Grady had taught her anything, it was that customers could love you one moment and hate you the next. Believing her own press had been her first mistake.

And then one of those high-rolling clients had

seen her as a liability and sent a killer to tie up the loose ends.

It had been three years since the man had come into her office, smiled at her, and then shot her point-blank in the side. She'd managed to escape to the bathroom off her office, barricade herself, and hold on until the cops had arrived.

She rubbed her side, her fingertips feeling the scar through the threadbare shirt. It was no longer pink, angry, and raised, but the scar would always be there. It would always be a reminder to her never to let her guard down.

Charlotte dug a loaf of rye bread from the refrigerator along with fresh slices of ham, cheese, and mustard. She made a simple sandwich and took a big bite as she walked into the living room and out onto her patio. She pulled in a lungful of air and savored this moment.

Her childhood had also taught her to savor the good moments. They could be fleeting and rare, and surviving the rough patches meant savoring the days of smooth sailing. A cool breeze blew off the water. In nine days she'd be living in a rented apartment near the Arlington border. There'd be no views. No doorman. No lap pool. Just a basic roof over her head.

This downward turn annoyed but did not devastate. The firm had several big fish in the pipeline, and if she were very careful with the condo sale profits, she could cover payroll until the new clients generated income.

"Cash flow is King." How many times had Grady said those exact words? Like it or not, the old buzzard had taught her valuable life lessons.

She finished her sandwich and then moved into her bedroom, where she carefully hung up her clothes and changed into athletic shorts and a T-shirt. Padding barefooted into the living room, she flipped on the lights and glared at the sea of unpacked moving boxes that she'd had delivered last weekend.

The décor of her place had always been simple but elegant. She'd never opted for new and sleek but rather had gravitated toward antiques and older pieces she'd had refurbished. The walls were painted a pale blue, and the couch, one of the few custom pieces, was covered in a toned-down ivory fabric that had cost three hundred dollars a yard. Lovely to look at, but when Charlotte really wanted to relax, she sat on the floor for fear she'd ruin the sofa.

On the other side of the room was a set of built-in bookcases filled with hundreds of books. The books weren't just for show. She'd read them all, which had always been a point of honor with her. Her name and persona might have been fake, but her intelligence and knowledge were the real deal.

So many books read. And so many books to pack. "They're not going to pack themselves, Grace."

Weary muscles and a throbbing headache began to argue that now was not the time to pack. Too tired. Too overstressed. Robert had hired the movers and they would pack most of her belongings, but there were private things she didn't want them handling.

Determination had her dragging a moving box down the hallway toward the storage closet. Charlotte had never been a big saver or collector, so the closet was in relatively good shape. There was her bike, which she'd ridden only a few times, tennis rackets, and golf clubs. She'd taken up all sports initially to meet clients, but when the work had rolled in, the sports had fallen to the wayside. Now staying in shape was heading to the building's gym and riding the elliptical trainer or tread-mill five days a week.

The right side of the closet was filled with out-of-season overflow wardrobe. An admitted clothes hound, she stared at the collection calculating what she'd spent over the years. The tally made her cringe. She lifted the hanging dresses and suits and carefully rehung them in the wardrobe box.

It took the better part of an hour to carefully reposition each item. As tempting as it was to rush, she knew buying new clothes might not be an option for a good while, and she'd best take care of what she had.

When the box was full, she dragged it back into the living room and grabbed another box. But as she dragged the box toward the closet, her balance tipped out of whack, and for a moment she thought she'd topple over.

She sat back on her heels and pressed the heels of her hands into her eyes. Her body protested the lack of sleep, and she realized she had no choice but to listen. Carefully, she made her way to her room and without turning on the lights went straight to her bed and folded back the silk coverlet. She fell into a deep sleep almost as soon as her head hit the pillow.

Grace woke to hear the baby crying. She quickly got off the sofa and ran to the cradle, where the little girl was chewing on her fist, crying and angrily kicking her legs. She glanced toward Mariah's bed and discovered it untouched. Mariah had never gone to bed last night.

"Damn it, where are you?"

Bleary-eyed, she lifted the baby, shushed her, and laid her on her shoulder. Unsteady, she moved to the kitchen and pulled a bottle from the tiny refrigerator, and then taking the nipple off, put it in the microwave for fifty-two seconds. The baby cried louder, and Grace carried her over to the little changing stand. Awkwardly, she struggled with the soiled diapers as the baby kicked and cried. Her hands began to shake. She shouldn't be doing this. Finally, she secured the diaper tabs and tossed the soiled diaper away. A quick wash of her hands and the microwave dinged. Pleased, she had to admit that she had this routine down to a science.

Grace settled at the dinette set and nestled the baby back in the crook of her arm. A quick check of the milk on her forearm and she popped the bottle in the baby's mouth. Greedily the baby suckled and ate.

With the baby's cries silenced, her own adrenaline dropped and her thoughts turned to Mariah. Where was she?

Grace glanced down at the baby, savoring the cooing sounds and the scent of milk. "God, you deserve so much better than this place."

She wasn't sure if she drifted but Grace startled awake and realized the baby had vanished from her arms. She jumped to her feet and ran to the cradle, but there was no sign of the child. Panicked, she searched every inch of the trailer and then ran outside. The summer evening was warm and the air thick with humidity. The circle of trailers, all homes to the carnival workers, were quiet in the predawn hours. There didn't seem to be any sign of life.

Grace's heart thudded as she thought where to go for help. There was Grady, but he'd be furious if he knew she'd lost the baby. The other carnies wouldn't care and the cops weren't welcome here.

Desperate, she shoved trembling fingers through her hair and ran toward Grady's black trailer. She was climbing the steps, fists clenched to knock, when she heard the first screams. Grace turned and scanned the darkness but could see no one.

　"Mariah," she called.

　At first the screams seemed distant and far away but they quickly grew and grew until they were so loud Grace covered her ears. The screams telegraphed crushing fear and such agonizing panic that Grace could feel the pain herself.

　And then out of the darkness, Mariah stumbled toward her. Her body and face were pale. Her lips were blue. And her clothes nearly torn from her body. Grace stepped back, fearing the sight of her sister.

　Mariah extended a hand and mouthed the words "Help her."

　"Help who?" Grace said.

　"Help our baby girl!"

　Charlotte jerked awake, her body glistening in a fine sheen of sweat and her heart racing so hard that she felt light-headed. "Damn it."

　She rose and paced the room, hoping the activity would wrestle the nervous energy from her body. Mariah had died eighteen years ago.

　So why the hell am I dreaming about you now?

Chapter 10

The guy who had appeared with Diane Young in the bank's video camera was a ghost. No one remembered seeing him, and those who had said they'd seen him could only offer vague and contradictory descriptions. Hood. Glasses. Tall. Short. Fat. Thin.

Rokov swallowed the dregs of the cold coffee in his mug and blinked hard as he stared at the columns of numbers. With little sleep in the last few days, reviewing the latest set of financials for Young was proving to be a challenge. He could go long stretches without sleep as long as he was moving. Sitting, however, reminded him that he needed sleep and a real meal.

He was rereading a column when he heard a commotion by the elevators. Standing, he glanced over and saw that his father and grandmother had arrived at the station.

Garrison and Kier had stopped to greet the pair, and he could see Sinclair's head moving in that direction. It wasn't like his father and grandmother just to show up. The haze of fatigue vanished and concern took root.

He rose. His grandmother surrounded by the cops looked old and frail. Her spine had begun to bend in the last couple of years and her once thick hair was now thinning. Despite time's effects, her gaze remained sharp and clear.

Rokov looked like his father, who at sixty-nine remained tall with broad shoulders. Gray had lightened once ink black hair and deep lines etched in his face, but he stayed fit and always donned a suit, tie, and hat when out in public.

When Rokov approached, his grandmother stared at Kier with a narrowed gaze. "You are smirking at me."

Kier raised his hand to his heart. "I promise, Mrs. Rokov, but I am not laughing at you. I just don't think it's gonna happen."

Rokov paused, nodded to his father and kissed his grandmother on the cheek. "What did you tell him?"

The old woman stared at her grandson and there was no missing the relief in her gaze. Seeing him seemed to ease the lines in her face. "Only the truth."

"Which is?"

"His wife is expecting a girl."

Kier raised an amused brow.

Rokov glanced at Kier embarrassed. It was no secret that Angie Carlson Kier was a cancer survivor, and though she'd been given a clean bill of health, she'd never give birth. In Russian, Rokov explained the situation quietly to his grandmother, who seemed unfazed by the entire exchange.

In English, she replied, "I see what I see."

Rokov nodded as he glanced at his father. "So what brings you here?"

"Your grandmother insisted," his father said.

"I was worried," his grandmother said in a clear voice.

Irina Rokov wasn't a worrier by nature and for her to be here now was out of character. And like many older Russians, she did not welcome trips to the police station, which in Russia could also house KGB offices. He'd told her many times that the KGB was not in this country, but she never really accepted his explanation. He kept his voice even. "I'm working. We are all working on the case."

"The witch case," she said in Russian. "I read about it." Every day since she arrived in this country, she had read the paper from front to back. In the early days when her English was not so good, she just looked at the pictures and used her Russian-English dictionary to translate as many words as she could.

"That's right."

In Russian she said, "I have something to tell you about that case."

"What is that?"

"The killer is not finished. He will do these terrible things again."

"How do you know this?"

"Like I know your friend Kier will have a daughter by the end of the year. And like I know your friend Sinclair must be very careful over the next few weeks."

"What does Sinclair have to worry about?"

She gripped his wrist with bent fingers that possessed an intensity he could not ignore. "She is going to be shot."

Sinclair did not speak Russian but recognized her name. "What did she say about me?"

"Nothing," Rokov said.

Sinclair glanced at the old woman. "What did you say about me?"

The old woman met her gaze. "I said that you must be careful."

Sinclair stiffened a fraction. Cops as a lot could be superstitious. "Why?"

"Because you just must."

Sinclair drew in a deep breath. "I'm always careful."

"Be more careful," Grandmother said. "You are too young to die."

Sinclair's face paled. "Damn."

Kier nudged Sinclair. "Lighten up."

"Hey, man, she was talking about you, too. Don't you want to know about the kid coming into your life?"

Kier shook his head. "Hell, no. Hearing fortunes is like reading the last page of a book. It's cheating."

"If I know I'm getting a happy ending, I don't read ahead," Sinclair said. "If I know it's going to end badly, hell yeah, I'll read ahead."

Rokov glanced at his father. "Grandmother has seen that I am fine. Now it is time to take her home."

Mr. Rokov nodded. "I am sorry for the intrusion. She would have no peace until we stopped by." He glanced down at his mother. "But now, Mama, you see that he is fine and we must go."

She nodded and kissed Rokov on the cheek. "Be careful, Daniel. This man won't stop for anything."

His grandmother's words echoed in his head as he watched his father lead her back to the elevators. When the doors closed, Rokov released a sigh.

"So you said she was some kind of seer," Sinclair said.

Rokov groaned. "Leave it alone."

She smiled. "When in your life have you ever known

me to leave anything alone?" She held up her index finger. "One, we know that I have to be careful. Two, little David Kier has got a kid sister headed his way, and three . . . we don't know three because you two were speaking in code."

"Russian."

Kier smiled, but his gaze had lost the humor and turned serious.

"Kier, I'm sorry about that," Rokov said. "I reminded her about Angie."

Kier shrugged. "This is not for public knowledge yet, but we filed adoption papers a few weeks ago. We're expecting a long wait so we thought we'd start early. But if what your grandmother says is true, we're looking at, what, eight weeks?"

Rokov would not discount his grandmother to his coworkers. "It's not an exact science."

Kier grinned. "Would be kinda nice, having a daughter." His expression sobered. "But none of you tell Angie. I don't want her to get her hopes up."

"Sure," Sinclair said. "Lips are sealed." She glanced at her partner, eyes narrowed. "What was the third?"

"Third what?"

"What was the third prediction she said? We don't speak Russian, my friend."

He sighed. "She said the killer is not finished."

When Charlotte glanced at the Entertainment section of the *Washington Post,* she nearly choked on her coffee. The lead article above the fold was a story on Sooner and the carnival. She was pictured standing in front of her Madame Divine tent, her arms folded and her gaze directly at the camera lens. Her dark hair swept down her shoulders and her olive skin added depth to green eyes that almost seemed to glow off the page. She wore a gold caftan, and dozens of bracelets decorated her arms. She looked mesmerizing.

Like Mariah.

Standing behind Sooner in the background stood Grady, the silent sentinel who watched over his prodigy carefully.

Charlotte read the article and found her blood pressure rising. Grady was quoted several times, referencing Sooner's psychic talent. He shared several stories about her predictions that had come true. He'd also alluded that the Alexandria Police might gain insights from Sooner on this latest murder.

Charlotte sat back in her chair. "That son of a bitch."

Angie appeared in the door. "Who is a son of a bitch?" On her hip she had her son, David, who had just turned two. He was a solidly built kid with curly white hair and a big toothy grin that had Charlotte forcing back the expletive. David played with the big chunky necklace hanging around Angie's neck.

Charlotte rose. Glancing at David, she smiled and tried not to think why Angie had brought him to the office. "It's an article about the carnival."

"Bad news?"

"Cheap PR."

Angie shifted David's weight and moved into the room. "Why is it cheap?"

"Because Grady just let the world know that his carnival psychic can not only tell the future, but she can find the killer that murdered that young woman earlier this week."

Angie frowned. "That is the Diane Young case."

"Yes."

She shook her head. "That is a rough one. And the killer has not been caught."

"Grady shouldn't have put Sooner at risk like that."

"She is the one you helped out in court?"

"You heard about that?"

"The courthouse is a small world." David tugged Angie's necklace toward his mouth. Gently, she pried it free and kissed his fingers. "Everyone was buzzing about the bigwig defense attorney Charlotte Wellington breezing into court and taking up this unknown girl's defense. You made an impression and raised a few eyebrows."

"Great. Just what I need." She smiled at the baby and grabbed his foot. Sooner should have had a mom like Angie.

The boy kicked and gurgled. "Young son and I are off to the doctor's for his checkup this morning. He needs his two-year-old shots. I'm dropping him off with the sitter and will be back by ten."

"Sure. Take all the time you need."

Angie laughed. "Oh, you so do not mean that. Time is money, remember, baby?"

Charlotte smiled. "Maybe I need to lighten up."

Angie raised her hand to Charlotte's forehead. "Are you feeling okay?"

She was worried about Sooner. "Fine."

She arched a brow. "I don't know. You're making crazy talk."

"Maybe I'm just a few quarts shy on the coffee. Give me a few hours."

"You do look tired," Angie said. "Makeup is a wonderful thing, but it doesn't hide the dark circles under your eyes."

"I've a new client presentation." No one knew she

was selling her condo or moving, and she intended to keep it that way.

"How is it going?"

"Good. We meet for dinner tonight. I'm doing a background check on him."

"And?"

"So far so good. But I keep thinking I've missed something."

"Knowing you, you haven't. You're pretty meticulous."

"I've made mistakes before. I've let money cloud my judgment. I need to make sure big bucks aren't blinding me to a fatal flaw."

Angie frowned. "Can I do anything to help?"

Charlotte shook her head. "No. Not now at least. Just get little guy here to the doctor."

"I will. I'll be back soon." David grinned at Charlotte.

She didn't remember Sooner grinning like that. "Take your time."

Charlotte took her seat back behind the desk and read the article again. *Sooner, what has Grady gotten you into?*

She'd read the girl's lease agreement, and they planned to meet for coffee today. She was going to suggest that Sooner pay no more than a thousand a month and that she reduce the length of the lease to six months. However, she doubted the girl would listen. Sooner wanted out of the carnival so badly that she was ripe to make a poor decision. Case in point: the article. She'd no doubt agreed to the article because of the publicity it would generate for her new business.

"Can you blame her?" Charlotte whispered.

Eighteen years ago, she'd felt like an animal caught

in a steel trap when Mariah had died. She'd have done anything, *anything*, to get free. And she had.

She just prayed Grady had not put the girl in danger or on some killer's radar.

"Have you seen the morning paper, Rokov?" Sinclair dropped the Entertainment section onto Rokov's desk.

He glanced up at her and then at the article. His attention was drawn immediately to Sooner Tate's bold, green eyes. "This is the girl that Charlotte Wellington defended in court a few days ago."

"I know. And according to this young girl's boss at the carnival, she can see into the future and could maybe find the killer of Diane Young."

"Really?" Irritation crept up his spine. There were always people that profited on the misery of others. From what this article said, this fellow Grady and this woman Sooner were doing just that.

"Do you know anything about them?" Sinclair said.

"The girl put Charlotte Wellington on edge when they were talking outside the courthouse. Wellington tried to brush the girl off as a pro bono case but there was something more."

Sinclair folded her arms over her chest. "Isn't there always something more?"

He frowned. There was so much he did not know about Charlotte. She wasn't a woman easily rattled, and yet Sooner had done just that. What had she said she wanted him to avoid? Tangles? "Grady's using the headlines to make hay while he's in town."

"Picked a hell of a way to do it."

"Let's visit the carnival. Diane's sister thought she

planned a visit there. And if this Grady has somehow stoked this killer's temper, maybe he'll show."

"Far-fetched?"

"What else do we got?" Rokov scanned the article. "The article says the carnival opens at five."

"I got no plans for tonight."

Chapter 11

Sooner had missed her one o'clock meeting with Charlotte. And when Charlotte, torn between annoyance and worry, had texted the girl, she'd gotten a few miserly words back. *Sorry. Can you come to carnival tonight?*

Charlotte had glared at the text. She'd tapped the phone's keyboard, the need to remind the girl of manners and professionalism. She should have told Sooner she had a dinner date with a paying client, but she did for the girl what she did for no one else. She capitulated.

So, just after five, she parked in the carnival lot, the sun hovering over the horizon, casting splashes of oranges, yellows, and reds across the sky. She shut off her engine. She stared out the front window at the carnival lights: the Ferris wheel, the giant slide, and the dozens of game huts. She'd forgotten just how lovely the lights could be at night, especially at sunset. The soft glow of the red, white, and green bulbs cast a magical air over the place. Lively organ music drifted out from an overhead speaker.

This place could be magical at night.

She remembered how she dreaded the mornings when she'd lived and worked there. In the hard light of the sun, all the flaws that had been magically whisked away by the night returned. All the soft dewy lines hardened, and what appeared new and delightful became weary and tattered. Even the carnival workers changed with the rising sun. The clowns scrubbed off their painted grins and white faces, and what remained were sullen men who had beer and cigarettes for breakfast. Trash littered the grounds and garbage cans overflowed. The carnies would rise by eight and wearily begin the task of preparing for the next night.

Her mother hated the mornings so much she rarely rose before noon. While her mother slept, Grace, Mariah, and some of the other carnie kids met with a tutor. The other kids had little interest in their studies, but she'd cared. Thankfully, the woman who had tutored them had cared enough to find her books that challenged.

By three her mother would have awakened, drunk several pots of black coffee, and begun to paint her face for the afternoon show. Her mother had been a beautiful woman with a long lean body, full breasts, and rich thick dark hair like Mariah's and Sooner's. When she'd begin to outline her eyes, pat the thick theater makeup on her face, and don the rich sparkling purple robe, she'd transform from a frightened woman who could not live her life without a man into an enchantress with all the answers. She'd relished her years as the mysterious Madame Divine. In those hours, she'd tell Grace and Mariah that she was not herself but better and more important.

Grady often said it didn't take special powers to read people. Just toss out bits of information and see what prompted a reaction. From there the guessing was easy. It didn't take much to fool people so bloated with hope and curiosity for the future. He'd said her mother could read anybody, but she was no psychic.

But as the years passed and life on the road took its toll, their mother began to break down, not psychically but mentally. She suffered wild shifts in moods, laughing hysterically in one moment and crying in the next. Grady had left her to her own moods until they had interfered with gate receipts.

Her last night in the mystic's tent had been nearly tragic. She'd been having more and more trouble distinguishing the real from the unreal, and when a young man had entered the tent, she'd taken one look at him and screamed. She'd called him evil—the devil's son. She'd lunged for him.

Grady, thankfully, had been close, and he'd caught her before she'd done the man any damage. Grady had loaded the guy up with free ride and food tickets and told him she'd never read again.

Her mother had wailed in her trailer that night until Grady had brought her a drink laced with something that knocked her out. Two days later her mother had died of a stroke and Grady had told a grieving Grace and Mariah and that it was time they became Madame Divine. Grace had been thirteen and Mariah had been fourteen.

And so on alternating nights, they'd each donned the eyeliner, the thick face paint and the purple robe, and taken a seat in the tent. And like their mother before them, they learned to read body language.

Grace, more than Mariah, had become adept at determining when someone sought a bit of fun and when they needed answers to find meaning and hope in their lives. She'd fended off drunken men and boys thinking to score with a carnie girl. She'd stopped thieves who wanted to steal from her till. A woman who'd resented her advice had even punched her in the face and knocked her off her chair onto the dirt floor.

"God, but I hate this place," she muttered as she stared at the lights.

She didn't want any part of this old life. Grace Wells was dead and buried. And yet, as she stared at the main entrance, it felt as if the last eighteen years had never happened.

The place had not changed a whole lot in that time. She could see that Grady had upgraded a couple of the rides and he'd created new games: the rifle shot was classic, but the petting zoo was new.

Straightening, she moved toward the ticket booth and pulled out her wallet. "How much to enter but not ride the rides?"

"All tickets are twenty-five dollars." The boy in the booth looked about seventeen. He had a dark crop of hair, a red carnival T-shirt, and his left ear had been pierced six or seven times with brightly colored studs. A few modest tattoos dotted his arms, but she imagined by the time he was twenty or twenty-five, they'd be covered.

"It's twenty-five dollars even if I don't want to ride the rides?"

"Don't matter. It's a flat rate." He glared at her as if he'd dealt with a million people haggling down the price. And no doubt this kid had seen more than his share of the public. If she knew Grady, he'd put him to work by the time he was twelve.

She pulled a twenty and a five from her wallet and handed them to the kid.

He raised a rubber stamp and rubbed it into a pad of red ink. "I need your right hand."

Reluctantly, she extended her hand and watched as he marked her white, slightly freckled skin with the red circular mark. She withdrew her hand, already anxious to remove the mark.

"Show that at each ride. That'll prove you've paid and they'll let you on."

She could have explained again that she had no intention of riding any rides but didn't bother. He didn't care. He had his money.

As she stepped into the carnival, she was assailed by so many familiar smells. Cotton candy. Popcorn. The funnel cake. Crisp fall air carrying the hint of grease paint.

She tucked her patent leather purse under her arm and walked over a dirt path deeper into the carnival. Lively organ music mingled with the peel of laughter from the children who'd boarded one of the evening's first Ferris wheel runs. Automatically, she glanced beyond the bright lights and lines of people to the man who operated the equipment, wondering if she recognized him.

For a moment his face was turned from hers as he held one hand on the machine's lever as another fished in his jeans pocket for a cigarette and lighter. He popped the smoke in his mouth and lit it. In the dim light she studied the lined profile and rawboned features. She thought she knew him but wasn't so sure.

The man she'd remembered had been lean and wore his thick hair loose around his shoulders. He'd had broad shoulders and a swagger when he walked. This guy just looked haggard, world-weary, and old.

She turned from the Ferris wheel and moved toward the brightly colored tents that housed the games. Ring toss. Basketball throw. Duck hunt. She'd played them all a million times and had gotten good enough to toss the rings just off center enough to compensate for the bottle's slightly tilted position. She knew which ducks had the winning number on the underside. She could even throw the basketball well enough to win an overstuffed bear, which come daylight would show signs of having been hauled from city to city.

She spotted the gold and red tent of Madame Divine and for a moment just stared. It hadn't changed at all and she half expected her mother to walk out and smile at her.

Costumed figures wandered the carnival. Ghosts, goblins, and vampires. According to both articles, Grady's carnival featured a Halloween theme in October. Clowns transformed into ghouls, the Ferris wheel became haunted, and the cotton candy turned pumpkin orange.

She passed by a funnel cake display when a guy dressed as Frankenstein stopped in her path. He growled and held up his hands.

"Thank, pal, but I'm not in the market for a fright."

He held up his arms and growled louder.

"Find a kid or a guy trying to impress a girlfriend."

Frankenstein's gaze lingered on hers, and this close she could see that his green paint did not stretch all the way to his collar, leaving a white strip of human flesh exposed. He growled and held up his hands higher.

"Look, pal, buzz off."

Frankenstein cocked his head, and then laughed.

"Mind telling me what the joke is all about?"

"You," the monster said in a clear Southern drawl. "I never thought I'd see you here ever again."

Her gaze narrowed. "Excuse me?"

His eyes sparked with recognition and surprise. "Grace Wells, right?"

It was bad enough having Grady utter her old name, but to have someone else speak it—someone she did not know—was more unsettling. "Who are you?"

He scratched the back of his neck, making his black wig shift a little. "Guess it's hard to tell with the getup. It's me, Obie Penn."

"Obie Penn." She scrambled through her memory and produced the image of a young man who had stood tall with broad shoulders. He'd had lean hips and auburn hair that brushed his collar. Grace had had a thing for Obie, who'd been five years her senior. Once he'd even managed to coax her behind the tent and get his hand up her shirt before Grady had caught them. Grady had been furious and had said he'd cut Obie's nuts off if he ever touched Grace again. Obie had backed off. Grace had been horrified. They'd never gone behind the tent again. But she'd been angry, and the seeds of rebellion had been sown.

"Obie, how are you?" His long calloused palm wrapped around her outstretched manicured fingers. She looked a little closer and recognized the brown eyes that had made her forget caution long ago.

He grinned. "You look great."

"Thanks."

He hesitated before he released her hand. "I always figured you'd end up living the high life. Grady said you were always meant for big things, and I guess he was right."

Grady had said that about her? All she remembered was the old man barking at her about being difficult. "You look good, too. I mean from what I can see."

He laughed, flashing small, yellowed teeth. "I'm usually not this green around the gills. Grady's got me working the costumes this week because the regular guy got arrested for drugs in Roanoke, Virginia."

In the carnival, everyone had to be prepared to fill in for anyone else. She'd worked the ball toss and even run the Ferris wheel for a few days around her fifteenth birthday. "Sorry to hear that."

"Ah, well, it wasn't the first time, and it won't be the last." He planted a hand on his hip. "So what brings you here? I think you are about the last person I'd expect to see here."

"Just curious, I guess."

"So what do you do now? Married to some fat cat?"

"I'm an attorney."

"And I'm still here."

Face makeup had already begun to dip into crow's feet etched deep by the sun. What would she have looked like if she'd stayed? Hardened to the point of being unrecognizable. Crazy like her mother. "Wow. Do you like it?"

"Can't complain."

"So what do you do when you're not scaring kids?"

The paint on his face cracked a fraction when he smiled. "Grady's got me managing the games most nights. I've got six I oversee."

"That's great. Sounds like it keeps you busy."

"Oh, it does."

She glanced around at the growing crowd. "Have you seen Grady?"

"He's probably working the rifle shot. Or maybe he's busting on the ghouls. Most were hung over and moving slow this afternoon."

"Never a dull moment."

"Not here."

An awkward silence settled between them. Whatever they'd once had in common had vanished over the last eighteen years. "It was good seeing you, Obie."

"You, too, Grace."

"I go by the name *Charlotte* now."

He eyed her for a moment. "Fits you and your fancy new look. But I can't say I like it." He leaned forward a fraction. "I like the plump little Grace who wasn't afraid to go behind the tent with me." His breath smelled of cigarettes and pizza.

She inched back and didn't hide the shiver of disgust too well. "She's long gone, Obie. I'm Charlotte now. So don't call me Grace."

Frankenstein's eyes narrowed. "I see you got an attitude to go with the suit. Mariah was like that. All attitude. Don't forget where you came from."

"Believe me, I haven't." But it wasn't for lack of trying.

He looked as if he had more to say when a little boy and his parents approached Obie.

"Can we take your picture, Mr. Frankenstein?" the kid's mom said.

Obie, annoyed by the interruption, knew better than to break character in front of a customer. That was Grady's number one rule: never disappoint the customer.

Nodding and grunting, Frankenstein raised his arms and grunted just like the movie character.

As the boy stood grinning in front of his monster and the dad snapped pictures, Charlotte moved away from him, letting the crowd swallow her. She continued to meander down the center aisle closer and closer to the Madame Divine tent. She thought she could see Sooner, maybe caution her about the article's exposure when she gave her the revised lease.

As she approached, she heard Sooner chanting in a low throaty voice that sounded, well, possessed. Intrigued, Charlotte ducked inside the tent and stood in the background as Sooner took the hand of the woman sitting before her. In her late fifties, the woman had graying hair that framed a round face made paler by a bright pumpkin-colored sweatshirt.

Sooner clutched the woman's hand and with her eyes closed said, "I am seeing your husband. He is smiling."

The woman cleared her throat. "He is? Is he smiling at me?"

"He is. And he wants me to tell you that he misses you very much."

The lady drew in a sharp breath. "Tell him that I've missed him, too. He really was the best husband in the world."

Sooner swayed back and forth as she held her hand. "And he says you were the best wife." Slowly she opened her eyes. She glanced briefly past the woman to Charlotte but her gaze darted back so quickly it was doubtful the woman noticed. "Is there a question you would like to ask him?"

"No, no question."

"I'm seeing the color red. Was that an important color to him?"

"No, I don't think so. He did like to hunt."

"Perhaps what I'm seeing is his own passion for you. He misses your touch."

The lady nodded and softly began to weep. Sooner pulled out a tissue and handed it to the woman. "I am so glad we were able to connect with your husband, Herbert. It's not always so easy to reach into the other world."

"Thank you so much for trying."

"I have one more message from Herbert."

"Yes?"

"He does not want you to be alone. He wants you to talk to the nice man at church who likes you more than you realize."

"He does?"

"Yes." She straightened her shoulders. "Now that will be thirty dollars."

The woman opened her cloth purse and pulled out two twenties. "Keep the change."

"That is very generous of you." Sooner slid the money in the locked box that Grady always provided. One of his first lessons was to get the money under lock and key.

The woman rose and, dabbing her eyes, passed by Charlotte without a glance.

Sooner waited until the woman was well clear of the tent before she rose and stretched the kinks from her back. "Going to be a long night."

Charlotte crossed into the room and took the seat opposite Sooner. This close, she could see that the girl had a knack for applying the makeup. She looked exotic without cosmetics, but with them, looked very ethereal. "Why didn't you get payment right up front?"

"I did. That extra thirty was a last-minute add-on. I could have asked for it up front but suspected if I waited I'd get a good tip."

"You might not have gotten paid."

"She's not the type to skip."

"How can you tell?"

"Just her aura, I guess."

"And the guy at church. How'd you hit that one?"

"The cross around her neck, and when she first arrived, she mentioned she'd be going to a church social. The blue eye shadow and rouge looked clumsy as if she'd applied it for the first time in years. Chicks, no matter how old they are, will preen for a man."

"Nice."

She leaned back in her chair. "So how is it sitting on the other side of this table?"

"Grady told you about me."

"He told me you and my mother worked the tent back in the day."

"What did he tell you about your mother?"

"Pretty. Drowned right after I was born."

"She loved you."

"Really?" The word sounded brittle enough to snap. "We don't talk about her much."

"I can tell you about her."

Sooner drew in a breath. "No."

When Charlotte moved to rebut, Sooner said, "Sorry again about the missed appointment. I was looking at paint colors and lost track of time. So what's the bottom line on the lease?"

Charlotte sensed she'd hit a nerve in the kid and

backed off. She gave her a detailed rundown of the lease. "You going to follow my advice?"

She reached below the folds of the tablecloth and pulled out a diet soda. She took a long sip and then hid it again.

"Some of it. Not all."

"It's all sound advice, Sooner. You should take it all."

"I might not have a deal if I play hardball with the landlord."

Charlotte crossed her legs. "Don't sell yourself short."

"I don't." The girl possessed maturity far beyond her years.

"I saw the article in the paper."

"Good press, I'd say."

"For Grady."

"And for me."

"He's put you out here like bait for a killer."

She cocked her head. "It's a bit we started doing this season in a lot of small towns. Pick a murder or crime and announce it can be solved."

"My God, Sooner, do you know how dangerous that is?"

"We've never had trouble before."

"Have you read the articles about Diane Young?"

"No." The girl glanced down and back up, a sign she felt defensive.

"She did not die easily, Sooner." Charlotte's words were clear, direct, and intended to be cutting. "Whoever killed her was making a statement."

She shrugged, indicating the event did not hold much interest. "I'm not trying to be hard, but bad things happen. That doesn't mean they'll happen to me."

"Grady paraded you in the paper as some kind of

psychic detective. If I saw it, there is a good chance the killer did."

Her chin tipped up a fraction. "I am going to be fine. Grady says it's good for business." Again another shrug. "Look, I'm the first to admit the guy can be a dick, but he does know how to drum up business and I want people to know who I am."

"There are better ways, Sooner."

"I don't have huge cash reserves. I've got to hit the ground running and make money." The girl ran long impatient fingers through her hair. She glanced toward the opening of the tent and saw a man hovering. "Look, I got a customer so I got to jet."

Charlotte glanced toward the opening. The man standing there was tall, lean, and wore jeans and a plain T-shirt. He could have been anybody. The killer was likely just anybody, someone no one ever noticed. The man who'd attacked her several years ago looked like just anybody. "Sooner, you need to back off this."

Sooner smiled at the man at the tent entrance and beckoned him in with the wave of her fingers. "You are not my mother," she said, still smiling at the man. "I appreciate what you did with the lease thing, but you need to back off. Now."

The man hovered just behind Charlotte, and she could smell the strong scent of Old Spice.

"Is it my turn?" he said.

Sooner's smile exploded with brightness and welcome. "Yes. Have a seat. This lady was just finished."

Charlotte stared at the young girl. A part of her wanted to grab her by the wrist and pull her out of this tent. But her carefully cultivated logical side understood that Sooner was eighteen and a legal adult.

Whatever rights Charlotte had had to the girl, she'd abdicated long ago.

She moved out of the tent, realizing that with Sooner, rights or no, this was not a retreat but a retrench. Like it or not, she had an obligation to the kid.

She scanned the carnival and quickly spotted Grady's trailer on the outskirts. During the day, he could be found there, balancing books, figuring work schedules, or handling whatever problem had cropped up the night before. And there were always problems: fistfights, drunks, stolen money, and even missing workers who'd just up and left the carnival.

But when the carnival opened its gates for the evening, Grady was on the go, moving past each ride, each food vendor, and each game to make sure his crew was working. Sooner had been right. Grady did have his faults, but anything associated with this business he did right. Obie had said the rifle shot.

The fairgrounds had filled with parents and their young children. The younger families would clear out by nine, and then the teenagers and singles would arrive. That was when the character of the place changed from soft to edgy.

She bypassed the Ferris wheel, which had been running steadily since she arrived, and moved toward the rifle shot, always a big draw for young families.

Dust now coated her high heels, and she was grateful it had not rained in the last few weeks. Rain would turn this place into a mud-soaked adventure. Grady would be happy about the weather. Crisp, cool air brought the customers out whereas rain and mud all but chased away people accustomed to the clean, paved walkways of amusement parks.

She found Grady standing by the rifle shot. Hands on

hips, his back was to her as he watched a customer raise his rifle and aim it at the red bull's-eyes. The man fired once, twice, and three times. Each time he missed. Charlotte could have told him the sight on the barrel was off but didn't bother. Frustrated, the man paid another five dollars for three more shots.

The extra moments gave her time to really look at Grady. He'd lost weight and his long, lean body hunched forward. He stood, his feet braced, hands on hips, and a cigarette in his left hand.

She moved up behind Grady and in a low voice said, "That was some article you had in the paper today."

Without facing her, he grinned. "I thought it would get your attention."

Anger snapped in her gut. "So that was for my benefit?"

Slowly, he faced her. The moonlight mingled with the glow of the game's light and deepened the crevices of his face. The air about swirled with a hard edge. "It's always about business. But if I can catch a few other fish along the way, all the better."

"Who else are you trying to catch?"

As the customer fired and missed again, he faced her, letting the full weight of his gaze settle. "Who else would I want to catch?"

He was the trickster. The game player. He had inspired her best courtroom tactics. "You said Sooner could catch the killer of Diane Young."

"Good drama sells tickets." He glanced toward her tent. "She's already got a line."

"You're putting her in unnecessary danger."

"She ain't a baby. She's a big girl now."

"Eighteen is so young."

"She's done all right for herself."

"All right? Grady, she deserved a real family. A mother and a father. Regular school. You've set her up as a side show freak."

"Good enough for you and your sister."

She shook her head. "If I'd known that you were going to keep her—"

"You'd what?" he challenged. "You'd have stayed with me and raised her?" He shook his head. "You wanted out of here so bad you'd have sold your soul to the Devil."

"That's not true." Tears choked her throat. "You said she'd get a real home. You promised."

He laughed. "You had me pegged for a con artist and a liar the day we met. How old were you? Eight? Even then you could see through all my tall tales, likely because you are just like me.

"I'm not like you."

He shook his head. "And when you wanted out of here so badly that you could taste it, you chose to believe me. You chose to believe the lies because it suited you."

Frustration scorched through her. "You're wrong."

"Who's the liar now."

They could stand here and pointlessly argue about the past, or she could worry about today and Sooner. "You need to protect Sooner."

"I am."

"How? You're standing here. She's over there."

"Ain't nothing happens in my carnival without me knowing it. Not ever."

"Mariah drowned. You never saw that coming." Pent-up emotion and anger coated the name.

The teasing light in his gaze vanished, leaving only

menace. "I got a close eye and ear on my girl, Sooner, so don't you worry none."

"That was what you said about Mariah."

"That girl was too damn boy crazy for her own good. I tried to protect her, but she never listened to good sense. Sooner's not like Mariah. She's like you. She's smart."

She stiffened. "Don't let anything happen to her."

"Or what?" He leaned toward her. "Why don't you just get back to your fancy life and leave us behind like you did before."

"Sooner is a great kid. She *is* smart and can go far. But she'll never see any of that here."

"She's doing just fine. Fact, I suspect she'll run this place one day."

"Is that what you want for her?"

"Sure, why not? It's a good gig and makes decent money."

"There are better ways to earn a living."

"Like being a bloodsucking attorney?" He laughed. "Look, you did like I asked and got Sooner out of trouble. And I do appreciate it, but now you need to pull that pretty little nose of yours out of my business."

She wasn't a scared sixteen-year-old so afraid of the big tall, grizzled man her mother had brought home. "Or what?"

His hand shot out and he grabbed her arm in such a tight hard grip, his calloused palms would likely leave a bruise. "You'd be surprised what this old body can still do."

She didn't flinch or try to twist out of his hold. "You don't scare me."

"I should."

So locked in their war of words, neither heard Detective Daniel Rokov approach. "There a problem here?"

Rokov had traded his suit for khakis, a dark polo, and a black leather jacket that covered all but the tip of his holstered sidearm. The dimming light had added some menace to Grady's visage, but it completely transformed Rokov into a darker, more dangerous man. No traces of her passionate, tender lover remained.

Chapter 12

Grady released Charlotte's arm and took a step back.

She flinched and rubbed the red flesh of her wrist. "I didn't hear you come up."

Rokov stared down at her, his gaze lingering and searching. "No, you did not. You were having an intense conversation with Grady."

"How do you know his name?" And then she caught herself. "Of course, the article. He claimed Sooner could catch the killer."

Grady sniffed and straightened his shoulders. "You've got me at a disadvantage. Mind making a formal introduction, Ms. Wellington?"

Her gaze remained on Rokov. "Grady Tate, this is Detective Daniel Rokov. He is a homicide detective with the Alexandria Police. I suspect he's investigating Diane Young's case."

Rokov sized up the old man with a glance. Most

underestimated the aging ringmaster as a threat, but Rokov seemed to understand that this old man could still do quite a bit of damage. "That was a bold statement you made in the paper."

Grady grinned, flashing yellowed small teeth, no doubt realizing that Rokov was no sucker. His body language relaxed, he spoke guardedly. "Bold is what gets the job done."

"Sometimes. And sometimes it creates a hell of a mess. Do you have information that could help the investigation?"

"Sorry, detective. It's all smoke and mirrors."

Rokov glanced at Charlotte. "What brings you here? This doesn't strike me as your kind of place."

"I came to see Sooner," she said honestly. "I was worried about the article."

"Kind of above and beyond for a pro bono client."

Rokov's height, six three or better, had her stretching every inch from her five-foot-six frame. In bed they were equals, but here he dominated. "The article caught my eye. It's out of the norm, and I thought I'd visit."

"No other agenda?" he challenged.

Amusement brightened Grady's gaze. The old man clearly loved this collision of her well-crafted present and unsavory past.

"Such as?" she said.

Rokov flashed even white teeth. "You lawyering out of the answer, counselor?"

She was. And she planned to keep doing it. "Am I?"

Rokov's amusement faded. "Did you know Diane Young?"

Charlotte shook her head. "No. Why would you ask?"

"Just checking to see if you're capable of a straight answer." He swung his attention to Grady. "Did you know Diane Young?"

Grady's pleasure draining away, he slid long fingers into his jeans pockets. "I did not."

"We found a note to visit the carnival on her to-do list," Rokov said.

Grady shrugged. "I'll bet you're gonna find that on a lot of to-do lists this week. We're having a record year."

"I don't care about anybody's list but Diane's and the killer's."

"Like I said, that stuff in the paper about Sooner catching a killer was all hype, detective. I saw a chance to grab attention, and I took it." Grady knew when to tell the truth.

Distaste sharpened the lines in Rokov's face. "I'd like to talk to your employees and show them her picture. Maybe someone here might have seen her. I also want to talk to Sooner."

Charlotte took a step back. "This conversation is clearly between you two, so I'll leave."

Rokov grabbed her elbow, his grip gentle steel. "A moment please, Ms. Wellington. I'd like to have a chat."

A rebellious urge rose and died under Grady's too curious gaze. "I really need to get going."

"You can give me a minute or two." Not a request but a statement. "Round up your men, Mr. Tate. I want to talk to them all."

"I'm a couple of men down tonight. Everyone's working full tilt."

"I'm sure you can pull a few at a time. It would be regrettable to call the Health Department for an impromptu inspection."

"We're up to code."

"So you'd like me to call the Health Department?" And Rokov was not a man who made idle threats.

Grady might be up to code, but health inspectors traipsing around food vendors drove off customers. "I'll get Tiny and Buster off their rides first. They both got backups."

"Great. I appreciate your help."

When Grady was out of earshot, Rokov turned to Charlotte. "So what aren't you telling me? And if you answer me with a question, I think I'll arrest you for obstruction of justice."

"I've told you everything that is germane to your case."

"Which means you have not told me everything."

"No, I have not. And I'm not going to. All you need to know is that I am here to check on Sooner."

"Why did Grady have a death grip on your arm?"

"Ask him."

He leaned close and she smelled hints of his soap mingling with his jacket's worn, smooth leather. He lowered his voice to a hoarse rough whisper. "I'm asking you."

She had outmaneuvered attorneys and CEOs in countless courtrooms and boardrooms. But here, right now, she sensed in Rokov a raw treacherous edge not easily escaped. If he took the gloves off, she might be hard pressed to win. "If it had a bearing on your case, I'd tell you. But it does not. Some things just have to stay private."

"The more evasions you feed me, the more curious I become. And I am not a pleasant man when I have an unanswered question."

"I guess you just have to deal."

A muscle pulsed in his jaw. "Walk with me to Sooner's tent."

"Why?"

"Just humor me."

She shook her head. "I'm not walking anywhere with you, detective. I've got a dinner date."

His energy became deadly still. "Really?"

She swallowed. "With a client."

Tension easing a fraction, he said, "The Samantha White case is behind you. You can take a little time." He'd used the same argument when he'd coaxed her back to his bed Tuesday morning.

"I never say no to a client." She caught sight of Grady, who moved toward them with two rough-looking carnies in tow. Rokov also saw them, and for a split second his attention shifted away from her.

Grabbing the opportunity, she pulled free and put distance between them. "Looks like your party is here. I'll leave you to it."

She suspected he could easily make a scene if that's what it took. But her past was not his top priority . . . now. It was Diane Young's murder.

"This isn't finished between us, Ms. Wellington. We'll be talking soon."

"Call my secretary. She'll tell you if I have time."

His grin telegraphed amusement and a very clear message: *I'll find you when I'm ready.*

Rokov watched Charlotte walk away, finding himself amused, frustrated, and most of all savoring the way she moved in the confines of her gray pencil skirt. She wasn't a tall woman, maybe five-foot-six, but she had lean taut limbs, breasts that filled out her white blouse, and a thick leather belt that cinched a narrow waist. He thought back to Tuesday morning and the way she'd touched him. This week's circumstances had severed their connection, but he'd get it back one way or the other.

A background check would tell him what she was hiding. But he didn't want to dig. He wanted her trust.

Grady, flanked by two young men, offered a wolfish grin. "Detective, I'd like you to meet Tiny and Buster." Tiny was indeed Tiny and couldn't have been more than five feet. He had long dark hair tied at the nape of his neck, wore a short-sleeved shirt that read *Danger*, torn faded jeans, and an endless flow of tattoos on his arms. Buster was taller but more muscular. He sported a blond crew cut, a swastika tattoo on his neck, and a buttoned-up long-sleeved shirt tucked neatly into pressed jeans.

Tiny and Buster. What a pair.

Rokov reached in his pocket and pulled out his Department of Motor Vehicles picture of Diane Young. The color picture was taken several years ago. "Gentlemen, did either of you see this woman last week?"

Tiny and Buster looked at each other and then at Grady, who nodded his approval.

Buster took the picture and studied the picture closely. "I don't remember her. We get so many people, she could have been here, and I just missed her."

Tiny accepted the picture from Buster. "Pretty. Too bad about her. I wish I could say I saw her but I just don't remember."

Rokov took the picture back. "She was about five-foot-six, and her sister said she walked with a slight limp because she'd sprained her ankle a month ago."

Grady, Buster, and Tiny shook their heads. If they'd seen Diane, he doubted they'd admit it. The carnies did not like any dealings with the cops even if it meant they could help.

"Want me to round up more men?" Grady said. "Can't say you'll get a different answer, but who knows, you might get lucky."

"Go ahead and grab a few more men."

"Could take a few minutes."

"No rush. I'll be at Sooner's tent having a chat with her."

"Why Sooner?" Grady's tone turned defensive with a hint of menace.

"That a problem?"

"No." Grady sniffed and waved away Tiny and Buster. "Just asking."

"Then I'll see you at her tent. And take your time." Not lingering for a response, he moved through the crowds, kicking up dust along the way. When he reached her tent, she had a line of ten customers outside. He produced his badge and walked past the line into the tent.

The tent was dimly lit with electric lights that resembled candles. Sooner sat at a table draped in purple silk and before her sat a client—a young girl with blond hair and a cheerleader's demeanor. Spread on the table were tarot cards arranged in the cardinal cross pattern. Oddly he recognized the cards. They were Russian and similar to the ones his grandmother kept tucked in the drawer by her bed.

Sooner looked up with expressive green eyes that were now heavily made up. The girl he'd seen at the courthouse had looked streetwise but young. This incarnation looked years beyond her age.

He held up his badge. "Sooner Tate?"

The sound of his voice had the cheerleader girl turning. Her face paled and her red lips parted into a surprised O.

Sooner couldn't have been much older than the girl, but her world-weary expression suggested the experience of a much older woman. "Yes."

"Ma'am," Rokov said to the cheerleader. "If you will excuse us."

The girl looked between Sooner and Rokov.

Sooner answered for her. "I have a few more minutes with my client. If you don't mind."

Young and ballsy. "Sure."

When he didn't move, she lifted a brow. "Do you mind stepping back? This is private."

"Sure."

He took a position in the back of the tent by the entrance. His hands clasped behind his back, he waited, not sure if he was amused or annoyed by the girl.

Sooner leaned toward the cheerleader and in hushed tones continued to whisper her reading. The cheerleader quickly forgot about him and leaned toward the cards as if they held the meaning of her life.

He watched Sooner, fascinated by the way she stroked the cards and turned each new one over with a dramatic flare. She waved her hands several times, making the bracelets on her arms clink with a dramatic effect. When she pronounced the reading done, the girl seemed satisfied and yet still hungry for more.

When the cheerleader asked for more information, Sooner shook her head and said, "Sadly our time is over and the cop in the corner has been patient enough."

Cheerleader's lips pouted but she rose, hugging her purse close. "Can I come back?"

Sooner rose. "Of course. I will be here for two more weeks. Come back anytime."

"I will." The girl hurried out of the tent.

Rokov moved toward Sooner. What was it about the girl that felt so familiar to him? He had an excellent memory for faces and names. They'd not met before, but still there was something.

He took the seat across from her, leaning back, relaxed as if he had all the time in the world and there was not a line outside. The heavy scent of incense hung around them, and he wondered if she ended up with a pounding headache by the end of the night.

"What can I do for you, detective?" she said. "Have you come for guidance from the stars in this latest murder investigation?"

"I'm not interested in your psychic talents but your powers of observation." He pulled the DMV photo from his pocket. "Did you see her here?"

Sooner took the picture. She studied the picture, and a frown formed and deepened on her face. "This is the woman that was murdered."

"Yes."

"I've seen her."

"You've seen her picture?"

"No, I've seen her."

"Tell me it was not in a dream."

"No. She was in this tent." Her face paled a fraction. "She was my first customer here. She said she wasn't crazy about crowds."

"You've not seen her picture before?"

"No." She looked at him, her eyes full and bright. "Grady was the one that told the press I could find a killer. I never said that."

He pulled a notebook from his breast pocket along with a pen. "When did you see her?"

"Last week. Early. Friday, I think. Opening night. She could read the cards and a couple of times challenged me. It was amusing at first and then it got a little annoying."

"Why?"

"I'm here to do a job. She was here to see how I handled my readings. Basically checking out and learning from the competition."

"That so bad?"

She shrugged with a casual elegance generally reserved for an older, more sophisticated woman. "How would you like it if another detective followed you around all the time and second-guessed you?"

"Point taken. So how long did she stay?"

"She paid for thirty minutes in cash. She stayed the entire time."

"What kind of reading did you give her?"

"Basic tarot reading."

"Do you remember her fortune?"

"I think I gave her the standard line of success on the horizon and foreign travel. But nothing stands out in my mind."

"And when you finished the reading, she left the carnival?"

"I don't know if she left. I was in the tent."

"You didn't see her talking to anyone?"

Amusement danced in her eyes. "Despite the advertisements, I don't see beyond the walls of this tent, detective."

"You've no special powers."

She chuckled and glanced toward the tent opening to see if anyone was listening. "None."

He rose. "Thank you for your time, Ms. Tate. How much longer will you be in town?"

"The carnival is here for ten more days."

"What about you?"

She'd been relaxed and confident up until this moment, but a rising tension froze the warmth from her body. "I plan to leave with the carnival."

"Do you?"

She grinned. "Why would I not?"

"Good question." He moved to leave and then stopped. "Why were you in court the other day?"

"How did you know that?"

He grinned. "I saw you with Charlotte Wellington."

Surprise gave way to knowing. "You noticed me or Ms. Wellington?"

Points for perception, kid. "All that matters is that I saw you. Why were you there?" He'd checked but wanted her version.

"A minor problem with a local shopkeeper. He accused me of stealing. I was innocent and the judge agreed."

"Were you found innocent or did Ms. Wellington do her magic and shoot holes in the Commonwealth's case?"

"The end result is the same." She glanced toward the tent. "Detective, I really must get back to work. Every minute you stand here is costing me money."

"Sure. I may be in touch."

"Of course."

He ducked as he moved out of the tent opening and

glanced at the growing line of people waiting to see Sooner. She had a dozen people waiting.

The sun had set and the lights on the rides had softened the carnival's hard edges. Excitement buzzed in the air as more and more families and couples started to arrive.

What the hell kind of connection did Charlotte have to this place? Why had she doubled back to see Sooner?

Puzzles or mysteries irritated him until he had the answer in his sights.

Sooner shoved out a breath full of tension and fear once the detective left. The man possessed a strong aura filled with steel and resolve. He was not a man to anger. Her mind tripped to the moment she'd mentioned Charlotte Wellington to him. Though his expression did not change, his energy shifted into high gear and he clearly inwardly bristled.

She grinned. "I wonder if Charlotte knows she is in his sights."

The next few hours were an endless stream of the lovelorn or those searching for some unattainable answer. Will I get the job? Will I find that ring? What are my chances with the lottery?

So weak were their auras, she barely could feel the energy around them. Later in the evening, a man entered her tent and caught her attention. Before he even crossed the ten feet from the door to her desk, she felt him. Like Detective Rokov, he had a strong powerful energy that had her sitting straighter and playing close attention to his features.

He wore a green baseball cap, glasses, and a dark jacket he'd zipped up to his throat. His hair was a deep brown and so long it brushed broad shoulders that appeared padded. Jeans and sneakers completed a look that was very nondescript.

As much as he tried to look like a Nobody, she knew there was more to this man. He had a need and hunger in him that teetered on starving.

Sooner cleared her throat and straightened her shoulders. "What can I do for you this evening?"

"Me? I thought maybe I could help you. I heard you were looking for me." He slid gloved hands into his pants pockets.

"I'm not looking for anyone." Her foot grazed the panic button Grady had installed under her table. Every bit of emotion in her screamed to press it as logic struggled to sooth her worries. "I am here to give help, sir. I am not searching."

"The article said you were looking for a killer," he said. "I might be able to help you find him."

Fear rolled over her skin in waves. She didn't know if he was a nut job looking for attention or something far more dangerous. It didn't matter. She pressed the button with her foot. "You need to leave this tent now. I have security coming."

"I don't think they're coming."

"What do you mean?" She pressed the button several more times and reached for the baseball bat she kept at her side. She'd only had to use it a couple of times, but each time it had been worth its weight in gold.

"I saw the wire and cut it. No one is coming."

Her confidence ebbed and she glanced around the tent wondering if she could reach the exit before he grabbed her. Instead of debating the issue or worrying about the buzzer, she summoned help the old-fashioned way.

She screamed.

"I'll see you soon." The man smiled and then quickly turned on his heel and left the tent. Bat in hand, she rose from her seat and moved to the entrance, where a few stunned and confused customers waited. The carnival's noise and music had drowned out her scream and only those at the front of the line had heard her.

"Hey, lady, are you all right?" The question came from the first woman in line. She sported an oversized Redskins T-shirt, a bag of popcorn, and a giant panda.

Sooner searched for the man but already he'd vanished into the crowds. Whoever Mr. Creepazoid was, he was gone now. Grady had said the article would jostle the nuts out of the trees. She considered telling Grady, but hesitated. Soon she'd be on her own and would have to handle situations like this alone. And calling Rokov, well, a lifetime distrusting cops was a hard habit to break. "Fuck."

"What did you say?" said Redskins lady.

Realizing she'd broken character, she straightened her shoulders. If Grady had taught her one thing, it was that it was the illusion that kept them in business. "So sorry. I was chasing away the evil spirits."

"So can I get my reading?" Redskins lady said.

"Yes, darling, please enter." Heart still pounding, she made a grand sweep of her hands and vanished into the tent.

* * *

It was past 1 a.m. when Grady was able to sit at his desk and plow through the night's earnings. Judging by the stack of cash and credit card receipts, it had been a very good night. He'd known Sooner would be the draw that he needed. The girl was just coming into her own, and her beauty and her talent with people could make her a grand draw for years to come.

Years to come.

He reached for the tumbler full of whiskey and drained half of it.

He didn't have years. He had months if he was lucky.

He glanced at the piles of cash, skimmed a couple hundred of the smaller bills away, and shoved them in his pocket. He wrote up the bank deposit slip, which he'd drop off in the morning.

When his work was complete, he glanced at the clock. Three fourteen. He should be tired. The doc in Nashville had told him to sleep more. But his head buzzed. Sleep had become harder and harder in the last year, and tonight he'd be lucky to get an hour or two. Glancing at his unmade bunk with a bit of resentment, he rose and moved to the window that overlooked the carnival. A few trailers remained lit up, and the sound of music drifted from Buster's trailer, but all in all the place was quiet.

He moved to the safe, opened the door, and dropped in the bank deposit bag. He was about to close the safe door when he spotted the folder in the bottom. Digging it out, he locked the safe and went to the dinette. He refilled his scotch before he sat down.

Opening the file, he leafed through the yellowed newspaper articles. WOMAN FOUND SLAIN, Raleigh. HIKER DROWNED, Charleston. WOMAN RAPED AND MURDERED,

Nashville. There were at least two dozen articles like these three. All featured women in the Southeast who'd been kidnapped, held, and then violently murdered.

The cities and times had been scattered enough that the cops in the different jurisdictions did not realize they were dealing with the same killer. But he knew.

Slowly, he turned each article over and over until he reached the last that he'd clipped out just days ago.

The article featured Diane Young.

Chapter 13

Charlotte's legs ached as she hurried up the courthouse's front steps. The last couple of days had been a blur of work. Friday's client dinner had gone well, and she'd spent the weekend drawing up contracts. He wasn't a huge fish but the work fees would help. Breaks had centered on visiting the new apartment, determining what she could keep, calling the clerk on the White case, and making sure the movers were ready to pack up her life on Friday.

She pushed through the glass front doors and hurried over to the line at security. She dumped her purse and briefcase in the bin and sent it through the scanner as she ducked under the sensors. The buzzer beeped and she glanced at the security guard, a tall black man with a shaved head and stern expression.

Without being told, she moved forward and held up her arms as he rose off his stool with his wand. "Morning, Ms. Wellington."

She smiled and tried not to look impatient. "Morning, Oscar. How's it going?"

"It's going just about like any other Monday."

"That sounds ominous." He brushed the wand and paused at her belt. She glanced at the large buckle and rolled her eyes. "Sorry, I wasn't even thinking today."

"Naw, just a lot of harmless fun."

Moving backward, she dumped her belt in a bin and sent it through the scanner. This time when she walked through, no alarm beeped.

"All clear." He watched as she refastened her belt and grabbed her purse and briefcase. "I'd say by those dark circles under your eyes, you could use a fun weekend."

"I never have fun, Oscar. Life is about work for me." Lately, she'd envied people like Oscar who could leave work behind and just break free. The only times she'd really acted without analyzing had been her nights with Rokov. Now, she couldn't even think about him without considering complications.

"So I hear the jury is back today?"

"It is." It had been seven days since the judge had given the jury instructions in the Samantha White case. Never in those seven days was the case far from her mind, and though the lengthy deliberations were a good sign, the constant worry was chewing up her stomach.

"You always got work on the brain."

"Always."

"You're too young and pretty not to have some fun."

The avuncular comment had her shrugging. "Tell that to the workload. When it eases up, I will, too."

"The work is always gonna be there, Ms. Wellington. Always."

As much as she'd earned a bit more fun, she'd never

resented the work or viewed it as a bad thing. Work meant money, and money meant freedom. And if she didn't have time to spend her money, then so be it. "I'll keep that in mind."

The good humor of the moment quickly passed as she moved through the throng of people toward the elevators. She had a half hour before court, which was time enough to talk to Levi, who'd requested another meeting.

She found the prosecutor in the conference room. He sat at the head of the table, his head bent over an open case file. He made quick, abrupt notes with his left hand. A line furrowed his brow.

"Levi," she said. "You wanted to meet before court."

He glanced up, and smoothing his hand down his red tie, he rose and pulled out a chair for her. "Glad you could meet me."

The soft scent of his aftershave wafted around him. As always, he was impeccably dressed in hand-tailored suits that drew attention to his lean waist. She'd heard he was a bit of a gym rat, but seeing as she'd never set foot in a gym, their paths weren't likely ever to cross.

She leaned back in her chair, noting the way the hard back dug into her spine. "What do you have?"

"Involuntary manslaughter. She serves four years."

Charlotte was shocked by such a generous deal. "My client doesn't want any deals."

"This is a great deal and can end this now."

"It is over. The jury is back."

"Take the deal, and we both win."

"My client loses four years of her life." Levi was a tough nut, and for him to cave was surprising. "She's made it clear. No deal."

He knitted his fingers and leaned forward. "Charlotte,

I'm not trying to be a hard ass. I feel for this woman. I don't want to see her suffer any more than you do."

"You sure tried to put her away."

"That's my job. And believe me, I did not enjoy it."

It was a good deal. "Let me place a call to the bailiff." She dialed and within minutes was on the phone with Samantha. As she suspected, the woman turned it down.

Charlotte turned off her phone. "She says no."

"You both could regret this."

"I don't think so. See you in court." The butterflies churning her stomach had her glancing at her watch as she moved down the hallway. She had fifteen minutes to show time.

Show time.

Funny she could think of court like show time. That was the term her mother had used as she'd left for her carnival shows.

"Mom, you look tired."

Mom finished underlining her right eye. "Really? I'm feeling great, kiddo."

"Can't you take a night off? We can watch a movie and eat popcorn. We've not done that in a long time."

"Kiddo, Momma can't say no to work because work is what keeps us together."

"One night won't make a difference."

"One night leads to two nights, and then before you know it, you're out of a job. I'll work until the day I die."

Until the day I die.

She'd suffered her stroke two weeks later.

Charlotte pushed through the double doors of the courtroom and moved to the defense table. The next few minutes moved along on a steady predictable course. The bailiff arrived. Deputies escorted in Samantha White, who took her seat by Charlotte. Levi took his seat. The courtroom filled, the jury took their seats, and the judge arrived.

Judge Winston Lawless struck his gavel against his bench and announced court proceedings to begin. Black robes broadened the appearance of his shoulders and accentuated dark hair combed back from stern features. In his late forties, he'd earned a reputation as a hard-ass.

Charlotte's back was to the courtroom door, but without turning, she knew the instant Rokov arrived. She couldn't say how she knew, only that the energy in the room had changed. It felt more charged, almost as if it buzzed with force.

Charlotte kept her expression neutral, and she did not dare turn and look to confirm his arrival. But the muscles in her body tensed, and she kept aligning her pencil with her yellow legal pad.

"Will the defendant rise?"

Charlotte and Samantha rose. Samantha dared a glance back, searching for her mother, who had returned from the beach but had not come to the courthouse for the verdict. Carefully, she smoothed the wrinkles from her prison jumpsuit.

Charlotte took her hand and squeezed it.

"Members of the jury," the judge said. "Have you reached a verdict?"

A short man with graying hair and a red tie stood. "We have, Your Honor." The foreman handed a slip of paper to the bailiff.

The judge received the paper and read it. He frowned, nodded. "What is your verdict?"

"On the count of arson, we the jury find the defendant . . . not guilty."

Charlotte and Samantha both remained rigid.

"And on the count of first-degree murder?" Judge Lawson said.

"We find the defendant innocent."

As a frowning Judge Lawless read his final instructions, a whimper escaped across Samantha's lips, and she leaned forward and buried her face in her hands. She started to weep. Charlotte tipped her head back, savoring the rush of this victory, and then wrapped her arm around her client.

"Thank you so much." Samantha looked up at her with red watery eyes. "Thank you so much."

Charlotte smiled, knowing she often came across as cold and unfeeling. "You are very welcome."

"You've saved my life."

Charlotte smiled. "I'm glad to have helped."

She watched the bailiff lead Samantha away and then hurried out of the courtroom quickly. She paused briefly to talk to reporters and then hurried toward the exit.

She had just cleared the courthouse steps when she heard her name. "Wellington. I want a word with you."

The masculine voice was rich with anger. Irritated by the rude delay more than fearful, Charlotte turned and faced the man. "Can I help you?"

Tall and thin, he wore khakis, a white shirt, and work boots. He'd slicked back his dark hair and sharply parted it on the right side.

"You can tell me why you helped that witch get

free." He closed the gap between them until he stood only inches from her.

This close, Charlotte could smell the hint of gasoline and motor oil on the man's flannel shirt and jeans. "Do I know you?"

"I'm Lonnie White. Samantha killed my brother."

And then she could see the resemblance. She didn't focus much of her research on Lonnie because reports indicated he'd been living in Atlanta for the last several years. What facts she'd gathered ticked back: auto repairman, married, military service with a general discharge. Lonnie and his brother hadn't been close. "I didn't notice you in the courtroom during the trial."

"I'm here now." He weighed at least a hundred pounds more, and he was a good six inches taller. "Hell of a show you put on in there. Made Samantha look like a fucking saint."

Ah, profanity, the language of scholars. "I've got better things to do than have this conversation, Mr. White." She turned to cut around him toward the street corner, but he blocked her path.

Clenched fists hovered at his side. "She killed him because she wanted the insurance money. She looks sweet and nice, but she is evil."

"The jury did not agree. Now, get out of my way, Mr. White."

A muscle in his jaw clenched. "Not until you've heard me out, bitch."

Her grip tightened on her briefcase. She glanced around at the crowds of people milling in front of the courthouse. "I've heard all I want to hear. Get out of my way." Each word was clipped and direct.

He shook his head. "Bitch, you made my brother

look like a monster in that courtroom. He was a good decent man who worked hard and who loved his wife and kids."

Anger egged on by impatience blurred her judgment. "He was a monster, Mr. White. He was having an affair with a woman at his office and wanted to marry her. But instead of asking for a divorce, he sealed every window in his house and then set it on fire. His plan was to burn the house down with his wife and children inside. Samantha hit him with that golf club because he stood between her and the only remaining exit out the house. Yeah, I'd say he was a hell of a great guy."

"Whore. Bitch."

"Get out of my way, now."

His fists clenched tighter as he raised them. "I read about you. Too bad that guy didn't kill you a couple of years ago. Scum like you and Samantha don't deserve to live."

The pure venom dripping from the words had her retrenching. Charlotte's temper had skewed her judgment, and she'd miscalculated the danger. She took a step back but bumped into a solid wall of muscle. Strong hands settled on her shoulders and immediately moved her out of Lonnie's reach. She didn't have to turn to know who had her back. Rokov's scent gave him away.

"Is there a problem here?" Rokov said.

Lonnie's face paled with more fury. "Someone needs to teach this woman a lesson. Samantha White is not a fucking saint. She's evil."

Rokov's dark sunglasses made it impossible to see his eyes, but his braced stance and hand on his hip next to his gun holster telegraphed menace. "Are you threatening Ms. Wellington?"

Lonnie's eyes narrowed. "I ain't making threats."

"Then what are you doing? Looks like threats to me."

Lonnie's sudden grin revealed several missing teeth. "I ain't like Samantha. I ain't a curse on the world."

"Then what are you doing here?"

"Hearing the verdict."

Charlotte stepped around Rokov. "I was doing my job. Read your bill of rights, Lonnie. We all are entitled to a defense."

"Not whores like Samantha." The veins in Lonnie's neck bulged. "She deserves to be burned at the stake."

"I'm telling you to back off and find a spot to cool down." Rokov shifted his stance in front of Charlotte. "One more word out of you and I'll arrest you."

"On what charge?" he challenged.

"I'll find one," Rokov said.

"And when he's done making his list of offenses, I'll add a few of my own," she said.

Lonnie shifted his gaze to Charlotte. "Sure, Ms. Wellington. Sure. I'll back down." He even managed a gap-toothed grin. "I'm just blowing smoke."

"Be very sure about that," Rokov said. "Or I swear, I'll be the first to haul your ass to jail."

"Yeah, whatever." Lonnie waved his hand, turned on his heel, and hurried down the steps. He soon vanished around a corner.

"Thanks," Charlotte said. "I didn't diffuse his temper so well. I should have known better."

His glasses tossed back her reflection. "You're good at stirring the pot."

"It's why I get paid the big bucks."

"You didn't get paid this go-around."

"Old habits die hard."

The danger had passed, the adrenaline had dwindled, and suddenly she felt shaky. She didn't quite trust her legs to work and hesitated, hoping a small delay would help her gain equilibrium. "Thanks again."

"You all right?" His gaze all but burned through the sunglasses.

"Me? Sure. I think the guy just caught me by surprise, and I'm not so fond of surprises."

"You're headed to your office?"

"Yes."

"I'll walk with you."

"You don't have to do that." She felt helpless and silly. "I can handle a two-block walk."

"I can use the exercise. I've been sitting too much lately." He nodded as if to say, *Get going*.

With a begrudging acceptance, she began walking. He kept his strides measured, setting a more balanced pace. She wasn't a fan of small talk but meatier topics had become explosive: Sooner, the carnival, the Young investigation, and God help her, the sex they'd had just six days ago.

Refusing to stoop to the weather or favorite movies, she chose the lesser of the evils. "How goes your investigation into the Young case? I've been keeping up with it through the papers."

"It's slow. We're still looking at her car and the man who got into it before she vanished."

"You'd think with all the cameras and people in this area that someone would have seen something."

"Yeah. But I'm starting to think our killer had his entire agenda well planned."

"Even the best killers leave clues."

"So I've heard."

They reached an intersection and he took her elbow in hand. Three cars passed. When the road was clear, they crossed the street. Taking her elbow was a protective, unnecessary, and kind gesture she appreciated.

"The organized killers often leave clues so small they are almost invisible," she said.

"If that's true, then this guy is very, very organized."

She'd never heard the faintest hint of self-doubt from Rokov. And even now it wasn't so much that she heard the doubt . . . she simply *felt* the doubt. If she sat in Madame Divine's chair now, she'd have said he had a strong aura, and he was destined for great things. "You'll find the killer, detective. You're a clever one."

He grinned. "Was that a compliment, counselor?"

"I give credit where credit is due."

He slid his hand into his pocket. "Let's hope I am that clever. This guy needs to be found."

Again she sensed the fear that another victim would die before he could find his killer. But to ask a question so personal meant opening a door she did not wish to open. And so they walked in silence.

When they reached her office, she faced him. "Here I am. Home sweet home."

He glanced at the three-story brick town house with its wrought-iron front rail, stone planter filled with red geraniums, and dark lacquer front door sporting the pineapple head doorknocker. "Fancy digs, counselor."

"Don't be fooled by the old world charm. The HVAC is in need of an overhaul, and I've got a couple of basement pipes that like to freeze in the winter." What had prompted this candor?

He tested the railing's sturdiness with a sound shake. "It still had to cost you a fortune."

"I'll let you in on a secret." It was a small, safe secret.

"I got the place in a bankruptcy sale a couple of years ago. I redid the first floor, electric, and plumbing, but the upper floors are a disaster. I wouldn't dare show them to you."

Humor and interest sparked in his gaze. "So Wellington and James is a facade?"

No truer words had been spoken. "One day I'll have the place finished."

"You could probably flip the building and make a good bit of money."

"A second mortgage financed the renovation. Seemed like a good move until the bottom dropped out of the real estate market and landed me upside down in the mortgage. I can't sell, but as long as I keep working, I'll be fine. The market will catch back up." And it would, just as the work would increase.

He glanced around to make sure no one was listening and then leaned toward her. "Why not just dip into the trust fund to finance the renovations?"

That made her laugh. "No trust fund, detective. It's just me with a big stick holding off the wolves."

"Alone."

"It's the way it's always been."

"Doesn't have to be."

She ignored the subtext. "It's less complicated that way."

"No tangles."

Tangles. The word of warning she'd used before they'd made love the last time.

"Right."

"Being alone doesn't bother you?"

Lately it did. Too many nights she'd lain awake wishing she could roll over into his strong embrace. But the cards didn't bode well for The Master at Bending Rules and The Boy Scout. "It's nothing I can't handle."

He pulled off his glasses, revealing a direct clear gaze. "I'd like to see you again."

"I would dearly love a few hours alone with you." Her voice was barely a whisper, and she was careful not to lean toward him, fearful someone would notice. "But I'm going to have to take a rain check. I barely have time to sleep."

He curled and uncurled his fingers as if resisting the urge to touch her. "When?"

"Soon."

"Very soon." Not a question but a statement.

"I can't make promises."

With an impatient jab, he shoved his glasses in his breast pocket. "Charlotte, stop worrying and just let this unfold."

"Into what?"

He took her hand in his and rubbed his thumb against her palm. "Isn't that the fun of it, not knowing?"

"I like being in control."

"So I've noticed."

Memories of her most brazen bedroom moves warmed her face.

Smiling, he gave her hand a gentle squeeze and then released it. "We'll work on that."

"Mighty confident, detective."

"I try." He glanced around as if scanning the streets for trouble. "Be careful. Lonnie doesn't strike me as a quitter."

She straightened, remembering they were in public. "I'll keep that in mind."

Rokov turned and strode down the street, leaving her to wonder why she was so afraid of the man.

* * *

On Mondays, Dr. Maya Jones went running at the local high school track, raced home to shower and change. Then she grabbed a coffee and bagel at Just Java, where she caught up with friends. By three she'd be at the school teaching class.

She was so predictable, as her on-again/off-again lover had once said. But she found comfort in structure and routine and had long ago decided to do what she pleased. She glanced at her sports watch as she strolled into the coffee shop.

The scent of coffee mingled with freshly baked pastries flavored with cinnamon. Warm and inviting, this place always made her happy. Mothers brought their children here. Writers read from their latest works. Business was conducted.

This was a good place. And to think a killer had invaded the neighborhood just days ago. She shuddered. There was always someone to spread poison and evil.

She strolled up to the counter, glanced at the glass jar filled with biscotti, the bin of mints, and the *We Accept Tips* cup. A young teen boy with shoulder-length blond hair, wearing a Georgetown T-shirt and jeans, moved up to the register.

"How's it going, Joey?" She dug her change purse from her pocket.

"All's well, Maya. You want the regular? Latte and sugar cookie seeing as it is Friday?"

She laughed. "Yes."

The kid stared at her with a clear direct gaze, and she had liked him from the start. "So how go your classes?"

He shrugged as he held a pitcher of milk up to the steamer. "Can't complain. Calculus blows, but I'm managing."

"I know tutors if you need help."

"So far I don't need the cavalry, but I'll let you know if I do."

Joey finished her latte, set a cookie on a plate, and rang her up. Seconds later she was sitting at a small round table by the large picture window that overlooked The Wharf. Drooping yellow crime scene tape still cordoned off the area. She'd read about the murder in the paper. There'd been suggestions it was related to the occult but details had been sketchy. Likely it was some ignorant kid who didn't even know how to spell *devil*.

She sipped her coffee. A couple passed by her table. They were laughing. Some days she wondered what it would be like to experience pure happiness. Or what it would be like to accept a man's smile at face value without searching for the kernels of evil. Or what it would be like to kiss a man and not fear he'd steal her heart.

This time when she raised the cup to her lips, the tension in her fingers threatened to crack the cup. Carefully, she set it down next to the uneaten cookie.

"Hey, welcome again."

She glanced up into Katrina's face. "Good afternoon."

Her smile brightened as she wiped down a table. "So how does that cookie taste?"

"Good and fattening."

"Please. You run so much, you'll never gain weight."

"You should have seen me forty pounds ago."

"Really?"

"Really."

"You look stunning."

"Thanks. Lots of blood, sweat, and tears." Her on-again/off-again had told her she'd looked a little puffy the other day.

Katrina moved on to the next table, leaving Maya to her cookie, her latte, and her book, which she dug out of her worn backpack. Today, she was giving the kids a test so there were no lessons to plan.

When a man sat at the table beside her, she was only vaguely aware of him. When he scooted his chair, the sound dragged her gaze upward. She'd seen him here before. He was quiet. Kept to himself. A reader. All traits she shared. As she lowered her gaze, she noted the book he was reading, *Salem's Lost*.

She had been reading it the other day. It was a historical biography of a woman accused of witchcraft in the seventeenth century. "So how do you like *Salem's Lost*?" she said.

He carefully marked his place before he glanced up. "I'm not buying the writer's hypothesis. I mean really, bacteria caused mass hysteria that led to the witch trials."

"It's a theory that has been debated a few times." She relaxed back in her seat. "Not many folks get into the history of Salem."

"There's a lot to be learned from history." He broke a piece off his muffin as if he were going to eat it. "But in this case, I think the writer has it wrong."

"Really?"

He didn't let his gaze linger on her too long. "Bacteria in the bread did not make the town lynch those women. It was fear and greed."

"Honestly, I agree with you. But it never hurts to explore new theories." On reflex she pushed up her sleeves to her elbows.

"However, the author provides some great historical detail."

She tucked a strand behind her ear and studied him closely for the first time. She liked what she saw. "Mind if I join you?"

He scooted his chair back and held out an open-faced palm in invitation. "The company would be nice."

She picked up her cup and took the seat across from him. "I've seen you here before."

"I like this place. Very homey." He glanced out the window toward The Wharf. "You hear about what happened there?"

"I did. Terrible."

"I hope the cops catch the nut soon."

She extended her hand, and the silver bracelets jingled on her slim wrist. "I'm Maya Jones."

He took her hand. "I'm Hunter. Hunter Thompson."

His hand was warm and soft. "Very pleased to meet you, Hunter."

They spent the next half hour talking and laughing, and for the first time in too long she felt as if the universe had tossed her a lucky break. Her watch beeped and she glanced down at the time. "I've got to go, Hunter. This has been great, but I've got to teach my class."

He checked his own watch. "I need to get going, too. Maybe we can grab a cup of coffee again?"

"I'd like that."

"Can I walk you to your car?"

"Sure."

They rose and he held the front door for her. So charming, so old-fashioned, so very nice. They strolled down the street.

"I have a book I think you'll like to read," Hunter said.

"What's that?"

"It's a history of this area. Fascinating stuff. If you've got a quick sec, I'll pull it out of my trunk."

She checked her watch. The side trip would make her late for class. She hesitated. And so what if it did? How many times had she waited on on-again/off-again or the kids in her class? "Sure."

She followed him down a side alley toward a Lincoln. He pulled keys from his pocket and clicked the lock open. As he leaned over and rummaged through piles of books, she caught his scent. Soap and soft aftershave. Nice. Normal.

"Here it is," he said.

She leaned forward a fraction and in that second felt the prick of a needle in the side of her neck. Her vision blurred almost immediately and her legs buckled.

Hunter grabbed her and quickly laid her in the trunk of his car on the books. "That was almost too easy. You are so predictable, Maya."

As her vision grew hazier and darker, her last image was of Hunter gazing at her with searing hate.

Chapter 14

Charlotte had scored a clear victory today in court. Innocent! Her client had been released from jail and now was free to get on with her life. The press for Wellington and James had been outstanding. Life was looking up.

So why did life feel so out of control? Why in the light of so many successes did she see only failure?

Because you are too tired and you need a break. Because you were on this case too long and you just can't let go.

She set aside the reports on her new client prospects and rose from her living room couch. Barefooted, she'd changed from her suit into short gym shorts and an old T-shirt. This was her go-to comfort outfit that made her feel like herself and one that she'd never wear in public.

In the kitchen, she set a copper teakettle on the stove and turned on the gas burner. She wondered what Sooner was doing now. Where was she going to sleep when she left the carnival?

The teakettle blew. She shut off the gas flame, poured hot water into a black and gray mug, and set the kettle on a cool burner. Moving into the living room, she stared at the mountain range of brown boxes. The movers would be here on Friday. She'd signed the closing papers, taken the buyer's check, and finalized the lease agreement on the modest two-bedroom apartment. In two days, the consignment store representative would arrive and she'd chosen what she wanted to sell and what she wanted to keep.

It was all necessary. All had to happen. Yet it was deeply unsettling. She'd moved around so much as a kid. And she'd hated it. There'd been no real school to attend. No long-term friendships. Everything had been temporary.

Had Sooner hated the endless moving? Had the girl longed for a permanent place, or was she part gypsy like her grandmother?

The movers had packed most of her belongings but she'd asked them to leave the back closet to her. She'd yet to tackle the task because all that stuff belonged to Grace Wells, stuff she should have pitched a long time ago.

Steam rose from the mug. *You go out of your way to forget, and yet you save all the evidence. Hell, you couldn't even bring yourself to leave Alexandria.*

She opened the closet, turned the light on, and set the mug on a shelf before kneeling beside a box marked *High School*. Carefully, she removed the lid. On top was the white cap and gown she'd worn at graduation. She pulled out the hat and flicked the gold tassel. She'd been seventh in her class. Though her GPA had been the highest senior year, the valedictorian was selected on the four-year average. It didn't

matter that she'd come to the party late. Or that she
was smarter than Nan Graham. All that mattered was
that she didn't have a four-year record to average.

Below the gown was a collection of school newspapers. She'd wanted to write for the *Jefferson Journal,* but
working thirty hours a week at the pizza place and
school had eaten all her time.

Charlotte closed the box and set it in the living
room inside a sturdier moving box. She sealed the box
and marked it with the word *Storage.* She stared at the
bold black lettering, her pen hovering. Why couldn't
she just let go? Wasn't everybody better off if she let
sleeping dogs lie?

"Shit." She scratched it out and then wrote *Trash.*
Afraid she'd overthink it, she recapped the pen and
returned to the closet.

The next few boxes were much the same. Bits and
pieces of a past she'd never been able to release. Like
the first box, she marked each as *Trash.*

The last and most battered box was shoved in the
back corner. This was the carnival box that held the
memories of her mother, Mariah, and Sooner.

Her hands trembled when she opened this box. Her
first image was of an old carnival program. It featured
Madame Divine on the front. The image was not
her mother's, hers, or Mariah's. The photo was of a
woman who'd sat in the tent long before them. Her
mother had wanted Grady to change the picture but
he'd refused. One night they'd gotten drunk and
begun to fight. Her mother had brought the picture
up and he'd told her the woman in the picture had
been a lover whom he'd adored more than his own
life. But she'd left him for a rich man.

Under the program, there was a photo of Grace in

costume. She couldn't have been more than sixteen but there she sat trying to look into the camera as if she had a lifetime of sophistication and experience behind her.

She traced the outline of the girl's rounded face. "I look like I'm twelve."

What the hell kind of man would put a kid like that to work?

She knew exactly what kind of man. A manipulator. A charmer. A man who used girls.

She dug deeper and found the pictures she'd tried to forget. They were of two young girls. One who looked awkward and scared. The other who looked like she owned the world. Sisters. And until that last fall they'd been closer to each other than anyone else in the world. That last fall had changed everything. Sooner had been born. And Mariah had died. A barely tolerable world had become unbearable.

She traced Mariah's face, which was so much like Sooner's. "Mariah, the girl doesn't know any different kind of life. She doesn't know it can be better. And Grady will see to it that she never does know different."

So what are you gonna do, Grace? Bitch and complain, cut and run, or stand and fight?

She checked her watch. The carnival would be open for another hour. Time enough to visit.

He stared at the woman Maya lying on the floor. Her eyes were shut and her mouth slack jawed. With a cattle prod he poked her in the chest. She didn't move. He pinched her arm. Hard. She didn't respond. Her breathing was so shallow and quiet he thought for a moment she'd stopped breathing. He leaned close and pressed his ear to her chest. Under the fabric, he felt the faint, but steady beat of her heart.

She was alive.

He'd overdosed her. He'd thought he'd not put enough in the syringe, and fearing she'd call out in public, he'd injected her a second time. Now he could see that he'd overdone it. She'd not awaken for another day at best.

As much as he wanted to begin the inquisition now, it would have to wait. Killing her now wouldn't be right. He needed the confession before God granted him the right to take her life.

He kissed her on the lips. They were soft and supple. He let his hand slide to her breast, and he massaged the soft mound and then pinched and twisted her nipple.

She moaned, and a faint line appeared on her forehead. Despite the drug, she felt the pain. He got hard.

He squeezed again and again. She moaned. His erection pulsed. "Even asleep, you have power over me."

He moved the edge of the gurney and grabbed fistfuls of her fabric skirt and dragged the hem up to her waist. He took a moment to stare at her long smooth legs. He grabbed a hold of her ankles and pushed them wider apart.

She lay limp, waiting for him, and already he found the lack of challenge deflating. Frustrated, he grabbed the folds of her blouse and ripped it. Buttons popped. He then pulled a switchblade from his pocket and sliced the center of her bra, which snapped open and freed her full breasts. He traced her nipple with the tip. When she didn't react, he sliced a little deeper into the areola. She whimpered and blood oozed from the cut.

His excitement returned. Of course, he'd not kill her now, but perhaps he could find something interesting to fill the time. He moved to a table where he kept several of his toys. Rummaging through the devices, he selected a thick, hard rubber shaft. He cut her panties free and tossed them on the floor.

"You'll be sorry you ever tempted me, witch."

He drove the shaft into her with so much force a tear ran down her cheek.

The night air had grown cool when Charlotte arrived at the carnival. The same familiar scents greeted her as it had the other night, but this time she'd been prepared for the memory triggers, and she'd not allowed herself to go back.

Digging her hands in the pockets of her suede jacket, she moved through the dwindling crowds toward Sooner's tent. She hesitated at the flap, wondering if this was really what she wanted.

Ignoring the warnings, she pushed open the flap and moved into the dimly lit room. A soft light glowed in the corner, and hidden speakers played a quiet soothing tune. Incense burned.

Sooner sat at her table, her gaze turned down onto tarot cards arranged into the Celtic Cross pattern. "So you've come back to offer me more advice?"

Charlotte moved across carpeted floor and took the seat in front of Sooner. Lavender incense burned and added a tang to the air. "I didn't see a line so thought I'd better jump at the chance."

"Traffic is always slow on Mondays."

She remembered. She smoothed her hands over

her jeans. "I've never sat on this side of the table before."

Sooner slowly gathered her cards. "All those years of readings and you never had one."

"No. I didn't have any interest." She tried not to marvel at the girl's resemblance to Mariah. "What's the old saying? The cobbler's wife has no shoes."

Sooner shuffled the cards and laid them out on the table between them. "Why don't you let me read for you? It's the very least."

"I can tell you what you're going to see."

Sooner arched a brow. She'd chosen just the right shade of purple and brown eye shadow to make her green eyes pop and even mesmerize. "Oh, really? What do I see?"

"Work. More work. A few thousand bills. More work."

Sooner studied her a beat and then lowered her gaze to the cards. She tapped a card featuring a heart with three swords driven through the middle. "Sorrow. You are not a happy woman, Charlotte Wellington."

"What tipped you off? The mention of nonstop work or a few thousand bills?"

Sooner shook her head. "It goes beyond that. This sadness runs deep."

Charlotte sat back in her chair. She folded her arms over her chest, nearly unfolded them but didn't, fearing she'd appear jittery or nervous. "You know I have a past with Grady. And if you've grown up with him, then you know it wasn't a lot of chuckles."

Sooner stared at her. "He's a prickly, possessive old man, but he has his good points."

"I take it you haven't told him you are leaving?"

"No."

"Tell him and then we'll chat about his good points."

The girl smoothed her flat palms over the silken tablecloth. "What was it like when you left him?"

"Not pretty."

"Tell me."

"I'm not sure how this turned into a counseling session." She did unfold her arms this time and shifted her position in her chair.

"You came to me. There must be a reason."

"I came here to talk about you and your future. Not me."

"I am not nearly as interesting as you. I find you curious."

"Why?"

"You lived this life. But you did not let it eat you alive as it has so many. You got out. I am getting out. I've a lot to learn from you, Aunt Charlotte."

"It wasn't easy. In fact, it was the hardest thing I ever did. But I can help make it easier for you."

Sooner ignored the statement. "I did a little poking around the carnival. You triggered memories with the older guys the other night when you paid us a visit."

"I thought I might."

"Grady was married to your mother?"

"Yes."

"What happened to her?"

"She died when I was thirteen. That's how my sister and I got the gig in this tent. She'd done it before us."

Sooner glanced at the next card. "The Devil. You were seduced by a man and then by the material world."

A smile, not so happy, tipped the edge of her mouth. "Guilty on both counts. Hence the thousands of bills."

"How did your mother die?"

"She suffered a stroke."

She drew in a long slow breath and then released it slowly. "At least you had her for thirteen years. My mother ran off and died right after I was born."

Charlotte sat very still for a long moment. "What has Grady told you about her?"

"He doesn't like to talk about Mariah. But on my thirteenth birthday I kept pushing. Finally he got angry and told me she ran off. He said she wasn't right in the head. She said a lot of crazy things before she took off."

"She wasn't crazy. She was young. And she was scared. But she wasn't crazy." She pulled a picture from her pocket and laid it over the tarot cards. "That's a picture of Mariah and me. We were about fifteen and sixteen." A lump formed in her throat and she swallowed to keep her voice even. "We were sisters and best friends."

Sooner's body went very still. She carefully picked it up. A frown furrowed her brow as she studied the image. "Mariah looks like me."

"And she looked like our mother. You look a lot like our mother. I nearly stumbled when I first saw you in court."

Sooner traced her face. "What happened the night she drowned?"

"She had a date, but she never said a word about leaving. Grady sent out search parties for her. We were all worried. Grady told me they found her by the lake."

"Where was the carnival then?"

"Here. It was very different then. More woods. Less houses. The carnival had two more nights to go before we wrapped and broke for the winter."

Sooner stared at Mariah's image.

"I was supposed to work the tent that night, but I

was tired so Mariah volunteered. I tried to wait up for her, but I must have dozed off. I woke up about three in the morning." No reason to tell the girl that she'd been awoken by a nightmare filled with Mariah's screams. Or that she'd heard those same screams in recent dreams. "I got scared and went to Grady."

"I've never seen a picture of her before."

Charlotte tried to ease the tension in her chest with a deep breath. "Grady never told you about Mariah?"

"No." She traced Mariah's face. "Did she love me?" Her voice was a bare whisper. "Did my mother love me?"

Tears choked Charlotte's throat and she couldn't manage a single word for several moments. Finally, she nodded. "She loved you very much. She wanted the world for you."

"Then why did she leave?"

"She was so young and so afraid." The explanation sounded paltry. "I'm so sorry it couldn't have been different."

Sooner stiffened. "But it wasn't, was it?"

"No." Charlotte straightened. "I want to help."

"Why? Why do you care?"

"Because we are . . . flesh and blood . . . all the family the other has."

The young woman's eyes glistened with anger and fear. "Maybe Mariah lied to you. Maybe she'd been planning to leave for a long time."

As kids, Mariah had stretched the truth, but she'd never lied to Grace. "No, she didn't lie to me."

"Whatever." She set the picture down on the table. "I don't want to talk about this anymore. I've got to wrap it up for the night. I don't want to dig into an old wound."

"Maybe you should. Maybe I should."

"Like I said, I don't want to. Just back off. Leave my tent." The last words were loud and tinged with so much anger.

Charlotte knew enough about people to know when she could get through and when she couldn't. And right now there was no talking to Sooner. "Okay."

She left the girl sitting at her desk, her gaze cast on the photo. As she walked through the carnival and listened to the organ music and the laughter, her anger grew.

She checked her watch. The carnival would be closing for the night soon, which meant that Grady was in his trailer getting ready for the final walk-through of the night. In long even strides she crossed the grounds to the black trailer that had been her home when she and her mother had first moved in with him.

Without knocking, she tried the door handle. It was locked. More frustrated and angry than she'd been in years, she pounded her fist until it hurt.

"Hold your damn horses!" Grady's gravelly voice cut through the metal door like a razor. "Shit. Someone better be fucking bleeding."

A little breathless, she stepped back. When he opened the door, his anger morphed to curiosity.

Behind him she could see the glow of a television set that he'd turned down. The scent of freshly brewed coffee and hot dogs wafted out of the room. "You're about the last person I figured I'd see here."

"I swear to God, Grady, if I had a bat, I'd knock you senseless."

Her statement made him laugh. "So the cold and level Charlotte Wellington is getting closer and closer to her roots every day. You can take the girl out of the carnival, but you can't take the carnie out of the girl."

"Why did you tell Sooner that her mother abandoned her?"

The humor vanished from his gaze. "How do you know what I told Sooner?"

"I just went to see her."

"I thought you were done with this place. I thought we wasn't good enough for you."

His attempts to make her feel guilty were a miserable effort compared to what she'd heaped on herself over the years. "I found pictures of Mariah and me. I thought she might like to have them. Seeing the pictures prompted her to tell me about her mother's abandonment."

Grady's expression hardened. "You and Mariah were so much alike. Always wanting more. You wanted school and she wanted a man to save her. She couldn't keep her legs closed for more than a few weeks."

"She was just a kid and she drowned. Did you ever wonder what happened to her?"

"Fucking right, I wondered." Energy rushed out of him like a tidal wave, leaving him drained and pale. "It was only a matter of time before that girl came to a bad end. She wouldn't listen to good reason."

"Good reason or your hard-ass rules and regulations."

He shrugged. "One and the same."

She pointed a shaking index finger at him. "You had no right to tell Sooner her mother abandoned her. She believes her mother did not love her."

"If her mama had loved her, she'd have stayed close to home."

Tears burned in her eyes. "Home? Or you?"

"One and the same."

Acceptance seeped into her bones. "I think you are right, Grady. You can't take the carnie out of the girl." She leaned toward him, her voice low and determined. "Carnies are fighters at heart, and we can be dangerous. And I can promise you, if you do not treat Sooner right, I will track you down and make you pay."

His face paled only a fraction. "What the hell could you do to me?"

"I'm not a kid anymore, and I swear I will crush you, old man. I will crush you."

She turned and left the carnival. In her car, the adrenaline had ebbed from her muscles and her body began to shake. She tipped her head back and let the tears pool in her eyes and fall down her cheeks. All those years ago she'd left the carnival because Grady had sworn Sooner would end up with a real family. And the bastard had lied!

She pounded the steering wheel. "What the hell kind of angle are you working, old man? You never do anything without a reason."

The air in the car grew hot and stale, forcing her to turn the key in the ignition so she could roll down the windows.

She'd been too young and afraid when Mariah had died to ask many questions. And then when she'd left the carnival, she'd been too busy running from her past to dare think about it.

However, her days of running were over. She wanted to know what happened to Mariah. And fuck Grady, the past, and whoever didn't approve of her.

Someone tapped on her window. "Charlotte?"

Hearing her name had her turning. There stood

Levi with a woman and two young children, his family, she presumed.

Forcing a smile, she swiped her cheeks and got out of the car. "Levi. What brings you here?"

"Brought the family," he said. He glanced fondly at a thin brunette standing beside him. "This is Marcia, my wife."

Charlotte extended her hand. "Nice to meet you."

Marcia took her hand and Charlotte immediately sensed nerves and worry. Small, petite, blond hair, she was conservatively dressed. Her only bit of jewelry was an angel necklace. Hardly the type she'd have paired with the supercharged Levi. "Nice to meet you. These are our children. Bailey and Jefferson."

The little girl, Bailey, was an eight-year-old version of her mother. And six-year-old Jefferson had his dad's build but his mother's nervous energy.

"Hey, guys," Charlotte said. "Did you have fun at the fair tonight?"

Both kids smiled and dutifully nodded.

"They're worn out," Levi said. "We got a late start this evening because of my work but we've been here for a couple of hours. I had to bring them. I loved this place."

She flashed to the moment she'd been pounding on Grady's trailer door. "There is a lot to see and do here. Did you kids try the Ferris wheel?"

"They loved it," Levi said.

Charlotte wondered if his family had the ability to answer for themselves. "Great."

"Didn't expect to see you here," he said.

"Just taking a break." She glanced up and saw Grady moving toward them. She held her ground and waited as he approached. "You all are in for a treat. This is Grady Tate, the owner of the carnival."

Grady hesitated as if surprised she'd held her ground. "Howdy, folks." He smiled at each, his gaze pausing on Marcia Kane for a split second. "Ms. Wellington giving you the rundown on the carnival?"

Confusion sparked in Levi's gaze. "You two know each other?"

She locked gazes with Grady. No more running. No more lies. "I used to work for this carnival when I was a teenager. Grady, was my boss. Grady, this is Levi Kane. He's a prosecutor in Alexandria."

Grady nodded, his smile bright but disingenuous. "Glad you could visit my show."

"We love the carnival," he said. He draped his arm around his wife's shoulders. Her smile was quick but stiff. Levi shook his head. "Charlotte, you worked in a place like this. I don't believe it."

All these years of hiding and now she had blown open the door to her past. "Believe it or not, I worked as the carnival psychic."

"Really? When was all this?"

"In high school."

"She was one of the best," Grady said. "One of the best."

Levi's gaze sparked with laughter. "There are times in court that I wondered if you weren't part sorceress."

Her laugh was humorless. "Madame Divine sees all."

He shook his head. "So did you read palms and tarot cards?"

"The whole deal. Even read tea leaves at one point." This was going to be all over the courthouse by Monday. So be it. Let the world know her past was a mess.

"Well, you learn something new every day."

"I was just trying to tempt Ms. Wellington to stay a little longer," Grady said.

"Sorry. Big day tomorrow." She checked her watch. "It's getting late and I've got a mountain of work to do."

"I'll be burning the midnight oil, too," Levi said.

"Well, nice seeing you." She got into her BMW. With a final wave to Levi and his family, she drove off, knowing she had to figure out what really had happened to Mariah.

Grady poured a healthy dose of whiskey into his half-full cup of coffee. He took several large gulps before the whiskey took a little edge off his anger.

He moved to a collection of newspaper articles and flipped to one featuring a large picture of Charlotte. The headline read: LOCAL ATTORNEY SHOT, EXPECTED TO RECOVER.

"Who the fuck do you think you are?" he said to the professional headshot the paper had used with the article. "You were a fucking nobody when I married that mother of yours. Living in motels. No sense of discipline. You were headed to a life of shit."

He took another gulp. "I warned Mariah that her behavior was going to get her in trouble. I warned her. And in the end she got what she deserved.

"I fucking came to you hat in hand and you've been nothing but a bitch." He pressed the mug to his temple and closed his eyes. Sudden hot tears pooled under the lids. "Nothing but a bitch."

Checking his watch, he slammed down the glass and disappeared into the night.

* * *

Maya woke to the heavy scent of urine and the cop-
pery aroma of blood. A tiny sphere of light dripped
from an overhead bulb that rocked and swayed over
her head. Confused, she stared at the light, trying to
clear the haze from her brain. Where was she? How
had she gotten here? She moistened her lips and tried
to roll on her side, but pain shot through her body like
a lightning bolt cutting through bone and muscle.
"Oh, God."

Had it been an accident? Tears pooling in her eyes,
she relaxed back and took deep even breaths. *Think!
Remember!*

And through the darkness and fog, her mind
tripped back to the coffee shop, the new man and . . .
the needle and the crushing fear. He'd drugged her
and tossed her in the trunk of his car.

Moaning her fear and frustration, she rolled her
head from side to side. How could she have been so
stupid? How many times had she told her students to
be careful and not trust strangers?

Carefully, she pried her eyes open, squinted past
the light above, and focused on her surroundings.
She craned her head to the right and saw a simple
workbench with everyday tools. Hammer. Screwdriver. Drill. Down here, the objects she'd never had
thought twice about took on a whole new and menac-
ing meaning.

The rattle of keys to the right caught her attention,
and she spotted a figure moving toward a workbench.
He set his keys on the bench, removed a rubber apron
from a peg, and slipped it over his head. As he tied the
strings at the base of his back, he turned toward her.

"You're lucky I don't have a lot of time."

"Why?"

He grabbed a fistful of her hair. "Because there are so many others I have yet to kill."

"I don't understand."

"Sure you do. You all talk to each other. I know you do." He shoved out a frustrated sigh. "But nothing has happened that I cannot fix."

"Fix what?"

"It doesn't matter. It's time."

Fear sharpened her senses. "Time for what?"

"Your confession."

Maya stared into dark, clear eyes that looked so sane. She had always made it a policy not to open herself to strangers—she'd heard enough horror stories. But he'd seemed like such a good guy. Normal. Grounded.

She turned her head away from his gaze. "Where am I?"

"My special place. It's where I do my work."

"Work? What kind of work?"

"God's work."

Evil shouldn't be so calm and attractive. It should be angry and hideous. Her body ached so much. Her insides felt like they were on fire. "Oh God, what did you do to me?" She tugged against the restraints securing her hands above her head.

His expression hardened. "How dare you call on His name?"

"What?"

He leaned over the table and pressed his lips right next to her ear. "People like you don't have the right to call to God."

"People like me?" Logic. Try to reach him. Maybe

he's made a mistake. "What kind of people are you talking about?"

"Witches. Those that have been sent by the Dark Prince to destroy all that is good."

Hysteria bubbled. "What are you talking about? I'm a history teacher. I barely date. I pay my taxes. I have a cat. I've never missed a mortgage payment."

"And you teach the dark arts." He unlocked something under her, which enabled him to move the gurney toward a wall. He butted the head against a big sink.

"I teach history."

"Of witches." He reached behind her and turned on a faucet. Immediately, water rushed in the sink behind her head and pooled and gathered.

"I talk about the history of Salem. Of the women who were persecuted." God, how many facts did she have to throw at this man to reach him?

"Witches."

"Not witches. Good women." She all but screamed the last words.

"You say they were good women. But after we've finished here tonight, I'd wager you will see it all very differently."

"What the hell are you going to do to me?" Her heart hammered so hard in her chest, she truly thought it would burst through her ribs.

He carefully rolled up his sleeve, and then slid his hands into gloves. "Let's find out right now."

Her brain scrambled to keep him talking. If he were talking, he wouldn't be doing what he was going to do. Keep him talking. "Who are you?"

"I'm a witch hunter. I find women like you and expose them for the evil they are."

"I'm not evil."

"Yes, you are."

He pushed another something underneath her and this time the gurney didn't roll but inclined. He tilted the edge back, forcing her head to dip. She clenched her fingers into fists and water from the sink rushed around her head and then her cheek. The water teased her mouth and then the end of her nose. Panicking, she closed her eyes and sucked in a deep breath just as her head went below the surface of the water.

Her heart pounded in her ears as she struggled not to lose her cool and hold her breath. She'd been a swimmer in college. Once she'd swum the length of the pool underwater. How long had that taken? Thirty seconds? A minute?

She counted. One. Two. Three . . .

Her heart pounded faster and faster. The jugular in her neck throbbed. She tightened her fingers into fists as if she were holding on to an invisible ledge. A rush of noise flooded her ears as her body begged for air.

And when her lungs could be denied no longer, she opened her mouth and on reflex inhaled. Water rushed into her mouth and lungs. Her eyes popped open and through the inches of water separating her from life, she saw his face. He studied her features closely. No humor. No joy. Just watching.

She tried to cough and gag, but it drew more water into her lungs. Her heart skipped a beat. Her vision blurred and then turned gray.

She could only think that this was a foolish way to die. So stupid. She'd always been so careful.

And then the blackness came, and her hold on life slipped. Maya drifted toward death.

Her next impression was of sucking in a lungful of air. She lay on her side and someone was patting her on the back. Water drained from her mouth. She breathed in long deep breaths and blinked.

She was alive. She was alive!

When the coughing ended, she rolled on her back, savoring a sense of relief that she'd never known before. Someone had stopped this madman and saved her. Saved her.

She blinked and focused, ready to thank her savior. But when her gaze sharpened, she didn't see a White Knight. She saw the Hunter, whose blue eyes still held a mixture of curiosity and determination.

The elation vanished as quick as a balloon pricked by a sharp needle.

"Why?" she whispered. Her throat felt raw and her chest ached. She suspected she had a broken rib because each breath now hurt. He'd drowned her, and then he'd brought her back to life. She pictured him pumping on her chest and then blowing air into her lungs, performing CPR until he'd forced the air and life back in her.

"Are you evil? Are you a witch?" he said.

"What? I don't understand."

"Are you a witch?"

He wanted a confession. But as much as she wanted to give him one to make this nightmare end, she sensed if she told him, he'd kill her. And she knew, despite the horrors of this room, she wanted to live.

"I am not a witch."

He shook his head. "The strong ones never admit to

the evil at first." He released the knob on the gurney again. "But in the end, they all do confess."

Terror burned through her body. She glanced over at her shoulder and he slowly tipped her toward the water. "I am not a witch! I am good! I don't des—"

Rushing water into her mouth cut off the last of her words.

Chapter 15

Tuesday, October 26, 10 a.m.

Rokov was called into court for a pretrial hearing, but the prosecution and defense has settled on a plea agreement. He hated the time spent in courthouses waiting to testify and doubted he'd ever fully accept it. Today, however, the summons to court had not bothered him as much because he'd half expected to see Charlotte. The White case was finished, but she was in the courthouse often enough that a chance meeting was possible.

He rubbed the back of his neck, wondering when he'd begun anticipating seeing Charlotte, not just in bed but also in public. They'd been intimate a half-dozen times and he'd learned things about her he suspected few knew. He knew makeup hid freckles on her nose. Knew her scent and the brand of her silk undergarments. Knew which touches made her coo. But beyond that, he knew little more than her public profile.

As he moved down the courthouse steps toward his car, the dark edges of his black suit flapping in the breeze, the cell in his pocket vibrated. He dug it out and paused on the sidewalk. "Rokov."

"I didn't think I'd get you."

"Sinclair. They released me. Plea agreement."

"This the stabbing on Van Dorn?"

"Yeah."

"What was the deal?"

"Manslaughter. Ten years."

She snorted. "I don't agree, but no one asked me."

He laughed. "Me either."

Papers rustled in the background. "So now maybe we can get some real work done."

"Would be a welcome change." He wanted to forget about the stabbing on Van Dorn, which in his mind was premeditated murder, and he wanted to forget about Charlotte. "What do you have?"

"I have a line on another one of Diane Young's more active clients."

They'd spent the last week slowly going through the list. Diane Young had hundreds of clients, but most were out of state. They'd decided to narrow the field by interviewing anyone in a fifty-mile radius. That had shrunk the list to thirty, and so far members of the homicide team had talked to twenty-eight of those. The remaining two had taken more legwork to find.

Most had been infrequent customers who'd hired Diane on a lark or for pure entertainment. A handful were hardcore believers in her psychic talents and consulted her on everything from new jobs, lovers, or trivial crap such as the best time to take out the trash. Sad cases, as far as he was concerned.

"Who did you find?"

"Victor Ingram."

He put on his sunglasses and, glancing both ways for

traffic, crossed to his black cruiser. "He's the one that did time for robbery?"

"One and the same. He's been a hard one to track down, but he did check in with his parole officer today. He was sick, he said. Wasn't real forthcoming about what made him sick but he's back at work today."

He slid behind the wheel of his car. The sun had warmed the leather and the heat eased his tense back. Too many nights at his desk and not enough exercise took its toll on him. In his twenties, he never had aches and pains. Now he did. He still blamed it on college rugby, not age. "Where is he now?"

"Works at a garage in Leesburg."

He fired up the engine. "I'll be by the offices in fifteen minutes. We can head out there now."

"Roger that, boss."

He hung up, pulled into traffic, and wove through the city streets. The drive from the courthouse to the police station took twenty minutes. When he pulled up, Sinclair was waiting.

She slid into the passenger side and rubbed her hands together. "Winter is on its way."

"It's sixty-five degrees. Hardly a cold snap."

She shrugged. "The cold gets to me more these days."

"You shouldn't have taken those two weeks in Florida. They spoiled you."

Sinclair shrugged. "I could get used to a life in the tropics on a beach easily."

He chuckled. "You'd go insane. And you know it."

"Maybe. Eventually. But I'd sure love to see how long it would take for the good life to bug me."

"One month. Max."

"You have little faith."

"You're type A, Sinclair. You don't rest well."

He maneuvered into traffic, which fed into the Beltway, the main highway artery around the Washington, D.C., Metro area. The westward drive to Leesburg took forty minutes, which in D.C. time was great. Rush-hour traffic, weather, or a fender bender could easily double or triple the drive.

They found Randall's Garage on Route 7 on the outskirts of Leesburg near a strip mall. Randall's was a one-story brick building with two garage bays, an office with a large picture window, and a couple of gas pumps out front. At one point the brick had been painted white, but time and weather had dulled the gloss and chipped the finish. A fluorescent sign in the picture window blinked *Randall's Garage* in bright orange.

Rokov parked on the side of the building next to a row of cars that appeared to be in the queue for service. The detectives got out of the car and walked to the front office, where they found a tall, slim man behind the register. Of Middle Eastern descent, the man had ink black hair graying at the temples, and his shoulders had hunched in a pronounced stoop, as if he'd spent a lifetime bent over a car engine.

When the detectives entered, the man glanced up, his gaze turning from curious to suspicious. "May I help you?" Perfect grammar blended with a thick accent, suggesting he had been in this country many years but had spent a good bit of his early life overseas.

Rokov removed his badge from the breast pocket of his suit. "My name is Detective Daniel Rokov. I'm with the Alexandria Police." Sensing the man's anxiety, he avoided using "Homicide Department." When people realized he was investigating a murder, they immediately tensed. "This is my partner, Detective Jennifer Sinclair."

Sinclair pulled out her badge and offered a fleeting smile. Warm and fuzzy was not her forte, and a lukewarm smile was a good effort for Sinclair. "Hello."

The man nodded.

"And you are?" Rokov tucked his badge back in his pocket.

"I am Mr. Randall. This is my garage." Apprehension rippled through the man's body, but Rokov didn't necessarily see that as a sign of guilt. This man was clearly from a country where a visit from the police could mean real trouble. How many times had his own grandmother hesitated around police?

"We're here to speak to an employee of yours. A Mr. Victor Ingram."

Mr. Randall expelled a small breath. "He is a mechanic. Is he in trouble?"

"No, sir. We just want to ask him a few questions. Routine."

Mr. Randall pulled a rag from his back pocket and absently wiped his hands. "He is in the third bay working on a Ford truck. You can go through the side door in the office and you will see the truck."

"Thank you," Rokov said.

Rokov and Sinclair moved through the door that led into a three-bay garage. On the first rack, five feet above the air, was a red Honda. The next bay was empty and, in the third, the white Ford truck that Mr. Randall mentioned. The heavy scent of oil and gas hung in the garage air, and the *buzz-buzz* of a pneumatic wrench blended with the rock music blaring from a radio.

"You should have taken the time to change," Sinclair said. "That pretty suit of yours could get trashed in a place like this."

"It won't."

"Want to bet?"

Rokov and Sinclair both reached to the straps on their gun holsters and unsnapped them. Neither were expecting trouble but were ready for it. "Ten bucks."

"You're on."

As they stepped around the red Honda, Rokov spotted a midsized lean man with a spotty beard. A mechanic's jumpsuit covered a white T-shirt and grazed the top of scuffed brown work boots. Thinning dark hair was slicked back. A spider tattoo clung to his neck.

"Mr. Ingram," Rokov said.

The man looked up and immediately gray eyes narrowed as he glanced from cop to cop. Ingram dropped the wrench in his hand and bolted to the other side of the Ford and out the front bay of the garage.

"Shit," Rokov said. Reacting instantly, Rokov ran out the front bay.

Sinclair, on his heels, reached for the radio on her hip and called local police, letting them know they were pursuing a suspect.

A car pulling into the lot cut between Rokov and Ingram, forcing Rokov to stutter-step sideways around the backside of the car. The delay allowed Ingram to put several more yards between them. Ingram ran across the asphalt parking lot toward Route 7, the four-lane artery that ran into town. The traffic was light enough for him to cross the first two lanes of traffic, but the heavy flow headed west stopped him in the median strip filled with tall grass. He glanced back at Rokov, who dashed toward Route 7.

"Mr. Ingram. Police. Stop!" Rokov shouted.

Ingram glanced at Rokov and then at the traffic headed toward him. He seemed to weigh the dangers of the police versus being hit by oncoming traffic. He ran into traffic.

Car horns blared. Brakes squealed. Ingram narrowly dodged an SUV and with no other choice turned on his heel and ran back toward the median. He cut right when he saw Rokov.

"Son of a bitch," Rokov muttered. He chased Ingram up the median.

With each step, Rokov closed in on Ingram, and when he was within feet, he lunged forward and grabbed the guy by the collar. Fabric in his suit ripped as he yanked Ingram to the ground. He quickly rolled the guy on his belly and put his knee into the small of his back as he reached for the cuffs on his belt. When Ingram struggled, Rokov shoved his knee harder into the guy's spine until pain forced him to still.

"You're fucking breaking my back!"

"Stop resisting."

Sinclair arrived as Rokov clicked the handcuffs in place and hauled Ingram to his feet. "Backup is on the way."

Rokov nodded, his teeth gritted. "Good."

When traffic in the eastbound lane cleared, the trio crossed the road. Two Leesburg Police squad cars, with lights flashing, arrived just as they reached their car.

A uniformed officer from each car got out and moved toward the detectives. The first to reach them was a short officer with broad shoulders and a thick black mustache. He appeared to be in his mid-forties. He introduced himself as Parker and the other officer, a tall slim man with auburn hair and freckles, as Adams, who couldn't have been older than twenty-five.

Officer Parker glanced between Sinclair and Rokov and then at Ingram. "And what has Mr. Ingram done to warrant your attention?"

Rokov glanced at the grass stain on his jacket and swallowed an oath. "All we wanted to do was talk to him about a case we have in Alexandria. He wasn't in trouble until now."

Ingram struggled with his cuffs. "These are too tight."

"Too bad," Rokov said.

Sinclair met Parker's amused gaze. "So how is it that you know Mr. Ingram?"

"He's been known to get a little loud when he drinks. Since he's been in town the last six months, we've had the opportunity to meet him a few times."

"I ain't never been arrested," Ingram said.

Parker shrugged. "Looks like you managed it now. Parole board is going to love you."

"I didn't do nothing!" Ingram tried to twist free.

Rokov jerked up on the cuffs until Ingram stilled.

"So Mr. Ingram is involved in one of your cases," Parker said.

"A homicide," Rokov said.

"Shit!" Ingram's head jerked around. "I didn't kill nobody."

"Why'd you run?" Rokov said.

Ingram grunted as he strained against his handcuffs. "Because you look like the fucking Mafia."

Sinclair glanced at Rokov. She often joked that he looked like a wise guy when he wore his dark suit. "We are investigating the murder of a woman named

Diane Young. She was tortured and then drowned. She ran an Internet site called *Beyond,* and Mr. Ingram was one of her biggest customers."

"What was she selling?" Parker said.

"Horoscopes and tarot reading," Rokov said.

Parker chuckled. "What do you need to know from the great beyond, Ingram?"

Ingram frowned. "I was getting picks on the horse races. I tried her the first time just for fun, and when I won, I kept coming back. Turns out she was right more than she was wrong so I kept coming back."

Sinclair arched a brow. "So how much did you end up losing?"

Ingram scowled. "I'm down six grand. I had to hock my watch and sell my car. But that's only because she didn't answer my e-mail, and I was on my own for the last race."

"Where were you last week?" Rokov said.

"I was down south at Colonial Downs near Richmond most of the week. Ask Mr. Randall. He nearly fired me for lost work. And I got stubs all over my apartment that shows I placed bets that day."

"We will check it all."

"We can hold him while you check his story," Parker said.

"I ain't done nothing," Ingram said.

"You ran, pal," Parker said as he took hold of the guy's cuffs. "Should not have done that."

"But he looks like the fucking mob!" Ingram complained. "He's got *collection* written all over him."

"I identified myself as police," Rokov said.

Parker shrugged. "Should have listened to him."

"Like the mob never lies?" Ingram complained.

Rokov waited as Parker switched a set of his cuffs for Rokov's. "Where do you live, Mr. Ingram?"

"On Route 15. I share an apartment with a few guys."

"Will you give us permission to search your place?" Sinclair pulled a notebook from her pocket.

"Shit, yeah. I didn't kill nobody. My keys are in my back pocket."

Parker fished out the keys and handed them to Rokov. Ingram supplied the address, and after a quick update with Mr. Randall, the detectives went to Ingram's apartment.

The apartment was located in a beige cookie-cutter complex within a three-story building. They found Ingram's apartment easily and opened the front door with the key he'd provided. The stench of old pizza and garbage greeted them.

"Damn," Sinclair said, raising her hand to her mouth. "It smells like something died in here."

Rokov had removed his suit jacket when they'd gotten out of the car and rolled up the sleeves of his white dress shirt to his forearms. He flipped on the light, and they surveyed the main living room, furnished with a third-hand green couch, a couple of folding chairs, and a wide-screen television resting on box crates. Trash, pizza boxes, dirty clothes, and beer cans littered the room. "Ingram said he shares with two other men. Likely, we're just smelling filth."

"It amazes me how people live."

Rokov jingled Ingram's keys in his hands. "I thought you said you never met an iron you liked."

"Hey, I might have a few wrinkles, but an extra spin in the dryer takes care of that, and my stuff and my apartment are clean. This is gross."

"We've seen worse." They moved toward the center

hallway to the back bedroom that Ingram said was his. A flip of another light switch revealed a mattress, no box spring, a rumpled quilt, and a pillow. "Ingram said to look for his black jeans."

"His lucky jeans. Shit." Sinclair slipped on rubber gloves and then moved to a pile of clothes. With thumb and index finger, she lifted a pair of jeans. "Maybe his luck would be better if he washed them once in a while."

Rokov donned his own gloves and dug into the pocket. He found a few rumpled dollar bills, a couple of pennies, and gum wrappers. It wasn't until he got to the back left pocket that he found the betting stubs. "Looks like he bought tickets on Monday, Tuesday, and Wednesday week before last."

"He was at Colonial Downs?"

"That he was."

"It's a two-and-a-half-hour drive from that track to Alexandria. A man could drive back and forth if he really wanted to establish an alibi. Diane appears to have been held for several days."

Rokov dug deeper into the pocket and came out with another stub. "Friday. And the time stamp is about the time Diane met our man in the van. And here's another stub for Monday."

"I'll call the track and have them pull surveillance tape and confirm it was Ingram who bought the ticket."

"Sounds good."

Sinclair shook her head. "The witch tattoo keeps coming back to me. What was the point of that?"

He dropped the pants and scanned the room for anything else that might tell him more about Ingram. The visual sweep, including a horse race poster and stacks of race bulletins, simply confirmed that Ingram's spare time was spent at the tracks. "I don't know."

Sinclair moved to a secondhand dresser and studied the collection of beer bottles, rumpled receipts, and loose change. "Maybe we should ask your pal Charlotte Wellington to look in her crystal ball and tell us what happened."

Rokov raised his gaze from a collection of well-read porn magazines on the edge of the bed. "What are you talking about?"

Sinclair grinned. "There was a little buzz about her at the station this morning. Fact, I'm surprised you didn't hear it at the courthouse."

"Spit it out, Sinclair." Annoyance snapped at the singsong tone in her voice.

She picked up on the irritation but it simply sparked delight in her gaze. "Apparently she ran into Kane last night at the carnival and told him she used to work at Grady's carnival as a psychic."

Out of the dozen past biographies he'd imagined for Charlotte, he'd never landed anywhere close to that one. "Didn't take Levi long to spread the word, assuming it's true."

"You know how it goes. Alexandria is a big small town. He likely told a few folks. And they told a few. There are enough in law enforcement who aren't crazy about the high-and-mighty Ms. Wellington and are happy to gossip about her."

He straightened and rested hands on hips. "You don't like her."

"How can you tell? Was it the way I choked a little on her name?"

Rokov moved out of the room. "What's your beef with her?"

"It's not personal. I mean she's professional, and you know where you stand with her. But she's a defense attorney, and I don't like them as a general rule."

"Everyone has a right to a defense."

"So they tell me."

He shook his head. He understood her sentiment. It was hard to work months on a case, secure an arrest, and see a scumbag walk. "We're done here."

When the place was locked up and both were headed back east, Sinclair studied Rokov. "You really like her."

He tightened his hands on the wheel, wondering when his partner was going to let this bone go. "Who?"

She brushed imaginary lint from her pant leg. "Please! *Wellington*. You like her."

"Why do you say that?"

"'Cause I've heard you bitch about defense attorneys before. But never Ms. Wellington. And we all have a right to a defense. Shit. You've never said that."

"She's smart. Owns a successful business. I respect that."

She snorted. "You like the way she fills out a tight skirt better than her brain."

True. But there was so much more to her. "What's with you trying to hook me up with her? You were busting my balls about her the other day."

She folded her arms over her chest. "Because it takes a lot to get a reaction out of you, and when I mention her, you become a windup toy with a hair trigger. All I have to do is sit back and watch the show."

"Sinclair, if anyone needs romance right now, it's you, not me. You need a life."

She shrugged. "True, so very true. But until I do get a man, I can live vicariously through your relationships."

"I don't have a relationship." Correct enough on so many levels that it wasn't far from a lie.

Rokov wondered what the cops would say if they knew of his connection to Charlotte. Shit. He knew. It would be open season.

Positioning a body was akin to a holy ritual.

Over the years, he'd grown quite rote in his approach. Eyes to the sky, arms outstretched, clothes neatly arranged, and of course, the *Witch* tattoo on the forehead of the slain. Today, however, he'd taken an extra moment to cover the windows. He'd had the growing sensation that someone was watching him. Grace, no doubt. So he'd taped garbage bags on the windows so that she could not see him and try to stop him.

"God is in the details," he whispered.

He adjusted Maya's head, so that it was a little straighter, and then he fanned out her hair around her face. Death had vanquished the evil from her body, and she looked so utterly peaceful.

He leaned forward and kissed her lips. "Go with God."

He glanced around the abandoned office floor. A sliver of moonlight illuminated the building's third floor. Wires hung from a dropped ceiling, the industrial gray carpets were still indented with the impressions of long-gone cubicles, and watermarks stained the west wall. Outside the large window, stars winked behind wisps of clouds above the Alexandria skyline.

By early morning the place would be filled with workmen ready to demo the building.

In the early days, he didn't take the time to position his prey. He simply dumped the bodies and ran. In those days he did mark his victims but only with crude lettering carved with a knife. Many times, the word was illegible and the warnings to the world unclear.

That's the way it had been with his first. He'd been so scared in the hours and days after her kill. Each time the phone had rung or someone had knocked on his door, he was sure it was the police. But the days and weeks passed and no one came for him.

Realizing he'd gotten away with murder, he'd been jazzed and had gone to a tattoo artist. He'd had the witch's name tattooed on his bicep as a reminder that real evil existed and that he must always be vigilant.

He glanced at the faded tattoo.

Grace.

He'd told the artist she was his girlfriend and he wanted her to be a part of him forever. The artist had suggested a heart wrapped in roses. He'd liked the idea but told the man to add thorns as well. They'd both shared a big laugh over the perils of love.

But he'd just come to realize he'd not killed Grace. She had sent a decoy to take her place.

He pulled the stakes and mallet from his backpack. Carefully, he positioned the pointed edge of the stake on her open palm, and then hammered it through the cold flesh into the hard floor. He repeated the task on her next palm and then her feet.

Breathless, he backed away from the witch, taking one last moment to admire her. He pulled a bag of salt from the same bag and drew a clean careful circle around her body. He etched a pentagram in the dirt just below her feet.

Perhaps God had denied him Grace, so that he would learn and grow as a hunter.

And now with the carnival in town again, he had to admit that life had certain symmetry. God had not only revealed to him Sooner, the witch's spawn, but gifted him with Grace.

Chapter 16

Wednesday, October 27, 6 a.m.

Rokov had gone home well after midnight and fallen into bed exhausted. For eight days they'd been chasing leads and talking to all of Young's clients. They'd walked the crime scene and the area around it until their feet ached. They'd revisited Diane's sister. Spoken to neighbors. But there'd been no leads on their killer. Dr. Henson had found skin scrapings under the victim's fingernails, but DNA results had yet to come back from the Commonwealth's lab. He wasn't holding his breath for a quick return. The backlog at the state lab was crushing, and even a high-priority case had weeks to wait.

The call from uniformed patrol came just after six in the morning. His buzzing cell phone woke him up out of a sleep so sound it had been dreamless. Sitting up bolt straight, he checked his watch and snapped up his phone. "Rokov."

"It's dispatch. Uniforms found the body of a young woman. She was killed like your victim."

His victim. He shoved out a breath and swung his legs over the side of his bed. "Where?"

He scratched out the address on a pad always on his bedside table and told dispatch he'd be on scene in a half hour. As he moved across the room, stiff muscles aired their grievances. *The bed is too small. The mattress too soft.*

Flexing his shoulders up and down, he kept moving. As he reached the bathroom door, he heard his grandmother moving down the house's center hallway toward the kitchen. He could tell her to go back to bed, as he'd done so many times in the last couple of weeks, but she'd simply wave him away as she brewed him a strong cup of black tea and toasted a bagel for him.

He ducked under a hot shower and let the water pulse over his face. He turned his back to the hot spray, wishing he could stand there for an hour and let the heat work the tension from the muscles in his shoulders. But there was no time for that.

He quickly toweled off and dressed in khakis, a long-sleeved shirt and brown-laced shoes. He slid a leather belt through the pant loops and attached his gun holster, cell, and cuffs. When he entered the kitchen, his grandmother had set the bagel and black tea on her small kitchen table. How many times had he sat at this table as a kid as she'd made him a snack after school?

He kissed her on the cheek. "You did not have to get up."

As expected, she waved him away. "Of course I did. You must eat."

"I can always grab something on the road." He bit into a bagel purchased at the Russian deli. Bagels from the chain stores were never as good as these.

"I saw your suit."

"Yeah. I'll get it to Dad."

"I've already taken it. He says to not dress up when you chase bad guys."

"I try, but sometimes the bad guys don't give me time to change." He sipped the black tea. She'd dropped a sugar cube into it to ease the bitterness.

"It will be ready by Friday."

"Dad does not have to rush."

"He does not mind." She moved to an avocado green refrigerator that dated back to the 1970s and pulled out a bottle of orange juice.

"I mind. He's busy enough."

"He is your father. He loves you. Let him do this for you." She filled a glass with juice and sat across from him. She sipped as he ate his bagel. "Daniel, it is time you move back to your apartment."

He glanced up at her. "Alexa will be back in a couple of days, and then I will."

"I am glad you two stayed with me while I was sick, but I am better now. Now you and your sister must leave my house."

"I like it here."

She arched a brow, sensing a lie behind the words. "I've said it before. A young man needs his own life. A young woman needs her own life." She raised her chin. "I change the locks in two weeks."

He laughed. "You are kicking us out?"

"Yes. I have spoken to your father and mother, and they agree that you and Alexa must live your own lives."

"Do they agree you should live alone?" She was old but no less cagey than a seasoned thief in a police interview room.

"That is my concern. Not yours or theirs."

He wasn't sure what was driving this or why she chose to tell him now. "I don't have time to talk about this now."

"There is nothing to talk about. You have two weeks." She hesitated. "I need my . . . space."

"Space?"

"That is the right word, no?"

"It's the right word. Okay. You need space. I'll talk to Dad."

"Talk all you want. But the locks will change."

"I'm in the middle of a murder investigation."

She shrugged. "Then after you catch your bad guy, I will change the locks."

He rose, kissed her on the forehead, and grabbed his thermos. "Aren't you worried Alexa and I will starve if we leave?"

She shook her head. "You both can cook. You just choose not to."

"We've got you."

"Which is the problem. You need a woman. She needs a man. Neither of you needs a doting grandmother. Now go and find your bad man." It was an order, not a request. And he had no doubt that if he didn't move his things back to his apartment, she'd put them on the curb. She loved him. Wanted the best. And she'd kick him and his sister to the curb to see that they got it.

Rokov left his grandmother sipping orange juice at the kitchen table.

All thoughts of his grandmother's edict had left Rokov's mind by the time he pulled up in front of the crime scene, an abandoned office building on Van Dorn. The parking lot was filled with seven police cruisers with lights flashing. The parking lot had been roped off with yellow crime scene tape and news crews had gathered across the street.

He rubbed the back of his neck and got out of his car. Sinclair was on the scene as were Detectives Deacon Garrison and Malcolm Kier. The three stood together, watching as a trio of forensics technicians moved into the old modular office building, likely built in the fifties. No doubt in its day, it had been cutting-edge design. Now it looked dated and old. The grass in the parking lot islands was tall and unkempt and the asphalt pitted and cracked. A large weathered *For Sale/Lease* sign lay by a demolition Dumpster. Now the land was worth more than the structure.

Rokov nodded to Sinclair as he approached Garrison. "What do we have?"

"A woman murdered. No signs of a gunshot or knife wound. Water in the mouth."

"Drowned?"

"No signs of a fatal wound. But I'll leave the final verdict to the medical examiner," Garrison said.

Tension crawled up his spine. "Was her body positioned like the first woman?"

"Yes. She was placed on her back, arms and feet extended and staked. Salt ring around her body. Tattoo on her forehead."

"Witch?"

"Yes." Garrison nodded toward the press. "The brass is going to be pushing us hard on this one. Two women murdered in less than two weeks."

Rokov glanced at the television news vans and the camera crews rolling film. "Have you made a statement?"

"Not yet," Garrison said. "I'd like to have more to say."

Rokov rested hands on his hips. "Did the victim have any identification?"

Sinclair moved up from behind him, her notebook flipped open. "None. Forensics is rolling prints. We're hoping for some kind of match."

"Any missing persons reports?"

"None that match her description. But that could change."

Garrison frowned. "All right, you two, go have a look. I'll talk to the press. Find me a killer, people."

Rokov and Sinclair ducked under the yellow crime scene tape and donned rubber gloves and paper booties before they entered the building.

Rokov glanced up at a surveillance camera posted by the front door and noted someone had spray painted black paint on the lens. "This son of a bitch is really thinking this through." He turned and surveyed the buildings around them. "He couldn't have gotten them all. We'll need to visit every building in the area, and if they've got cameras, watch their tapes."

"It's like finding a damn needle in the haystack."

They climbed the stairs, passing several uniformed officers on the way up to the second floor. The third floor was a large wide-open box illuminated by large fluorescent ceiling lights.

Red crime scene tape, which forensics reserved for the most sensitive areas, greeted them. The detectives moved to the edge of the tape, where Paulie stood just inside the room, snapping photographs.

Paulie, still aiming his camera, said, "Your boss has already been here."

"We saw him."

"And he told you the killer has a distinct pattern. This crime scene is very similar to the last scene."

"Yeah."

The technician stepped aside, so Rokov and Sinclair could look into the room. The victim lay in the center of the floor, positioned on her back, limbs outstretched and staked to the ground. Fully dressed, her hair was splayed out behind her head, and a ring of salt encircled her body. Pentagrams were drawn on two of the walls and three large glass windows had been blocked off with large plastic garbage bags and duct tape.

He moved into the room and stared at the woman's face. She had a wide-set jaw, high cheekbones, and dark hair. She'd not been stunning but pretty. She appeared to be in her mid- to late forties, wore a blue peasant skirt and loose-fitting white blouse and jean jacket.

The word *Witch* had been tattooed on her forehead in careful, block letters that measured an inch high and an inch wide.

Rokov forced out a breath. "The skin on the forehead is thin."

"I know. Pretty fucking painful." Sinclair was careful to keep her emotions checked, but there were moments when her anger bubbled to the surface.

"Covering the windows is different," Rokov said.

"Maybe he wanted more privacy," Sinclair said.

"Or he's scared."

"Let's hope."

"The circle is as defined as the last. He likes to take his time. He likes precision."

"He picks places where no one goes," Sinclair added.

"Abandoned places. He's got a system. He's obsessive-compulsive about getting the details right." He stared at the neat circle. "He's done this before Diane Young."

"There have been no ViCap hits." ViCap was the Violent Crimes Database. Though effective, it wasn't foolproof because not every jurisdiction inputted crimes into the system.

"Maybe this is the first time he decided to show off his work to the world. Maybe whatever he did before he hid because he didn't want to be discovered."

"So why go for an audience now?"

"Ego. Maybe he's tired of working in obscurity. He wants the world to know what he's doing."

"A master needs his work recognized." Bitterness dripped from the words.

Rokov studied the salt circle and tried to imagine the killer painstakingly dribbling it out. "He had more control over this scene."

"Think he needs more control?"

Rokov nodded. "If he thinks he's slipping. Sure. Control is important to him."

"Control and attention."

"I'm wondering if something has changed in his life. Maybe he lost a job, his girlfriend broke up with him, or he is sick."

"Or his boss yelled at him, or his dog died. It could be a million reasons. These guys don't need much of an excuse to do what they do."

"You're right." He stared at the blacked-out windows.

"But something has changed for him. And I'm willing to bet it's fairly drastic. First, he goes public with his kills. Second, he is getting more precise with his crime scene. This is more than ego. This is anger."

"At a woman in his life?"

"It would be my guess."

She shoved out a sigh. "We need to find out who Jane Doe is ASAP."

"I agree. And I'm going to resubmit to the ViCap system and see if I get a hit this time. I'm also putting heat on the forensics lab. I want the DNA put in CODIS sooner than later."

"Detective Rokov," Paulie called out.

Rokov glanced back to find the technician holding up a small orange ticket stub. "What is that?"

"Found this in her pocket. It's a ticket stub from the carnival."

"Does it have a date?"

"Four days ago."

"Thanks." He looked at Sinclair. "That's two for two and the carnival. We need to figure out where that carnival has been in recent years and check the jurisdictions to see which ones might have had murders not submitted to ViCap."

"The carnival visits a lot of small rural areas. This area is the big exception. Smaller localities don't always input into ViCap, which might explain the lack of hits."

"Once you get their travel schedule, we'll check with the jurisdictions directly."

"Want to talk to Grady again?"

"I sure do." Rokov thought about the grizzled old man, who he suspected lied as easily as he breathed.

"But I think what I'm going to do is talk to Charlotte Wellington."

"Why her?"

"If your gossip is true, Sinclair, and she is linked to the carnival, she might have some interesting information."

"What about Sooner Tate?"

He thought about the Life Style focus on Sooner. Effective for public relations but reckless when it came to the girl's safety. "You talk to her. I'll talk to Charlotte."

Chapter 17

Knowing Charlotte would likely be at her office, Rokov headed to the offices of Wellington and James. He rang the front bell and waited for the receptionist to buzz him inside.

"Detective Rokov," the receptionist said. She was in her mid-fifties and wore a dark dress, matching headband, and flats.

"You know me, but I'm afraid I don't know you."

"I'm Ms. Wellington's secretary and basically manager of all things that have to do with Wellington and James. Call me Iris. And I know you. Alexandria Police."

He'd heard Charlotte had hired a top-notch assistant with an uncanny memory for names. "Is Ms. Wellington here?"

"She is. You'd like to see her?"

"I would."

"Be right back." She vanished down a carpeted hallway, giving him time to study the reception area. The place was sleek and had a moneyed, old world feel that fit the public Charlotte. She'd always carried herself as if she'd been raised with a silver spoon, and it still amazed him that she might have grown up in a carnival. Perhaps this place, like the carnival, was just an elaborate set designed to support the fantasy.

"Detective."

Charlotte's smooth clear voice had him turning from a hunt country painting toward her. She wore a black pencil skirt, white fitted blouse, heels, and the pearls she'd had on the last time they'd made love. She'd swept her hair into a French twist, accentuating her long neck and high cheekbones.

"Ms. Wellington."

Suspicion darkened her eyes. "What can I do for you, detective?"

"Is there someplace private we can talk?"

Green eyes grew wary. "Why?"

"You'll see." A narrowing of her gaze told him she wanted to give him the bum's rush. She wasn't comfortable. Was she simply busy or embarrassed by his visit? Just the idea he embarrassed her set his nerves on edge. And so he waited, determined not to budge an inch.

"This can't wait?" she said.

"No." In the past when they were alone, he'd allowed her to run the show. However, this was no game, and he called the shots.

Sensing the steel in his resolve, she nodded. "In my office."

He followed her down the hallway to the back office. It didn't appear to be the largest of the offices, but it was the most private and remote. She'd placed a large decorative screen behind her desk that blocked the view of the street. Was that a holdover from her attack three years ago?

She closed the office door and motioned for him to take one of the club chairs in front of her antique desk. "Have a seat."

He waited until she'd moved behind him and took the seat behind her desk before he sat. "Taking up a defensive position?"

She knitted her long manicured fingers together. "Do I need to?"

Five feet and that damn desk separated them, but it might as well have been a million miles and a brick wall. "I heard through the grapevine that you used to work for the carnival."

Surprise and then acceptance crossed her face. She raised a brow. "Is that the latest gossip about me?"

"Is it true?"

She hesitated. "Does it matter?"

"I have a second victim. There might be a link to the carnival."

Her face paled. "Oh, my God. I didn't know."

"No one does yet."

"What does the murder have to do with me and the carnival?"

"Always the attorney scoping the lay of the land before you answer."

"Second nature." She shrugged. "It's true. I grew up in the carnival."

He sat back in his chair, realizing this was the first bit of personal information she'd acknowledged. "You cultivate the impression that you come from a very different place."

She released a breath. "It was deliberate."

"Why pretend to be something you are not?"

Her gaze narrowed. "Did you come here to quiz me about why I don't talk about my past? Because if that is the case, I've got too much work to stroll down memory lane right now."

He made no move to rise. "There is a method to my madness. Why the deception?"

"Why do you care?"

He managed a grin that wasn't so friendly. "Humor me."

She offered a small shrug. "I wouldn't exactly call it a deception. I wanted to go into defense law and discovered back in law school that the people with money like to work with people who have money. I figured out the nuances of being from a certain world and embraced them."

"Spoken like a defense attorney."

"I've never lied about my credentials on my CV. I don't mention high school but I did graduate from George Mason and Georgetown."

"On scholarship?"

"Partly. I also worked my butt off."

"Doing what?"

She sat back in her chair. "I still don't see where this is headed."

"It relates to a case, I promise."

She pressed fingertips to her temples as if they now throbbed. "Can you keep it to yourself?"

"Sure, if it has nothing to do with the case."

She released a breath slowly and then met his gaze. "I was a stripper. I worked in a club called Gold's."

If not for his own firsthand experience with the prim

Ms. Wellington, he'd have discounted the story. He knew under the ice was fire. "I know the place. In D.C."

"That's right."

"I worked undercover there a couple of years ago." He'd watched the strippers, appreciated a few, but had not given any of them much thought at the time. Placing Charlotte on one of those stripper poles did not set well with him.

She seemed to read his disapproval. "That would have been long after my time."

"How long were you there?"

"Five years. From eighteen to twenty-three."

"No one recognized you from those days?"

"I wore a wig and a half mask. It was part of my mystique. A trick I learned at the carnival. It also protected me from the embarrassing run-ins with professors and friends."

"Always hiding behind a mask."

"Not so much anymore."

"Did you have run-ins at the club with people you knew?"

"I saw them. They didn't see me beyond the costume and act." She traced imaginary circles on her ink blotter. "It's amazing how many people turn their noses up at places like Gold's and still slip by when the sun goes down."

"I'm not turning my nose up."

"Aren't you?"

"I don't like the idea of any man leering at you." His tone had lowered to a growl. "But I'm not judging."

She didn't answer. He now knew when she was silent it didn't mean she was cold or unfeeling but worried or stressed.

"Did you turn tricks?"

"No." The word was clear, crisp, and without hesitation. "What if I'd said yes?"

"I'd have to find my way around it. Better to know the truth than nothing at all."

Again, she was silent.

"When did you leave the carnival?"

"When I was sixteen."

"Why'd you leave?"

She shook her head. "I've given you far more than I've ever given anyone. Now it's your turn to give back. Where is this going?"

"I'm asking the questions."

"Not until you tell me why. What does my past have to do with your murder investigation?"

"I could arrest you and we can talk at my office."

She laughed. "Don't pull that cop line on me, detective. Don't. You would not arrest me."

"I would. In a heartbeat."

"And I will drag out the question-and-answer session until we all go insane. Tell me why, and I will help you."

He could force this. And no matter how long she dragged out a Q and A, he'd win in the end. But he wanted them on the same team. "What I'm sharing with you now isn't public knowledge. I don't want the details getting out to the media."

"Seems to be the day for secrets."

"They always crawl into the light eventually."

"So it seems." She sounded resigned, sad even. "Why the interest in the carnival?"

"We found a carnival ticket stub in the second victim's pocket. The stub was dated four days ago."

Her brows knitted. "So both women were at the carnival."

"Yes."

"Have you talked to Grady Tate, the carnival's owner?"

"Not yet. But I will. Right now I want to know what you know about the carnival."

Charlotte stared at Rokov. When it came to stone cold stares, he easily matched hers. They both could be unreadable. She sat forward in her chair and pressed her fingertips to the desk. "Do you think Grady has something to do with these women's deaths?"

"I don't know. Could he have killed them?"

"I don't think so but I'm discovering there is a great deal that I don't know about Grady."

"Start from the top. How did you two meet?"

"He married my mother. I was eight and my sister Mariah was nine. We were living in a motel. Mom was waitressing when he came into her diner. They hit it off. He asked her to marry him and she said yes."

"Just like that?"

"My mother was quite impulsive. She was also quite moody. I think if she'd ever seen a real doctor, they'd have diagnosed her as bipolar. Grady met her when she was up and full of energy and life. She was a lovely woman and not even thirty. Before I knew it, we'd traded the motel for Grady's trailer and were traveling around the country with his carnival."

"He's your stepfather."

"He was my stepfather. My mother died when I was thirteen."

"Is that when you left the carnival?"

"I didn't leave for a couple more years. I stayed because I had no real place to go. I knew my mother had an older sister, but I didn't know how to find her. So I stayed. Grady put my sister and me to work in the Madame Divine tent as the carnival psychic just as he had our mother. We wore the same costume but rotated shifts."

His jaw tightened a fraction.

"You don't approve?"

"A child should be in school."

"We did have a tutor of sorts within the carnival. She was good, but I quickly was asking questions more detailed than she could answer. She was good about getting me books to read. And when I finally was placed in a real school, I was on par with most of the kids."

"Why did you finally leave?"

She moistened her lips. "Mariah drowned. I freaked out. I was sure someone had murdered her, but Grady kept telling me it was an accident. When I refused to believe him, Grady found my aunt and told me I could go live with her if I wanted to leave the carnival. I did."

He leaned forward. "Where did Mariah die?"

"We were in Alexandria. It was the end of the season as it is now. She went to work that night and never came back." She swallowed.

"Did Grady call the cops?"

She closed her eyes. "He said he did, but I'm not so sure now. He's a liar."

He pulled out his notebook. "What was her full name?"

"Mariah Angel Wells."

"What happened that last night?"

"I'd drifted off to sleep. Sooner was less than a week old and she was with me. I woke up to the sounds of a woman's screams. I bolted out of bed, checked on the baby, and then ran to Grady's trailer. He had just come back from somewhere. I told him Mariah was missing, and he organized a search party. They found her by a lake. Later he said she must have fallen into the water and hit her head."

"You don't sound so sure."

"I believed him then but I don't now. He's told me too many lies." She flexed her fingers on the mat like a starfish. "In the days after Mariah's death, I kept hearing her screams in my sleep. Finally, I thought I'd go insane, so I demanded that he let me go live with my aunt. I also told him I was taking Sooner."

"He refused."

"How did you know?"

"She grew up in the carnival, not with you."

"Grady told me he'd put her up for adoption. He said I was too young to raise a baby. And I knew she deserved a real home."

He didn't respond. For the first time he wondered if she did indeed come with far too many tangles and baggage. He'd just dug his way out of a mess with his ex.

"I wish now I'd taken her with me. The carnival was no place for her. I wanted to take her and raise her. And I knew Grady was a liar. I knew it. And still I let myself believe."

"How old were you?"

"Sixteen."

"So young to be a mother."

"I would have made it work." She reached in her desk drawer and pulled out the photo. She held it out to him and he accepted the other side. For a moment the yellowed photo connected them. "This is how I remember Mariah."

He took the picture. "Sooner looks a lot like her."

"She does. She even sounds like her."

"Could Grady have killed Mariah?"

"He really did adore her. I know he can lie and cheat better than anyone, but he loved Mariah."

"Women are often killed by people they know."

"I've read the statistics." She shook her head. "We had a lot of people in and out of the carnival that summer."

"Any still around?"

"A few. I saw them the other night."

"Are you sure you didn't wake to hear Mariah really screaming? Maybe she was killed near your trailer."

She stiffened as if she'd never considered the option. "All these years I assumed the screams were a dream." She shook her head. "I wasn't awake. I know that."

"How do you know that?"

She closed her eyes, not wanting to see his reaction. "Because the dreams and screams have returned."

"When?"

The lack of censure had her raising her gaze. "A few weeks. I thought it was because the carnival was back in the area and old stuff was getting stirred up. But they are so vivid."

"Who is Sooner's father?"

"A boy in a small town in Franklin, Tennessee. When the carnival left Franklin, the relationship ended."

"Maybe he still had an interest in Mariah?"

"No."

He blinked. "What was Sooner's father's name?"

"He gave the name of Matt Davis, but that proved to be a lie when Grady tried to find him. He'd come to the carnival with sweet lies looking for fun and no intention of ever being found. And in retrospect, he was smart. Grady wanted to kill him."

His jaw tensed.

"I can only imagine what you are thinking."

"Not as dire as you might think."

She nodded. "You're going to ask around about Mariah?"

"I am."

"Do you think her disappearance is related?"

"Maybe."

"Why?"

"This killer has a thing for witches. He's drowned one and likely the second and marked both with tattoos. Both had connections to the carnival and at least one had a fortune-teller thing going on. So yeah, I think Mariah fits the profile."

"Honestly, you could be talking about me as well."

"I know. Which is why I want you to be very careful."

She offered a smile she was not feeling. "I am careful."

"We all think we are careful until we're faced with a nut who is determined to kill and has nothing to lose."

She offered him a wan smile. "I've been faced with a nut and survived."

"You were lucky."

"I'll be careful. I promise."

He rose and so did she. However, he moved around the desk and closed the gap between them. "So is the past the reason you wanted to keep things cool between us?"

Color rose in her face. "It's not wise to mix business with pleasure."

He stood at least six inches taller than her. "I'm not

asking you what's wise or not. I'm asking if your past has built that wall of ice around you."

"I don't know." She shook her head. "I know. The answer is yes. I saw my mother win and lose more men than I can count, and I witnessed enough girls at the club fall for a guy, reveal all, and then lose all. So, let's just say I've not seen many successful relationships so I keep mine light."

"I've been thinking about the ground rules you set up."

"Nothing has changed."

He cupped her chin in his hand. The touch was gentle but possessive. He kissed her softly on the lips. "Time to renegotiate the rules, counselor."

For an instant she stood stunned, the soft pressure of his lips lingering on her own. "I don't renegotiate."

"I do."

Grady stood in the growing shadows staring at the little curio shop located on Washington Street. Ageless had closed twenty minutes ago, and the entire brick building was dark except for the light in the room facing the side street. Sooner was in that room, moving, carrying, and unpacking boxes.

Tonight Sooner had told him she was leaving the carnival when it closed next week. He'd thought she was kidding at first and had laughed. She'd gotten pissed and stalked out of his trailer.

He'd decided to give her time to cool off and realize she had nowhere to go. He was her life.

Tonight was her scheduled night off and in years past she always spent her night off alone in her trailer reading. When he'd knocked on her door ready to make peace, he'd realized she wasn't there. He'd scrambled around the fairgrounds looking for her until Obie had told him she'd driven into Old Town. Two years ago, he'd put a tracker on her car, and so he'd activated it. He'd found her easily.

Now as the evening cold seeped into his bones, he was torn between dragging her home and letting her learn firsthand some of life's nasty lessons. He'd taken care of everything since she was a baby. She'd wanted for nothing. And now she was leaving him.

She passed in front of the window again and stared out almost as if she knew he was out there. He sank deeper into the shadows.

God, but she looked so much like Mariah. It was easy to watch and listen to her and be transported back to the time when Mariah had been alive and so full of life.

He closed his eyes and tried to imagine Mariah's laugh and the way her eyes lit up when he gave her a new shiny piece of jewelry. Just having her close had breathed life into him and made him excited about getting up each morning.

And then just as quickly, she was gone.

He glanced at his hands, remembering how cold her body had felt the last time he'd touched her. He fisted his fingers. He'd have given his own life in that moment if he could have taken back the events of that day.

As he'd raised his poor dead Mariah in his arms, he'd held her close to his chest, whispering in her ear that he forgave her and would take care of her. She didn't need to worry anymore. No one, not even he, could ever hurt her again.

On that long-ago night, he'd glanced around the isolated stretch of woods and knew he could not leave her out in the woods for the animals to find. So he'd carried her body to the lake and laid her down, knowing she'd soon be found. He'd returned to camp and found Grace banging on his trailer door demanding to see Mariah. Grace was more like her mother than she'd ever dare admit. She had the Sight, though she'd done her best to deny it all her life. He'd organized a search party and soon led the group to Mariah.

And now as he stared up at Sooner's window and watched her pass, he had to wonder what she was doing with this new shop of hers? Did she really think she could make a new life?

A car pulled up in front of the shop and parked. He recognized the BMW and wondered how Charlotte knew about Sooner's secret place. "Figures you'd be mixed up in this, Grace. You always were the one that stirred up trouble."

He watched as Charlotte made a call on her cell phone. Upstairs Sooner answered hers and seconds later was downstairs to greet Charlotte. The two vanished back inside the building.

Grace had put stupid, terrible thoughts into Mariah's head back in the day. Education. Independence. Life doesn't have to be this way. She'd done her best to shit all over the world he had built.

And now she was trying to do the same thing again.

He'd brought Sooner back to her for a specific reason that had nothing to do with Grace. If not for Sooner's arrest and likely incarceration, he doubted they'd ever have stood face to face. But the kid had gotten into trouble and his back was to the wall, so he'd been forced to call Grace. He'd not expected to find her so changed and so well, and her success had stuck in his craw. He'd given in to pride and rubbed salt into her old wounds and he'd taken pleasure in her pain. But once he'd had his fun, he'd expected that to be that. He would keep what was his and she would be left alone.

But as always, Grace had her own plans. "Well, you ain't winning this tug of war, bitch."

He'd have dealt with her right here and now, but he had a more pressing matter—another person to hunt down.

The smells of fresh paint mingled with the moo goo gai pan, fried rice, and steamed veggies packed in Charlotte's takeout bag. The room was now a soft purple. The color had softened the stark white and gave the room a warm and serene feel. "The place looks great."

Sooner wore her long hair up, a red sweatshirt now splashed with purple paint, and cutoff jeans. "I'm really loving this place."

"Hey, I'm sorry things didn't end so well for us the last time. I seem to have a talent for irritating you."

"You piss me off."

Charlotte shrugged. "It's a talent."

Sooner laughed. "I can be pretty irritating as well."

Charlotte relaxed, grateful they were back again on peaceful ground. "I can see you've worked hard. So what's next?"

"I found the coolest bureau at a yard sale. The owner is a sweetie and he's promised to deliver it to me tomorrow. Also, I bought a mirror from him and a couple of chairs. The space will be sparse at first, but it will fill in with time."

The girl's excitement had stripped away the cool sophisticated air, and she looked just like an eighteen-year-old kid. "You're making real headway."

"I can't wait until it's all done."

"Don't suppose you're hungry?"

"I'm starving."

"Good."

Sooner pulled up two folding chairs and placed them by a large box. "It's not a fancy table, but it will do."

"I don't mind if you don't."

They each took a seat and Charlotte handed out napkins, forks, and a couple of sodas. "So what's in this box?"

"Fabrics. A store was just gonna throw them out. I took them, knowing there will be something I can make."

She handed Sooner a bento box. "Dig in."

"This is great. You didn't have to do it. Especially considering I was a bitch to you the last time I saw you."

"I was worried about you." She stabbed a piece of broccoli with her fork. "You tell Grady you were leaving?"

"Yeah."

Charlotte stared at her food. "How did it go?"

"I don't think he believed me. He laughed. He said I didn't have anywhere to go, and I had to stay with him. I told him to piss off and stormed out."

"He didn't follow?"

"No. He understands it's final with me."

Charlotte shook her head. "Grady doesn't let go very easily, Sooner. He's not going to just watch you walk away from his carnival. There is always a price to pay."

"You walked away."

She set her fork down. "I was more trouble than I was worth."

Sooner's eyes twinkled. "Really."

Charlotte smiled. "I can be a bitch, if you haven't noticed."

"No. Really?"

"Smart-ass."

They both laughed and settled into a silence. "Did he get along with Mariah?" She kept her voice low and her gaze down.

"He liked her because she was beautiful, and she was sweet-tempered and so full of life. She could light up a room. I could be a handful."

"Why'd you leave?"

"It was after Mariah died. I was having a lot of bad dreams and had to leave." For a long moment neither spoke. "I wanted to take you with me, but Grady said he was going to put you up for adoption. I thought he'd let us both go. I thought, if I let him put you up for adoption, we'd both have a chance at a real life."

Sooner stared at a fork full of food. "Grady always said you didn't want me."

Charlotte set her plate aside and laid her hand on Sooner's. Eighteen years of sadness threatened to overflow. "That's not true. I always wanted the best for you. He swore you'd have a normal life." She shook her head. "I should have known he'd have a trick up his sleeve. I should have tracked him down and followed up. But he swore . . ."

Sooner shrugged. "Shit happens."

Charlotte kept her hand on Sooner's arm. "I'd like us to be friends."

Sooner's gaze filled with frustration and sadness. "Why?"

"We're family."

Tears filled her eyes and several spilled down her cheek. She shook her head and looked as if she wanted to say something, but then rejected it. "Did my mom love me?"

Tell her. Tell her. "She loved you very much."

She swiped away a tear. "I think I've hated her all my life."

"She never hated you." For several minutes they sat in silence. "Look, Sooner, I'm not so foolish to think we're going to come together like the Brady Bunch."

"The who?"

"Never mind. I just want us to be close. No strings. Just friends. Wouldn't it be nice to know you have someone to call if there is trouble?"

"Sure. I guess."

"I'm here if you need me." She reached in her coat pocket. "I want to give you some cash. Think of it as a housewarming gift."

"Thanks, but no money."

She dug deeper in her purse for her wallet. "Why not? You can use it to furnish the place."

"No charity. I work for my money. Period."

She'd not expected that. "Please take the money."

"No."

She shoved out a breath, realizing her respect for the girl had risen sharply. "I'm throwing a charitable fund-raiser. It's kind of a Halloween theme. Actually my partner is doing all the work. Proceeds go to cancer research. It's this Saturday."

"Good."

"We could use a card reader. Someone to liven up the party. I mean Angie's got a band and food and jugglers but no card readers. It's honest work. And it pays well."

She stared at Charlotte for a long moment. "It's for charity."

"Yeah."

"Sure, I'll do it. But I'll donate my services."

"I want to pay you."

"No. I can give just like everyone else."

"I want to pay you."

"If it will make you feel better, I'll bring my shiny new business cards and pass them out. I'll consider it a marketing event."

Charlotte shook her head. "Why won't you let me help you?"

"No one helped you."

"No. And I took some shortcuts that I regret. It would be nice if you could avoid mistakes like that."

"I won't make those mistakes."

Charlotte arched a brow. "Sooner."

"You'll keep me on the right path, I've no doubt."

She smiled. "I'm going to do my best."

The two ate in silence for several minutes before Charlotte said, "I want you to be very careful. There is a nutcase out there killing women."

"I read about that woman in the paper."

"You'll be reading about another one in the morning paper. She was killed the same way."

"That doesn't mean I'm in danger."

"This guy seems to have a thing for strong women and the carnival."

"Grady's carnival."

"I think you could be his perfect victim."

He dug the knife blade into the end of the wooden shaft and pushed hard until the wood splintered and slid free. Without much thought he repeated the process over and over until the tip of the wood reached razor sharpness. Setting the knife down, he pressed his thumb to the tip, watching in fascination as his skin tore and bled. Smiling, he laid the stake down next to the seven others he'd fashioned.

Four were reserved for Sooner and four for Grace.

Two witches.

Two deaths.

Excitement sent his heart gaveling against his ribs. Their deaths would be a great triumph that he would savor for a very long time. Drawing a breath as he stood, he wiped the blood from his thumb with a rag.

As much as he wanted to stay in this room, sequestered with his thoughts and fantasies, it was time to focus on his life outside. He had another life with people who loved him despite his dedication to justice. Tonight he'd promised his love a real date. It would be time for just the two of them. He would find the right words to say, listen as a lover should, and win back her love.

Even a warrior needed a life outside of battle.

He carefully rolled down the sleeves of his shirt, fastened his cuffs, and then tugged them down over his wrists. The cuts in his arms were bandaged but he still had to be careful. It wouldn't do to start bleeding again.

As he slid on his jacket, he glanced at the wall where he displayed his photos. They were the faces of evil, the witches he had slain. Maya had brought the number of images to eighteen. Gently he traced the photo image of her terrified face.

Satisfaction collided with anticipation. By Saturday night, the number of photos on his wall would be twenty.

Chapter 18

Rokov had expected a needle in the haystack when he'd started searching for Mariah Wells. Armed with her name, a picture, and the date she died, he didn't hold out much hope that he'd find anything. He contacted the surrounding jurisdictions, gave them her vital statistics, and asked them to check morgue files. He also called Dr. Henson and asked her to review old autopsy files.

It was just after eleven when Sinclair appeared in his doorway, file in hand. "I've got all the missing persons reports on women who match our second victim."

He took the files from her. "Great."

"Word is you're asking about another missing persons case. What gives?"

"How do you know everything?"

"It's a gift. And I've also got a file from Fairfax. An officer just dropped it off. It's the file you requested."

"Mariah Wells."

"Jane Doe as far as he's concerned." She glanced at the folder tab. "Murdered eighteen years ago."

Rokov sat back in his chair and dragged his hands over his short hair. He opened the file and examined the autopsy picture. She'd been dead at least a day. Her lips had turned black and her skin a sallow gray. But this was Mariah.

"Who is she?"

"She was Charlotte Wells's sister. Mariah Wells."

"Charlotte doesn't know her sister is dead?"

"She knows. She believes she drowned in an accident."

"That chick did not die accidentally."

"You looked at the file already?"

"Sure. It isn't often you call in favors. That's not your style. I had to see what all the fuss was about. I take it she's related to Sooner Tate? Mother?"

"Has to be. She gave birth at seventeen and was murdered shortly after."

"So Charlotte is the girl's aunt? Explains why she was with her in court."

"Yeah."

"So how did you find out about Mariah?"

"I asked her about working in the carnival. The rumors are true. When I told her about the second murder and that both victims had been to the carnival, she opened up about Mariah. I'm worried that the carnival owner might be involved."

"What do we know about Grady?"

"He wasn't at the carnival when I went by. No one has seen him today. I was just reading up on the old guy. Seems he has more than his share of trouble with the law."

"A carnie butting heads with the law. Shocking."

"Most of his crimes happened in his teens and early twenties. Stealing. Assault. Drunk in public. But he seems to have settled down by his late twenties. Or at least he got older and wiser and just managed to stay out of trouble."

"How does he know Charlotte?"

"Her stepfather more or less. I'm not sure if the marriage to Charlotte and Mariah's mother was legal."

"How long has he been running the carnival?"

"Thirty years."

"Wow. Okay. Thirty years."

Rokov read the file. "Mariah Wells did die. The medical examiner also reported severe bruising around her face and neck, and the report claims she had sex hours before dying."

"Nasty way for a girl to die."

"Yeah."

"How did Grady end up with baby Sooner?"

"He swore to Charlotte that he'd put Sooner up for adoption, but he never did."

"And that makes him evil why?"

Rokov sat back in his chair. "Because Charlotte said he was jealous of Mariah's dates. That they fought a lot. And he's reminding me more and more of a lover rather than a father."

"Lover to Mariah?" She wrinkled her face in disgust. "He'd have to been about forty to her sixteen when Sooner was conceived."

"Not the first time an older man took advantage of a young girl."

"So he knocks up his stepdaughter and then flies into a jealous rage when she dates another boy and kills her. It's not out of the realm of possibilities. A DNA test would confirm Sooner's paternity."

"That will take weeks. And it doesn't explain how he could be linked to the current murders." Rokov flipped through the pages of the medical examiner's report. He clicked through the details: defensive wounds on her hands, tissue fibers under her fingernails, bruises on her arms. And then he found a detail that made him sit a little straighter. "Shit."

"What?"

"The killer wrote on her body with a pen."

"What did he write?"

"Witch."

"Shit."

"The letters are faded, but the word is unmistakable." He tapped his finger on the desk. "Let me see the current missing persons reports."

"We have an ID on the victim," Rokov said. He stood in Deacon Garrison's office door not a half-hour after he'd spoken with Sinclair about Mariah. He held a missing person file in his hand.

Garrison motioned for Rokov to come into his office and have a seat. "Tell me."

"Her name is Dr. Maya Jones. She's a history teacher at the local community college. She missed all her classes on Monday and Tuesday and so her boss went by her apartment to check on her. She wasn't home and newspapers had piled in front of her door. Her colleague got worried and called the cops."

"You're positive."

"Fingerprints match."

"Did she have any connection to Diane Young?"

"The carnival stub. But neither woman was seen at

the carnival. Young made her living in astrology and tarot. Dr. Jones researched witches."

"Our killer has a thing about the occult."

"Specifically women." He shifted his stance. "We also have a cold case. A Mariah Wells. She grew up in the carnival and was drowned eighteen years ago. The coroner noted that the killer wrote on her chest. The murder was never solved." Rokov pulled out the picture and handed it to Garrison."

"Witch. But no tattoos. He used a marker."

"Maybe she was his first kill."

Garrison sat back in his chair and pinched the bridge of his nose. "Any hits on ViCap?"

"None yet. I'm trying to track down Grady Tate, the owner of the carnival. I want to talk to him, and I want a list of the towns he's visited in the last eighteen years. Lots of small jurisdictions that might not put a murder in the system."

"Assuming the bodies were even found."

"The responding officers in the Mariah Wells case noted that her body had been moved after she was murdered."

"Was she positioned like our victims?"

"No. In fact, her face was covered with a handker-chief."

"The killer showing signs of remorse?"

Rokov pulled out a photo of the crime scene. "I think so. Her hands are crossed over her chest. It's almost like we are dealing with two different people."

Garrison studied the picture. "Or our killer is simply evolving. He's just gotten better, more efficient, and less remorseful."

"Saying she was his first. What was it about her that made him snap and cross over into the world of killers? He had not fully developed his system when he killed her."

"And because she was his first, maybe the killing was more emotional than he'd expected."

"Maybe."

"He's certainly gotten over his guilt."

"What's next?"

"I'm headed over to the community college to speak to Maya's department chair. See if she had any stalkers or trouble makers."

"Keep me posted."

Rokov arrived at the community college's campus, parked, and made his way into the third industrial brick building and down a polished hallway to the last office on the left. The sign outside read: *Max Boxwood, Ph.D., Department of History.*

He knocked. "Dr. Boxwood?"

A tall trim man lifted his red-rimmed eyes from a German newspaper. Thick dark hair swept over his turtleneck collar, giving him a boyish look despite crow's feet that suggested he'd passed forty. "Yes."

"Detective Rokov. Alexandria Police. Thank you for waiting for me."

Dr. Boxwood folded his paper and rose. "Of course. Anything I can do to help. We're all really torn up about Maya. No one can believe it." He motioned for Rokov to sit in the chair by his desk.

The office was small but neatly organized. The wall behind Boxwood's metal desk and the one to the right were filled with floor-to-ceiling shelves packed full of books. Neat stacks of periodicals covered the floor behind his chair. The desktop was clean, cluttered only with a closed laptop and a coffee cup.

Rokov took his seat and pulled a slim notebook and pen from his breast pocket. "You knew Dr. Maya Jones well?"

Boxwood nodded. "We worked together the last few years. And I'll tell you before anyone else does. We were sleeping together. But it wasn't like we had a relationship. It was just sex. What's it called? Friends with benefits?"

Rokov hated the term because Charlotte had used it. Hell, he couldn't even say they were friends, or if there'd be more benefits. "It wasn't serious between you two?"

"No. In fact, I'm engaged to marry another woman."

His irritation grew. "And Maya was okay with that?"

"Sure. She knew the ground rules."

Rokov sat back in his chair. "When's the last time you slept with Maya?"

"A few weeks ago."

"And you two parted on good terms?"

Boxwood's brows rose. "Of course. We were friends."

"Your fiancée know about Maya?"

"Hey, it's not how it sounds." An edge had crept into Boxwood's voice.

"How does it sound?"

"Like I'm betraying my fiancée. I'm not. I love her. I want to spend the rest of my life with her."

"So your fiancée doesn't know about Dr. Jones."

"Helen? No."

"You sure?"

Boxwood frowned. "Helen would never hurt Maya."

"She might not see the benefits as inconsequential as you do."

Boxwood shook his head. "Helen does not know about Maya. So she cannot be a suspect." He cleared his voice. "And I'd like to keep it that way."

"As long as it doesn't get in the way of the investigation."

"Look, I'm trying to be open with you."

"And I appreciate that. But my guess is that you are open because your relationship was so secret."

"Not in the department."

"And no one would have leaked your affair to Helen?"

"No. Why would they?"

"Maybe you pissed someone off. It doesn't take much with some people."

"Everyone likes me here. I am respected and valued."

"Right." He noted Helen's name in his book. "Was Dr. Jones seeing anyone else?"

He seemed grateful for the shift in conversation. "I don't think so, but I don't know."

"I'd like a list of her students."

"I'll get you a printout."

"She have problems with her students?"

"Not that I know of. And if she did, she didn't tell me."

"She have any favorite hangouts?"

"She was crazy for the Just Java coffee shop. Went there almost daily."

Just Java was the coffee shop near The Wharf. He wrote the name in his book and circled it. If her killer had been stalking her, someone could have noticed him. "Her field of expertise was the Salem witch trials?"

"It was. She'd been working on a book and even got herself written up in the papers last year at just about this time. The reporter was writing a piece on the history of witches, and he interviewed Maya. The article ran right before Halloween."

So Maya had not been toiling away privately. Her work had gone public, which unfortunately expanded the field of suspects. "Do you have a copy of the article?"

"I'll take you to her office. It's framed and on her wall." Boxwood grabbed a set of keys from his desk and led Rokov three doors down the gray hallway. He opened the door and clicked on the light.

This office was thirty percent smaller than Boxwood's, and it contained double the books, paper stacks, and magazines. A poster of Salem, Massachusetts, decorated one wall. On the other wall was a poster of *Bewitched* next to *The Wizard of Oz*. Behind her desk was the framed article of her featured in the *Post*. The large article took up most of the Events page and featured Dr. Jones holding a broomstick and wearing a hat.

"She was fascinated about society's view of witches," Boxwood said.

"Looks like the author is making fun of her."

"She agreed to the getup because she knew it would catch readers' attention."

"And it did?"

"Her class enrollment for the spring semester rose twenty percent."

He leaned in and read a quote. "'I am fascinated by the fact that society is so afraid of witches, who for the most part were simply strong women with strong opinions.'"

"Maya spent most of this past summer in Salem digging through archives. She'd chosen one woman who was hung during the trials and was trying to re-create the woman's life."

Rokov glanced at the stacks of papers on her desk. "Did she receive any threats?"

"If she did, she never said a word to me or anyone else."

"Did she ever mention Diane Young?"

He flinched. "The other woman killed. No. She didn't know her."

"Did she visit the carnival?"

"She didn't usually go in for that kind of thing, but a student left tickets on her desk so she went."

"Which student?"

"She never could figure it out." He pushed trembling fingers through his hair. "Christ, who would do something like this?"

"That's what we're trying to figure out."

Tears welled in Boxwood's eyes, and his voice cracked when he spoke. "She didn't deserve this."

"No one does."

Rokov and Sinclair arrived at Just Java a little after four thirty. Most of the round tables were full with patrons holding coffee cups, and the place buzzed with conversations punctuated by the hiss of cappuccino machines. As it had before, it smelled of cinnamon and coffee.

The detectives moved to the front cash register and showed the young cashier their badges. The kid doled out change to a customer and wiped his hands on his green apron. "You guys back again?"

"Afraid so." Rokov pulled out the DMV photo of Maya Jones. "Has she been in the shop lately?"

The kid shrugged. "That's Dr. Jones. Haven't seen her in a few days. She's a regular. She in trouble or something?"

"No," Rokov said.

"She wasn't the woman killed at The Wharf."

"No. Did you serve her?"

"I did. She always gets the skinny latte with extra foam and a cookie on Fridays. Nice lady."

"Did she meet anyone here?" Sinclair said.

"Honestly, I couldn't tell you. But ask Katrina. She's our waitress, and she gets around the room. I'm stuck behind the metal dragon." He patted the cash register and smiled.

"Is she here?" Rokov said.

"Yeah. On the floor." He pointed to a tall slim woman with long dark hair.

"Thanks."

"Sure."

The detectives cut through the crowd and approached the waitress. She balanced a tray full of dirty dishes as she approached.

"Katrina." Rokov pulled out his badge.

"That's right." She blew long, dark bangs out of her eyes. "What do you need?"

"We're looking for this woman." Again he showed Dr. Jones's picture.

"Maya. She's cool."

"When's the last time you saw her?"

Dark eyes grew wary. "Last Friday."

"You're sure?"

"Yeah. It was cookie day. She always gets cookies on Fridays. And she always tips well on Fridays."

"Was she alone?"

"She came in alone, but then moved to the table of a man."

Rokov tucked Dr. Jones's picture back in his breast pocket. "Did you recognize the man?"

"He'd been in a couple of times. Kept to himself. Always tipped exactly fifteen percent."

"Did he approach her?" Sinclair said.

"I don't know. But they seemed to be talking about a book. Maya loves to read. She moved to his table, and they chatted happily. I know she's been dating a louse, so it was nice to see her meet someone else."

"What did he look like?"

Katrina frowned. "Medium height. Light-colored hair. Mustache. Baggy sweatshirt. Acted like he was in his fifties, but he gave off a younger vibe."

"Good memory," Sinclair said. "Folks don't usually remember so well."

"I remember how people tip. I'm kind of a savant that way. But I don't usually remember people."

"Why was he different?" Rokov said.

"He bled on the table."

"What?"

"Yeah. Not when he was here with Maya but about a week before. He came back and wiped up something on the table and then left. I checked behind him and saw drops of blood on the floor near his chair."

"Did he appear injured?"

"No bandages or anything. But it was definitely blood I cleaned up. I threw the wash cloth right in the trash."

"Would you be willing to meet with a sketch artist and help him work up a picture?"

"Sure. Who is this guy?"

"We're trying to find that out."

"Did something happen to Maya?"

"I can't say right now."

She shoved out a breath. "Shit. You'd have told me she was fine if she was."

They asked Katrina a few more questions before releasing her back to work. Outside Rokov rested his hands on his hips. "He came back because he knew he was bleeding."

"Why was he bleeding?"

"I wish the hell that I knew."

"Too bad she threw the rag out."

"Yeah." He glanced down the street at The Wharf. "He dumps one victim down the block and kidnaps another from here. He knows this area. It's his hunting ground."

"So what now?"

"We beat the pavement and canvas the shops and ask about Dr. Maya Jones and mystery man."

When Charlotte shut down her computer, it was past eight. Bone tired, she had a throbbing headache. She glanced at her calendar. Each day was packed with appointments and notes. She flipped the page to November and noted the first week of the new month was just as slammed as October. She didn't see white space—breathing space as she liked to call it—until mid-November. Longingly she glanced at the Saturdays in November. The first few weeks would be spent putting her new place in order, and of course, Thanksgiving was open as always. For the last few years she'd worked on the holiday but perhaps this year she'd invite Sooner over for a meal. *Home-cooked* took on a whole and not so positive meaning when linked to her, but she'd see that the girl had a decent meal.

The front bell rang, startling her. She glanced at the monitor behind her desk. Rokov stood by the door, his hands casually in his pocket. *Casual.* That was probably the worst word anyone used to describe him. He possessed an intensity that carried over from his work into the bedroom.

She closed her eyes and imagined the look on his face the last time he'd pushed into her. He'd been staring at her, gauging her reaction, even trying to read her mind. They'd both promised the sex was just sex. No attachments. No commitments. But she'd sensed in that moment he was starting to have feelings for her. That's why in the parking lot she'd told him no more meetings.

No sex. No touches. No contact.

And yet he was here now.

Sighing, she rose, smoothed her skirt, and walked to the front door. She flipped the locks and opened the door. "Detective. What brings you to my neck of the woods?"

His expression was unreadable even as his gaze lingered on her. "Have you seen Grady?"

"No, I haven't." The edge of disappointment did surprise her. Of course he'd come about work.

"What about Sooner?"

"I saw her last night." She stepped aside and motioned for him to enter. She closed and locked the door behind him. "She's opening a shop on Washington Street. She's leaving the carnival."

"Does Grady know?"

"He does, and he's not happy about her leaving." She sighed.

"What kind of relationship did he have with Mariah?"

The shift tipped her off balance for a moment. "I've told you. He was her stepfather."

"Was there more to it?"

"More?" Her face paled. "You mean sexually?"

"Yes."

Her stomach felt hollow. "He couldn't have done that."

"Why not? She was lovely."

"He was thirty years her senior."

"Age doesn't stop abusers."

She shook her head in denial even as the old memories flooded. "Grady always favored Mariah. He'd spent extra time with her. He didn't like it when boys wanted to date her." She closed her eyes. "It explains so much."

"Like what?"

"The way she'd tease him with news of a date. She knew he hated it."

"Is he Sooner's father?"

"No. I told you it was that boy. The one with the fictitious name. Matt Davis."

"How can you be sure?"

"I know."

His eyes narrowed. "And she never told anyone who had fathered Sooner?"

"We never talked about the baby's father."

"Maybe that's why Grady kept Sooner because she was his."

"No. Grady is not Sooner's father." He'd kept Sooner to punish her for leaving. "Why are you asking all these questions? What have you found out about Mariah?"

His jaw tensed. "I found out what happened to her."

She closed her eyes and immediately they filled with tears. He was about to tell her what she'd sensed for years. "It wasn't an accident."

"No."

She hadn't cried since the night she'd left Sooner with Grady at the carnival. Over the years she'd kept tears and sadness buried so very deep. But now she couldn't stop the tears.

Rokov pulled her into his embrace and held her close. He didn't say anything but just held her as the sadness and worry and old fears poured out of her.

Finally she pulled back and swiped the tears. "I'm sorry."

"It's okay." His tone was soft and firm.

"I guess I've known it all these years, but to hear it is another matter."

"I'm sorry."

She shook her head. "You shouldn't be sorry. You gave me the answer I've needed for too many years." She pulled back away from the heat and the touch of his fingers on her arms. "How?"

He hesitated. "She was drowned."

"Like the other two women?"

"Yes. And she was marked with the word *Witch*."

"Oh, God."

He enunciated each word carefully. "Could Grady have killed Mariah in a jealous rage?"

She felt sick.

"He's a liar. You know that."

She shook her head. "I can't believe he'd kill her."

Rokov was silent for a moment, and then in a low dangerous voice said, "Did he ever try anything with you? You two were the same age. Did he ever touch you?"

She paled.

"Charlotte?"

"I was too argumentative. Grady used to say if I could just be more like Mariah, his life would be easier."

His gaze burned into her. "Is that a yes or a no?"

"A no. Grady never touched me."

A grim smile tipped the edge of his mouth. "Okay. Okay." The question satisfied, his mind seemed to return to the matter at hand. "You said you both worked the Madame Divine tent."

"That's right. We took shifts."

"You wore the same costume."

"And the same wig and mask. Grady didn't want folks knowing Madame Divine's identity. He never wanted the mystique ruined."

"Or he never wanted the public knowing his psychic was two underage girls."

"That, too, I suppose."

"If Grady didn't kill Mariah," he said carefully, "could the killer have come into the Madame Divine tent as a customer and become fixated on her?"

"Sure. Maybe. We saw so many people. I lost track."

"The killer could just as easily have gotten a reading from you as Mariah?"

Her stomach dropped. "You're saying whoever killed her was really after me."

"Maybe. Maybe he just wanted Madame Divine. If the public didn't know she was two people, then he wouldn't either."

"Oh, God."

"What?"

"We switched at the last second that night. I wasn't

feeling well and Mariah was happy to get out of the trailer and away from the baby."

He frowned. "Did anyone odd come into your tent before Mariah died that set off alarm bells for you?"

"It has been eighteen years. I've blocked all that out. And after Mariah died, I was gone for good in less than a week."

"When was the last time you worked in the tent?"

"About a week before she died. After she was gone, I refused to go into the tent again."

"Grady give you a hard time about not working?"

"Yes. He was furious. He said . . ." She paused and swallowed jagged emotions. "He said it should have been me."

Rokov opened the manila folder at his side. "These are Mariah's crime scene photos and they are rough."

She moistened dry lips and tried to dismiss the growing nausea in her gut. "Let me see."

He hesitated a moment and then opened the file.

She stared in horror at the colored picture of Mariah lying on her back, her face covered with a handkerchief, and her limp body lying by a road. Tears choked her throat. "I don't see a connection."

"Have a closer look."

She clenched her fists. She lowered her gaze and drew in a sharp breath when she fully took in the image of her sister lying in the grass. She'd seen her share of autopsy photos, and though she'd found them sobering, they'd never been as devastating as these.

"You all right?"

"Yes."

He flipped to the next picture. It was another angle of her lying down.

"He wrote on her."

"Yes."

All she saw was the violence and the hatred that had spewed out of a monster onto her sister. But as she'd allowed logic to elbow and subdue emotion, her mind locked on a detail. "That handkerchief is Grady's. He always carried one like that."

"It appears fairly generic."

"He bought them by the dozen because he always needed one in his pocket. He called them his good luck charm."

Her knees gave way, and he quickly closed the file and caught her elbow, preventing her from crumbling. He guided her to a cream-colored sofa. "I still hear her screams in my dreams. Her last moments must have been a nightmare."

He sat beside her. Though he didn't touch her, his presence gave her the strength to stay calm. She wasn't going to cry this time.

"It's no shame to cry," he said.

"My mother taught me never to cry. A foolish lesson for a mother to pass on to a child, but until today I've not cried in a very long time."

"I'm sorry I was the cause."

"It wasn't you. You gave me the answers I needed for so long." She tossed him a sidelong glance and found him staring at her. "Where is she? Grady said he had her buried in Fairfax but he wouldn't let me see the grave."

"She was never claimed so she was cremated."

She pressed her fingertips to her eyes. "She should have been claimed. We should have gathered and honored her."

"Let's go," he said.

"Where?"

"Get away from here. Get something to eat."

"I'm not hungry."

"You need a break. You need an hour to get away from this place and the White trial and the worries you are carrying about Sooner."

"I don't need a break."

"Get your purse or whatever it is you carry. Break."

"Detective."

He shook his head. "I think we moved beyond the formal titles a long time ago. My name is Daniel."

She shook her head. "Detective, I told you we were not going to move on beyond the formal titles."

"As I remember, we did. Five times."

Color rose in her cheeks. "That was different."

"Really? How?"

"It was a diversion for both of us. We both knew it was what it was."

"Meaning?"

"Not personal."

"When a man and woman get naked, it's personal." He rose and pulled her with him. "Now get your purse. We're getting out of here."

Chapter 19

Too tired and overwhelmed to argue with Rokov, Charlotte grabbed her purse from her desk drawer and shut off the lights. Rokov waited on the front porch beside her as she set the alarm and locked the deadbolt. He guided her down the stairs to an un-marked police cruiser, opened the passenger side door for her, and waited as she slid into the car. He closed her door. The car's interior had remained warm and immediately subdued the chill clinging to her bones.

Without a word, Rokov got behind the wheel and fired up the engine. A quick glance in the rearview mirror and he was driving down the street. Before long they'd maneuvered around the latest patch of road construction, so much a part of this area, and were on I-495 south. She didn't ask where they were going, knowing she was safe and for these few moments with him she did not have to worry.

When he pulled into a residential neighborhood,

she sat a little straighter. The houses were small, many built in the fifties, but the lawns and properties were neatly kept. "Where are we?"

"I have to stop by my parents. They're having dinner so we might as well grab a bite there."

Immediately, she tensed. "I shouldn't be here."

"Why not? Their food is good, better than any restaurant, and you're hungry."

"No. They're not expecting me." She stared down the street, wondering if they'd passed a Metro stop, a bus, or a subway line.

He ignored her. "Mom cooks enough for an army. Besides, it's late and some of the clan will have cleared out."

"I don't like being around real families." They were reminders of too many personal disasters. "I can wait in the car."

"No." He parked behind a black Lincoln and came immediately around to her side of the car. He opened the door. "Don't be a baby, Wellington. It's just a meal."

"Breaking bread with family is personal."

"More personal than sex?"

"Absolutely." She got out, hugging her purse close.

Rokov followed and pressed his hand into the small of Charlotte's back, guiding her toward his mother's front door decorated with dried cornstalks. He could have called his mother and begged off the meal. God knows he'd done it enough times. But he'd wanted Charlotte to meet his family. Why? And to fully answer that question required more time than he had. All he knew was that they were both hungry, and there was no better place to nourish her than here.

Without knocking, he opened the front door. Immediately, the sounds of laughter and music rushed out to greet them. Charlotte's muscles stiffened under his palm, and he could feel her pushing back. If he'd not been there, she'd have run.

"You can cross-examine a man to shreds without breaking a sweat, and yet a little family time scares you?"

"It scares the shit out of me," she whispered.

The uncharacteristic remark made him laugh. Which was how his mother found them, him smiling down at her and her looking at him with a bemused if not embarrassed expression. An outsider might have thought he'd just kissed her or they'd shared an intimate exchange.

"Daniel?" His mother's voice was loud and excited. "We did not think you'd make it."

He nudged Charlotte closer to his mother with more than just a little push in the small of her back. "I don't have much time. I've got to get back to work soon."

His mother's bright blue gaze had shifted completely from him to Charlotte, and there was a curiosity there that could only be described as hungry. "And who is your friend?"

His mother had learned English well over thirty years ago but she still spoke with a pronounced Russian accent. Streaks of white had turned her blue-black hair to salt and pepper, but erect shoulders gave her the presence of a much taller woman. A strict code of eating had kept her figure trim, and she still wore dark dresses instead of slacks or shorts.

"This is Charlotte Wellington. We're working on a case together."

His mother arched a brow. "You are a policeman?"

Charlotte extended her hand. "I am an attorney, Mrs. Rokov."

His mother took her hand in both of hers. "My name is Nadia Rokov. Daniel's mother. And please call me Nadia."

More laughter and conversation bubbled from the kitchen. "I don't mean to intrude."

"Intrude! That is the last thought to cross my mind. My son knows I feed all hungry people. Now come and please sit at my table."

His mother led the way and Charlotte tossed him a glance filled with a mixture of worry, relief, and payback-is-a-bitch. He winked at her.

They moved into the kitchen, decorated with Formica and white wallpaper with strawberries and vines. The stainless round kitchen table now sported two extra middle extensions to accommodate the mountains of food and the crowd, which included his parents, two brothers, a sister, and a grandmother.

All the Rokov children looked eerily similar. Growing up, they'd been known as the Rokov Rat Pack, infamous for close ties and a readiness to fight anyone who challenged the Pack.

When Daniel and Charlotte entered the kitchen, all conversation stopped.

Rokov stood at her side, his hand on her back. "Family, I'd like you to meet Charlotte Wellington. We work together."

The group stared in stunned silence, and for a moment he wasn't sure if they'd heard him. However, his father broke the shocked stillness. "Welcome, Ms. Wellington. I am Dimitri Rokov."

"Charlotte, please."

He nodded. "And you will call me Dimitri. These are my children, Nathan, Ivan, and Joanna. There is another daughter, Alexa, but she is traveling for her business."

They all raised their hands and nodded. Dumb grins ignited and spread across each face. He'd be catching shit about this later. So be it.

At the other end of the table sat his grandmother. "Charlotte, this is my grandmother, Mrs. Rokov."

She smiled at Charlotte. "Daniel, get this poor girl a chair. She is hungry."

"Sure, Nona. Sure." He pulled two extra chairs from the dining room and set them at the table. His sister scooted to the right to make room for them.

"I have a lovely dining room," his mother said. "And of course no one ever eats in there. Everybody wants the kitchen."

"Family gatherings are often impromptu here," Daniel explained. "One kid figures out what Mom has on the stove, and he texts the others. Before you know it, there's a crowd."

Charlotte sat on the edge of her chair as if she could jump and run with little prompting. "That's nice. You're lucky to be so close."

"Do you have family in this area?" Mr. Rokov said.

"No," she said smoothly. "They're out of town."

Charlotte had never talked about family until tonight when he'd informed her Mariah had been murdered. There was Grady, niece Sooner, and an un-named aunt who'd taken her into her home. They were a ragtag group with loose ties at best.

Rokov took two plates from his mother and gave one to Charlotte. "Dig in."

Charlotte accepted the plate and glanced at the table with a bit of panic. "Oh, my. I don't know where to start."

"It's all guaranteed to bust any diet." The comment came from a tall slender brunette with ice blue eyes. The dad had introduced her as Joanna. "Mom likes to cook with gallons of butter."

Mrs. Rokov shrugged. "A little butter is good for the soul. Much better than all that junk in the stores today."

Charlotte had no idea what dish to choose or where to start. She'd not felt this awkward since she'd argued her first case in law school. Without much thought, she grabbed the first serving spoon and heaped what looked like a cabbage dish onto her plate. Next was a meat dish, something marinated and spicy. And then potatoes. It smelled tantalizing, and she realized she was hungry. She'd been so nervous when she'd visited Sooner that she'd barely eaten.

Grateful to have a plate and something to do, she ate and listened as the family chattered around her. Rokov's brothers razzed him about cleaning his stuff out of the backyard shed, discussed who would rake Nona's leaves and Alexa's latest text from Boston. He took it all in stride, letting all the good-natured razzing roll off his back.

When Charlotte had first suggested they sleep together, she'd not really thought of Daniel Rokov as a person. She'd sensed he was honorable and good but that had been secondary to her primary goal: ending a very long and lonely dry spell. And he'd done it. In fact, he'd done such a good job, she'd been unable to forget him. She'd called him the second time, half hoping it wouldn't be as good as the first time. Better to be disappointed early and move on. But the second time had been as good as, if not better than, the first. Before she realized it, she couldn't stop anticipating the next time.

She'd convinced herself it was just sex. A basic need, not so different than food or water. But she'd been fooling herself. It was more than sex. And Daniel Rokov was so much more than a man in a motel room. He was a man who could be gentle with horrific news, who was loved by his family, and who was respected by his coworkers.

She'd not only learned a lot about Daniel Rokov these last few days, but had broken all the rules she'd established for their relationship. What emotional price would she eventually have to pay for allowing too much familiarity?

Better to pull back. Just sit, eat, and make a quiet retreat from the conversation. The Rokovs had a different plan.

"You were representing that woman who murdered her husband, weren't you?" The question came from Joanna.

"That's right," Charlotte said.

"I read about you in the paper."

"You did?" She smiled but didn't expand.

"Have you spoken to Ms. White since the trial? She must be pretty relieved."

"She's putting her life back together," Charlotte said.

"Many of the editorial pieces suggest she killed her husband," Joanna challenged.

"That is their opinion," Charlotte said, grateful for something businesslike to discuss. "The jury found Ms. White innocent."

Joanna shared her brother's intense gaze. "The evidence could have gone either way."

"The jury did not agree."

"Juries can be swayed by emotion."

Rokov set his fork down and glanced at his sister. "Be nice, Joanna."

Joanna arched a brow. "Hey, I was just asking questions."

Charlotte laid her napkin by her plate. "Your questions don't bother me, Joanna. I believe Samantha White is innocent, and that is why I took her case. There will be those that do not agree but I cannot help that."

Joanna cocked her head. "How could you know she was innocent?"

Charlotte shrugged. "A gut feeling."

"That's it?"

"That was it."

Joanna leaned forward, a signal she wanted to kick the discussion into high gear. Charlotte met Joanna's gaze with a mixture of challenge and amusement. The girl reminded her of herself when she'd been in her mid-twenties: full of fire and fight. "That's not very scientific."

Rokov cleared his throat and glanced at his father. "I'll be by to work on that shed as soon as this case is closed."

His father waved a dismissive hand. "The shed will wait. Your work is more important. I know this."

Mrs. Rokov cleared away their plates. "I've been following the case in the papers. It is horrible what I am reading. Those poor women."

The mood in the room shifted from jovial to

solemn. Charlotte thought about Mariah and the moment's respite from her thoughts ended.

"Do you have any leads?" Ivan said.

Rokov set his fork down. "We're working on it." He glanced at Charlotte, seemed to note her change in mood. "And Charlotte and I have early calls in the morning."

"Daniel, do not leave," Mrs. Rokov said. "You just got here."

"Sorry, Mom. I didn't realize how late it was." He stood and kissed his mother and grandmother.

Charlotte stood and smoothed her skirt flat. "Thank you for dinner, Mr. and Mrs. Rokov. It was a nice break."

"It was lovely to meet you, Charlotte. I hope you'll come again sometime."

She nodded, touched by the woman's genuine tone.

"Charlotte, can you take some dessert?" Mrs. Rokov said. "I've got enough to feed an army. You can put it in your refrigerator at home."

"Normally I would. But I'm moving in a couple of days and trying to clean out what I have. But thank you."

Rokov said his good-byes again, shook his father's hand, punched a brother good-naturedly in the shoulder, and escorted Charlotte to his car.

The day's stress hadn't drained from her shoulders and she seemed, as she always seemed, braced for a fight.

He started the engine. "You're moving?"

The comment had slipped out so easily when she'd spoken to Mrs. Rokov that she'd not thought about the fact that she'd told no one she was moving. "Yes."

"Don't you have a swanky condo overlooking the river?"

"Yes. It's been great."

"You moving to a bigger place?"

"Smaller. I don't need so much space as I thought."

"Mind me asking where?"

"You're full of questions."

He shrugged. "Just making conversation."

She smiled. "I doubt you've ever just made conversation, detective."

"You might be surprised. I do have my moments."

"I've no doubt."

He took the exit off the Beltway and wove through Alexandria toward her office. When he parked in front of her car, he shifted in his seat toward her. The light from a street lamp shone through and sharpened the angles on his face. "So where are you moving to?"

"Just a smaller place in Alexandria. Near Seminary Road."

"Nice area, but not as nice as where you are."

"It's more convenient."

His gaze narrowed. "How so?"

"Again with the questions, detective."

"Just wondering why the step down."

Her defenses strengthened. "It's not a step down."

His wrist rested easily on the steering wheel. "From river views to Seminary? Don't kid yourself. Why?"

"Maybe I want a change."

"Is your practice in trouble?"

He had a talent for striking to the heart of a matter. "It's fine." And it would be when she pumped in the profits from the condo sale.

He tapped his fingers on the steering wheel. "Why can't you just tell me?"

"There is nothing to tell."

His smile wasn't pleasant. "What's made you so guarded? Was it the shooting three years ago?"

She arched a brow. "Are you always this direct?"

"Yes. Are you always this evasive?"

"Yes."

"Charlotte, just tell me." He laid his hand on hers.

The warmth coupled with the strength and the cover of the night was her undoing. "I've been guarded since before I could walk. If you don't have loving parents, you learn to hold your cards close. And the shooting didn't help. In the moments I was in that bathroom waiting for that man to return and finish the job, I knew there was no one in the world that was going to save me. I had to save myself. And I did." She released a sigh. "And I'm selling the condo because too much pro bono work and not enough high-profile cases have chewed into the firm's bottom line. Selling my condo is the only way I can save the firm. The money should buy me six months."

"And then?"

She smiled, hoping the simple gesture would bolster her confidence. "By then I will have landed another big fish, and I'll be fine."

"Just like that?"

"Don't worry about me, detective. I'm a cockroach. I'm a survivor in every sense of the word."

As he studied her, a smile that held no warmth curled his lips. "Good. Because I want you around for a long time."

"I've redefined being careful. I'm all about security." A quip danced on the tip of her tongue, but she let it pass. "See you soon, detective."

"Sooner rather than later, counselor."

A sad smile tipped the edge of her lips. "You know that's where Sooner got her name."

"How?"

"She was born a month early and Mariah took her first look at her and said, 'The kid came sooner rather than later.' Somehow Sooner just stuck."

"It's a catchy name."

"It seemed pretty cool when I was sixteen. Now, I wish she had a more conventional name." She gripped the handle of her purse tighter. "One more thing to add to the Things-I-Wish-I'd-Done-Differently list."

"What else would you do differently?"

"It's too late to get into that discussion. Maybe some other time."

He nodded. "I'm sorry again about Mariah."

"Thanks."

She got out of his car and hurried to her own car. She clicked the lock open and slid behind the wheel. As he waited and watched in his car, she started her car. Pulling out onto the street, she glanced in the rearview mirror and realized he was slowly following behind her.

When she reached the stop sign, she paused and then took a left toward her house. He followed her for two more blocks and then took a right. She gripped the wheel, grateful and sorry he no longer followed.

"The number one rule is not to care," she said. Since she'd fled the carnival, she'd never broken the iron-clad rule. Not once. Now it was becoming a habit.

First with her employees.

Then with Sooner.

And now with Rokov.

* * *

It was close to midnight when Grady stood outside the two-story brick home. The neighborhood tidy look-alike lawns, neat curbs hugging well-paved streets, and houses that all spoke of stability, money, and decency. He knew firsthand how much shit hid behind respectability. Folks who lived in places like this might think they were better than him, but they were just as dishonest.

Nearly every house on the block was dark. Good. He exhaled a lungful of cigarette smoke, and ground out the butt in the ashtray of his truck. "Tight-ass fuckers. You don't fool Grady."

He got out of the car, cringing against the cold, hurried across the street. He crossed the lawn of a neat little house and hurried to the back fence. Carefully, he opened the gate. In the distance a dog barked.

His lungs burned as he jogged around the side of the house to a small side door. Pulling a screwdriver from his jacket pocket, he wedged the tip under the lock and pushed. The wood cracked and splintered and the lock slid open. A turn of the handle, and he was inside the house.

The utility room was small and painted a bright yellow. Across from the door stood the washer and dryer, piled high with freshly folded laundry. A basketball, scooter, and baseball mitt filled a corner and there was a cat's litter box to his right. A cat wouldn't be a problem but a dog was another matter. Those fuckers made a lot of noise.

He waited, listened, but didn't hear a sound. Carefully he moved into the house, which smelled of Pine-Sol and pizza. He'd watched the house for a couple of days and knew the woman here lived alone with her two young children. He wasn't sure what had happened to her old man but right now didn't care. She was alone, defenseless, and that was all that mattered.

He moved down a carpeted hallway and up the stairs past dozens of framed pictures of her two children. The little girl reminded him of a cleaned up, suburban version of Grace. The top step creaked and he paused, ready to dash back down the stairs. But the house remained quiet, except for the hum of the heater. He moved to the back room and opened the cracked door. Moonlight filtered in through a window, casting a beam of light on the bed where the woman slept. She lay on her side, away from the dresser and window.

He stood at the edge of the bed, watching her sleep. She had no idea that monsters didn't just lurk in the imaginations of children. Monsters lived in the real world, and sometimes they were so close you could feel their breath on your neck.

She groaned, rolled on her stomach, and let out a sigh. She was pretty in a mousy sort of way. Monsters ate mice like her for breakfast.

He turned and moved toward the dresser. It wasn't littered with makeup and perfume bottles like Sooner's but was neat and clean. Carefully, he opened the top drawer, and found a jewelry box. He removed it, closed the drawer, and set it on the dresser top. The hinges of the box squeaked when he opened it and inspected the contents. He smiled, removed what he'd wanted, and pocketed it.

Instead of replacing the jewelry box, he set it on the floor and unzipped his pants. He fished out his dick and pissed on the box.

Grinning, he zipped up his pants and glanced at the Mouse. He wanted her to know he'd been in her room, standing next to her bed and watching her sleep. He wanted her to know that at any moment he could have taken that same jewelry box and beaten her to death. And he wanted her to worry and wonder when he would be back.

Chapter 20

"We have two hits on ViCap," Sinclair said. She stood in Rokov's door with the file in hand.

The fatigue that had been weighing him down vanished. "Where?"

"Raleigh, North Carolina. Twelve years ago. And Athens, Georgia, ten years ago." She moved into his office and sat at his desk.

"Hold on a minute, I want to get Garrison and Kier in here." He placed calls to both and it was agreed the four would meet in the conference room. Five minutes later, they were assembled around the large rectangular table in the windowless room.

Garrison and Kier both showed signs of fatigue. Like Sinclair and Rokov, they'd been chasing down interviews on anyone who might have known something valuable about either victim.

Sinclair opened the file, which like most ViCap reports contained crime scene descriptions and photos, victim profiles, lab reports, and any other information that might help create a link between the crime and others like it.

"According to this report, the victim's name was Margaret Day, age thirty-two." She pulled photos of the crime scene and dispersed them to the team.

Rokov studied the picture, which had eerie similarities to his two crime scenes. Margaret Day's body had been laid out in a green field, her hands and feet tied to stakes hammered in the ground. She wore a black dress and had a thick shock of dark hair, which flowed out around her head. Rain had dampened her body and the ground around her, and a thick mist hovered in the distance. Written on her forehead was the word *Witch*.

"Tell me about the victim," Garrison said.

Sinclair flipped through the pages. "She was a prostitute. She didn't work the streets but kept an apartment where she welcomed regular clients managed by her pimp. According to her pimp, her thing was dominance. She was called the Sorceress."

"They checked out all her clients."

"The ones that they could find. No one gave last names, all transactions were in cash, and there were no cameras watching the building."

"Who reported her missing?"

"No one. She was found in a wooded area by a couple of hikers who'd ventured off the trail. According to the medical examiner, she'd been sexually assaulted several times before she died. At the time she was found, she'd been dead about five days. She was staked to the ground."

"How did she die?" Rokov said.

"The medical examiner suspected drowning." Sinclair

tapped an agitated finger on the file. "Why drown them? Kicks? Excitement?"

"Maybe he needs information or proof?" Rokov said. "He needs to assure himself that they are witches."

"Why does he care about a confession?" Garrison said.

"Maybe he's got a perverted sense of justice."

Garrison nodded. "Go on."

"Maybe he doesn't feel justified killing an innocent. He's only about destroying the guilty. Think about the crime scenes. He's almost warning whoever finds the body that they have found something evil and dangerous."

Garrison shook his head. "That's one hell of a theory."

Rokov took the next file from Sinclair. "This ViCap report is from Georgia. Ten years ago." He flipped through the pages. "Alice Carrington, age thirty-five. She worked as an Athens librarian and vanished after a Halloween party. Found two weeks later, wooded area, staked to the ground."

"Let me guess, she was wearing a witch costume," Sinclair said.

Rokov nodded. "That's correct. And like the others, she was sexually assaulted."

"There are no other hits?" Garrison said.

"None," Sinclair said. "And I've checked."

"So assuming his first victim was Mariah Wells, his first recorded kill is eighteen years ago, in Alexandria, Virginia; the next in Raleigh, North Carolina, and the last we know of is Athens, Georgia. Assuming there are no other victims, his cooling-off periods lasted six years and then two years. For almost a decade he doesn't kill?"

"Assuming there are no others," Garrison said. "The

first three bodies were left off the beaten track. There could be others never found."

"Mariah was by the road," Sinclair said.

"But she'd been moved," Rokov said. "And I'd bet not by the killer."

Garrison traced his jaw line with the edge of his reading glasses. "Still no trace of Grady Tate?"

"No. He's crawled under a rock."

"Was there any DNA in the other cases?" Kier said.

Rokov scanned the file. "In Austin. Traces of semen were found on the victim. We can see if we've got a match between that case and what the medical examiner collected from under Diane Young's fingernails."

"He's so careful about his planning. I can't believe he'd leave behind DNA," Sinclair said.

"Maybe because it's not on file anywhere," Rokov said.

"His pace is much faster now," Kier said. "And a faster pace means he's going to make a mistake very soon."

"I'd like to think he's already made that mistake and we've just missed it," Rokov said. He studied the locations of the murders. Virginia. North Carolina. Georgia. "All the murders we have took place in the Mid-Atlantic and South."

"Grady Tate's carnival travels the Mid-Atlantic and South," Sinclair said.

"We've got to find Grady. He is the key to all this." Kier said.

Rokov glanced at the files. "One other thing. All the murders took place in October."

Perfection was its own brand of holiness. This, he understood, had been the key to his survival all these years. He'd been careful to control his impulses, knowing a man who let his emotions run amuck was a fool doomed to fail. He'd made a lot of mistakes in his past and had let emotions rule him. He'd been in danger of falling prey to his own needs when he'd met the woman that had brought calm to his life. She'd given him hope. Showed him that goodness was all around. And she had given him the strength to maintain strict control over his life.

And then she had turned on him.

A glass of whiskey in his hand, he stared down at the letter that had arrived this morning. He'd gone to her with hat in hand and opened his heart to her. She'd been quiet and told him she needed to think, all the while knowing this letter had been posted.

Neatly typed wording. Precise. Not a word wasted. And cutting to the core.

If she thought she could leave him, she was wrong. She was his and she belonged to him. He wanted to kill her tonight. He wanted to strap her to his board and dunk her head into the cool waters until she screamed for mercy and confessed her sins.

But he wouldn't kill her. Not yet. But soon.

There was work to be finished before month's end. He needed to vanquish more evil. Cleanse his soul.

Draining the last of the whiskey, he carefully folded the letter and tucked it back in the cream-colored envelope.

He glanced at the razor on the workbench and longed to make a few quick slices into his flesh to ease the tension. Simple straight cuts that weren't too deep would make him feel so much better. But as tempting as it was to release into the pain, now was not the time for games that would weaken him.

He reached for a piece of wood and a knife. He began to carve the rounded end into a sharp tip.

He didn't need more stakes, but he needed restraint. Strength. Courage.

This time he was killing The One that had enticed him to the dark side eighteen years ago.

She'd been called Grace then. Now she fancied Charlotte. Either way, she and her assistant were next.

Chapter 21

Early Saturday morning, Charlotte wore her faded cutoffs, a black T-shirt, and tennis shoes. Her hair was pulled into a topknot. She'd been working since dawn assembling the last of the boxes and getting ready for movers scheduled to arrive between eight and ten. Sleep had been impossible. Thoughts of Mariah tumbled and prodded her each time she'd closed her eyes, so in the end she'd just given up on sleep.

As she glanced around the condo at the piles of boxes, she conceded to a sense of relief. There was a time when she'd convinced herself that this place had fit her like a glove, but much like the too expensive outfit that couldn't be returned, she'd often not felt wholly comfortable here. She'd never gotten past the feeling that the real owners would burst into the space and demand that she leave.

The front bell buzzed and she glanced at her red sports watch. Seven forty-five. The movers were early.

The one time she needed them to be late, they were early.

She hurried to the door and, without looking in the peephole, snapped it open. Rokov stood at her threshold holding two cups of coffee.

"Detective."

"Counselor." He handed her a coffee. "Moving day?"

"It is. And it is not a good time to visit."

"Never a good time to visit with the cops." He smiled and sipped his coffee. "Let's chat."

"I can't. Not now. I'm under the gun with this move."

A smile that wasn't a smile tipped his lips. "I'll help."

"I don't need your help."

He shrugged. "Too bad."

"Leave."

"No." He stepped over the threshold and brushed past her. He surveyed the collection of boxes, set down his coffee cup, and shrugged off his sport jacket. "When did you say the movers were coming?"

"About an hour. And I refuse to pay them extra while they wait and watch me pack."

"Then we better get busy. Where do we start?"

"The kitchen."

He nodded and moved into the kitchen. He whistled his appreciation. "So this is how the other half lives?"

She'd only heated soup and made toast in the space, but it was a designer's dream. A muted palate of blues and greens stood as a backdrop to white Carrera Marble countertops, a crystal backsplash that mirrored hanging lights, stainless steel Wolf appliances, and a wine refrigerator stocked with expensive wines.

This was the kind of kitchen she'd dreamed of as

a kid, and for a time all her dreams had come true.
But now she could no longer support the dream.

She grabbed an empty box and handed it to Rokov.
"You can start wrapping the dishes in the cabinet."

"Why not have the movers do this?"

"I don't trust them with the delicate stuff."

She turned her attention to a stack of pots, which
she'd laid out on a farmhouse-style table surrounded
by eight upholstered chairs. Grabbing newspaper, she
began to wrap.

"You mentioned that Mariah had a date that last
night."

"Yes. I got the impression he was a local and he'd
come to see the carnival. We always had a lot of local
boys coming around the carnival looking to hook up
or seeing if they could score drugs."

He raised a brow.

"You're wondering if I'm guilty of either."

"I'm a cop. I'm paid to wonder." He filled a box with
wrapped plates and sealed it with a packing tape.

She shoved aside the old defensive feeling. "Sorry. I
guess you can take the girl out of the carnie but not
the carnie out of the girl. I'll never forget how people
looked at me when I was a kid."

"That why you've perfected the polished image?"

Two pots clanged together as she dropped them in
a box. At this point she didn't care so much about
her stuff. She just wanted it moved and gone. "After
Mariah died, I knew I had to leave. I swore the rest of
my life would be different."

"So you rejected all things carnie and became the
uptight snob?"

The fitting description rankled her nerves. Several
counterpoints danced on the tip of her tongue.

"Trying to decide which argument to hurl at me first?"

She smiled. "Am I that obvious?"

"I'm learning to see through the veneer." He winked at her and carried the two packed boxes to the foyer by the front door.

Irritated, she picked up another empty box and dumped a couple of never-used copper pots inside. "You cannot read me."

He reappeared with an empty box in hand. "Yes, I can."

"Just because we had sex doesn't mean that you know me."

"But I do." When she opened her mouth to argue again, he shook his head. "Tell me about the night Mariah died."

Sighing, she shook her head. "She was working and then she had a date with a boy I'd never met. He was taking her to dinner and a movie in town. She was excited because he was taking her on a real date. Meaning, a lot of boys showed up with a bottle of wine and an offer to park somewhere. This guy, she said, had been a gentleman."

"Did she date a lot?"

"From the time she turned fourteen, it was impossible to keep her around the carnival. She searched for every chance she could to get away." Sudden emotion choked her throat. "Mariah was so desperate for another life. I saw it, but I couldn't help her. I was consumed with my own fears and dreams. I wish I'd paid more attention to her. Maybe she would have stayed in that last night."

"You were just a kid. Don't carry that burden."

But she did carry the burden along with another far

heavier. "That last night, Mariah said that Grady was very angry about her date. She took pleasure in making him worry. She bragged that he had given her an expensive necklace, and she was going to wear it on her date."

"He was possessive."

"Very."

"Where was Grady that night?"

"Working the rides. Making sure everything ran smoothly. We only had a couple of nights left in town, and it was the big push to make cash."

"But he could have been anywhere that night?"

"Yeah."

"Could he have killed Mariah?"

"You asked me that last night."

"And you've had a chance to sleep on it."

She sighed. "I don't know now. Maybe. He wouldn't be the first man to kill someone he loved." She was unable to say the word *lover*. "Her date gave her a rose when he asked her out." She'd forgotten that detail. "But I guess that doesn't help too much. Eighteen years and a rose purchase."

"Not likely."

She closed her eyes and let her mind drift. She'd spent so many years forgetting that her ability to remember had grown rusty. "She also said he was uptight. A straight arrow. He had taken a semester off from school but planned to return in January."

"Why had he dropped out?"

"He'd been sick." Images were pushing their way to the forefront of her mind. "And he was worried about going back. It was important to him that he succeed in school."

"Did he say which school?"

"No."

"A fall dropout eighteen years ago from a college near Alexandria."

"He told her he could barely afford the instate tuition."

Rokov retrieved his notebook from his jacket pocket and scribbled down the details.

"Why would he start killing again here and now?" she asked.

"We think he's killed other women in Raleigh and Athens."

"Those towns were major carnival stops."

"What were some of the other cities?"

"Nashville. Charleston. Roanoke, Virginia. Asheville, North Carolina. Atlanta. Grady would have the full list. He was good about keeping notes on the different stops."

"Did you keep any kind of log?"

"No. No records. It was all informal."

"You ever read anyone that really gave you the spooks?"

"Well, there were the guys that tried to get more than a reading. I kept a baseball bat under my table for those guys. But there were times when the random person came through, and you could feel the resentment and anger."

"You felt it?"

"My mother taught me how to read people. She was good at it, but I was great at it. The problem with Mom was that she stopped believing that it was science and started thinking her talents were really psychic. Toward the end she believed she could read minds. I never made that mistake. I read people's body language, which I guess is what generates the feeling."

"You think you could read me?"

She shook her head. "I don't think that's such a good idea."

"Why not?"

"Given our history."

"You said yourself it was no big deal."

"It wasn't."

He held out his hand. "Then read me."

The challenge in his voice had her folding her arms over her chest. "You won't like it."

He grinned. "Try me."

This was a test. She didn't know why he was testing her but he was. "Give me your hand."

She took his hand and turned it over. His skin was warm and his fingertips calloused. Strong lines creased his palm. For some the lines had significance. Past lives. Future. Love. Death. A reasonably smart person could make anyone believe. The trick was guessing what the client wanted to hear.

So what did Daniel Rokov want? "You are young."

"Not so young."

"Younger than me."

"Not enough to count."

"You have ambition. Hate obstacles." She glanced at his military college ring. "You are used to command. In school you rose to the top."

He nodded, his eyes keen with interest. His pulse quickened just a bit. "You are from a hardworking immigrant family, but you dress like a man who wants to rise to the very top, just as you did in college."

"You've met my family. No magic there." He stared at her with an intense gaze.

"It's never magic. It's all observation and guesswork." She traced her index finger over his palm. The

faint callous on his left ring finger told her something
she'd not realized before. "You dress as if you would
like to be a chief, a mayor, or a senator. But those titles
hold little interest for you. I think that is why your first
wife left you. She wanted the big titles for you, but you
see the real power behind the scenes."

He was silent for several moments. "I never told you
about my first wife."

She frowned. "A slight callous at the base of your
ring finger."

"Then how did you determine why she left?"

"Lucky guess."

He captured her hand in his and slowly turned it
over. His grip wasn't gentle or painful, but it was un-
breakable. "Now it's my turn."

The grim set of his jaw told her she'd struck a nerve.
"I don't need a reading."

His grip remained firm. "Turnabout is fair play."

"You asked for your reading. I do not wish one."

He traced her lifeline. "You are at a crossroads."

She arched a brow. "What tipped you off? The hundreds of boxes?"

"It's more than that," he said. "You are questioning."

Charlotte arched a brow. "You mean like when the
movers are going to be here?"

"Like why you do what you do. You can catch the big
fish, but the question is do you want to?"

"You mean I'm afraid that I might get bitten by another big fish with teeth? Believe me, I'm not afraid of
teeth, and for the record I know how to bite hard."

A smile tipped the edge of his lips. "I remember."

Immediately color rose in her face, and she remembered the second time they'd slept together. She'd
been beyond excited to see him, and they'd barely

made it to the hotel room before they'd each dropped their clothes. He'd stripped the coverlet from the bed, and they'd fallen onto the mattress. When her orgasm shuddered through her, she'd bitten his shoulder.

"You hate letting go more than anything in the world. It's why you only drink at home and then only moderately. You are drawn to the idea of family, but fear it as well."

"You've noticed my wine refrigerator in the kitchen and my reputation for being a nondrinker. No one wants an out-of-control attorney."

"You take control to the next level. And I know why that is now."

She didn't want to ask why and show him she cared. However, her voice failed her, and all she could manage was a cocked eyebrow.

He leaned forward, his lips close to her ear. "You're afraid."

"No, I am not."

"You are. You're afraid the real truth will come out."

She cleared her throat as her heart pulsed rapidly under his fingertips. God, did he know? "And what truth is that?"

He shook his head. "I want you to tell me."

If he didn't look so serious, she'd have called him a con man. She wanted to tell him he didn't know anything, but somehow she feared he did know the truth. "Everyone says they want to know the truth, but they really don't. Once the fantasy is destroyed, the fun ends."

"Not for everyone."

She wanted to connect with him, but the words would not form. All she had at this moment was her body and her ability to touch. She kissed him.

He cupped the back of her neck and pulled her to him. His kiss began gently but quickly intensified before he broke the contact. "Has sex always been an escape for you?" The whispered words didn't soften the challenge.

A good attorney knew when to avoid and when to attack. No more of either. "Sex was a cold lonely place . . . until you."

His gaze darkened, but the meaning in their depths escaped her. Was he pleased? His hand traced her palm, and then rose up her arm to the back of her neck. His hold wasn't urgent. It was possessive.

With deliberate pressure he guided her face to him. She could balk. Say no. Demand that he leave her alone with her secrets. But she'd never said no to him in bed and knew she'd soon confess.

When his lips touched hers, a frisson of desire shot through her body. Her muscles tightened, she clenched handfuls of his shirt and pulled him toward her. His hand roamed up her shirt to the underside of a lace-covered breast. He cupped her nipple, squeezed. Her heartbeat thundered against her ribs as she arched into him. The movers would be here soon. She had so much to handle. And all she could think about was Rokov inside her.

She reached for the buckle of his pants.

He stilled her hands. "Bedroom."

"This way." She guided him quickly through the maze of boxes to her room. The room was entirely packed, and all that remained on the bed were the sheets and a few blankets for this last night in her place.

He pulled her shirt off and reached for the elastic waistband of her athletic shorts. "I want to see you naked."

She gripped his hand, her breath stopped in her throat.

He stared at her unmoving as she listened to the fast beat of her heart. "Yes or no?"

"Yes." Her voice sounded ragged, like a stranger's.

He pulled down her shorts and let them drop around her ankles. As he pushed her back toward the bed, she reached for his belt buckle. Seconds later he was on top of her and then inside her, moving with hard, even thrusts. Her breasts bounced with each push. Tense urgent fingers ran up his thighs.

"I've been thinking about this for days," he said. "It's been all I can do not to touch you."

She understood. During the frenetic hum of her days or the silent still moments of the night, her thoughts often strayed to him.

The tempo between them rose, and energy in her swelled until finally it exploded inside her. She tipped back her head and growled his name, too lost in desire to be ashamed.

He waited until the last of the shudders had passed through her body and she opened her eyes. He cupped a handful of her hair in his fist and held her head steady as he moved faster and faster in her.

"Look at me," he growled.

She couldn't take her gaze from his features as he clenched his fingers tighter into her hair. His power snapped between them as she watched the play of agony and ecstasy on his face and finally his body went rigid.

He collapsed on top of her and his rapid heartbeat thrummed against her chest. For several long seconds they lay, too spent to speak.

Finally, he rolled on his side facing her, his arm

draped over her belly. Again, it felt as if he wanted to stake a claim.

"You do that to me," he rasped. He took her hand and laid it on his beating heart. "No one else does that to me."

The muscle drummed wildly under her fingertips. "What is it with you? Why can't I just do this and walk away?"

He opened his eyes and looked at her. "Admit it. It's more than just sex."

"Yes."

He traced a circle around her belly button. "How can an attraction be so strong?"

She turned her head toward him. "We are all about adrenaline. Pure energy. Both burn hot, but don't last."

"Are you tired of me?"

"No."

"Good. I can't imagine I'll get tired of you."

"You will. It is the nature of men and women."

"Maybe I will get tired of you. But I'm thinking it will take time. A long, long time."

Even a long, long time didn't feel adequate.

He traced a strand of hair out of her eyes. "Tell me your secret."

In this moment she felt closer to him than she had to anyone in her life. The walls dropped, and she felt so vulnerable. She didn't want to lose him, but it was better to tell him now and cut her losses. If he hated her for what she was about to say, then better now than later.

She shifted her gaze to the ceiling. Tears filled her eyes and trailed down the sides of face. "Sooner is my child. Not Mariah's."

The silence in the room was heavy and broken only by the hammering of her heart.

He rolled on his side and faced her. His gaze was unreadable. "She doesn't look like you."

"No. She looks like my mother and my sister. There are no traces of me in her. But she is mine. I was sixteen when she was born." Fear lingered behind the words as she waited for rejection and censure. "You see, I told you the tangles were thicker than you realized."

He shifted his weight on top of her so that they were almost nose to nose. "Who is her father?"

"A boy who lied about his name and his love so that he could seduce me."

"Not Grady."

"No."

His gaze searched hers an extra beat before relief flickered. "She's a lot like you. She's got your spirit. When I interviewed her, she felt so familiar to me, but I couldn't place her."

Tears fell down the sides of her face and dripped on the mattress. "Aren't you disappointed in me or angry?"

"No."

"Why?"

He traced a strand of hair from her eyes. "My heart breaks for the kid that was alone and desperate for a better life for herself and her baby."

"I'm not that kid anymore."

"She's still driving the bus, Charlotte. That kid, Grace, is the reason you are where you are."

"For so long I just wanted to forget Grace."

"Stop trying to forget her. She's not going anywhere, and I don't want her to. She's a part of you and

I like all your parts." He kissed her on the lips. "Have you told Sooner?"

"No. She thinks Mariah was her mother. Grady lied to Sooner about her mother. I'm sure he was doing it to spite me for leaving and punish me for Mariah's death. And I've been too scared to correct her."

"But you are going to tell her."

"Yes. I have to tell her."

"Do you want me with you?"

"No. I'll have to do that one on my own."

"Let me know what I can do."

"You do not want to get dragged in my family drama."

He brushed a strand of hair from her forehead. "You act like I'm afraid of a little trouble."

She stared into his dark and determined gaze. "Why do you want me? Why don't you find yourself someone sweet, uncomplicated, and who isn't terrified of commitment or has an eighteen-year-old kid? You are a good-looking man, Daniel Rokov. I would think you could find someone a little more perfect."

The creases around his eyes deepened when he smiled. "I got a thing for you, counselor. And as much as I've tried, I can't shake it."

"My baggage could get a little heavy."

"Let me be the judge." He kissed her. "You ever reconsidered breaking bread with me?"

Nervous laughter bubbled as she swiped away another tear. "You should be running for the hills at this point."

"Is that a yes or no to dinner?"

"I did break bread with you. At your mother's kitchen table no less."

"I was thinking more along the lines of a date."

She smiled. "Us on a date. I'm not sure if I can picture that, detective."

"Daniel. Call me Daniel."

She traced the strong line of his jaw. "I haven't told Sooner the truth, and when I do, my life could get messy."

"Give me a real obstacle, Charlotte." His hand slid up her belly, and his knuckle brushed the underside of her breast.

"The one I just gave is fairly significant."

"You're going to have to do better than that." He frowned. "Let me share this with you."

She traced the line of his jaw with her thumb. "I won't blame you if you change your mind."

"Stop yammering. We need to get dressed. The movers will be here in minutes."

"That would be embarrassing if they found us. What would people say?" Her tone was light but the meaning wasn't. People were going to talk a lot. Not just about them but her past and Sooner.

He nudged her side. "Break bread with me, counselor."

Any kind of real relationship with him was so, so foolish. It would end. It was a matter of time. Tangles ruined things. "Fine. Dinner."

As she rose, he grabbed her by the waist. "Is that a tattoo on your lower back?"

Immediately she pulled free and righted her pants. "No."

He rose up off the bed and refastened his pants. "It's kind of sexy."

"It's not."

"Sure it is. Let me see it."

She faced him. "No. And please do not tell anyone."

"No one knows about it?"

"No."

"If it bothers you so much, why didn't you just have it removed?"

"It's a reminder that Grace Wells was capable of doing some really stupid things. It is a reminder that I should think long and hard before I act."

He brushed the hair off her forehead with his index finger. "You didn't think too hard about us."

She hadn't thought at all. She simply reacted. "And that is what worries me."

His hand dropped to her waist. "Can I see it?"

She clamped her hand over his. "No. No you cannot."

His hand easily slipped out of her grip. "Pretty please."

"Why?"

"I don't want any secrets between us. Plus, I'm thinking it's going to be pretty hot."

"It's not hot."

"Let me be the judge."

Again she could say no. But why start now? She gave him her back and lowered the elastic.

"It's a tiger."

"Mariah and I thought we were so clever when we got these. We thought we were different."

He traced the tiger with his finger. "I like it. And it suits you. You are a tiger." He kissed her on the shoulder in such a tender way that it made her still. She had the urge to melt into his body, and forget about the movers. She wanted to make love to him. Love. Not sex.

The front door buzzed. She sighed. "That must be the movers."

"I'll help you finish packing."

"There's not much to do. Just get back to your case, and I'll finish up as they carry out the rest."

"Are you tossing me out?"

"Yes."

"Why?"

"Because I can't think with you around. And I need to think to make sure this job gets done right. Too many things going in too many places."

"You're not keeping everything?"

"No. I'm downsizing and simplifying big time."

"Why?"

"It's time."

Chapter 22

Sooner flipped the *Closed* sign on her shop to *Open* and stood back smiling. She hugged her arms over her chest feeling a thrill of excitement. She was officially a business owner. She backed away from the door and slowly took a seat behind the table she'd set up for her readings. With a critical eye she surveyed her shop. Mark had gone home sick for the day so she was officially in charge. And it felt good.

The deep purple walls gave the room a soft moody vibe that would enhance her readings. Setting, Grady had always said, was important to the right mood. She'd draped swatches of purple fabrics on the walls, which she'd hoped would hide her bad paint job and the uneven spots in the wallboard. She was too early in the process to have retail items for sale but that would come. She had big dreams for this place.

The bronze Indian bells Mark had allowed her to hang over the front door clanged, and she tried not to smile too much. She didn't want to look excited or desperate, but mysterious—almost as if she was doing the client the favor. She started to shuffle her tarot cards.

A man stepped in and glanced around the shop. He was dressed in khakis and a dark blue collared shirt cuffed with gold links at his wrist. He wore his hair short and neatly combed and a wedding band that had a soft patina that suggested he'd been married several years. Conservative. Uptight. Those words clanged in her head and she couldn't imagine a guy like him here, searching the cards for answers.

Immediately her heart dropped. "Can I help you?"

He glanced around the shop, assessing and cataloging. "I was looking for the card shop."

He wanted directions. Of course. She almost laughed. "Down the street on the corner and next to the pizza shop. You can't miss it."

Smiling, he looked at her for the first time. "Thanks."

Ask for the sale. It had been one of Grady's mantras. If you don't ask, you'll never know. "Interested in a reading?"

He held up his hands. "I don't think so. I'm just looking for an anniversary card for my wife."

Anxiety churned and she reminded herself that he was no different than any dude that wandered into her tent. "Let me read you and then I'll tell you the perfect note to write in the card." Most guys couldn't write much beyond *I love ya* on a card. Nice but not totally inspiring.

The guy laughed but hesitated. "The perfect note."

"Perfect. The goodwill that comes your way will be well worth the twenty bucks."

"Twenty bucks. I can write 'I Love You' for free."

"If you want a hot steamy night on your anniversary, you're gonna have to do better than those three words."

He let the door close behind him, and he took a step into the shop. She imagined herself fishing, line in the water, and the fish had just grabbed a hold of her bait. What guy, even an uptight dude like this, wouldn't explore the possibility of hot steamy sex with his wife?

"So what do I have to do?" he asked.

"Sit in the chair and let me read your cards. I'll give you a few insights and then tell you what to write."

"This is a con?"

"No con." She sounded calm, maybe even a little ethereal, a word she'd looked up online just yesterday. "Spiritual insights." Shuffling the cards, she nodded to the chair by the desk. "It will be the best twenty dollars you ever spent."

He shrugged, glanced around as if checking to make sure no one was peeking in the shop. "Yeah, sure. Why not?" He pulled out the twenty and handed it to her.

Tucking the twenty in her empty cash drawer, her smile warmed. "Do you have a name?"

"Honestly," he said, leaning toward her. "I'd rather not give it. This is just a little weird for me, and I half expect someone to jump out with a camera and tell me I've been punked."

"No cameras. No worries. Just you and me and the cards."

He relaxed back in his chair. "Great."

She set the shuffled deck in front of him. "Now I need for you to shuffle the cards."

"Why?"

"So you can put your energy into them. And once you've shuffled them three times, divide the stack into three even piles."

"Will do." Long neat fingers shuffled and divided the cards.

She set a timer at her side for fifteen minutes and then arranged the cards carefully and deliberately in the Celtic cross pattern. She'd give her first customer a reading that gave him some answers but raised others as well. The other questions often prompted people to buy more time or return later.

Carefully she studied the ten cards. The Judge. The Destroyer. Nothingness. It was an unusual spread for a man that seemed so mild. "I think there is more to you than I first realized."

"That's what I keep telling my boss." His eyes danced with laughter.

She lowered her gaze back to the cards. Death sat in the center, and this, of course, could simply mean change. But . . . this grouping did not feel like change. It felt like emptiness, and when she closed her eyes, she had the sense that she was falling into a great abyss. A cold chill passed through her body. She'd never experienced a reading like this.

That man leaned forward and studied her with an intensity that made her stomach churn. "You look so much like her," he whispered.

Her eyes snapped open. "What?"

"You look like her."

"Who?"

He smiled. "A woman who once read my cards. You look so much like her."

"Are you certain I've not read your cards before?" she said. "Perhaps at the carnival last week?"

"This is my first time in this shop."

"Our paths have crossed before."

She stared at him, feeling energy buzz from the cards into her fingertips. On reflex, she moved her foot to the panic button Grady had always maintained under her desk. But it was not there. Grady was not at the ready to save her. Mark had gone home sick. She was on her own.

He cocked his head. "Are you going to give me my reading? I need to know what to say to my wife so that she'll forgive me and take me back."

"You said you were buying her an anniversary card."

"It is our anniversary. She hasn't gotten her divorce yet."

She opened the cash drawer and laid his twenty between them. "I don't think that I can help you. Sorry."

"Why not? Now you've got me curious. What do you see in the cards?"

Tell him what he wants to hear. "She loves you. And she will take you back. She will remember her love for you."

His gaze sharpened. "Really?"

"Yes. Really. Now I must go, sir. I've a party to work this evening."

He didn't touch the money. "I don't want a refund. I want you to tell me what you see."

"That your future is bright and wonderful."

He rose, but this time when he stood, tension gripped him, sharpening every muscle in his body. He'd first seemed affable and a bit of a fool. But no more. "I think that you are right. I feel good about the future."

"Good."

"Do you feel good about the future?"

She rose. "Me? Of course I do."

"That's good. You should feel good about it."

A tentative smile teased the edge of her lips. "Because of my new business."

"Because God is going to cleanse you of your sins and set you free." He smiled and rose.

"Who are you?"

"Doesn't really matter."

He turned and very calmly left the shop. For several seconds the bells jangled and swayed. She got up and ran to the door and locked it.

"Shit. A nut on the first day."

She glanced at the clock, and seeing she was going to be late even if she hurried, she grabbed her satchel and moved to the back of the shop. She'd parked in the back alley.

Sooner shut off the lights, except for the three glowing lava lamps that Mark kept burning, and exited the back door. She shoved her key in the lock, twisted the bolt in place, and then jingled the handle to make sure the door was locked.

Under the glow of the moonlight and a blinking street lamp, she moved to her beat-up Ford pickup truck. She shoved her key into the lock.

She was looking forward to tonight. She liked Charlotte and thought the two of them might be good for each other. She could use a little polishing and Aunt Charlotte could use a little mussing up.

As she opened the door and tossed her purse on the seat, a strong hand banded around her waist and another clamped over her mouth. She immediately kicked and clawed at the hands. She jabbed an elbow and heard her attacker grunt. *Hope I broke a bone, motherfucker.*

"You are an abomination. But I won't send your worthless soul to hell before it is cleansed."

She dug under the folds of her gown and found her phone. He snatched it from her, dropped it to the ground, and smashed it with his boot.

He jabbed a needle in her neck and shoved in a plunger. Spots quickly formed in front of her eyes as her body lost control. God, was she going to die at the very start of her new life?

Maybe Grady had been right. Maybe she should have stayed with him where she was safe.

Her vision went dark and her legs slumped. Her world went black.

Charlotte's nerves were in shreds after her confession to Daniel today. And tattered emotions aside, the movers had also arrived—a half hour late. She'd spent the morning supervising the move, cringing when movers dinged a wall and yelping when they'd dropped her sofa. A panicked call to the handyman and a little pleading had him at her condo by three to patch and paint the wall. By the time she'd written him a check, the paint on the newly smoothed wall corner was drying.

By five, everything had either gone into storage, to charity, or to her new apartment, a cramped, unorganized mess. Thankfully, she'd kept her evening dress she'd planned to wear to Angie's fund-raiser in her car along with her hair and makeup gear. Tomorrow would be all about sorting, organizing, and making sense of her new place.

It would have been so easy to sequester herself behind the boxes in her new apartment, pour a glass of wine, and hide in a hot tub. There were enough legitimate reasons to bail on Angie's charity event. But Angie had worked hard on her Halloween fund-raiser, and it did mean a lot to her. Charlotte could be a bitch and a ball buster, and there were many who didn't like her. But no one truthfully could say she'd ever broken a promise.

She'd told Angie she'd be at the party, and so she shoved her raw emotions down deep inside her and put on a grand smile. Faking-it was a specialty she'd honed over the last eighteen years.

She wouldn't talk to Sooner about the truth tonight, but the day fast approached. To avoid it now, no matter what her personal cost, would be far too cruel to Sooner.

By seven, she stood in the hotel staring at the ball-room decorated with drapes of orange and black fabric, pumpkins, and black and white lights that gave off a spooky glow. There was a buffet table on the long wall and three bars set up around the room.

Angie deserved real credit. Not only had she cajoled the Regis into donating their ballroom for the night, but she'd also managed to get a band to donate their services, the caterer to give her a great deal, and a dec-orator to dress the room for a nominal fee.

Angie had called upon all the areas rich and elite to come and be entertained, so they'd open their wallets. And it appeared they had come in force.

Charlotte had worn her hair loose and curled around her shoulders. She'd chosen a sleek black dress that skimmed her curves and dipped low in the back. High heels and diamond earrings and bracelet completed a simple and elegant look. She'd been

unable to bring herself to wear a costume as Angie
had requested, but she had compromised and purchased a lovely mask to carry and wear if need be.

Angie, wearing a sleek red dress, wore a red witch's
hat and makeup that made her green eyes pop like a
cat's. "I should be grateful for the mask."

Charlotte smiled as she saw a group of noted busi-
nessmen and their wives chatting. They were dressed
as members of the Starship *Enterprise*. "I'm feeling un-
derdressed."

She smiled. "Good."

"You've outdone yourself, Angie."

"So far it's going well. I think it will be a profitable
night." A waiter passed with a tray of champagne and
both women declined. "I was hoping your girl, Sooner,
would be here by now."

Your girl. "She's late?"

"By almost an hour. I'd asked her to be here early
for set up."

"That surprises me. She was looking forward to
this."

"Tips alone would be generous."

"Have you called her?"

"Twice. No answer."

She opened her slim black purse and checked her
cell. No calls. Worry crept up her spine. "I can go track
her down."

"She was my big draw. I mean the clowns are fun
and the juggler entertaining, but people like the idea
of walking on the dark side."

"The dark side?"

"You know what I mean. I don't care how rich or
famous someone is, they are just as curious about
the future as the next guy." Angie waved away her

concerns. "She's likely forgotten and working late at her shop."

"Then why doesn't she answer her phone?"

"Maybe she turns it off during readings. I mean a cell sure would break the vibe."

That made sense. Sooner, like her, had been raised never to break character. "I'll have a seat at her table and fill in until she gets here."

"She was going to read tarot cards. Do you have cards?"

"No. I generally don't carry tarot cards," she said, smiling. "But I can read palms." Maybe Sooner had just blown them off. She was young and pretty and men loved her. And she'd missed that one appointment with Charlotte.

"You can read palms?"

Angie's relief prompted a smile. "You haven't heard the tidbits about my carnie days?"

"I had, I kinda thought you'd cracked a joke, and it had gotten blown up."

"No. No joke. I worked the circuit when I was a kid with my family."

Angie laughed. "One day you're going to have to tell me all about it."

The band filed onto the bandstand in the corner and started tuning up. "It's not so very interesting."

"Charlotte, you were raised in a carnival and not in high society as we'd all thought. Sorry to burst your bubble, but that's interesting."

Charlotte let her gaze move across the room. "Where's my table?"

"The red draped one over there. I've posted a sign, and I think you already have a line."

Charlotte arched a brow. If you'd bet her two weeks

ago she'd be here now, reading palms, she'd have wagered everything she owned against you sure she'd win. And yet here she was with no time to fret or worry but simply to perform. "Okay."

"Are you any good at this?"

"I used to be pretty good back in the day."

"Kinda like riding a bike?"

"Let's hope."

Angie stared at her as if seeing her for the first time. "So were palms your thing or did you read cards?"

"Angie, do you want me to trip down memory lane or read palms?"

"Honestly, I'm dying to hear your story. But I can wait."

"Good."

As she moved toward her table, her worries about Sooner grew with each passing minute. Had Grady told Sooner the truth to drive a wedge between her and Charlotte? *No, you wouldn't do that. You know Sooner's too curious and direct. If you told her about me, I'd be the first person she'd find.*

She flipped open her phone and called Daniel's cell. It went to voice mail on the first ring. She listened to his deep clear voice, "You have reached Detective Daniel Rokov. Leave a message."

"Hey, this is Charlotte. I'm at Angie's thing. Sooner never showed. Might not be anything, but something doesn't feel right. Could you send a car by her shop?" She dropped her voice a notch. "I appreciate it, Daniel. Thanks."

She closed the phone, knowing Rokov would take care of the matter. A sense of calm washed over her anxious nerves when she thought about him. Like it or not, he had worked his way under her skin.

She moved toward her table, stopping and chatting with people she knew from the community. She made a point to ask folks for their names, what they thought about readings, and what they hoped to gain. She filed away the tidbits and invited all to stop by and visit her so she could read their palms. She'd been working the crowds since she was thirteen, and it was something she did better than anyone.

Judge Lawless and his wife appeared at her table. "Counselor."

Charlotte's grin was broad and welcoming. "Judge and Mrs. Lawless. Have a seat, be my first customers."

The judge looked grim and his wife reserved. Neither looked as if they wanted to be here. But the judge understood politics and never missed an opportunity to shake the right hands.

He pulled two twenties from his pocket and tucked them in the fish bowl on Charlotte's table. "It's for charity?"

"All proceeds go toward the children's cancer wing at Alexandria Hospital." She grinned and waved her hand toward the seats in front of her desk. "This is an opportunity you cannot pass up."

Mrs. Lawless smiled coolly. The judge scowled.

Charlotte sat. "Now who is going first?"

The two looked at each other, he nodded, and Mrs. Lawless sat in her seat. "Me, I suppose."

Charlotte grinned. She'd heard faint rumors that the couple's marriage wasn't doing well. Some said he'd moved out, but the judge, to her knowledge, had not spoken of a separation. No doubt her past, like their separation, would soon be churning on the rumor mill for months.

"So let me see, what you have going on here?" She

studied the deeply rutted lines in the woman's palm. "You have a very strong lifeline. You've lived many past lives."

"I have?" Polite but not impressed.

"At least eight." Charlotte traced the line. "And I think you're going to live a long life."

Mrs. Lawless stiffened a little. "Good."

"Not impressed, Wellington." The judge rolled his eyes and walked away.

Mrs. Lawless sighed as she watched her husband walk away. "He can be blunt."

"I've noticed that in court." He had a reputation for being a real hard-ass and most attorneys groaned when they drew Lawless.

Charlotte suspected the judge's wife was just as hard a sale as him. However, she'd met, welcomed, and conquered similar folk. "Let's try this again."

Without her husband looming, she relaxed a little. "Sure."

Charlotte traced the woman's lifeline. "The judge has promised you a vacation, but he is hesitating."

Mrs. Lawless's eyes narrowed. "We've canceled some of the best vacations. No secret there."

She glanced at Mrs. Lawless's small diamond engagement ring sandwiched against a larger, brighter solitaire diamond. Life had been good to them, but she still cherished the ring he'd given her on their wedding day. "But he loves you very much. Vacations don't matter to him, but you do."

Mrs. Lawless stiffened and pulled her hand free.

Charlotte knew she'd hit a nerve. "I see more. Don't you want to hear it?"

She hesitated. "I'm not sure."

"A faint heart never wins."

Challenged, the woman extended her hand.

"I see vacation pamphlets lying about the house and notes on trips." When Mrs. Lawless didn't respond, Charlotte knew she'd missed the mark and quickly turned the negative into a positive. "These pamphlets are old. From vacations never taken."

Mrs. Lawless's grip softened. "Yes."

"Get more brochures, Mrs. Lawless. Plan your dream vacation, and I believe you will find that for which you search."

The older woman's face had softened, and she stared at Charlotte, clearly surprised. "What am I searching for?"

"For the marriage you had when you first married. I believe it is there, but you must dig for it."

"What if he doesn't want to find it?"

Charlotte glanced up and looked beyond Mrs. Lawless to her husband, who kept stealing glances in their direction. "He wants it."

"Thank you."

"Thank you for your donation."

After Mrs. Lawless left, Charlotte had a stream of customers. The old tactics of using body language as well as the bits of information she'd collected as she walked to the table added credibility to her readings.

The evening progressed smoothly enough. She read palms, joked with attorneys, judges, and clients, but all the while she kept glancing toward the door hoping to see Sooner rush in, harried and full of good excuses to explain her no-show status.

Sooner never arrived. And when Charlotte could break away to call, she never answered her phone. Though the event was proving to be a real success, Charlotte's worries grew.

"So you are a popular attraction." Levi Kane's comment had her raising her head.

Charlotte smiled out of habit rather than joy. "It seems to be going well."

He sat at her table. "You've had quite the line for the last hour."

"Most love their fortune read."

He pulled two twenties from his wallet and stuffed them in her jar, already crammed full of bills. "It's for a great cause."

"That it is." She held out her open palm to him. "Let me read you."

He grinned. "I don't go in for that kind of thing. Just a little out there, if you know what I mean. Shame my wife isn't here. She loves that kind of stuff."

"Where is she this evening?"

"Home. Our youngest is sick with a cold. We were both looking forward to a night out, but when your kid gets sick, that's the way it goes."

Without the distraction of work or a palm reading, there wasn't much to say. "Sure I can't offer you a glimpse into the future?"

He laughed. "It's all hocus-pocus."

"Harmless hocus-pocus."

He studied her a moment. "Harmless? You sure? Old Darren on *Bewitched* was always getting turned into a rock or sporting donkey ears."

Laughter eased some of her tension. "I promise I won't turn you into a black cat or give you donkey ears."

He glanced from side to side, always aware of who was watching. Nearby a photographer from the paper snapped pictures. Levi reminded her of herself. Once you stepped outside your front door, it was game-on. "Thanks, but I'll take a pass."

She smiled. "You are always thinking. Always looking to the next horizon."

"I'm ambitious."

"I see you running for state office. Perhaps even national office."

He shrugged. "It's no secret the sky is the limit for me."

He wanted office, true. But he possessed a hunger for power. He wanted power over life and death. "I think you'll be a judge, maybe even a senator in the very near future."

"I like the sound of that."

Rokov had been in the medical examiner's office when Charlotte had called. He'd felt his phone vibrate but had been unable to check messages for several hours. As soon as he played her message, he broke away and drove over to Sooner Tate's shop. When he finally stood outside Ageless, it was past ten. The building was dark, and there didn't seem to be any signs of trouble. But calm waters often hid trouble.

He got out of the car, flashlight in hand, and crossed the street to the front door. The doorknob was locked. He shone his light in the picture window, letting it skim over the front counter, glowing lava lamps, books, and all sorts of crap. He didn't see anything out of the ordinary.

"Kid, have you blown Charlotte off?"

He shook his head. Damn kid. He was half tempted to walk away when he thought about the alley that ran behind the store. Five minutes to check and confirm the kid was well and truly gone and then he'd call Charlotte.

He got back in his car and drove around the corner

and into the alley. His lights shone on the narrow alley and landed on the truck parked by a dented blue Dumpster. He parked beside the car, unclipped his sidearm, and rested his hand on the gun's handle. He walked toward the truck, and shone his light into the interior. His feet crunched on something, and he glanced down to see a smashed cell phone. "Shit."

Inside the truck, Sooner's satchel purse lay on the seat as did her keys. He tried the door. Unlocked. He removed his gun from its holster as he reached for his radio.

"Dispatch, this is Detective Daniel Rokov. I need units at 101 Washington Street. I've got signs of a possible attack."

"Will Dispatch units, Detective Rokov."

He called Sinclair. "I need you to get over to Sooner Tate's place on Washington. I think the killer has been here."

"How do you know?" She was at the office, but her voice sounded rough with fatigue. They'd all been putting long hours into this investigation.

"Her truck is here and so are her purse and keys, but someone smashed her cell phone."

"Sooner was his perfect victim."

"I know." What would Charlotte say when he told her that her child had been kidnapped?

Sinclair must have picked up on the extra tension in his voice. "He holds his victims for several days."

"Which is why we might have a chance this time."

Patrol cars arrived in minutes, and soon the scene was filled with uniforms and a forensics team.

The shop owner was summoned and he arrived blurry-eyed and annoyed to unlock the front door. While forensics worked inside the store and around the truck, Rokov and Sinclair walked up and down Washington Street showing copies of Sooner's mug shot, which Sinclair had brought.

Most of the stores were closed this time of night but a couple of restaurants and a movie-rental store remained open. The clerk in the movie-rental store reported that he'd seen a black SUV parked in front of Sooner's.

"What made you notice it?" Rokov said.

The kid with red hair and freckles shrugged. "Everyone on the street has noticed Sooner. She's something to look at. We all knew she was set to open today."

"And did she?"

"Not until the end of the day. I saw her flip her sign from *Closed* to *Open* late in the day."

"Late as in when?" Sinclair said.

"I'd been watching *Braveheart,* and it was the final battle scene. What's that, a couple of hours into the movie? Anyway, I started the flick when I arrived at three. So about five."

She'd been scheduled to arrive at Charlotte's party by seven. "How was she dressed?" Rokov said.

"Smoking H.O.T. She had on this long white dress that hugged her curves. Her hair was pinned up, and she wore a lot of makeup. Not too much, but enough to make her look supersexy."

"You saw all that from here?" Rokov said.

The kid grinned and pulled a pair of binoculars out from behind his desk. "I like to keep an eye on stuff."

"What can you tell me about the SUV?" He glanced toward the store's security camera and wondered if it cast its lens toward Sooner's.

"Black. Tinted windows. I kinda thought she had a

date with a big shot. She's the kind of gal who dates big shots. But the car pulled away and drove off."

"You see the big shot?"

"He never got out of the car." Maybe he pulled around back and picked her up in the alley? Maybe the big shot didn't want to be noticed.

"You see anyone go into the shop?"

"I had a couple of customers so I got a little distracted. I don't know. Hey, is Sooner okay?"

"We hope so." He glanced toward the surveillance camera. "That work?"

The kid glanced at the camera. "Not exactly."

"What's that mean?"

"It works, but the outlet it's plugged into is dead. The owner has an electrician coming."

"Great."

"But check with the pub on the corner. I hear he keeps his cameras on and running all the time."

"I'll do that."

They moved four stores down and into the pub. The sound of laughter mingled with the steady beat of music. Smoke filled the air. A bouncer, a six-foot-eight black dude with a name tag that read RJ, greeted Rokov and Sinclair.

"What do the cops want?" RJ said.

There'd been a time during Rokov's undercover days when he'd never have been pegged for a cop. He'd been the master at blending and vanishing. Rokov tucked his ID back in his pocket. "We need to see your tapes."

With a nod, RJ indicated a reed-thin white guy talking to a waitress. The guy had dark, balding hair slicked back away from an angular face. His side vision caught sight of Rokov and Sinclair, and he quickly excused the waitress and moved toward them.

"What can I do for you officers?"

"Surveillance tapes," Rokov said.

The thin man shrugged and motioned them toward a side office. Once he shut the door, the blare of the music eased. "There a problem?"

"We don't know," Rokov said. He glanced at a bank of six television screens behind a desk abutting a wall. "But I'd like to see the tapes from the camera you have out front."

The thin man turned. "Number one. East on Washington. Sure." He punched a couple of buttons. "What time frame?"

"Let's start with today around five."

"Pretty specific."

"Can you pull it up?"

"Sure." He tapped a couple of buttons and the image of 4:45 p.m. popped up. The camera didn't take in all of Sooner's storefront, only the far west side. The thin man played the images frame by frame. Cars passed. People passed. But without a direct angle on the front door, it was impossible to see who entered the shop.

The black SUV that the video kid had mentioned drove slowly by the shop.

Rokov leaned in. The tape caught a portion of the license. ADEJ. "Can you copy that for me?"

"Sure."

He downloaded the images, shoved a CD into a slot, and hit record. "You'll have a copy in a minute. What happened?"

"You noticed the new age shop across the street?"

"And the new psychic? Yeah. She's a looker. What's she done? Drugs. Prostitution?"

"What makes you think she's done something?"

"She's been in business less than a day, and she's got cops on my doorstep. Plus that weird old guy has been lurking around."

"What weird old guy?"

"I don't know who he is, but I caught him watching her shop a couple of times. He never stayed long."

Grady Tate. "If I get a few pictures, could you identify him?"

"Sure."

Charlotte saw the flashing police lights in front of Sooner's the instant she pulled onto Washington Street. She parked and got out of her car. It was easy to spot Rokov.

She hurried to him, her high heels clicking against the pavement. "Daniel."

Rokov turned, as did his partner.

Sinclair raised a questioning and amused brow. "Daniel? Christ, can I call them or what?"

Rokov moved toward Charlotte. "You were right to call. There were signs of a struggle in the alley."

Her stomach clenched. "Did you find Sooner?"

"Not yet. But we're doing all that we can."

Feeling both helpless and angry, she shook her head. "I knew something was wrong."

"Detective." Rokov turned toward a forensics tech. "Yes."

"We found a twenty-dollar bill in the desk. I dusted it and pulled two nice thumb and index prints from the edge."

"Thanks. Let me know the second you have an ID."

"Do you think the killer gave it to her?" Charlotte gripped his arm, uncaring if anyone saw her.

He patted her on her hand. "If he did, then we might be able to identify him and find her."

Sooner awoke in stages as the fog cleared from her brain. Her eyelids felt heavy and her mouth dry. She realized she was sitting in a metal chair. Her arms were tied to the chair's arms and her feet to the legs. She tried to rock from side to side and knock the chair to the side but discovered it was bolted to the floor.

Her vision cleared to a dimly lit, plain windowless room made of concrete. All she could see in front of her was a metal door. The room was empty to the right and to the left. She craned her neck behind her but could only make out some sort of tub and a stack of cinderblocks.

Heart now hitting her ribs, she tried to twist her hands free. All she managed to do was cut the tender flesh of her wrists as she twisted and turned.

"Shit. Where am I?" She screamed but the thick walls boomeranged her voice right back. She'd been in fixes: drunken townies looking for fun or a mugger aiming to grab her cash. But nothing, nothing like this had happened to her before.

The door opened and a brighter light switched on and drowned the room in light. The brightness made her wince and turn away.

"What do you want?" she said.

"Your confession."

Her pupils adjusted and she looked up. Whoever this creep was, he stood just behind the light so that she couldn't see his face clearly. She did make out the outline of a robe and hood. What was he, some motherfucking monk? God help her. This wasn't about sex or money. This guy was crazy. "Why do I have to confess?"

"I can't send you to God without a confession."

She strained against her bindings, letting the rope dig into her skin. Pain kept her mind focused and her panic tethered. She'd been dealing with crazies since she was a kid and knew the futility of arguing. They believed what they believed. "God doesn't want me with or without a confession."

"God wants you clean and pure," he said.

His kind got off on fear and control. He had control, but she'd withhold fear as long as possible. She managed a laugh. "That ship has sailed."

"Redemption is always possible no matter how unclean you once were."

"Not in my case. God will want more from me than just a simple confession. I've lied so much. The words will be meaningless to him."

Tension rippled through his body. Good. Keep him off balance. Keep him thinking.

"How would you know what God wants?" he said.

"I know." Her voice didn't wobble or betray the fear tearing her gut.

He crossed the room, grabbed the back of her hair, and jerked hard. "How do you know what God wants, witch?"

Pain pulsed across her scalp. "I know He wants more. You need to find more like me or He will be angry."

Her captor released her hair and stepped back. He

studied her with narrowed eyes. "He wants the other witch, too, doesn't He?"

"That's right. He wants us both."

"I'd thought to wait and save her for last, but maybe not."

She didn't know who he referenced, but hoped she could buy enough time to get free and get out of here before he returned.

He stepped back and moved to the door. "I'll take care of you both. It seems right that you two go to God together."

When he slammed the door behind him, she closed her eyes and started to weep. "Forgive me."

Chapter 23

Daniel had told Charlotte to go home. He wanted her locked behind her apartment door, safe and secure. But just sitting on her hands and waiting for someone else to save Sooner wasn't an option. She did go home, but only to change quickly into jeans, a thick sweater, and sneakers.

As she hurried back to her car, she thought about Sooner lost and afraid and calling for her. She hoped to put aside all the time and memories they'd lost. She'd hoped they'd make new memories. Now she feared that window into the future was closing quickly.

She stiffened her spine. "Feel sorry for yourself later, Grace."

Daniel was still trying to get a warrant to search Grady's trailer. Likely it wouldn't be until midday when the judge signed it. But she didn't need a search warrant. She wasn't concerned about convictions or due process. She simply wanted to find Sooner.

She slid behind the wheel, fired up the engine, and backed out. "Find Sooner. Find Sooner."

Finding signs to the I-395 on-ramp, she headed south and then followed the interstate and back roads to the carnival. Even this early the road was crowding with traffic. When her phone rang, she was glancing in her rearview mirror at a black truck that was annoyingly close to her bumper. She slid into the right lane as she hit Send. "Charlotte Wellington."

"It's Angie." Her voice sounded rough with fatigue. "Have the police found Sooner?"

"I haven't heard. I'm headed to Grady's now."

"Are you going alone?"

"I'll be fine."

"Malcolm says Grady is a suspect."

"I don't care what they are calling him now, I just want to find Sooner."

"Charlotte, does Daniel know where you are?" Concern dripped from the words.

"No."

"He needs to know."

"I'll be fine. I've handled Grady before and I will again."

"Daniel should know what you're doing."

"I'll tell him." The SUV's headlights bounced off her rearview mirror, temporarily blinding her.

Angie hesitated. "Is there anything I can do to help?"

"No. No." She softened her tone. "But thank you."

"I'm sorry."

Charlotte raised her chin. "Thanks."

"I know this isn't the best time, but thanks for last night. You were a big hit. We raised over two hundred thousand."

The truck passed her and zoomed ahead. "Well done."

"I couldn't have done it without you."

"Sure you could have." Her exit approaching, she put on her blinker and took it.

"Call me when you find Sooner."

"I will."

Tears glistened as she hung up, checked her screen to make sure no one had called while she was on with Angie, and then wove through the back streets toward the carnival. As she approached the carnival entrance, she picked up her phone and called Daniel. It rang once. Twice.

"Charlotte." His deep even voice sounded tired yet chocked with a familiarity shared between people who were intimate.

She could have argued, dismissed, or ignored the tone but didn't. She loved him. "Have you found her?"

"Not yet, we're running those prints through AFIS now."

She parked her car. "No one has seen her?"

"No."

"Have you found Grady?"

"He's still missing. We've had cruisers at the carnival several times, but no one can find him. The cops walked the grounds, but without a warrant, we can't search the structures. We should have that warrant in a couple of hours."

She set her handbrake and turned off the ignition. "Good. Call me if you find something."

"Charlotte, where are you?"

"I'm at the carnival."

"What are you doing there?" The urgency rocketed in his voice.

"I'm looking for Grady. And when I find him, I'll call you."

"Damn it, Charlotte. Go back home. Stay in your apartment today. Keep the door locked. Unpack. I'll call you when I have something."

"I'm not very good at staying put, Daniel."

His voice dropped to a low growl. "Charlotte, get in your car now and drive home."

"I can't do that. I have to find Grady."

"That's my job." He sounded as if he wanted to come through the phone and shake her.

"I know his little tricks and hiding places. I'll find him before you get your warrant."

"Exactly. And then I won't be able to use the evidence."

"Your warrant has nothing to do with me."

"Do not go looking for Grady."

She got out of her car. A breeze blew, chilling her skin. "If it's any consolation, I think I love you."

"Charlotte," he groaned. "Please, go home."

"I'll call back in a few minutes."

She closed the phone and shut it off. The carnival was quiet and all but deserted. The crew would have had a late Friday night and everyone would be sleeping for at least another hour because tonight was the closing and the place would see big crowds.

She spotted Grady's trailer and moved toward it. She tried the silver, chipped handle but discovered it was locked. "You're going to have to do better than that, Grady."

Digging in her purse, she pulled out a metal nail file. Mariah had taught her how to wedge open the lock on Grady's trailer when they were kids. A couple of times they'd pry open the lock and take beers from the fridge and cigarettes from his desk drawer. Mariah had handled the beer and smokes well. Charlotte, after half a cigarette and some beer, had grown light-headed and nauseated. She'd thrown up several times.

"Good times," she quipped.

She reached for the lock when she heard the crunch of footsteps behind her. "Ms. Wellington."

She slid her file between her fingers, a defensive technique she'd learned after the attack several years ago. Slowly, she turned and saw Lonnie White striding toward her. Behind him sat the black SUV she'd noticed following her on the highway.

He jabbed his index finger at her. "I want to talk to you."

She moved away from the trailer, knowing it cut off one of her avenues of retreat. Keeping her expression neutral, she searched around him for signs of anyone else. They were alone.

"It's time you and I talked." Red-rimmed eyes broadcast a hangover, sadness, and anger.

"I don't have time for you."

"We need to talk."

"We have talked. There is nothing else to say." Her hands trembled as she walked toward her car.

He moved quickly in front of her and blocked her path. "Bullshit. You bitched at me enough, but I didn't get to say my piece."

"Sober up, Lonnie, and then we'll talk." The sternness behind the words belied her rising fears. She tried to sidestep him.

Lonnie blocked her, curling dirty, rough fingers into a fist. "You saw to it that Samantha went free. She's a damn witch, and she doesn't deserve to live, let alone walk the streets free."

"What did you call her?"

"A goddamned witch. She cast a fucking spell on my brother, and she killed him. Then you used that legal bullshit and made the jury think she was innocent."

She took a step back. He'd talked about witches and spells. He lived in Raleigh, but he'd been back in Virginia for several weeks. He could have killed those two women in Alexandria.

"Go home, Lonnie. Get some sleep and we will talk later." She fished in her purse for her phone.

His hand shot out, he grabbed her by the collar, and he tugged hard. She stumbled forward and her phone flew out of her hands and skidded across the hard ground.

In a panic, she drove the flat of her hand into his nose, just as a self-defense instructor had explained. The nose was a sensitive spot, and if hit hard enough, could kill. The force of her strike wasn't deadly, but the sharp painful jolt would slow him down enough so she could get to her car.

He seized her throat and squeezed. "I've been wanting to do this for weeks."

She clawed at his hands, screamed, and kicked at his shins. He dodged her kicks and tightened his grip. White spots appeared as she grasped for a full breath. Was her life going to end on the grounds of the carnival? Grady would have a laugh over that.

Somewhere her fogged brain registered the thunder of footsteps running toward her. Daniel? Hope exploded. As he got close, she realized her savior wasn't Daniel but Levi. Where had he come from?

Levi grabbed Lonnie by the back of his head and twisted hard. Lonnie screamed and, now off balance, was forced to release Charlotte's neck. She sucked in a breath and stumbled back as Lonnie fell to the ground. Levi had Lonnie on the ground and his knee in his back.

"Levi?"

"Yes. You're fine."

Lonnie lay on the ground, struggling and squirming. "Let me up. That bitch is gonna pay!"

Levi ground his knee deeper into the man's spine until Lonnie winced and cried out in pain. "I will break your spine in two before I let you get away."

Lonnie shouted several expletives but pain forced him to go limp on the ground. "Charlotte, are you all right?"

"Levi. Where did you come from?"

"I brought my kids back out here last night. My daughter left her coat behind. It's her favorite. Shit, what are the chances I'd be here?"

"I'm just glad you were." Her fingers traced long scratches made by Lonnie's fingernails as he gripped her neck. As adrenaline faded, the wounds grew painful.

"You better get those looked at," Levi said.

"Yeah. You're right."

Lonnie growled. "Let me go. You ain't a cop and you can't hold me."

Levi ground his knee again into Lonnie's spine. "And yet I am."

"I'm gonna sue."

Levi laughed. "I know a good defense attorney who just might help me out with the case."

Charlotte nodded. "My services will be free of charge."

Levi winked at her. "Appreciate it."

Charlotte spotted her phone on the ground and reached for it. "I'll call the cops."

"Open your trunk."

"Why?"

"I need to stow this bird somewhere."

"You can't put me in a car trunk!" Lonnie screamed.

Levi twisted the guy's thumb until he screamed. "Get in the trunk, or I will break your hand."

Lonnie screamed when Levi manipulated his thumb backward. He scrambled to his feet and moved toward Charlotte's BMW as she hurried ahead and fumbled for her keys. With a shaking hand, she opened the trunk. The rising trunk blocked her view of Lonnie and Levi for a moment, and she used the interlude to run a shaking hand through her hair and gather her wits.

Thankfully, Daniel had not been the one to rescue her. He'd have been upset and she sensed he wouldn't have been afraid to lecture. At least Levi didn't have an emotional stake in her life, so he would be cool.

As she tried to calm herself, she heard a grunt and the whoosh of air. She moved around the open trunk door and saw Levi moving toward her. Blood covered his hands.

She glanced at him and then at Lonnie, who now lay on the ground in a thickening pool of his own blood.

"Levi?"

He jumped forward, and before she could process the situation, he drove a needle into her arm and jammed his thumb down on the plunger.

She stared at him, struggling to mesh realities. "Levi?"

He held her as she relaxed involuntarily into his arms. "I've been waiting for you for eighteen years, Grace."

"What?"

Instead of answering, he scooped her up in his arms

and laid her in the trunk of her own car. She stared up
at his smiling face as he slammed the lid closed.

Rokov got the call fifteen minutes after he'd hung
up with Charlotte. Annoyed, tired, and frustrated as
he sped toward the carnival, he'd snapped into the
phone, "Rokov."

"This is Garrison."

He shoved out a breath. "Yeah."

"A patrol returned to the carnival. They found
a body."

His thoughts jumped to Charlotte. "Who?"

"Lonnie White. His throat was cut."

"Was there any sign of Charlotte?"

"No. Why would there be?"

"She called me just minutes ago and told me she was
looking for Grady. She thought he could help us find
Sooner."

Garrison hesitated, clearly detecting the concern
and familiarity. "According to patrol, they spotted a
black BMW driving away from the scene."

"Charlotte drives a BMW."

"A man was behind the wheel."

He took the carnival exit. "I'm almost at the carnival."

"Good, because patrol opened Grady's trailer
searching for the killer. And they found some disturb-
ing images. News articles on several murdered women.
And Levi Kane."

"Levi Kane?"

Garrison shoved out a breath. "Yeah. The prosecutor, who is not answering his cell, home, or office
phones. In fact, I am standing in his office and have

spoken to the night security guards. He's not logged in the building for two days."

"What about his home address?"

"Kier and I can be there in fifteen minutes."

"I'll search Grady's trailer."

"I'll call you as soon as I know something."

Rokov hung up his phone and pulled into the carnival parking lot, now filled with a half-dozen cop cars with flashing lights. He showed his identification and rushed toward the yellow crime scene tape. A white, bloodied sheet covered Lonnie's body.

He moved past the scene to Grady's trailer, where a uniformed officer stood guard. He showed his badge and identified himself before gaining admittance.

The trailer wasn't large. There was a front section with a bed covered with rumpled blankets, a small galley kitchen along the wall, a bathroom with dozens of prescription bottles on the sink, and in the back a larger space with a table and several bench chairs around it. Spread on the table were dozens of articles featuring murders over the last eighteen years. He recognized the two murders that had been picked up by ViCap, but there were others that hadn't been gathered by the system. Not surprising considering they were all in small towns.

Why had Grady saved the articles? Was he the killer or working with the killer? Shit. Mariah was the first to die. And now he was back and two other women had died.

Garrison and Kier arrived at Kane's home just after four in the morning. The Kane home was a neat suburban white clapboard house on a small green lawn.

Leaves peppered the neat front yard. There were pumpkins on the front steps, mock spiderwebs strewn across the bushes, and a ghost made out of an old sheet dangling from an oak.

Garrison checked his watch and then moved to the front door and rang the bell. Several seconds passed and there was no sign of movement. He rang the bell again. Finally, a light flickered on and he heard footsteps. The footsteps paused at the front door and he stood in front of the peephole with his badge held high.

"Alexandria Police," he said.

The door opened to a small, fragile woman. A thick well-worn robe swallowed her slim body, and dark hair framed a pale face. She held a metal baseball bat in her hands. "Can I help you?"

"I'm Detective Garrison with the Alexandria Police. This is my partner, Detective Kier. Is Mr. Kane at home?"

She frowned and lowered the bat. "Levi moved out over three months ago. I can give you the address of his apartment."

Kier glanced at Garrison, his shock mirrored his own face. "I saw him at a fund-raiser last night. He said you weren't there because one of the kids was sick. He gave us the impression that you were happily married."

She glanced behind her as if fearing the noise would have awoken the children. "I've told him to stop doing that. I've told him our marriage can't be fixed. But he won't leave me alone."

"What has he done?"

"Someone broke into my house the other night. They stole jewelry, set the box on the floor, and urinated on it. I knew he could be foul, but he has no limits."

Garrison flexed his fingers. "Did you call the police?"

"No. Levi has too many connections. Why are you asking about Levi?"

Levi is a person of interest in a missing persons case."

"What? Who?"

"Charlotte Wellington. She's a defense attorney."

"I know who she is."

"How?" Garrison said.

She set the bat down. "Levi used to speak about her often."

"What did he say?"

"He didn't like her. He thought she manipulated the law." She twisted the ties of her robe in her hands. "He called her a witch."

"Witch," Garrison said. "Are you sure about that?"

"Yes. I'm sure." Thin lips flattened. "Levi never dealt well with strong women. I'm hardly what anyone would consider aggressive, and we even had our issues."

"Can you tell us what they were?" Kier said. "I wouldn't ask but this is important."

"It doesn't matter. All that matters is that I convinced him to leave."

"How?" Kier demanded.

"I found some things in the basement. Terrible things. I found an attorney and gave what I discovered to him. I told Levi if he didn't leave, I'd go to the media."

"What did you find?"

"Photos of women."

"Who?"

"I don't know who they were. They appeared to be asleep."

"Asleep or dead?" Kier said.

Her shoulders stiffened. "I don't know for sure. But it was enough to make Levi leave."

"You said he came back?"

Her lips flattened. "Yes."

"Who has the pictures now?"

"Like I said, my attorney." Her gaze narrowed. "Where is Levi?"

"Why didn't you come to the police?" Garrison said.

"Because they were just pictures, and there is no proof that Levi took them. And like I said, he has connections."

"Do you have any idea where he might be if not at his apartment?" Garrison said.

"I don't know."

"I think you do," Kier said.

She pursed her lips. "I should get my attorney."

Garrison leaned forward, using the full measure of his height to intimidate her. "You should get an attorney because I am going to prove that you knew those women weren't sleeping but dead."

"I didn't know."

"You've lived with the guy for how long? A decade? You are clearly afraid of him so you know what he can do."

She shoved a trembling hand through her hair. "Our marriage is in trouble. That doesn't mean anything."

"And yet you had to blackmail him into leaving." Garrison shook his head. "I'm going to arrest you if you don't tell me what you know about Levi."

"I'm trying to protect my children."

"You won't be able to protect them from jail," Garrison said.

Tears welled in her eyes. But he had no pity for her. She held evidence that could have prevented the murders of two women. "Where are the photos?"

"Max Green. He's in Fairfax." She rattled off the address.

Garrison wrote it down. "Does Levi have a place where he goes?"

"His father had a house. Levi inherited it a couple of years ago when his father died."

"Where?"

"In Manassas. It's a small house in an old neighborhood. I asked him several times to sell it but he refused."

"What else can you tell me about your husband?" When she hesitated, he said, "We think he has Charlotte as well as a young woman named Sooner."

She wrung her hands together then gathered the folds of her robe tighter. "He's disturbed. I always thought he was quirky early in our marriage, and it didn't bother me. Since his dad died, it's gotten worse."

"What about his mother?"

"I never knew her. She died when he was young, but there was no love lost between his father and his mother. Mr. Kane hated his late wife."

"What else can you tell me about Kane?"

"He reads a great deal about the occult. Witches. In fact, if he saw the Halloween decorations here, he'd have a fit. This is the first year the kids have celebrated Halloween."

Garrison's pulse pounded in his head. As he and Kier raced to the car, he dialed dispatch and asked for squad cars to come to the Kane house. He then spoke to Rokov and told him what was happening. "Kier and

I are headed to Manassas. I'll call Fairfax Police and alert them."

"Tell them not to go in hot," Rokov said. "I don't know what this guy is going to do if he hears sirens."

"Got it." He checked his watch as he started the engine and pulled into traffic. "I can be there in twenty minutes."

"All right."

Shit. Twenty minutes. Almost no time and also a lifetime.

Chapter 24

Sunday, October 31, 7 a.m.

"Charlotte, wake up!"

Charlotte groaned as the annoying voice got louder and louder. She wanted to swat the voice like a pesky fly, but no matter how much she tried to get away from the noises, they just kept getting louder. All she wanted to do was sleep. But the voice pleaded, cajoled, and demanded that she open her eyes.

Slowly, she pried open her lids. The room was dimly lit and at first glance appeared to be quite barren. "Who's there?"

"Oh, thank God! You've got to open your eyes."

Charlotte blinked, and her mind cleared a few more degrees. "Sooner?"

"Yes. It's Sooner."

"Where are you?"

"We're in some creepazoid's basement and he's going to kill us."

Her eyes opened wide and full now. Her brain still lingered under a haze but it was improving. "Levi."

"I don't know what his name is. I've never seen him before."

"Tall. Blond."

"He wears a hood, like one of those wizards on television."

"Where is he?"

"He's preparing."

"For what."

"Shit if I know." Sooner's voice cracked with fear. "But I can promise it isn't good."

Charlotte tried to sit up and realized her hands and feet were secured to bolts on the floor.

"He keeps calling me Mariah."

"How would he know about Mariah?"

She sniffed, trying to hold off tears. "He said it is hard to kill witches."

"He killed Mariah." Her brain scrambled to get back to the past as her hands twisted to get free of the bindings. "I never saw him before."

"Eighteen years changes people."

"Yeah. Sooner, where are you? I'm in a chair. I'm tied." Charlotte paused. "I hear running water."

"There's a big ass tub in the corner. I don't know what he uses it for."

"It's where he drowns his witches."

When Levi descended the stairs to the underground chamber, he wore only his robe and nothing underneath it. His body hummed with excitement. He'd never before been in the presence of such overwhelming power. Two witches. One was reborn from the dead and the other destined to have been his first kill.

He opened the door and flipped on the lights. Both women tensed and both stared at him.

He met the young one's gaze head on. "You should have stayed dead."

The girl stared at him but it was the other one that spoke. "You killed Mariah?"

He faced her. "I did, but as you can see, she came back. I never realized that she was so powerful."

"Mariah was a young girl, barely seventeen. This girl is Sooner, not Mariah."

"Don't be fooled, Charlotte," Levi said. "She is the reincarnation." He studied Charlotte. "It makes sense now. You used your power to bring her back. I always knew you were strong, but I didn't know just how much."

"She was my mother, you sick son of a bitch!" Sooner yelled.

Levi turned and looked at Sooner. "She wasn't your mother. You are one and the same."

Tears welled in Charlotte's eyes. This was not the way for Sooner to find out the truth. But if they were to die, Sooner deserved the truth now. "Levi, she was born before Mariah died."

Levi moved toward Sooner and from his pocket pulled a knife. He grabbed a handful of her hair and yanked her head back, exposing her neck. He pressed the tip of the knife to her neck. "I should just kill her now and be done with her."

Charlotte jerked at her bindings. "Don't hurt her. She's a child."

"She's no child."

"She's *my* child!" Charlotte screamed.

Sooner's frantic gaze darted from Levi to Charlotte. "What?"

"Grady lied to you," Charlotte said to Sooner. The weight of eighteen years pressed hard on her chest. "I'm your mother. Not Mariah."

"What?"

"I gave birth to you, not Mariah. Grady lied."

Tears ran down Sooner's face. "Liar."

The word scraped over her brain. She had lied. She could have told Sooner the truth immediately. But she hadn't. Levi pressed the knife against Sooner's throat.

"You are a coward, Levi." Charlotte injected venom into her voice. "A spineless coward."

He pressed the knife into Sooner's flesh. "Watch what you say!"

Charlotte yanked hard at the ropes around her wrists. "Why, you are a fool! A fucking coward! If you had any balls, you'd be coming after me, not her."

He lowered the knife from Sooner's neck. "What?"

"You go after a child when you could take me. Spineless. Pitiful." She spat at him.

His eyes narrowed. "Bitch."

Good. Good. Get mad at me. Leave her alone. "You go after helpless women who are alone and vulnerable because you know you can't handle a ball buster like me." She coated the words with all the anger that had been building since Grady had contacted her ten days ago.

He crossed the room and grabbed her by the throat. Murder burned in his gaze. He wanted to choke the life from her lungs.

"Take me and leave her," she gasped.

"Not yet, Charlotte." He released her and she coughed.

"Why, Levi?" Tears spilled down her cheeks. "What are you waiting for?"

"It's about Justice. About ridding the world of evil. Something you would not understand."

"Why wouldn't I understand?"

"Because you are dedicated to releasing Evil on the world."

"What evidence do you have?"

"You're The One that read me all those years ago. When you held my hand, I knew you were destined to be my first. You were the one that would enable me to cross from the light to the dark."

"But you killed Mariah."

"I didn't know there were two of you. The wig and the mask . . . I was confused. All these years I thought I'd killed you, and then I saw you at the carnival. And you said you'd worked there. I realized my mistake. And now I am correcting it."

"How do you know I'm evil? What if you are wrong again?" She hoped his brain would connect with some shred of logic. "You're a lawyer. You know we are all entitled to a defense."

"There is no defense for true evil." He backed away fearing he'd lash out and kill her. "Did you really think Samantha was innocent?"

She hesitated. "Yes."

"She is not innocent."

"How can you say that?"

"I know. Just as I know you are guilty."

Rokov and Sinclair arrived at the little home in Manassas, Virginia. It was a one-story white brick home with a neat front yard. The mailbox by the front door was not overflowing with mail and only today's paper sat on the front step. Levi had been here recently.

The house's large front window was curtained off with heavy drapes. All the shades on the other windows were drawn. There were no signs of life in the house.

"It looks deserted," Sinclair said.

Frustration ate Rokov. "Yeah. Let's have a look around back."

Guns drawn, they moved around the side of the house through the gate of a chain-link fence. He lifted the latch and carefully opened the gate. It squeaked and groaned. He stepped around a green hose, neatly rolled into a circle, and moved toward a set of three stairs that led to a back door. The drapes on the door's windows were also drawn.

"There's no way to look inside," Rokov said.

"Garrison is working on the warrant. It should be here any minute."

Time had never carried such weight for Rokov. Minutes even hours didn't matter in the big scheme, but today both could span the rest of Charlotte's and Sooner's lifetime.

Daniel. She'd spoken his name with such urgency. For the first time he'd seen her vulnerable. God, but he did not want to lose her.

He reached for the door handle.

"The warrant will be here soon."

"I hear something inside. Someone sounds like they're in trouble."

Sinclair cocked her head and listened to the silence. "I think you're right. They sound pretty scared."

Rokov hesitated one more instant as if to give her

the chance to change her mind. They were investigating a prosecutor's home, and they better damn well be sure they understood the consequences. Rokov understood he would risk all for Charlotte.

Sinclair raised a questioning brow. "What are you waiting for?"

He tried the door and discovered it was locked. Stepping back, he shoved his shoulder into the door. It bowed and groaned but didn't give. His shoulder stinging, he hit the door a second time, and this time wood splintered and gave way. The door swung open to a neat kitchen outfitted with avocado green linoleum floors, a green countertop, and white appliances.

Rokov flipped on the lights. He studied the room, which looked as if it hadn't been used in a long time. As he crossed the room to the door that led to the front of the house, he heard the flip of a deadbolt and the slam of the front door.

Rokov raced toward the front of the house while Sinclair ran out the back.

Blood now racing, he yanked open the front door as a hooded figure dashed toward a truck across the street. Rokov chased the suspect, his long legs quickly eating up the space. He grabbed the guy by the hood and yanked back just as Sinclair came up, gun drawn. The man teetered off balance and fell to the ground. Rokov grabbed his cuffs from his belt, handcuffed him, and rolled him over.

Grady glared back up at them, his breathing sharp and quick. "Get the hell off me."

Rokov hauled him to his feet. "What are you doing here?"

"I don't have to tell you shit," the old man spat.

Rokov pushed him against the side of the truck.

"Old man, I don't have time for you. I'm trying to find Sooner and Charlotte, and if you know something, tell me."

Thick brows knotted. "Charlotte and Sooner are missing?"

"Sooner twelve hours ago. Charlotte just this morning."

"That son of a bitch Levi took them," Grady ground out.

"How do you know about Levi?" Rokov said.

"Because he's the bastard that killed Mariah."

"How do you know?"

"When I saw his wife at the carnival. She was wearing an angel necklace. I recognized it. It's the one I gave Mariah."

"There are a million angel necklaces in the world."

"Not like this one. I had it made for her. I know it was hers."

"That doesn't mean he killed her."

"The bastard that drowned her in that lake took the necklace. It wasn't on her when I found her."

"You're the one that moved her body?"

"I couldn't bear to leave her like that. It just wasn't right." Old eyes filled with tears before he coughed and wrestled his emotions back in check. "When I saw the necklace, I started digging. That's what I been doing the last couple of days."

"What did you find out?"

"That he was in this area going to school eighteen years ago."

"Thin."

"Other women have died like Mariah. Raleigh. Ashville. Greenville. I got a look at Levi's credit card statements. Levi traveled to all those cities around the times of the murders."

Rokov would find out later what Grady had done to dig up the information on Levi. "Do you know where he is?"

"He's not in that house. I searched every inch of it."

"Then where?"

"There's another house. In Alexandria."

"Who told you this?"

A bitter smile tipped the edge of his lips. "I don't worry about legal channels. I know how to get around and ask questions."

"Where is the house?"

"First you're gonna have to promise me something."

Levi reached behind Charlotte's head and tested the strength of the ropes. "Since you are so anxious to die, let's get started."

Charlotte stared at Sooner's tear-streaked face. She was doing her best to be brave, but Charlotte only saw a young frightened girl. "So you want me to confess?"

"The faster you do, the faster this will all be over."

And the longer she held out, the more time they might have for help to arrive.

"Don't, Charlotte. I don't care if he kills me," Sooner said.

"I do, honey. I do." She jerked at her chains. "I have nothing to confess to you, you son of a bitch."

"I was hoping it wouldn't be too easy." Levi moved behind her, where he retrieved a large flat board, which he laid over her body. The weight pressed down on her chest, and though she could still breathe, the increased pressure made the effort more conscious.

Smiling, he moved to the pile of cinderblock and hefted the first. He laid it on the center of the board.

"Are you ready to confess? No? I didn't think you'd give up so early. The tough ones are the hardest and most satisfying to break." He placed another cinderblock on the board.

How long could she last? A half hour? An hour? Fresh tears welled in her eyes. They were not for her own life but for Sooner and for the fact that she wouldn't see Rokov again. For a moment, she nearly let despair wash over her. Surrender beckoned.

She closed her eyes and in that instant heard Mariah scream. *"Coward! Baby! Quitter!"*

"I'm not a quitter," Charlotte whispered more to herself.

Levi leaned closer studying her. "What did you say?"

She met his gaze. "I said I am not a quitter."

"We'll see about that." He laid another block on the center of the board.

She struggled to breathe but still managed a grin. "So what is your story, Levi? When did you become the protector of the faith?"

He hesitated, the fourth cinderblock in his hand. "It's a duty I was born to do. I've know it since I was very young."

"So you always knew?"

"I had glimpses of my destiny. But I didn't see the clear vision until eighteen years ago when you read my palm and told me to follow my heart."

"What is it with you nut-jobs and destiny?" Sooner said. Her fists clenched, she glared at him. "I mean, who told you that your destiny is such hot shit?"

He glared at Sooner. "Shut up!"

"It's a valid question," Charlotte said. The longer he talked, the longer he delayed, and the better their chances. "Most of the crazies either think they are destined for greatness, or they hate their mothers."

"I'll bet he hated Mommie Dearest," Sooner said.

Levi swung around and leveled his gaze on her as he clutched the block. "Shut up."

Charlotte felt no humor but forced a laugh from her laden lungs. "Hit a nerve."

He stared at Sooner, and then as if wrestling a demon from his own shoulders, he turned and placed the block on Charlotte's chest. "Keep talking. Soon enough the weight is going to crack your ribs, and you will barely have the weight to confess."

Breathing now was deliberate and a struggle. Soon her body wouldn't be able to tolerate the weight. And when she died, he'd go after Sooner. A tear trickled down her cheek, and Levi leaned forward and gently swiped it away with his index finger.

"How many women have you killed, Levi?" Charlotte whispered.

"Not women. Witches." He retrieved another block. "After tonight, twelve."

Charlotte struggled to breathe. "Levi, I've met your wife. This would break her heart."

"My wife has no heart."

And then it made sense. Levi's wife's tense manner at the carnival. The slight fear in his children's eyes. "She left you."

"Not for long. Soon she will burn. I plan to take a page from Samantha White's book. Nail the windows shut and set the house on fire. I offered the five-year plea agreement because I knew I could wait to kill my family. I planned to make it look like she did it to get revenge on me. And when she's arrested again, there won't be anyone to save her."

Levi laid another cinderblock on Charlotte's chest. Five blocks now weighed down her lungs. Her ribs had bowed to the point of cracking and breaking. Sweat dampened her brow as she labored to pull in breath after breath.

He laid another and then another on her chest. Her breaths were short and shallow and her chest burned with pain.

Death, she imagined, stood in the shadows, and she sensed he wanted her but couldn't take hold of her soul because Mariah stood in his path.

"Mariah," she whispered.

Levi leaned toward her. "Who did you say?"

In that moment the basement door exploded open. Levi reacted instantly, snatching a gun from his workbench.

Charlotte, dazed, watched in horror as Levi turned, raised the weapon, and pointed it at Rokov. However, Levi shifted his aim and fired at Sinclair. The bullet hit her squarely in the chest and she dropped to the ground.

Rokov's face darkened and instantly he fired and hit Levi in the chest. Levi stumbled back, raised his gun a second time. Rokov fired again twice. The bullets sliced into Levi's chest, knocking him dead to the ground.

Rokov glanced at Charlotte. She could barely keep her eyes open and wondered how much longer she could shove air into her lungs.

"Sinclair," he shouted. "You better be alive."

Sinclair groaned. "I'm okay. Hit me in the vest."

A rush of relief so pure washed over his features as he raced to the pit and started pulling the blocks off

Charlotte. When he lifted the board, she pulled in painful but deep breaths.

He glanced at the chains and then returned to Levi. He dug through his pockets and found a key. He unfastened her manacles and pulled her free.

Sinclair stumbled to her feet and untied Sooner. "Fucker broke my ribs."

Charlotte leaned heavily on Rokov. "How did you find us?"

"Grady. He saw the necklace Levi gave his wife. It had belonged to Mariah."

"Where is he?" She hated the old man for what he'd done to her sister. And was grateful he'd saved her and Sooner.

"Outside."

"Thank you, Daniel."

He hugged her close and she could feel the raw energy tightening his muscles. "Anytime."

The rising sun greeted Charlotte and Sooner as the two stumbled outside, arm in arm. Squad car lights flashed and EMTs rushed to help them. Charlotte clung to Sooner, refusing treatment until she knew the girl was okay. Only then were the EMTs able to coax her back on a gurney and give her oxygen. The next minutes were an odd haze of frenetic activity.

Daniel with Grady, his hands cuffed behind his back, approached Charlotte. "He wants to speak to you."

She smiled at Daniel. "It's okay."

Daniel took one step back but remained close enough to act on an instant's notice. "I'm right here."

Grady shifted his stance. "Sooner is good. Tough as nails. Like her mother."

A part of her would always hate Grady for what he'd done. But another part recognized he'd also saved her daughter's life. "Is she speaking to you?"

"Only in four letter words."

She pulled the oxygen mask from her face. "She's got a lot to process."

"Yeah, I know." He cleared his throat. "I been looking for Mariah's killer for eighteen years. I knew whoever was doing the killing was shadowing the carnival. But I never could figure it out." He inhaled. "I'm dying and knew this was my last season so I used Sooner and the press articles to flush him out. I was sure he'd see an article eventually."

"You nearly got her killed."

"If I hadn't flushed him out, he'd have come after her when I was dead and couldn't protect her."

"Why did you lie to her about Mariah?"

"'Cause I was pissed you'd left. Once the lie was out, it just took on its own life. And it was easy enough for folks to believe 'cause Sooner looks so much like Mariah."

"None of the old carnies said a word to her?"

"They knew I'd kill them if they did."

She closed her eyes. Her chest still ached and pulling in a deep breath hurt.

"Are you all right?" Daniel said.

She opened her eyes. "Yes. I'm fine."

"I ain't asking forgiveness," Grady said. "But I'd appreciate it if you could help Sooner get past hating me after I'm dead. No matter what anyone says about anything, I loved that kid like my own."

Charlotte nodded, unable to forgive and unable to hate.

Epilogue

Four Months Later

Charlotte stared at Daniel across the crowded living room of the Rokovs, who'd gathered for Mr. and Mrs. Rokov's thirty-fifth wedding anniversary. All of Daniel's brothers and sisters were present along with assorted cousins, aunts, and uncles.

Charlotte still felt out of place at Rokov family functions. Though the family had always made a point to make her and Sooner feel welcome, she couldn't shake the feeling that she wasn't deserving of a real family.

She'd never voiced her worries to Daniel, but of course, he knew. He always seemed to know when she was worried either about a family gathering, a case, or Sooner. Sooner. Most of her worries these days were reserved for Sooner.

Sooner was doing well and, with Charlotte's encouragement, had closed her shop and enrolled in the community college. She lived with Charlotte in her spare room. Not having a great deal of formal education, the girl had had to backtrack with many of her courses, but she was proving to be a good student and a hard worker.

The adoption experts had told Charlotte that she and Sooner were still in the honeymoon phase of their relationship. Reunions between children and birth parents often started well but could sour. Charlotte prayed every day that never happened.

That didn't mean to say that they didn't have their disagreements. Sooner's bull-headed temperament mirrored Charlotte's, and both were quick to argue. But so far they were seeing their way past it all.

The new apartment had not been the adjustment that she'd expected, maybe because she spent spare nights at Daniel's place. She'd been determined to take their relationship slowly, but somehow he'd gently coaxed her closer and closer each time they were together. She'd always prided herself on independence, and now she couldn't imagine living without him. Nor could she imagine not having Sooner puttering around the apartment leaving her piles of clothes on the floor, her endless shampoo products in the bathroom, or her dirty dishes in the kitchen sink. Daniel and Sooner had become friends. He was an easy man to like, but Charlotte believed Sooner would never forget the night he charged into the basement and saved them. That terrifying moment had bonded them all in a way that could never be forgotten.

From across the room Daniel raised his glass to Charlotte and winked. She smiled, warmed that soon they'd be alone in his bed.

"My Daniel is a good boy." Grandmother Rokov's voice crackled behind Charlotte and had her turning.

"Yes, he is."

"He worries about you."

She raised her wineglass to her lips and pretended to sip. "He doesn't need to. I can take care of myself."

The old woman glared at Charlotte as if she were prying away layers. "Do you still have the dream?"

She frowned. "Daniel told you about the dreams?"

"No. Daniel would never speak of things so private. Do you still hear the woman's screams?"

Charlotte studied the old woman. "How did you know?"

"Some things I just know." She smiled. "Do you hear them?"

"No." And it was a relief to say it. "I've not heard her since . . . that night." The night Levi had tried to crush Charlotte to death.

Sooner had suffered no lasting physical injuries. However, Charlotte had suffered three cracked ribs and bruising all across her torso. All would be fixed by time.

Mentally, she recognized a new fear of confined spaces. Elevators and crowded rooms were the worst reminders of Levi laying the cinderblocks on her chest. So she'd become adept at taking the stairs and remaining close to the door. Her quirks were improving, but they still bothered her enough that she did not enter the family fray for the toast Daniel gave to his parents.

"You stay on the fringe. You do not go into the room," Grandmother said.

"I don't enjoy tight spaces right now."

The old woman nodded. "It will pass. Time will make it better."

"I hope you are right." She felt a bit like a cripple at times and it made her angry. Levi had taken something from her and she wanted it back.

"I am right."

She stared at the old woman's lined face. It was easy to look past the wrinkles and gray hair and see the vibrancy in her eyes. Despite nearing ninety, she remained mentally sharp.

"Where is your friend, Angie, and her family?"

"An unexpected appointment came up." Angie had called early this morning. She'd been talking so quickly and so excitedly that Charlotte had thought something was wrong with David. Finally Angie had calmed and explained that David's pediatrician had another patient, a sixteen-year-old girl, who was pregnant and about to deliver. Would she and Malcolm consider adopting? Angie didn't want anyone to know of the offer for fear it would fall through, but she and Malcolm were beyond excited about the idea of being parents again. Charlotte had been waiting for the text, which would tell her if the baby was a boy or a girl.

"I've always liked the name *Vivian* for a girl," Grandmother said. She raised a glass of red wine to her lips and sipped.

Charlotte had not even told Daniel of this latest development. First the dreams and now the baby. What was it with this woman? "Excuse me?"

"For the baby girl, I like the name *Vivian*."

"What baby?"

Grandmother smiled and patted Charlotte on the shoulder. "The one Angie and Malcolm now await. It's a girl." She winked. "But I won't tell just as they requested."

"Who told you?"

"No one."

"Someone had to have told you."

She smiled. "I see your Daniel headed this way."

And before Charlotte could ask Grandmother another question, Daniel arrived, and she slipped away. He was dressed in a dark suit that fit the lines of his broad shoulders and trim waist so well. Faint lines around his dark eyes creased when he smiled down at her.

He kissed her on the lips. "You look surprised."

"Your grandmother says the oddest things. Not bad things, just odd."

Laughter danced in his eyes. "She's been known to do that."

"I mean she's kind of eerie about what she knows."

"How so?"

"Does she sort of know when things are going to happen?"

He shrugged. "If she does, she rarely says."

She let the questions fade and hooked her arm in his, rose on tiptoes, and kissed him on the lips. He smelled of soap and the faint hint of aftershave. As fearful as she could be of tight spaces, his touch, having him close, had not bothered her once.

Levi's wife and children had moved out of the home they'd shared when the police had determined that he had, in fact, been plotting to kill his family and blame it on Samantha. Upstairs windows had been nailed shut and incendiary devices had been planted. Most believed he'd planned to return to finalize his trap after he killed Charlotte and Sooner.

Grady, satisfied that Levi was dead, had released his hold on Sooner and Charlotte and had left town with the carnival. There were charges pending against the old man, but it was likely he'd never see trial. He had stage four lung cancer and wasn't expected to make it to summer.

Even despite his illness, Sooner could not bring herself to talk to him. All these years he'd lied about her mother's identity and Mariah's death.

Charlotte, too, resented the old man. If he'd given Sooner up for adoption or if he'd simply told the girl about Charlotte, it all could have been so different. If, if, if.

However, she was careful to keep her thoughts private. Grady was the only family Sooner had known, and if one day she needed to forgive him, Charlotte wanted to keep the door open. After all, Grady had tracked down Levi. If not for him, Daniel never would have found them in time.

And thanks to Grady, the police had ten murders across the country that could now be marked *Solved.* Levi could be placed in all the cities where the other women were murdered. The DNA that had been collected in Raleigh matched Levi's.

What Grady had never understood was Levi's obsession with his carnival. The answer had been painfully simple. Levi's mother had been one of Grady's psychics—the one, in fact, still pictured on his brochure. Apparently, Grady and Levi's mother, Greta, had had an affair years ago. When Greta had realized she was pregnant, she'd left the carnival and married Levi's father. When the boy's paternity had been finally discovered, Levi's father had killed his mother. From then on, the father set out to poison the son that was not of his blood.

Charlotte knew, *knew*, that Mariah was now at peace. In an odd strange way, the pieces of her life had fallen into place.

"What are you worrying about now?" Daniel traced his finger down the frown line in the center of her forehead.

She looked at him and smiled. "With you, I have no worries."